Praise for *Midwife of the Blue Ridge*

"A terrific book! A riveting tale of love, struggle
and savagery on America's colonial frontier."
—Bernard Cornwell

"Love and adventure, pride and passion . . .
A vivid evocation of time and place . . . An unforgettable
novel that will capture your heart. There is simply no
way to put it down once you have begun."
—Rosemary Rogers

"A splendid novel of passion and danger in the early Virginias
by a talented new author. I highly recommend it!"
—Bertrice Small

"Full of action, passion and period detail."
—*Historical Novel Review*

"Blevins doesn't soft-pedal the brutal realities of
women's lot in the colonies, but gives strong,
skilled Maggie pluck and hope."
—*Publishers Weekly*

"Lavishly and minutely described . . . an in-depth and up-close
look at what life was really like in those times."
—*Booklist*

Berkley Titles by Christine Blevins

MIDWIFE OF THE BLUE RIDGE

THE TORY WIDOW

The
TORY WIDOW

Christine Blevins

BERKLEY BOOKS, NEW YORK

THE BERKLEY PUBLISHING GROUP
Published by the Penguin Group
Penguin Group (USA) Inc.
375 Hudson Street, New York, New York 10014, USA
Penguin Group (Canada), 90 Eglinton Avenue East, Suite 700, Toronto, Ontario M4P 2Y3, Canada
(a division of Pearson Penguin Canada Inc.)
Penguin Books Ltd., 80 Strand, London WC2R 0RL, England
Penguin Group Ireland, 25 St. Stephen's Green, Dublin 2, Ireland (a division of Penguin Books Ltd.)
Penguin Group (Australia), 250 Camberwell Road, Camberwell, Victoria 3124, Australia
(a division of Pearson Australia Group Pty. Ltd.)
Penguin Books India Pvt. Ltd., 11 Community Centre, Panchsheel Park, New Delhi—110 017, India
Penguin Group (NZ), 67 Apollo Drive, Rosedale, North Shore 0632, New Zealand
(a division of Pearson New Zealand Ltd.)
Penguin Books (South Africa) (Pty.) Ltd., 24 Sturdee Avenue, Rosebank, Johannesburg 2196,
South Africa

Penguin Books Ltd., Registered Offices: 80 Strand, London WC2R 0RL, England

This book is an original publication of The Berkley Publishing Group.

This is a work of fiction. Names, characters, places, and incidents either are the product of the author's imagination or are used fictitiously, and any resemblance to actual persons, living or dead, business establishments, events, or locales is entirely coincidental. The publisher does not have any control over and does not assume any responsibility for author or third-party websites or their content.

PRINTING HISTORY
Berkley trade paperback edition / April 2009

Library of Congress Cataloging-in-Publication Data

Blevins, Christine.
  The Tory widow / Christine Blevins. — Berkley trade paperback ed.
     p. cm.
  ISBN 978-0-425-22601-8
  1. New York (N.Y.)—History—Revolution, 1775–1783—Fiction.   2. Widows—Fiction.
I. Title.

PS3602.L478T67 2009
813'.6—dc22

                                                                    2008053564

PRINTED IN THE UNITED STATES OF AMERICA

10 9 8 7 6 5 4 3 2 1

For Brian
My Dearest Friend

Acknowledgments

From story conception to holding this real book in my hands, I have been fortunate to draw support from many quarters.

The sage advice goes, "write what you know," and I would first like to acknowledge the many historians and writers whose diligent work enabled me to understand and "know" Revolutionary New York.

I must thank my fabulous literary agent, Nancy Coffey, for the boatloads of encouragement and advice, especially as the deadline loomed. I am grateful to artist James Griffin and art director Judith Langerman for the production of a beautiful and arresting cover. Thanks to copy editor Jacky Sach for her particular eye, and to diligent managing editor Crissie Johnson for pulling it all together and overseeing the details. Special thanks to my terrific editor, Jackie Cantor, whose keen insight and remarkable story acumen led me to write a better book.

It is hard to imagine finishing this novel without the kind and earnest advocacy of my good friend David Blinderman. I'm also quite grateful to my friend Farheen Dogar for finding time to offer valuable critique on my manuscript pages.

I thrive on encouragement from my wonderful family, and they have never failed to be there for me. For their constant love and support, I'd like to thank my mother, Anela Zownir; my sister, Natalie

Frank; my brother, Robert Zownir; my sons Jason Blevins and Bob Blevins; my daughters Grace Blevins and Natalie Momoh; and my son-in-law, Lucky Momoh. I love you all very much.

I am grateful to all of my in-laws—Mary Ann Zownir, Darlene and Larry Kaplan, and Wayne and Jeannie Blevins—for cheering me on. I appreciate the support shown by my crew of nieces and nephews—Joey Morris, Aaron Frank, Madeline Frank, Lisa and Kurt McKenzie, Wes Kaplan, Rory Moore, Brad and Marnie Morris, Casey Morris and Zoe Morris.

And last—but never least—for helping me maintain the discipline and dedication it takes to research and write, I am most grateful to my husband, Brian Blevins. He is without doubt the finest story-brainstormer, first-reader, web-designer, foot-rubber and bolsterer-of-sagging-confidence-and-fragile-ego in the whole wide world. Nothing would be possible or any fun without you, honey.

—CB

May 20, 1766
St. Paul's at Broad Way and Fulton Street, New York City

T HE bright new chapel had yet to be furnished with pews, leaving the floor an uninterrupted chequerboard of gray and white stone tile. Anne Peabody stood centered on a single square—twisting and untwisting a damp handkerchief in her hands—a wretched pawn on this, her wedding day.

The old minister did not spare a glance at the worn book open on his palms. He faced the bride and groom and by rote recited the matrimonial service in a brisk monotone.

"Dearly beloved, we are gathered together here in the sight of God, and in the face of this congregation, to join together this man and this woman in holy matrimony . . ."

The words provoked a thrum in her head, and Anne felt herself go pale. She ached to reach back and loosen the taut knot of chestnut hair laying heavy at the nape of her neck. Blue eyes shiny with restrained tears darted maniacally from the minister, to the man standing at her left and down to her mother's best lace-edged hanky wadded in her fists.

Anne took in a long breath. To regain a modicum of composure, she began to mimic her betrothed. Standing stiffly erect, she focused beyond the scowling cleric's shoulder, on the dust motes dancing in the sunbeams streaming in through sanctuary windowpanes.

The church door opened on squalling hinges. Without a by-your-leave, two men entered, struggling to carry a bulky section of ornate balustrade between them. The older of the two groaned when he noticed the ceremony taking place.

"*Blood and thunder*—now we'll catch it."

Anne's groom kept his eyes fixed straight ahead, but the minister paused and glared as the workmen shuffled past the spartan wedding party to drop their burden at the base of one of the columns support-ing the vaulted ceiling. The carpenter and his apprentice were quick to swipe the caps from their heads.

"Beg pardon, Vicar." The elder carpenter shoved his apprentice to take up positions behind the bride's father and brother.

"Fine day to tie the knot," the younger carpenter offered.

Satisfied with the comportment of the two unexpected guests, the minister resumed.

"Peter Merrick and Anne Peabody, I require and charge you both, as you will answer at the dreadful day of judgment when the secrets of all hearts shall be disclosed, that if either of you know any impediment why you may not be lawfully joined together in matri-mony, you must now confess it . . ."

Any impediment? Anne suffered a sideways peek at her soon-to-be husband. *He's old. He reeks of cabbage and onion. His wig is in dire need of powder. His cuffs are frayed, his cravat stained . . . and there is hair growing out of his ears!*

"Mr. Merrick, wilt thou have this woman to thy wedded wife, to live together after God's ordinance in the holy estate of matrimony? Wilt thou love her, comfort her, honor and keep her in sickness and in health; and, forsaking all others, keep thee only unto her, so long as you both shall live?"

Peter Merrick did not hesitate to answer. "I will."

Struck by a sudden notion that her father might yet muster up a shred of paternal love and rescue her from impending doom, Anne cast a desperate glance over her shoulder. Standing beside her brother,

Amos Peabody seemed oblivious to his daughter's plight. He winked and nodded, quite puffed up by the brilliance of the match he'd engineered on her behalf.

"The man's a respected printer, bookseller *and* stationer—can you imagine, Annie?" her father had boasted on the day he'd negotiated the marriage. "A two-press shop with a steady clientele—the carriage trade! Merrick has a fine suite of rooms above his shop to bide in, and servants to tend you when you call. Oh, daughter, you will not want."

On the surface, the match was more than a dowerless eighteen-year-old of her station could expect. Merrick's enterprise in New York City dwarfed the failing Peabody Printshop upriver in tiny Peekskill, where Anne and her brother, David, struggled with their father to produce third-rate work using worn type and a rickety old press that needed repair more oft than not.

Amos Peabody had negotiated a shrewd deal with his old friend, exchanging his only daughter's hand for a complete set of hard-to-come-by Dutch-made type, much-needed replacement press parts and ten reams of quality bond. A boon to the Peabody family fortune, Anne's marriage to Peter Merrick put an end to the unsettling talk of sending young David out to be bound as an apprentice and ensured continuance of the family business.

"Anne Peabody, wilt thou have this man to thy wedded husband, to live together after God's ordinance in the holy estate of matrimony? Wilt thou obey him and serve him, love, honor and keep him in sickness and in health; and, forsaking all others, keep thee only unto him, so long as you both shall live?"

"I will."

The moment she uttered the fated words forsaking her happiness, her future and all she'd ever known, a distant church bell tolled. The one bell was soon joined by another, and another, till it seemed every steeple and belfry in the city echoed in an unending, doleful peal.

The minister grew agitated and rushed to finish the service. Erratic bursts of musket fire and the far-off boom of a cannon added to the clamor coming from the street. No longer able to withhold curiosity, the two carpenters and David sprinted out the sanctuary door.

Pronouncing bride and groom "man and wife," the clergyman clapped his book shut and also abandoned the wedded pair.

The father of the bride stepped forward. With a hurried, "Congratulations!" accompanied by an abrupt slap to the groom's back, he, too, was quick on the minister's heels, out the door.

Peter Merrick turned and faced his new wife. He bent awkwardly at knees and waist to plant a tight, dry kiss on her cheek. Without further ado, he rushed to join the others.

All alone, Anne Merrick gave herself over to all the self-pity, anger, loneliness and fear she'd suppressed for weeks. Sobbing, she wadded her tear-drenched hanky and scrubbed hard at the spot on her cheek where Mr. Merrick had sealed their union with a kiss.

Heaving a ragged sigh, she sniffed and fussed with the lace at her elbows and adjusted the gauzy kerchief at her neckline. Somewhat composed, Anne gathered the beryl blue silk of her best dress, and joined the men congregated near the northernmost stone column supporting the portico roof.

The air was alive with bells clanging and sporadic gunfire. Across Broad Way, a sizable crowd formed on the green of the Commons, and people spilled from shops, houses and narrow alleyways onto the dusty road. Her brother, David, stood at the far end of the chapel stoop in a glum huddle with the two carpenters, the minister and Peter Merrick.

"What news?" Anne asked.

David shrugged. "Father went to find out. He bade us all stay put."

The minister lamented, "It takes some time for word to make its way here, to the edge of town."

"There come the newsboys now." Peter Merrick nodded, folding his arms across his chest.

Several young men in shirtsleeves and leather aprons ran down Broad Way armed with thick sheaves of paper. Fresh off the press, the broadsides being distributed were greeted with rousing cheers. One of these fresh-faced young men ran up to St. Paul's, handing his last pages to Merrick and the minister. Breathless he blurted, "Arrived on the express from Boston . . . the Stamp Act's been repealed!"

"Huzzah!" David and the two carpenters leaped up and punched the air. "We did it! We did it." The ridiculous trio of instant friends ran out to the crowded street in a tumbled camaraderie of backslapping and jovial shoving. They linked arms and marched onto the Commons to join with the singing and dancing celebrants.

"I-I don't believe it!" The minister patted his pockets for his spectacles.

Grim-faced Merrick held the paper at arm's length, squinting at the news. "Our King would never accede to the whim of Whig radicals." He rattled the sheet at the messenger. "Who is your master? Which Whig press manufactured this flummery?"

Unflinching, the young man squared broad shoulders. "I'm Jack Hampton, sir, apprenticed with Parker's Press, and that"—Jack tapped the broadside in Merrick's hand—"is excerpted word for word from the *London Times*, that is."

"Parker's Press? A rabid dissenter—he is no friend to the Crown." Peter Merrick crumpled the broadside into a ball and flung it to the ground. "Your master ought think twice before publishing lies that excite the rabble into disobedience and sedition."

Dark brows knit, jaw tight, fists clenched, Jack Hampton mounted the stoop. "John Parker is nothing but a true Son of Liberty, sir, and he publishes only the Truth." The young man turned and noticed Anne and the minister, standing off to the side. He stepped back, took a breath and brushed back a shock of black hair that'd escaped his queue. "But I think this is neither the time nor place for a debate on the rights of freemen and the merits of civil dissent, is it?" A white-toothed grin flashed and with a brash wink he turned to Anne and said, "Cheer up there, lass. We stood toe-to-toe with Parliament and we showed 'em what's what!"

Jack stepped forward, grasped Anne round the waist with ink-stained hands and swung her up through the air, shouting, "Joy to America! Huzzah the Liberty Boys! Huzzah the King!" Setting her back to her feet, he pulled her close and kissed Anne full on the mouth.

Peter Merrick sputtered, "Why . . . I . . . you—you . . ." But before he could enunciate his outrage, one of Hampton's likewise apron-clad cohorts called from the street.

"Hoy, Jack! Quit sniffin' after petticoats—the lads are a-waitin' on us . . ."

Bold young Jack took Anne by the hand and raised her fingertips to his lips in a gesture so suddenly genteel as to take her breath away. In that moment, Anne's life seemed in her grasp—the bells rang bright, the world was happy—then Jack Hampton bounded down the stair and out onto the street to join his mates.

"Scoundrel!" Peter Merrick shouted, with fist raised. "I shall make a report to your master!"

Jack turned and thumbed his nose. "Take heart, you ol' Tory! Meet me at Montagne's—bring your pretty daughter . . ." He blew Anne a kiss. "We can all toast our good King's health!"

While Merrick cursed and grumbled, Anne marked Jack and his friend dodging their way across Broad Way onto the Commons. She so wished she could drum up the courage to shed her misspoken vows and forced-upon obligations—the courage to run after the wild lad and take him by the hand. As Jack Hampton disappeared amid the raucous throng, Anne felt her heart spin away and clatter, like a bucket lost down the depths of a deep, deep well.

No. It was never in her nature to own that kind of reckless courage.

Anne flinched when Peter Merrick grasped her by the shoulder.

"Come along, Mrs. Merrick . . . your father assures me you've a deft hand at setting type. We've work to do today—a special edition at the least."

Anne took her husband's proffered arm and he led her beyond the joyous din to begin her new life.

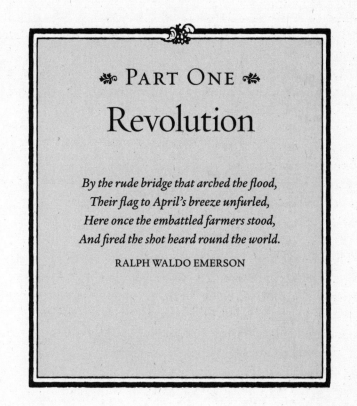

❧ PART ONE ❧

Revolution

By the rude bridge that arched the flood,
Their flag to April's breeze unfurled,
Here once the embattled farmers stood,
And fired the shot heard round the world.

RALPH WALDO EMERSON

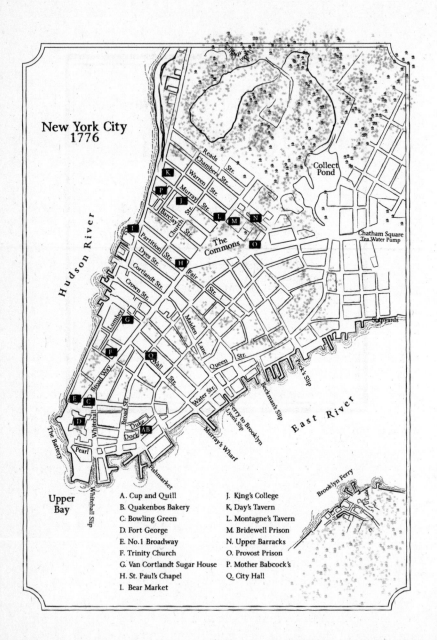

New York City
1776

Hudson River

Reads Str.
Chambers Str.
Warren Str.
Murray Str.
Barclay Str.
Partition Str.
Dyes Str.
Cortlandt Str.
Crown Str.
Lumber
Broad Way
Fair Str.
Maiden Lane
Queen Str.
Water Str.
Duke Str.
Pearl
Dock
Fishmarket
Whitehall Slip

The Commons

Collect Pond

Chatham Square
Tea Water Pump

Shipyards

Peck's Slip

Beekman's Slip

Ferry to Brooklyn
Lyon's Slip

Murray's Wharf

East River

The Battery

Upper Bay

Brooklyn Ferry

A. Cup and Quill
B. Quakenbos Bakery
C. Bowling Green
D. Fort George
E. No.1 Broadway
F. Trinity Church
G. Van Cortlandt Sugar House
H. St. Paul's Chapel
I. Bear Market

J. King's College
K. Day's Tavern
L. Montagne's Tavern
M. Bridewell Prison
N. Upper Barracks
O. Provost Prison
P. Mother Babcock's
Q. City Hall

CHAPTER ONE

O ye that love mankind!
Ye that dare oppose, not only the tyranny,
but the tyrant, stand forth!

THOMAS PAINE, *Common Sense*

May 1775
New York City

A strong breeze blowing in off the bay caught in the black wool of her skirts, propelling Anne Merrick across Broad Way at a smart pace. Dodging carriages and carts, she clutched the jute string wrapped around the package with her right hand, kept the plain cotton bonnet from flying off her head with her left, and zigzagged a path across the cobbled thoroughfare.

Anne was not in the habit of making deliveries, but her pressman, Titus, was busy finishing a print run, and Sally, her servant girl, was late in returning from the ink seller. The rector at St. Paul's paid a premium to have copies of his latest sermon delivered by Evensong, and times being what they were, Anne could not afford to lose yet another customer.

Merrick Press & Stationers was located at the tip of the island off the corner of the narrow alley connecting Duke and Dock streets, and Anne did not often find reason to stray to the west side of town. With French heels tapping a brisk rhythm on the redbrick walk, she coursed a straight path past a row of stately mansions, noting many were shuttered and deserted by their owners. When news of Lexington and Concord galloped into town, more than a few Loyalist New Yorkers fearing Patriot malcontents closed their homes and boarded the first available packet bound for England.

Patriots and Loyalists . . .

How quickly the tides had shifted. Rebels and Englishmen was how Mr. Merrick would refer to them if he were yet alive. Her husband's Loyalist sentiments had earned him the custom of a likewise devoted clientele and he prospered by his beliefs. A staunch supporter of the Crown until his dying day, Merrick was.

Anne had once been avid to follow the politics of the day, collecting pamphlets and broadsides, always combing the papers for the latest news from London, Boston and Philadelphia. She weathered several of Merrick's stern rebukes in regard to her pro-Whig sympathies, and quickly learned to keep her reading material and her opinions to herself. After Jemmy was born, Anne found little opportunity to indulge in clandestine intellectual pursuits, and her interest in current events waned.

In truth, the simultaneous loss of both her husband and her little boy to smallpox three years before sapped Anne of ardent feeling for anything—politics in particular. On most days, it was all she could do to swing legs from bed and tend to her printing business, much less give a fig for the ever-fickle ideologies of men. Anne lifted her skirts and picked a path through a rank pile of dung occupying the center of the walk. *Loyalists and Patriots . . .*

The city teemed with newly professed Patriots who'd not a month before boasted lifelong fealty to their Sovereign. It was beyond her ken as to who were the worse—those with ideologies malleable enough to bend with whatever wind enriched their purses, or the fanatics, who by threat and violence forced their unyielding notions down the gullets of all.

Taxation, tyranny, the rights of free men—Anne spent no time trying to make sense of the concepts and ideals filling newspapers and pamphlets, posted on walls, and spoken on street corners at every turn. She was only concerned with the rights of one woman. Keeping Merrick's Press prosperous enough to remain free of her father's tyranny and predilection to marry her off again—that was what kept Anne fully occupied.

Marriage.

The word alone was enough to set her teeth on edge. As a propertied young widow, she drew many a zealous suitor to her shop these days, but she had no problem rejecting every offer. She'd had more than enough marriage for one lifetime.

Anne skirted around the tea-water peddler's cart and donkey blocking the walkway, the sight making her wistful for the convenience of fresh, clean water delivered to her door. Merrick's death coupled with new taxes and political strife had severely affected trade, forcing her to dispense with many such luxuries. Still, she could not bear for her coffee to be tainted by the brackish water drawn from the nearby public well, so every dawn she and Sally joined the stream of women toting buckets, making their way to the city's only truly potable source, the Tea-Water Pump in Chatham Square.

A trio of denizens came up from the dingy streets west of Trinity Church and fell in behind Anne on her northward trek up Broad Way. She glanced over her shoulder.

Prostitutes.

It was a bit early in the day for these women to have emerged. As a port and garrison town, New York City proved a haven for such women of ill repute. Doxies and whores of every ilk had, until recently, plied their trade with ease. But when the British military vacated the city to take up arms in Boston, these garish women in their ridiculous wigs and brassy petticoats suffered a harsh economic adjustment.

How ironic, Anne thought. *Losing all their Loyal customers, just like me.*

To Anne's relief, and contrary to a typical streetwalker's languid stroll, the women set a brisk pace and the threesome was quick to pass her by.

Half a dozen dockworkers in red knit caps with lading hooks dangling from the waistbands of their baggy sailcloth trousers swaggered out from the Boar's Head tavern across the street. One of them shouted, "How much?"

Without a hesitation, a prostitute squawked, "Only four shillings, darling!"

"Hoy! *Ladies!*" the shortest and slightest longshoreman called, wagging his hips. "How about *you* pay *me* four shillings and I'll treat yiz to the biggest and best cock in Christendom."

The women stopped dead in their tracks, causing Anne to halt abruptly as well.

"You've got it all wrong, sweetie," shouted the youngest and prettiest whore with a jut of her hip. "*We're* the ones what get paid to tell the lies about the size of your cock."

The whores flounced off in a giggle and the dockworkers fell about laughing at their mate's expense.

Anne put a kick in her step and outpaced the bawds, but as if she were the lead bird of a migratory flock, the prostitutes cruised along in her wake, matching her step for step. Past Crown Street, the sidewalk grew even more congested. Apprentices, mechanics, housewives, shopkeeps, schoolboys—the entire population of the town, it seemed—streamed onto Broad Way from all directions, and Anne found herself caught up in a rush toward the Commons. She clutched her package to her breast, swept along in the human wave like so much flotsam and jetsam. Every opportunity to escape from the throng eluded her. She asked one of the whores who were now crowded beside her, "What is going on?"

The woman smiled, her fuzzy yellow teeth a high contrast to her pitted face painted with a thick layer of white face powder. Fleshy cheeks were heavily rouged, and in a fruitless attempt to hide a scabby sore, she'd applied a crescent-shaped black silk patch at the corner of her crimson mouth. "A rally on the green. Them Liberty Boys put out the word."

"Liberty Boys!" the eldest prostitute sneered from behind. "Liberty Brutes is what I calls 'em. I wouldn't give 'em the time o' day, exceptin' I'm likely to garner some custom in a crowd this size." This clearly mercenary pronouncement earned the woman many baleful glares.

Anne, for one, agreed with the old whore. The Liberty Boys lost all check and reason the very day the British Garrison shipped out to quell the rebellion in Boston. They immediately formed a militia and commandeered the munitions in the armory. They marched about town provoking incidents, harassing Loyal citizens and vandalizing Loyal businesses. In the name of Liberty, these men manufactured much mischief and mayhem when times were troubling enough.

Sighting St. Paul's steeple over her shoulder, Anne realized she had overshot her destination, and she strained to get a bearing on her position. Above the many heads and shoulders before her, she could see the upper half of the Liberty Pole—a red ensign fluttering beneath the gilt weathervane affixed at the very tip of it spelling out the word *LIBERTY*.

The first pole erected to celebrate the repeal of the Stamp Act had been a simple affair, an old ship's mast haphazardly planted in the ground with a board affixed at the top inscribed *George III, Pitt and Liberty*. The display was an affront to the British soldiers quartered in barracks facing the Commons, and they hacked the pole to pieces. The original pole was soon replaced, and soon destroyed. The back and forth continued for years, escalating to violent mob action on more than one occasion.

On the day the Liberty Boys with much pomp and circumstance installed this fifth and enduring pole, her Jemmy had been no more than three years old. Together they watched the sixty-foot mast being drawn by six draft horses bedecked in ribbons and bells, as it was paraded up from the shipyards with drums drumming and tin whistles whistling—how Jemmy had laughed and clapped! She had held tight to his little hand that day.

Anne slipped her hand inside her pocket, and fingered the little brooch she kept pinned there. It had been three years since Jemmy's passing, and the simplest recollection could still bring on a sting of tears.

Overcome by the press and stench of the crowd, Anne pulled a hanky splashed with lavender water from her sleeve. Holding it to her nose, she rose up on tiptoes to catch a bit of the same fair wind that turned the weathervane taunting her with the word *liberty*.

"I can't see nothin' either." The youngest prostitute complained and grabbed Anne by the hand. "C'mon . . ."

The girl ducked down; tugging Anne along, she wriggled, wormed, bumped and nudged toward the front of the throng. "Move away! Step aside! Comin' through . . ."

Anne tucked her head and joined the effort. Paying no heed to grunts and complaints, they bullied forward and broke onto the green to the right of the Liberty Pole.

"Better, aye?" The prostitute gave Anne's hand a little squeeze before letting go. "We'll be able to see everything from here."

This girl was much younger than her well-worn companions—Anne judged her to be no more than eighteen years. Despite her youth, or perhaps because of it, she seemed to be a bit more astute and subtle in regard to the presentation of her wares. Eschewing the heavy makeup and high-styled wigs her sorority sported, this girl wore her thick raven hair swept up, with a fringe of loose curls framing her pretty face. A tiny black heart-shaped patch on her right cheek drew attention to the girl's best features—a clear complexion and wide blue eyes.

A gust of wind blew across the Commons and lifted Anne's starched cap from her head to flutter away. The gilded weathervane began to spin erratic and the ironclad pole loomed against dark clouds menacing the eastern sky. A pair of young boys poked at a crude, straw-stuffed figure hanging from the pole. Pinned to the effigy's breast, paper signs scrawled with the words *Rivington* and *Tory* rustled on the breeze.

Mr. Merrick's colleague, James Rivington, published the Loyalist leaning *New York Gazetteer*—the most widely read weekly newspaper in town. A good percentage of Anne's earnings was derived from the odd jobs deemed too small by Rivington that he kindly sent her way. The effigy did not bode well for Mr. Rivington's fortunes or, for that matter, her own.

A large packing crate lay on its side at the base of the Liberty Pole. "Ooooh!" The young prostitute pointed with excitement. Two bulbous tick sacks marked H. MYER, POULTERER sat propped beside the crate next to a steaming pair of buckets caked with amber pine pitch.

Off to the side of the packing crate, two men were held at bay by half a dozen cudgel-wielding sailors—one man was writhing and spitting in protest, the other stood stiff, defiant and stoic—neither of them James Rivington. A tight huddle of men some ten yards back broke and solemnly came forward to form a semicircle around the packing crate. *The Liberty Boys.*

Laborers, tradesmen and artisans stood side by side with merchants, bankers and lawyers, representing New York City's faction of the Sons of Liberty. Anne scanned the diverse group, recognizing a few faces—Mr. Tuttle, her banker, and her neighbor Walter Quakenbos, the bread and biscuit baker—but her breath caught in her throat when she spied the man at the far end. Arms folded across his chest, his stance wide, there stood Jack Hampton.

Anne hugged her package tight. Ten years had past, and the kiss under the portico at St. Paul's remained emblazoned in her brain— the only pleasant remembrance she treasured from her wedding day. With crystal clarity she could call up the defiance in Jack Hampton's dark eyes, the feel of his strong hands gripping her waist, his soft lips on hers . . . This vivid recollection formed the inkling, the wild imagining of a life she might have had.

He must have come to the Commons straight from his press. Jacketless, he was dressed in leather knee breeches and his linen shirt was open at the collar. His sleeves were rolled up to elbows and his thick forearms were daubed with ink. In the years since she had last laid eyes on Jack Hampton he'd grown taller and broader through the shoulders—daily lifting wooden forms heavy with lead type tended to build strong arms and backs. Anne decided he must be prospering in his trade. His muscular calves were encased in fine clocked hose, and his leather shoes were not laced, but buckled with silver.

He ought shave more often. The heavy stubble he wore put a dark, hard edge to an expression Anne had always recalled as being hopeful. He still wore his thick black hair parted and queued, and he still battled a stray lock that slipped the blue ribbon at the nape of his neck, but his angry eyes darted from the buckets of tar to the stormy skies, and two deep creases of consternation formed between his drawn brows.

"Captain Sears," Jack shouted to a thin, graying man wearing a cocked hat and a brown suit. "If we're doing this thing, then let's get it done."

This irked and annoyed Jack Hampton did not mesh well with her fond recollection. Anne always imagined him happy.

"All right, Hampton, let's get it done." The captain mounted the crate and the crowd erupted in cheers and applause. Sears pushed the tricorn back on his head and began. "Brothers and Sisters of Liberty!" The crowd calmed. "With Patriot blood newly spilled on the fields at Lexington and Concord, we must all be diligent to expose and expel the Loyalist traitors lurking in our midst . . ." The captain gestured to the sailors and they prodded the stoic captive to stand in front of the crate no more than ten yards from where Anne and the prostitute stood.

The whore nudged Anne with a sharp elbow. "Best seat in the house, eh?"

The captain resumed. "John Hill, will you redeem yourself by damning the despot George and swearing your loyalty and your life to the cause of liberty?"

The crowd grew hush. Hill spoke, "As God is my judge and God is my witness, I can swear to this: I will never draw my sword against my country, but neither will I raise my hand or my word against our Sovereign, King George."

The groans and snorts of disdain were audible. Anne knew full well this kind of prevarication would not hold sway with the mob assembled on the Commons that evening.

"Tory rot!"

"Traitor!"

Wild hissing and jeering turned to laughter when a flung turnip hit John Hill square on the side of his head.

"As a slave to the king who would make us all slaves," Sears charged, "this man is an insidious enemy to the liberties of us all."

Hill did not offer any resistance as he was stripped of jacket and weskit. A sailor grabbed hold of each arm and he was forced to his knees.

A knot formed in Anne's throat. Her base instincts called on her to leave—to cut across the Commons and run full speed back to her shop—but her better sense forced her to stay put. It would not do to draw the attention of the Liberty Boys and risk being labeled a Tory herself.

A bucket was swung up to the captain. The crowd sang out with encouragement. Pistols fired into the air and a boy pounded on an upended barrel with a pair of sticks. To this rude music the bucket tipped and hot pitch poured in a thick stream onto the poor man's head. Luckily for Hill, the tar had cooled some. Flowing slow, like clover honey, it oozed over his face, down to his back and shoulders. The man shuddered and hunched in pain, for pitch hot enough to pour was hot enough to burn and blister. Anne supposed Hill should be grateful, for he had not been stripped of his shirt. As tar and featherings went, his proved to be a more benign sort.

"Now to enliven your appearance . . ." Sears tore open one of the poulterer's sacks and shook feathers over the poor man. Some feathers stuck to the tar—adding the ridiculous to Hill's pitiful humiliation—but most of the feathers caught up on the strong breeze to form a blizzard of fluff flying in faces, up noses and into the mouths of the Liberty Boys and onlookers alike. Rather than cheer and applaud as they should, the crowd sputtered and slapped at feathers clinging to wool jackets and felt hats.

"Move him along now." Sears gave Hill a nudge with his booted foot. The crowd parted. With cudgels, two sailors herded the pathetic, staggering figure to parade down Broad Way.

Anne thought to join this procession as a means to escape the crowd, but she hesitated to mix in with the rough cabal trailing along behind the tarred and befeathered victim, instead deciding to weather the mob and make a discreet exit when the crowd winnowed away on its own.

Anne looked over to where Jack Hampton stood, his arms folded and his expression a dark cloud of impatience as Captain Sears waited for the tumultuous multitude to reform and shuffle close in anticipation of the second tarring. Taking advantage of the lull, a pie man, as wide as he was tall, skirted along the front edge doing a brisk business.

At last, the second man was brought to the fore. Writhing and spitting, his voice grated the ear like an iron nail drawn across a quarrel of glass. "Fuckin' sods! Whoresons! Bugger yiz all! Bugger yiz *all*!"

The young whore leaned in. "Now there's a pinheaded, pinched-faced Tory sniveler if ever I saw one."

And that was an apt description. Tall and exceedingly thin with drooping shoulders and a sunken chest, the man's head was at least two sizes too small for the rest of him. In a vain attempt to conceal a balding pate, sparse brown hair thick with pomade was plastered into a slick sheet curving over the top of his head. The wind reached under to lift the greasy flap of hair and it slapped up and down like some sort of macabre hinged lid.

Just as with the first man, this one was allowed to keep his shirt. Captain Sears mounted the packing crate. Poised with a pitch bucket in his hand, he called the crowd to order.

"This man is also a slave of the monarchy and a betrayer of his country. William Cunningham, you are charged as an obnoxious and blatant Royalist. Redeem yourself in the sight of your neighbors by damning the tyrant George and swearing your loyalty and your life to the cause of liberty."

Cunningham squawked, "I will not forswear my King."

"Tar the Tory!" shouted the old whore, starting up a chant.

"Tar the Tory!"

"Tar the Tory!"

Two burly sailors wrenched Cunningham by the arms, forcing him to his knees. The chanting continued, the drumming began and the captain tipped the pail.

The pitch—having cooled to a thick mass—would not pour. The mob began to hoot and jeer. Jack Hampton, along with a few of the other Liberty Boys, did little to hide his disdain and threw up his arms at the lack of planning and order. Sears tossed the bucket aside and leapt from the crate to salvage his spectacle. "Damn the tyrant, sir!" he demanded.

From his twisted position, Cunningham responded by hawking a wad of sputum onto the captain's chest. This defiance earned him a cudgel to the head and a sharp kick to the ribs. Sears grabbed the man by his shock of greasy hair and bent his head back.

"Damn the King, I say!"

Dazed and coughing, Cunningham blinked at the blood trickling into his eye. "I say . . ." he panted, ". . . I say *God bless King George . . . God bless good King George,* ye bunch o' bung-buggered, cock-sucking rebel bastard boys . . ."

The sailors let loose with clubs and boots, unleashing a violent beating. Cunningham curled into a ball as vicious blows rained down upon him from every direction. The crowd surged forward with a roar.

Pistol fire. The dockworkers kicked and tore the packing crate apart and people crowded around to wrest a club from the debris. Throttled into the midst of this instant riot, Anne struggled to escape the press. Stretching on tiptoes, she craned her neck, searching for Jack Hampton. Her package squirted from her arms. She dropped to her knees to save the vicar's sermons from being ground into the green. Someone grabbed Anne hard by the upper arm and yanked her to her feet.

"C'mon . . . away from here!"

The young prostitute shoved Anne along, plowing a path through the incensed mob to where the pie peddler sat on his fat hind end. He'd slit the ticking on the remaining sack of feathers and with mad glee tossed chubby armfuls up into the darkening sky.

The whore took Anne by the hand and they ran—cutting across

the Commons, through the Presbyterian churchyard, down a narrow alleyway—skittering to a stop on Williams Street, leaning back against a rough stone wall to catch a breath. A group of boys went dashing past, flinging a lit string of squibs to fizzle and pop at their feet. Startled, the two women clutched at each other, then giggled in relief.

"The world has gone mad for sure." The prostitute laughed, plucking feathers from her hair. "It looks as if we're the ones what were tarred and feathered!"

Anne brushed at her skirt, thick with chicken feathers. "It's getting dark . . ."

"If you need me to, miss, if it would make you feel safer, I can walk along with you—or behind, if you like."

Anne stopped grooming and held out a hand. "I'm Anne Merrick . . . Your name?"

"Patsy," the girl answered, suddenly serious with a bob of the knee, barely grazing Anne's fingertips with her own. "Patsy Quinn, m'am."

"Well, Patsy Quinn, you most likely saved me from a trampling, and I'm grateful to you. I appreciate your offer and all your kind assistance, but I need not trouble you any further. I can make my way from here."

"Aye, then. A good evening to you, miss."

"Good evening, Patsy." Anne set off. Upon reaching the next corner, she looked back to see smiling Patsy Quinn in an animated conversation with a portly gentleman wearing an old-fashioned curly wig.

Back to business for me as well. Anne marched a quickstep to her shop. She crossed her fingers, hoping Titus had not yet scattered the form composed for the vicar's sermon, or she would have to spend half the night resetting type by candlelight. She would pay a call on the vicar with fresh copies and the tale of her exploits with the mobocracy, and perhaps she might not lose his custom.

Up ahead, a gang of youths came running pell-mell from the narrow alleyway her shop shared with the baker. Anne rounded the corner and stopped dead in her tracks. Shards of plate glass were strewn over the dirt lane in front of her shop. She moved forward slowly.

Anne found every diamond-shaped pane on her shop-front windows broken. With the tip of her shoe, she toed the shattered bits mingled with scattered eggshells. She glanced up. Raw egg dripping from the shingle touting *Merrick's Press* plopped upon her shoulder. She reached for the door with a trembling hand. Across the faded oak, scrawled with bootblack in thick, angry letters:

Tory Take CARE.

CHAPTER TWO

❧❧

Suspicion is the companion of mean souls,
and the bane of all good society.

THOMAS PAINE, *Common Sense*

November 1775
In Merrick's Pressroom

WITH the handle of an inkball gripped in each fist, Anne beat an even coat of ink onto the composed type—a crucial and exacting task. Poor coverage resulted in a faint impression. Too much ink filled in the letterforms. Either extreme produced illegible material, a costly waste of precious paper.

As one pressman beat, the second pulled. Titus fixed a sheet of paper to the points that held it in place and pulled the lever to move the heavy brass platen down, pressing the paper against the inked type. Today, Beater and Puller worked in lovely concert, producing perfectly executed folios. Later that evening, when the pages were good and dry, Anne and Sally would fold the folios into four-page pamphlets titled "A Friendly Address to all Reasonable Americans."

Sally peeled the last sheet from the press and hung it to dry on the racks stretching along one wall. Titus tidied the press and cleaned the inked form, and Anne saw to the inkballs. After a hard day's use, her inkballs looked much like a pair of big black mushrooms. She pried the tacks free from around the wooden handles and removed the sheepskin covers and wool stuffing. She dropped the ink-soaked sheepskin into a bucket of stale urine, and used a wire brush to tease the stuffing smooth and fluffy for the next use.

Anne crinkled her nose and moved the acrid pissbucket into the far corner, hung her leather apron on a hook and sank exhausted onto her stool. As a young girl, she was always relegated to the tedious task of typesetting, but her father would often allow her to beat. Merrick ran an altogether different operation, and for years she was never allowed to wander from the dreary compositor's stick. Anne enjoyed working her press together with Titus and Sally. Knuckling the muscles at the small of her back, she viewed with no small pleasure the fruit of their labor—two hundred and fifty copies.

"Sally." Anne fished in her pocket for some coin. "Run over to Bellamy's and buy us all a pie for our supper."

Sally unwound the wide kerchief she'd used to protect and contain her ginger braids, and stuffed it in her pocket. "Might be today Bellamy has those lobster pies ye fancy so much, aye?"

The thought of flaky pastry filled with steaming chunks of lobster meat in cream and butter caused Anne to slip Sally another coin. "It's been a long, hard day—two pies each."

"None for me, Mrs. Anne," Titus announced as he slipped his bib apron over his head, its ink-stained cowhide a shade darker than his smiling brown face. "Supper and darts with my mates at the tavern tonight," he explained, squeezing his big arms into a heavy overcoat. He fit a cocked hat trimmed with fancy gold braid over wooly black hair.

Titus Gilmore had come to Merrick's twenty years before—a sturdy twelve-year-old purchased at the slave market on Wall Street. In a deathbed fit of conscience, no doubt spurred by selfish concern for the state of his immortal soul, Peter Merrick had set Titus free.

Anne had endured seven years under Merrick's roof as an uneasy slaveholder, and Titus's change in status soothed her conscience immeasurably. Titus moved into a room above Fraunces Tavern, his favorite haunt down the street. He worked for a generous wage on the days Anne needed him, but otherwise he was free to accept opportunities from other print shops. An accomplished journeyman, skilled dartsman and shrewd gambler, Titus had no problem augmenting the erratic income earned at Merrick's.

"I'm off!" Sally whisked her crimson wool cloak about her shoulders, popped hands through the vertical slits and took up her market basket. Anne bade Titus good evening and he followed Sally out the door.

Fading daylight angled in through the windows over her compositor's table. Anne usually bemoaned the coming of winter, for the shorter days offered little quality light by which to work type. In truth, lately it did not matter, as she had little business to occupy her press. She looked down at the form Titus had left on her table—row upon row of lead type set square and tight within the frame, the title bracketed with fancy ornaments—

꙰❧ A Friendly Address to all Reasonable Americans ☙꙰

Anne could not recall when she'd learned to read backward, but it seemed as though she had always been able to do so. She and her brother, David, likened the ability to knowing a secret language. Sometimes, though, when she worked quickly, the set type became so much gibberish—where she almost didn't recognize the words and phrases.

These words—this title—she saw very clearly. *A Friendly Address to all Reasonable Americans.* Anne heaved a sigh. It seemed so harmless, so . . . *friendly.* As she'd composed the text, she'd tried hard to convince herself that printing this pamphlet was no more dangerous than reprinting one of the vicar's sermons. But when she proofed the first galley, she did so with her heart in her throat. There was no doubt this windfall job—which she'd needed so desperately and accepted so gratefully from Mr. Rivington—was a virulent Loyalist treatise. Upon its first printing weeks before, its author barely managed to elude a murderous mob and flee the city with his parts attached. Anne eyed the sheets drying on the racks. It would behoove her to get this material folded, wrapped and delivered with speed.

Anne marched over to the fireplace, stirred the embers and tossed in another log. She went back to the form, loosened the quoins and began to sort the letters back into the thin, flat cases where she stored her fonts. Capital letters, numbers and ornaments were sorted into the individual compartments of the upper case. The lower case housed the rest of the letters, including punctuation. The leading—smooth lead slugs used to separate lines of type—those she kept apart in a different container.

With a sensitivity developed over the years, Anne was able to identify most of the letters by touch, and with practiced ease she dismantled the form, running fingertips along the sentences, plucking up the bits of lead as she was taught—first the As, and then the Bs, and so on—careful to mind her p's and q's. The metal bits tinked funny little tunes as she dropped them into their compartments.

All type foundries were located in Europe, and for colonial printers, fonts were never cheap or easy to come by. Anne was lucky in that Merrick would have nothing but the finest Dutch-made Caslon for his presses. It was one of few traits she admired in him.

With the advent of open armed rebellion, trade vessels laden with British manufacture had ceased coming to port, and New York's merchants and tradesmen were beginning to feel the pinch. The lack of ready-made ink from England was an easy work-around for Anne. She had experience mixing varnish and lampblack from her years in her father's shop, so she simply returned to the habit of using home-brewed ink.

But paper—paper posed a considerable problem. Colonial paper mills were few and far between, and the paper manufactured in them was at best suited for newspapers, pamphlets and broadsides. The finest American mill did not come near to producing a grade that could compare with English and Dutch made bond. One was more likely to find a basin of holy water in hell than find a ream of quality paper for purchase in New York City.

With good paper so hard to come by, Anne could not replenish her blank form stock—deeds, wills, bills of sale, bills of lading and the like—the mainstays of her stationery business. Merrick's Stationery was reduced to selling homemade ink, quills and the slow-moving inventory of expensive imported books left over from better days.

Tory Take CARE—the angry warning Anne had scrubbed from her door with a stiff bristle brush became watchwords engraved into her brain—a reminder to pay heed to the goings-on in the world around her. Anne determined she must be ever supple and shift to and fro with the winds of the political clime in order to protect her property and livelihood.

The day after witnessing the tar and feathering on the Commons, she had Titus dismantle the better press and store it away in the closet beneath the stair. The second-best press and compositing tables were relocated to the far back end of the shop. The stationery counter and bookcases were moved center, perpendicular to the large hearth, serving to divide the long, beam-ceilinged space in two. Titus banged together a pair of trestle tables and accompanying benches and installed the new furnishings at the front end of the shop. Anne repainted her shingle with the image of a steaming cup framed by a curving quill pen, circled with the words MERRICK'S COFFEEHOUSE STATIONERY & PRESS.

Putting a copy of *The Art of Cookery Made Plain and Easy* to good use, Sally found she had quite a knack in the kitchen. Tuesdays through Saturdays, Sally and Anne offered light fare for a fair price at the sign of the Cup and Quill—the best coffee, scones, cakes, custards and puddings in the neighborhood. Good word spread, and in three months alone Anne realized enough profit to consider replacing the glass in her boarded-up windows.

And ol' Merrick scoffed so when I taught Sally to read, Anne gloated, trickling the last handful of s's into the lower case.

Four years before, with little to recommend Sally Tucker save for the low price of her contract, Merrick purchased the timid fourteen-year-old girl from the master of a schooner just in from Glasgow. Indented as their maidservant, the quiet girl was diligent at her chores, but she tended to hover when Anne would teach Jemmy his letters—sweeping, dusting and polishing the pewter—never very far from earshot. When Anne discovered Sally tracing the day's lesson on a sooty window, she decided to include the girl in her classroom. Quick-witted, it was not long before Sally graduated from the primer to more complicated works. One often found Sally's freckled nose buried in a book or a newspaper.

The front door opened and slammed shut.

"A mob, Annie!" Sally flew in, flinging her basket to the table.

Anne jumped from her stool. "Where?"

"Rivington's!" Sally pulled the folios from the drying rack into a sloppy pile. "They say poor Mr. Rivington's fled the town."

Titus opened the door. The handle was wrenched from his grip by a wicked gust off the East River and the door slammed *bang* against the wall. The wind tore in, creating a swirling maelstrom of paper flying erratic about the shop. Titus pushed the door shut, putting an equally sudden end to the sudden hurricane. He clacked the three brass bolts home—bottom, top and center.

"Och, but tha's an ill wind." Sally scooped up one of the wind-strewn pages and stared despondent at the copy. "This Tory business'll surely do us in."

"Into the fire with them, Sally," Titus ordered as he threw off his coat and hat. "Mrs. Anne—you and I must see to the type."

Anne did not waste time bemoaning all the fine work going up the chimney. She knew the drill. Following Titus to the back of the shop, together they pulled and pushed the unwieldy supply cabinet away from the wall to expose a short, wide door—access to the triangular closet space beneath the stairs. Anne unlatched the door and Titus pulled out a few heavy cases filled with old worn fonts they kept stored there. While Sally darted about plucking up pages and tossing them on the fire, Anne and Titus worked like a pair of stevedores loading a ship's hold, lugging the expendable old type to the compositor's table and tucking the precious cases of fine Caslon into the closet.

Titus maneuvered the last case into the closet when a raucous pounding sounded at the front door. Sally helped to push and shove the supply cabinet back into position, concealing the closet door. The hammering at the front door and boarded windows became more boisterous, accompanied by much shouting and sharp whistling.

Anne swiped the ink-stained mobcap from her head and stuffed it into the box with the leading. She twisted her tumble of chestnut hair into a quick knot and secured it with the pair of pins from the pocket at her hip. Spying a streak of black ink on the kerchief tucked about the low neckline of her blouse, she stripped it off and tossed it into the fire. There was no time to change from the old brown skirt she wore on press days, or the linsey blouse, now made immodest for lack of a neckerchief.

The knocking at the door shifted to an incessant thudding, but the sturdy brass hinges and bolts withstood the weight of determined shoulders being heaved into the oak door. Anne took a position at the front of the shop next to one of the trestle tables. A good foot taller, Titus stood behind her, the iron poker snatched from the hearth gripped in one fist. Anne waved Sally to the door. "Go, go, go . . . afore they break it down."

Sally snapped the bolts back, one by one. "Hoy, lads!" she shouted. "Keep yer breeches on, aye?"

The door swung open, and a dozen men spilled into the shop like so many slippery cod from a fisherman's net—young men smelling strong of rum and ale—dockworkers, mechanics and apprentices by the looks of them. Having gained entrance, the raiders blinked in momentary confusion, floundering to form slipshod ranks. Most were armed with clubs, though Anne noticed several muskets and one man with a brace of pistols tucked at his waist.

The last three men came through the open door bearing grim expression—all three familiar to Anne. Walter Quakenbos, the baker in apron and shirtsleeves, must have come straight from his shop next door. Captain Isaac Sears and Jack Hampton were dressed for cold weather in boots and caped wool coats, their cocked hats tucked beneath their arms. Hatless Quakenbos, a burly man, folded his arms across his chest. Sally shut the door and backed away to stand together with Anne and Titus.

It disturbed Anne to see Jack Hampton once again mixed with vulgar company, but then, the man who'd just stepped into her shop was not the celebratory, smiling Jack of her memory. Tar-and-feather Jack had come to call this day. Beat-a-man-senseless Jack.

Isaac Sears took the lead, and came to stand before her. "You are Widow Merrick, the proprietress?"

Anne nodded. "I am, sir. Indeed."

"Why did you bolt your door to us?"

Her knees had gone as soft as Sally's egg custard and she braced a hand on the tabletop beside her. "Bolted with no prejudice on my part, I assure you, sir. All comers will find my shop closed Mondays." Anne forced a smile. "Why, my neighbor Mr. Quakenbos knows this for the truth. He can attest."

"'S truth." Quakenbos shagged his head up and down. "Always closed Mondays, even back when ol' Peter was alive."

The baker's confirmation did not serve to ease her plight, for Sears was not persuaded. "Why did you hesitate to come to the door when called to it?"

"Habit, sir. I am a widow alone living in uncertain times"— Anne pointed to her boarded windows—"with ample cause to be wary."

"But you are not alone today," Sears noted.

"My journeyman and maidservant are here cleaning shop." Anne pointed to Sally's basket sitting on the table. "We were making ready for supper when you and your companions arrived."

Sears peeled back the napkin covering the basket. He picked up a crescent-shaped pie, sniffed it and took a bite from one flaky end. Chewing this mouthful, he stepped closer to eye Titus and the poker tight in his fist. A spattering of crumbs sprayed from his mouth when he spoke. "Your nigger seems to have violence on his mind."

"I hold no slaves," Anne asserted. "Mr. Gilmore is a free man in my employ and a good friend to Sally and me. As such, he is concerned for our protection." Anne turned to her journeyman. "Please put the poker by, Titus. I'm sure these men mean us no harm."

Titus hesitated, then flipped the poker to bounce and clang onto the table. Disarmed, the big man still bore a threatening countenance and Anne was grateful to have him at her back.

"Mr. Sears," Anne brooked a conciliatory tone. "I do sincerely apologize if my locked door and Titus's fervor caused you and your friends alarm. You need not waste any more of your valuable time with us. As you can see, we are up to no mischief here."

"Very nice. Very civil indeed." The captain popped the last bite of the lobster pie into his mouth. "And yet"—he reached into the basket again—"I still wonder why you were so long in opening the door . . ."

Jack Hampton shifted from one booted foot to the other and loosened the horn buttons on his overcoat. "Isaac! What does it matter? Let's get on with the search."

"Search!?" Anne squeaked.

"A thorough search." Hampton looked her square in the eye without a flicker of recognition. "Rivington's apprentice informed us we'd find Tory swill originating from your press."

"Well, sirs," Anne dithered, "I—I . . . I'm absolutely shocked to hear you lend credence to such charges. Your source is obviously suspect—a terrified boy who would no doubt say anything to gain this lot's good graces—including pointing a finger my way." Anne dismissed the notion with a flip of her hand. "So much stuff and nonsense. My press has been idle for weeks for lack of paper and ink." Interlocking her fingers she clasped them at her waist to keep the men from seeing her trembling. "Times are hard, sir. Our living at Merrick's is earned from the sale of coffee, quills and scones these days."

Jack squared his shoulders. "We have cause to search. If you've nothing to hide, you've nothing to fear."

"I fear for the loss of my common rights." Anne took a step and blocked the aisle leading back to the print shop. "I will not allow a search. I recognize neither your cause nor authority."

"We do not seek your permission, madam." Sears came to stand before her. "We cull traitors from our midst by the authority of the people."

"The people?" Anne scoffed. "This drunken mob?"

"Liberty must be protected."

"And who's to safeguard my liberty?" Anne gritted her teeth, anger displacing fear. "My rights are being trod upon here. Am I to be tarred and feathered for not flinging my door open quick enough?"

"Widow Merrick," Quakenbos interceded. "Be reasonable. We've no tar and feathers here . . . Allow the lads a quick look around and then we can all be on our way."

"Bugger that!" Sears swiped the back of his forearm across his mouth. "We will search these premises at will. We're not a mob. We're militia, duly recognized by the Committee of One Hundred."

Anne's ire sparked a fury. "Militia—mob—it is a pity that most of us citizens are hard-pressed to tell the difference these days."

Sears towered over her. "You are glib, madam."

"And you, sir, are a brute."

"Search the shop," Sears shouted.

The militiamen pushed past Anne and fanned out to begin poking about. Sears sent half a dozen men up the stairs to search the living quarters. Titus followed after them, calling out, "Don't worry, Mrs. Anne. I'll mind they don't steal anything."

Smug Isaac Sears made himself comfortable at one of the tables. Quakenbos joined him. Jack Hampton set his hat down and made a beeline for the press.

Anne paid no mind to the militiamen rifling through drawers and cupboards. Her eye was locked on Jack Hampton. He strolled around her press, stopping to give the rounce several turns—moving the carriage in and out from under the brass platen. He swung open the tympan and pressed a palm to the marble imposing stone still damp from its recent cleaning. Jack wandered to the compositor's table and poked through the disorganized pile of quoins, gutter sticks and leading—the miscellaneous parts and pieces from the form she had just dismantled. He found the pissbucket in the corner and hoisted it onto the compositor's table. Using a gutter stick, he fished up one of the leather inkball covers, studying the urine-drenched sheepskin for quite some time before dropping it back to the bucket.

Blast his eyes. In all the hubbub, she had not thought to clear the bucket away. She called to him, "Cleaning day, sir! Long overdue." He nodded and continued to poke through the mess on the back table.

Sally came up and whispered. "Tha' one's a nosy bastard, in't he? Dinna fash, Annie, these rebels canna arrest ye fer keepin' an untidy shop."

"I don't know . . ." Anne grasped Sally by the hand. "Who's to stop them from doing whatever they please?"

Hampton looked out the back window and called two militiamen over. "Go search those outbuildings there," he ordered, sending the men through the back door to search the privy and the kitchenhouse.

"Och! My kitchen . . ." Sally snatched up her cloak and bustled after them.

Jack turned his attention to the other items on the table. Picking through the type cases, he held the inferior bits of type up to daylight. He tugged Anne's mobcap from the box of leading and spread it out on the tabletop. After contemplating it for what to Anne seemed an eternity, he took the leather aprons hung from their hooks and laid them on the table.

A loud noise erupted from the Stationery and Anne turned to see a big man—a fisherman by his wooly cap and cuffed seaboots—standing before her case of Books for Sale, sweeping shelf after shelf of leather-bound volumes to the floor like so much rubbish.

"Have you lost what little wits you possess?" Anne rushed round and gathered up an armful of books from the floor, piling them onto the countertop. "Fish-stinking lout!"

"Mouthy Tory bitch." The fisherman swept his arm across the countertop and redistributed the books she had just set there back to the floor.

"*Blount!*" Jack Hampton came over, boots pounding hard on the floorboards. "There's no call for that!"

"Bugger off, Hampton. Who's to say I won't find some Tory

scribblins hidden here?" Blount pretended to study the gilt-stamped title of the book he was holding upside down in his filthy hands.

Anne winced at the sight of his coarse fingers reeking of fish offal fanning through the pages, muttering, "It might be easier to read if you held the book right-side up . . . you illiterate ape."

Blount paused from his feigned perusing of the pages. He grimaced at Anne, baring filmy gray-green teeth, and slammed the book hard against the edge of the countertop, flipping the broken volume onto the floor with the others.

"Enough!" Jack clapped a hand to Blount's shoulder and shoved him toward the door.

Blount shrugged free, rubbing his shoulder. "Leave off. You ain't the cap'n here . . ."

In a single swift motion Jack took a step forward and freed a nasty dagger from his left boot. With eye dark and voice low, he growled, "Off with you."

"Yiv no call t' pull yer sticker on me, ye correy-fisted devil. I'm on my way." Blount backed away slow. Pressing a crooked knuckle to his brow in sullen mock salute, he exited the shop.

Jack slipped the knife back into his boot. "I just can't abide a fellow like that . . . only in it for the mayhem he can cause and the free grog he can swill." He picked up the broken book just flung to the floor and handed it to Anne, its loose binding strings and pages dangling at a distressing angle from between the cover boards, like the broken wing of a bird.

A soft "Oh!" pushed from Anne's lungs as she cradled the damaged book on open palms. More stunned than frightened by the wanton destruction, she opened the book and turned past its torn frontispiece to the title page—*The Life and Strange Surprising Adventures of Robinson Crusoe* by Daniel Defoe. Shoulders slumped, she squeezed her eyes tight to contain a rush of tears.

"A beautiful edition, this." Jack took the book from her hands and examined the damage. "*Crusoe*—one of my favorites. You know, Fletcher's Bindery on Wall Street . . . they can mend it for you good as new. Tell 'em Hampton sent you."

Anne swiped her tears away, and tilted her head back to meet Jack square in the eye. "Why are you in it with them?"

"What do you mean?"

"That man Blount—in it for the grog you said. Quakenbos there . . ." Anne flipped a thumb to the baker sitting across from Sears. "He's had his eye on my shop since the day Mr. Merrick died— he is sure to prosper by my being run out of town. And Sears—well, everyone knows he's plain power mad. Why're you in it?"

"Fair question." Hampton cocked his head, a half smile crinkling the corners of his eyes a bit. "A few months ago I would have answered you with much rabble-rousing zeal—something dramatic like, *'For I prefer Liberty to wearing shackles and licking the hand of a Tyrant, madam!'*"

Overhearing Jack's loud pronouncement, Quakenbos thumped the tabletop with a beefy fist and uttered a "Hear! Hear!"

Jack lowered his tone. "But there's more to it now. Much more." He shifted his weight and twin furrows creased the spot just above the bridge of his nose. "We are at war. Blood has been shed, and our countrymen are dying. I do all I can for our cause—wholly in it, heart, mind and soul, for I will not have our men perish for naught."

Face-to-face with Jack's pure conviction, her cynicism began to dissipate, lifting like a misling fog on a sunny day. The man's sincere expression reminded Anne of her brother, David, and of herself, so long ago when she once felt strong for the American cause. Anne bent to gather the books from the floor to hide the sudden shame coloring her cheeks.

"Let me help . . ." Jack joined her, rattling off the titles as he gathered an armful of books. "*Tristram Shandy, Gulliver, Don Quixote, Tom Jones, Pamela* . . . a very fine selection."

"I ordered this stock after Merrick died," Anne said with some pride. She took up a rag, giving the embossed covers and gilt edges a good swipe before shelving each book. "My husband—he would not tolerate a novel in his Stationery."

"Husband . . ." Jack said with a shake of his head as he set a stack of books on the countertop. "I thought he was your father."

Anne glanced over her shoulder. "What?"

"Merrick . . . the day the Stamp Act was repealed . . ." Jack clarified. "Truly, I thought him your father."

"You remember that day?"

"Everyone remembers that day. You remember it as well."

Anne nodded. "That I do, sir, for every woman remembers her wedding day."

"Wedding day?" Jack winced and groaned. "My deepest apologies, Mrs. Merrick—I was filled with brash and more than a few pints and . . ."

"Never mind . . ." Anne was amused by his fluster. "T'was a lifetime ago."

Jack handed Anne another book, and she wiped it clean, basking in his genuine smile, once again allowing it to comfort her on a day of despair.

Sally strolled back in with the two militiamen trailing behind, each of them munching on a raisin scone. She winked at Anne and waggled her brows. Anne looked up at Jack, a good head taller than she, and caught him admiring the view down the front of her blouse.

Titus and the six militiamen came clattering down the stairs. One of the men announced, "We din't find no Tory contraband anywhere up there, cap'n."

"Alright then, it's off to the pub with us." Sears stood, brushing pie crumbs from his coat. "Let's get going, boys."

As the men shuffled into ranks, buttoning jackets, pulling on hats and rewinding woolen mufflers against the winter chill, a warm wave of relief wafted over Anne. She issued a silent vow to never, never again be lured by crown silver into another such precarious position.

Jack and Anne bent together to gather the last few scattered books. It caught Anne's eye first and Jack followed her gaze—a lone surviving freshly printed folio, hiding in the shadow cast by the bookcase, one corner caught under the edge of the skirting board.

Anne reached for it, but Jack was far too quick. He snatched up the sheet and straightened, holding the page to the light. At that moment his expression reminded Anne of the time she had fed her trusting little Jemmy a dose of bitters—sheer surprise turning to utter betrayal and in an instant, shifting to the vehement anger hooding Jack's eyes and sending the muscles at his clenched jaw a-twitch.

Anne grasped his forearm and whispered, "I'm no Tory . . . I swear to you, I'm not!"

Jack swiped his thumb over the damp ink, smearing the word "Reasonable" illegible. Jerking from her grip, he stumbled back a step and held the page aloft. "Isaac! Have a look—"

Sears strode over and read the sheet in Jack's hand.

"Well, well, well . . . so the indignant widow is not so innocent." Sears smirked with such pleasure. "Alright, boys, the pints will have to wait. Go and work up a thirst—have at the Tory's press."

With a whoop and a holler, the militiamen ran to the back of the shop. Three dockworkers in thick-soled hobnail boots kicked and kicked at the press's wooden frame until it splintered. They pulled and wrenched the pieces apart, sending the imposing stone to the floor with a crash. There was a mad scramble for the machined parts, as they would fetch a good price for anyone lucky enough to wrangle one free.

Sally and Titus pulled Anne away. Urging her up the stairs, they could not get her to progress beyond the first three steps. Gripping the banister tight, she stood frozen and watched the broken bits of her press march out the front door.

Sears yelled out, "Don't leave the type behind, boys."

A sandy-haired apprentice produced a tin whistle and tooted a crude "Yankee Doodle" as the cases of worn type were carried out the door. Quakenbos and Sears fell in at the rear and Sears waved his tricorn in salute. "The Sons of Liberty thank you, Widow Merrick! Tory type makes for the best musket balls."

And they were gone. The door hung open, banging against the wall in time to the fading "Yankee Doodle," while the evil wind once again whipped through her shop. Anne stumbled from her perch on the stairs, agog at the militia's swift ferocity and the sudden silence of its departure. She pushed the door shut and saw Jack

Hampton's hat on the trestle table. She grabbed the hat and looked to where Hampton stood lingering near the back window, intent on comparing a few bits of type spilled from the carted-away type cases, to the damning folio he'd laid out on the compositor's table.

Anne dodged Titus and ran back, tossing the tricorn onto the floor. "I hope you're happy. My press is in ruins; my types are all gone . . ."

"All gone? I don't think so . . ." Turning slowly on his heel, Jack studied the perimeter walls.

"I'll have you leave my shop at once, sir."

Titus came and placed a hand on her shoulder. "Mrs. Anne, you go on upstairs with Sally now. I'll see this fellow to the door."

"No need for that," Jack said, folding the page into quarters. "Fine work this, very fine—my compliments to you both." He slipped the paper into his coat pocket and squatted down for his hat. He rose eyeing the floorboards, quickly traversing the space between himself and the supply cabinet in three long strides.

"Your work is done here, sir," Anne said, scurrying after him. "I would have you leave."

Jack paid her no mind. He traced the toe of his boot along the raw scrape marks in the floor. Grasping the edge of the cabinet, he angled it a few inches away from the wall, enough to peer behind and see the hidden closet door.

Anne lurched forward and pulled him back by the arm. "Haven't you done enough?"

Jack shrugged her off, looking behind the cabinet. "It seems I haven't."

Anne's voice grew shrill. "Just go . . . Why can't you just go? I've been punished enough . . ."

Jack set his hat on his head and made an abrupt about-face back to the compositor's table. He grabbed up the wire bale handle on the tin pissbucket, marched straight for the bookcase and splashed the stale urine over the fine volumes, tossing the empty bucket to land with a spin and clatter at speechless Anne's feet.

"That is your punishment, madam. Be grateful I don't call the boys back to give you the tarring and feathering you so richly deserve." He answered her openmouthed astonishment with a stern admonition. "I will have my eye on you."

Jack Hampton hiked up his collar and stormed out the door.

Chapter Three

We have it in our power to begin the world over again.

THOMAS PAINE, *Common Sense*

April 1776
At the Sign of the Cup and Quill

THE new day candled at the edge of the horizon. Through a dewy haze, soft dawn illuminated church spires and gabled rooftops, inching in to color the docks and quays, and light the dirt lanes between storehouses, taverns, shops and homes. A crisp, clean breeze bespoke a fine, clear day—welcome change after a long spell of rain. With spade on shoulder, Jack Hampton slogged through the sucking mud, glad to see the early-morning streets alive with like-minded men on the move.

The Continental Army had been massing on the island for weeks—almost fourteen thousand soldiers arrived to defend the city. Jack was among the New Yorkers who were glad to hear General Washington would soon be setting up his headquarters at #1 Broad Way.

A month before, British General Howe woke in Boston to find rebel cannons mounted on Dorchester Heights, and he withdrew his forces and evacuated the town. Attention turned south, for it was clear as glass to anyone who could read a map—the Redcoats needed to take New York City.

Unfortunately, Jack's beloved hometown provided the perfect base from which to quell a widespread rebellion. The quality of her protected harbor was unsurpassed, and the mouth of the Hudson provided as excellent an access to the north as the Atlantic did to the south. British warships menacing the bay gave proof of intent to take New York and nothing could be done to drive them away. Unopposed by naval force, the *Asia* alone with her sixty-four guns could pound the city to a fine powder in a matter of hours.

While Patriot soldiers marched into town, the civilian population headed out. The daily influx and exodus clogged Broad Way all the way to the Post Road. Docks sat empty. Trade idled. Shops closed. Normal living turned absolutely topsy-turvy.

Jack was proud to be one of the staunch New Yorkers who stayed put and supported the effort to fortify the city against invasion. But many Tories remained as well—those who held quiet hope for reconciliation, and to Jack's utter dismay and disgust, those active collaborators who supported the monarchy. It galled him when the Provincial Congress did nothing to put a stop to the Loyalists who provided food and fresh water to the British warships lurking off Bedloe's Island. Like a pack of well-fed wolves, the *Asia*, the *Mercury*, the *Phoenix* and the *Duchess of Gordon* cruised the bay at will, presaging certain perdition.

Jack turned off Duke Street and headed for the sign of the Cup and Quill. Just as he arrived, Sally unbolted the door and opened the shop for business. Jack Hampton filed in along with the ready crowd of eager customers, grabbing his regular seat to the left of the door that Sally had propped open with a tin of lead slugs. Before immersing himself in the latest issue of the *Philadelphia Gazette* he'd stuffed into his coat pocket, Jack perused the day's collection of customers.

Citizen soldiers.

Farmers and tradesmen from every colony volunteered for service, and lacking uniforms, many served their stint dressed in their everyday garb. It was easy enough to identify the origins of the two men in fringed hunting shirts and leather leggings. Propping their long rifles against the wall, the pair of backcountry Virginians doffed battered felt hats and settled in at the far corner table. A group of uniformed soldiers sat at the table across from Jack's.

New Englanders.

It was difficult to keep track of the sundry uniform types sported by some of the colonial companies. Such a hodgepodge affair, this Continental Army—nigh on impossible to tell officer from enlisted man save for bits of colored cloth General Washington ordered worn on shoulders, or ruffled into cockades and sewn onto hats. Sporting bright ribband sashes worn across the chest, the highest-ranking officers were the easiest to identify.

The young fellows sitting across from Jack—enlisted men, all—wore matching striped waistcoats, blue jackets and round felt hats. Jack caught the eye of one. "Where do you boys hail from?"

"Massachusetts. And you?"

Jack leaned back, tipping the two front legs of his chair from the floor. "New York City, brother."

The young soldier grinned easy, admiring Sally's rear end as she circled their table distributing wooden mugs and plates. "A native son! Not many of you around. We're told this is the place for the finest coffee in all of New York City."

Jack laughed, examining the inside of the empty mug Sally had set before him. "I'd say this is just about the *only* coffee in all of New York City."

Anne Merrick sidestepped through the open back door, balancing a tray of baked goods on each hip. She slipped the trays onto the stationery counter, which had been pushed to the back of the shop. Since the day the Liberty Boys had relieved Mrs. Merrick of her printing press, the entire length of the first floor was devoted to serving comestibles. The rebel occupation proved an enormous boon to the Tory widow's business, and she did not want for customers.

True to his word, Jack Hampton kept his eye on Anne Merrick, making it a habit to take coffee in her shop at least once a day. He had to admit a grudging admiration for her resilience. Even the most steadfast Tories fled the town once visited by the Liberty Boys. But not Mrs. Merrick—she simply swept up the mess, repainted her shingle to read LIBERTY COFFEEHOUSE and reopened for business.

She came in from the kitchen, hefting a steaming coffeepot onto the countertop. For a wife who had not seemed overly fond of her departed husband, Jack had never seen the woman dress in anything other than mourning-wear. Today the widow wore a gauze kerchief tucked about the square neckline of a plain gray gown. Her skirt was protected by a brilliant white apron, its crisp starched bow at the small of her back being the only adornment added to her Quakerlike simplicity. A frilled mobcap covered her chestnut hair, framing her flushed face with a pretty ruffle.

Contrary to her mistress, the Scottish servant girl favored cheerful patterns and colors. Sally brightened the shop in her green skirt and blue-checked apron; her riotous red hair was tied back with a matching checked head scarf.

Crisscrossing the room, Mrs. Merrick carried a tray and Sally handled the coffeepot. Together they visited each customer, filling mugs and this day offering a selection of raisin scones and corn muffins. As usual, Jack's table was the last stop on their route.

"Good morning, Mr. Hampton!" The women greeted him in unison and together dipped a silly, florid curtsy.

"Good morning, ladies," he answered, equally jovial.

"Coffee today, Mr. Hampton?" Sally asked with a grin.

"Please . . ." Jack offered up his mug, and as usual she poured him the dregs from the bottom of the pot—a bitter sludge of grounds mixed with eggshells—coffee so thick he could easily get his spoon to stand upright in it.

Widow Merrick tipped her tray, which was empty save for a lone raisin scone. "Can I tempt you today, Mr. Hampton?"

"Thank you, Mrs. Merrick—I think the scone."

"Good choice." Mrs. Merrick plucked up the scone and placed it on his plate. "Sally baked this one special for you."

Sally peered into his mug with some concern. "Och! The coffee seems a bit on the strong side this morning. Shall I brang ye a lump of sugar and a wee bumper of cream, Mr. Hampton?"

"No need, Sally, this coffee is perfect." Jack pushed his spoon through the muck in his cup. No amount of cream would salvage this brew, and at any rate, as he knew from past experience, any cream brought to him would be curdled, and the lump of sugar would more than likely be a lump of salt.

"Well then"—Anne Merrick smiled—"enjoy!"

Jack was subjected once again to the ridiculous tandem curtsy before they left him to stand at the back of the shop, arms akimbo, watching his every move.

Jack eyed the scone on his plate. Sprinkled with a generous amount of brown sugar and baked to crusty golden perfection, it looked delicious. The regular customers always raved about the quality of the fare produced in the widow's kitchen. He broke the scone in two to expose a soft, crumbly interior, loaded with plump black beetle bugs. Jack pushed the tainted scone and coffee aside. Sally and Anne scampered back to the kitchenhouse, giggling.

Among the many dreadful things he'd been served since becoming a regular at the Liberty Coffeehouse were scones burnt to a charcoal crisp, muffins sprinkled with mouse droppings, cakes frosted with dung and puddings drenched in what smelled like horse piss. The clever women contrived to couple the friendliest, most charming service with the meanest, most rotten fare. The most insidious being the servings where the food seemed perfect and he could discern nothing amiss—steaming coffee, rich cream, sweet sugar, lovely baked goods. Suspecting the food might be laced or injected with some undetectable poison or emetic, Jack could do nothing other than pay for the wonderful fare left uneaten on his plate. Those were the days when the laughter coming from the kitchen was the loudest.

Anne began to clear tables, and Sally began another round, pouring coffee and serving scones and muffins to the new customers. Jack flipped opened his newspaper to catch up on the latest news from Philadelphia.

A breathless boy came in off the street. He pulled the widow to the side, and after a short but excited exchange, Mrs. Merrick slipped him a coin from her pocket and sent him on his way with a pat on the head. She ran up the stairs untying her apron strings and was soon on her way back down with a black wool shawl thrown around her shoulders and a shallow-crowned straw hat pinned to her mob-cap, its black ribbons tied in a bow beneath her chin. Calling, "Mind the shop, Sally!" she sped out the door.

Jack folded his paper, tossed a few coins on the table and slipped out as well.

ಛ ಛ ಛ

ANNE darted up Whitehall toward Broad Way. The city's refuse col-lection, which had been erratic even during the best of times, be-came negligible with the coming of Washington's army. Anne gave wide berth to the pigs snuffling through piles of rubbish and puddles of stagnant water. She slowed her pace at the Bowling Green to skirt a crowd gathering around an effigy dangling from a mock gal-lows, and she stopped to read the label attached to the straw-stuffed figure.

> *Our Royal Governor—the bloody tool of the sanguinary Despot who is using his utmost efforts to ENSLAVE you!*

Adding drama to the display, the gilded equestrian statue of King George dressed in Roman toga and laurel leaf crown loomed from beyond the iron fence surrounding the green. The Liberty Boys had truly honed their craft.

A day did not pass without some poor Loyalist being hauled out by a mob, pelted with brickbats and run from town—often astraddle a rail. The crier had even taken to tolling the names of accused To-ries along with the hour. No longer able to depend on wealth or in-fluence for protection, many avowed Loyalists—the Royal Governor included—fled for their lives, taking sanctuary aboard one of the four British warships menacing the harbor.

Shading her eyes, Anne took a few steps toward the waterfront and scanned the bay. She could just make out the bright pennants and Union Jacks fluttering from the masts poking up through the morning mist. That pretty sight drove the bulk of the populace from the city.

A newsboy pressed a broadside into Anne's hand. She read it quickly—an offer of reward for information on any "traitor" associating with Royal Governor Tryon and his "nest of sycophants."

By far the most valuable commodity supplied to the British Navy was the information being passed along by Loyalist supporters—accurate reports on Patriot troop numbers and placements, fortifications and armaments. Anne eyed the effigy and noted the fierce anger bubbling among those gathered. *Dangerous work, Loyalism.* She crumpled the paper in her fist and dropped it into the gutter.

By repainting her shingle Anne acquired instant Patriot status. In times so ridiculous and volatile, she was quickly learning to roll with the swell and chart an ever-changing course to maintain her own independence. On this day she embarked on a quest for things sweet.

With invasion literally on the horizon, trade disrupted and an army encamped, Anne competed for hard-to-come-by but oh-so-necessary commodities like sugar and coffee. The boy from Van Cortlandt's Sugar House brought word of a rare shipment arrived from the West Indies. If Anne intended to get her hands on a share before the limited stock was depleted, she could not spare the time to make a patriotic show by joining the brewing mob at the Bowling Green. She continued on her excursion up Broad Way.

The cobbled main thoroughfare was daily clogged with the confused hubbub of fleeing citizenry, soldiers on the move and enough beasts, overloaded carts, and heavy artillery to create a daily writhing quagmire rivaling Dante's fifth circle of hell. Anne kept a hand on her hat to keep it from being knocked to the ground as she melded in with the throng.

Overnight, her hometown had become an armed camp. Lacking warships and armament, the Patriot army had no other choice but to transform New York City into an advantageous battleground.

Trenches were being dug and redoubts thrown up. Martial law was imposed in full effect—complete with a set curfew, sentries posted and passwords issued.

No place for a widow on her own . . . as her father was wont to remind Anne in letters admonishing her to return home to Peekskill. And she might well follow his advice, if it were not always coupled with the endorsement of some old friend or ancient widower in need of a wife.

In need of a slave or a whore, more like. Anne repressed a shudder. It did not speak well for filial affection when she'd rather brave the perilous clime in an occupied and dangerous city than risk coming under her father's dominion. Her father was more than happy to profit by another "advantageous" match as the means to provide for her security.

Anne shuffled along the crowded sidewalk, bypassing a large gang of trench diggers. She made slow progress past the row of elegant mansions with doors and windows uncharacteristically thrown open to the dirt, clang and clatter of the street. Hundreds of the same men who toiled the day long mired in muck and mud now occupied these fine homes. The soldiers cooked their mess on hearths framed by ornate mantelpieces, and crowded the parquet floors every night to sleep lying shoulder-to-shoulder.

Anne shook her head in wonder at the instant ruin befallen these premium properties. The fear of having her own home commandeered for quartering soldiers fed her resolve to remain entrenched and in business. And though business at the Liberty Coffeehouse boomed like a mainsail filled with strong wind, Anne was careful to husband her resources and hoard her profits. *For fair winds do not forever blow . . .*

At last reaching the picket fence delineating the graveyard at Trinity Church, she turned off crowded Broad Way and shifted pace to march a snappy quickstep. The breeze grew heavy with a cloying sweet smell, announcing the presence of sugar to one and all.

An imposing five-story stone building, Van Cortlandt's sugar refinery took up the corner of Thames and Lumber. Ahead, Anne could see two big men off-loading large barrels of unrefined muscovado sugar from an ox-drawn dray. One by one the barrels were rolled, rumbling down a ramp through the double doors leading to the lowest level.

Anne followed the caramel perfume up a flight of stairs and through the main door. Louder than intended, she cursed, "Adrat!" upon finding several customers already formed in a queue. Samuel Fraunces, the owner of the tavern where Titus kept his room, stood at its head. A pair of Continental Army officers and her neighbor, the baker, had also beaten her to the sugarhouse door.

"Good day, Widow Merrick." Quakenbos tipped his hat.

Anne acknowledged the baker's greeting with a vague nod directed at the empty air to his left. She slipped her woolen shawl to drape over one arm, fanned her face with her fingers and waited her turn while watching the sugar boilers feeding charcoal to the fires beneath three steaming cauldrons.

Sugar making was a tricky business. The temperature must be carefully controlled—the cauldrons must be kept hot enough to liquefy the coarse brown muscovado sugar, but not so hot as to burn it. One of the sugarworkers stirred a quantity of sticky bull's blood into a ready batch, to bring impurities to the surface. He quickly skimmed the dross, and poured the sugar slush into cone-shaped vessels. As the sugar hardened, dark molasses drained down to drip out through an opening in the cone tip. A valuable by-product of the refining process, the molasses was collected in shallow pans.

When fully cured, the solid loaves of pure white sugar were drilled from the earthenware cones, wrapped in blue paper and sent to market. White sugar was expensive, and Anne only offered small nipped bits of it to her customers for a price. She was more interested in purchasing quantities of unrefined muscovado and molasses. These products held the rich flavor suited to Sally's recipes and a frugal price that suited Anne's pocketbook.

Fraunces, having completed his business, tipped his tricorn to her as he passed on his way out the door. "Mrs. Merrick . . . you are quick to take advantage of opportunity."

"Well, I try to keep my hook cast these days—you never know when a fish will happen by."

"Speaking of happening by . . ." Fraunces stepped in close, and spoke low. "Are you in need of coffee?"

"Always."

He slipped his tricorn from his head to shield his mouth. "There is a small shipment of coffee berries at King's Wharf—the same Dutch trader who brought in this muscovado. I am on the prowl for rum, if you should hear of any . . ."

"I will surely let you know. Thank you, Mr. Fraunces."

At her turn, Anne placed and paid for her order, arranging to have it delivered to her shop. King's Wharf was a little more than a mile from the refinery, and she must make haste before word spread. It would not do for the army's quartermaster to get his hands on all that coffee.

"Good day, sirs," she said in passing to the officers and the baker in serious conversation at the foot of the stairs.

She sped down Thames Street only to be thwarted by a tall pile of logs barricading access to the Hudson. Altering her course to travel north, Anne found every street offering a route to the river similarly barricaded. Coming to yet another dead end, Anne drew her shawl tight about her shoulders.

The most recent exodus had left these back streets in eerie desolation. Anne startled when a hog rushed out from a space between two buildings to commence snuffing and rooting in the open sewer that ran the length of Crown Street. She pondered the dark access between the tenements when a lone peddler emerged from the same gangway, slumped under a heavy bundle of birch brooms.

"Pardon, sir, but does that way lead to the river?" She pointed from whence he came.

"Aye . . . ye can cut through t' Cortlandt Street," he said. "They've yet to set a barricade on Cortlandt."

Anne thanked the man and turned into the dank, narrow gangway, immediately seeking the handkerchief kept stored up her sleeve. Pressed to her nose, the lavender water she'd splashed on it did little to mask an unwholesome compound of ordure and rotting offal. The awful stench served to put kick in her step.

A sustained whirr caught her ear and grew louder as she progressed along the mazelike path running between ramshackle buildings. Through an open doorway, Anne spied a woman with hair as fair as the pile of flax at her side, working her spinning wheel in earnest. Without missing a beat of the treadle, the spinster waved merrily. Anne waved back, heartened by the woman's industry in such forlorn circumstance.

A warren of mean hovels and dilapidated clapboard sheds clustered behind and between the tall brick tenement walls. Here and there Anne spied smoke wiggling up from a mud-daubed chimney, and though she did not see another living soul, she could not squelch the uneasy feeling of being watched. The gangway she followed angled onto a long alley. With palpable relief, Anne could at last see twenty or so yards ahead, to the opening onto sunny Cortlandt Street.

The alley was strewn with the detritus of concentrated human habitation, and the happy song of the spinning wheel was replaced by blowfly buzz, rooting pigs and squalling gulls scavenging through the rotting garbage piles. A pair of barefoot boys dressed in naught but grubby shirts sat on haunches at the edge of a foul puddle, intent on poking a bloated gull carcass with sharp sticks. The urchin heads turned as she passed, red-rimmed eyes wide in their thin, dirty faces. As if hearing a call from their mother, the two leapt to their feet to dart past Anne and disappear behind a slamming door at the end of the alley.

A moment later, a squat, hulky fellow stepped out onto the stoop from the same doorway. He spotted Anne, tugged a sword from a scabbard belted round his waist and hit the alley running, barreling straight for her.

Anne hiked her skirts with both hands, turned and ran in an all-out, full-legged stride back the way she came. Heedless of the puddles and rubbish she ran through, her shawl blew away and her straw hat flew from her head. She glanced over her shoulder and saw the bonnet crushed beneath her pursuer's boots.

Skittering to turn into the gangway, Anne ran square into another man blocking the narrow path. A head taller, he leered down at her with a death's-head face—bulging, wicked eyes and an openmouthed grin exposing blackened teeth loose in gray gums. In a swift movement, he spun her round and pinioned her arms back.

The man's scrawny pigtail coated with stiff pine tar whipped about as Anne screamed, kicked and thrashed, trying to break free of his grasp. His dry fingers tightened, twisting into her skin like corded rope as he pulled her into a piss-smelly corner.

"Ye skivin' bag o' bones!" the breathless running man arrived. "That one's mine!"

"Ah, look at you—ye great greedy-guts," Bagobones sneered as he struggled with Anne. "Barely breathin' you is. I'm shamed to name ye Brother Tar."

Greedyguts brandished his weapon. "Shove off, I say. I spied her first."

"She'd've outrun ye if'n I hadn't stepped up, aye?"

Dressed in baggy tarpaulin trousers and checkered shirts, both men were clearly beached seamen. Greedyguts stood and pondered the situation, scraping at the stubble on his cheek with the honed edge of his sailor's sword.

Shouting, "Thieves!" at the top of her lungs, Anne raised her knee high and stomped a sharp heel down on her captor's toe. Yowling in pain, Bagobones loosened his grip enough for her to wrest free.

Greedyguts snatched the back of her dress and whipped her up against the brick wall, rendering Anne silent and still with the sharp edge of his blade pressed to the base of her throat.

"Arrah! She's mine now." His tarred tricorn slipped from his head and Greedyguts leaned in so close Anne could discern his breakfast— ale and fried kippers.

The skin above Greedy's left eye was pink, shiny and tight. The extent of this recently healed wound was made apparent by the loss of his hat, revealing wiry tufts of steel gray hair growing betwixt large patches of the smooth scar tissue that covered most of his bulbous pate.

"Ah now, brother." Bagobones turned genial. "What say we splits this plunder—even shares—fair and square?"

Greedyguts grunted in assent and Bagobones shoved a hand down the slit in Anne's skirt that gave access to the pocket tied about her waist. With a practiced jerk, he freed it, emptied the contents into one palm and tossed the pocket aside.

"Fuck all! Naught but eight shillings and pence . . ."

"She's stashed it somewheres . . ." Greedyguts shoved a hand down Anne's neckline, his furry tongue poked from gap teeth as he foraged between her breasts for hidden valuables. Anne could not help but jerk away and she felt the bite of his blade. Bright blood beaded to trickle down and slide over the curve of her breast.

Furthering his search, Greedyguts thrust his free arm under her skirts, and his roving hand stopped to cup between her legs. He bent his monstrous head and lapped the blood from her neck with one long swipe of his tongue, all the while keeping the sharp edge at her throat, strangling her scream to a pitiful whimper.

"Eight shillings . . ." he muttered. "Hoy, mate! Take m' blade . . . keep her quiet while I butter her bun."

"Then I gets a turn," Bagobones asserted. "Fair is fair."

The weapon exchanged hands. Bagobones stood duty at her left, licking his flaking lips and emitting a series of encouraging grunts while the stout man fumbled with his trouser buttons.

The pitched scream she dared not unleash shrieked in her head. Anne pressed back against the rough brick wall, wishing she could will herself to seep through its pores and crevices and break through to the bright light she imagined on the other side. She stared past the greasy knotted kerchief tied too tight to Greedyguts's thick neck, and let her eyes lose focus as he struggled to find a way through her skirts.

Bagobones suddenly blurted, "Hoy . . . mate . . ." and the worried utterance snapped Anne back into awareness.

Jack Hampton's angry face loomed in clear, perfect focus just beyond Greedy's shoulder. Swinging a wide arc, the barrel stave wielded in his two-fisted grip sounded a sickening *thwack* as timber met skull bone. Greedyguts flew from her line of vision.

Bagobones pulled her in close, keeping the blade tight to her throat. "Back off, or I'll cut her . . ."

Jack stepped up, raising the club over his shoulder. "Throw down!"

"Slit her windpipe, I will . . ."

"Throw down—*now!*"

Anne ground her heel into her captor's slipshod foot. Bagobones yelped and she pulled away, scuttling sideways as Jack leapt forward swinging, knocking the tall man to his knees with a brutal blow to the neck.

Tossing the sword aside, Bagobones raised his stringy arms in shuddering supplication. "Quarter, sir! I beg quarter."

His request was answered by the ragged end of the barrel stave rammed into his gut. Bagobones doubled over with a miserable groan, and Jack dealt him a fierce, felling blow to the jaw.

Anne snatched up her discarded pocket. Jack grabbed Anne by the hand and began pulling her down the alley. "C'mon—afore the rest of their mates come after us."

Anne glanced over her shoulder at the two broken men lying bleeding in the dirt. "Are they killed?"

Jack shrugged. "Who cares?"

⚭ ⚭ ⚭

Jack's heart pounded a retreat in his ears and he ran hard with the widow's hand squeezed in his. Once they emerged onto Cortlandt Street, she began to drag and stumble. Without warning, Anne Merrick tore her hand from his, and slumped back against a wall. Her words expelled in exhausted puffs, "Please . . . I need . . ."

Loose strands of hair escaped from the mobcap askew upon her head. Gasping for breath, her face shone as bright as a polished pippin. In a sudden panic, she turned her rescued pocket inside out, revealing a little gold brooch pinned to the inside. With an audible moan, she leaned forward, a bit wobbly with hands propped on knees, and studied the dirt patch in front of her feet like a drunk contemplating the best place to vomit.

Jack paced a short course, checking up and down the street. The muscles corded taut in his arms and across his back like the springs in an over-wound clock. Waving the blood-spattered stave clutched in his fist, he checked over his shoulder and urged, "C'mon, c'mon—we need t' get going!"

Jack bounced on the balls of his feet and Anne pulled upright. Tugging the gold pin free and tossing the pocket, she slipped the brooch between her breasts. "It's all I have from him." Avoiding his eye, her thin voice cracked on his name. "Mr. Hampton . . . I don't know how to begin to thank you . . ."

"No. No time for that." Jack grabbed her by the arm and pulled her along.

"Stop pulling at me!" Anne's angry eyes flashed lively as she struggled to jerk free.

Jack gave her a rough turn, drawing her attention to a gang of sailors stepping out from the alley. He rasped in her ear. "I will not fare as well against six. Now run!"

And she did—hand in hand they reached the crowded safety of Broad Way. With a palm pushed firm at the small of her back, Jack rushed Anne across the cobbles and down Maiden Lane. He pulled up to a halt at the corner and tossed his club into the gutter. Having lost both his hat and the ribbon from his queue in the tussle, Jack brushed his unruly hair from his face and drew a deep breath, releasing it in a whoosh. Fists on his hips, anger denting his brow, he demanded, "Now tell me—what in bloody hell were you up to?"

Anne dropped her eyes. "I was going to see about a shipment of coffee beans . . ."

"Coffee beans! Have you lost your wits?"

Intent on her shuffling feet with fistfuls of skirt clutched in each hand, she did not answer.

"Coffee!" Jack threw his arms up. "You stepped willingly into that nest of . . . of vipers, for coffee? What is wrong with you?"

She shifted her weight from one foot to the other. "It seems foolish now, but I . . ."

"Foolish?" Jack loomed over her, jabbing a finger in her shoulder.

"Foolishness does not begin to explain your recklessness. I question your sanity, madam—I do."

"You are right—" Anne's head bobbed in assent. "I am truly so thankful you found me, and . . ."

"Ravished with your throat cut on a pile of rubbish is how and where you would have been found if I had not been following you."

Anne's head popped back. "Following? You were following me?"

"I was—and lucky for you. Come along now." He offered his hand. "I'll see you safe home."

Anne ignored his outstretched hand. "Though I am apparently a witless idiot, I need trouble you no further. I can make my own way from here."

"Don't be an ass." He grabbed her by the hand and pulled her along.

They tramped along in silence. Coming up to the little lane her shop was located on, Anne tugged Jack to a standstill and pulled him to the side.

"Mr. Hampton—I would ask a favor . . ." she began, then dropped her chin to her chest.

"What's that?"

Her fingernails bit into his palm, and before his very eyes, she crumpled like a piece of newsprint. Shoulders shaking, she cried and cried for what to Jack seemed an eternity, all the while clutching his hand. For lack of knowing what else to do, he was about ready give her a good hard shaking, when she caught a breath and gazed up at him with sad eyes saturated in shame.

"Please . . . can we not keep this . . . incident betwixt ourselves?"

"Oh . . ." Jack shook his head. "I don't know about that . . . For one, we ought to make a report to the provost so . . ."

"*No!* I beg you—not a word to the provost. Not a word to Sally. N-not a word to anyone—you understand?"

"But the city militia at least should be made aware of . . ."

"Please, Mr. Hampton." Her grip tightened. "Promise me, not a word to anyone, ever."

Jack shrugged, nodding. "Alright. Not a word."

"Swear it."

He pried his hand from her grip and crisscrossed his thumb over his heart. "I'll never tell a living soul."

"Thank you." Her face softened in relief. "Now I'd best carry on alone. Sally is bound to ask questions if I show up with you in tow."

"Wait." Jack produced a handkerchief. "You know," he said, wiping her face dry, "Sally is nobody's fool." He dabbed the moistened fabric at the thin line of blood beaded where her neck met her collarbone.

Anne fiddled with her neckerchief, pulling and fluffing the fabric to mask the slight cut. She lifted her chin, squared her shoulders and held out her hand. "I owe you a debt, Jack Hampton, and I can't see how I'll ever be able to repay it."

"Well, you know," Jack said, "I could use a *good* cup of coffee now and then."

At that Anne almost smiled. She slipped her hand free and turned the corner.

ȸ ȸ ȸ

THE next morning, Jack shuffled in with the morning crowd. The Cup and Quill was doing a brisk business and Sally buzzed from table to table with her coffeepot. Anne came in from the kitchenhouse, tying an apron round her waist. She seemed to have gained some strength and ease by virtue of being within the bounds of her own domain. Scanning the crowded room, she spied Jack as he took his usual seat, and called to Sally, "I'll take care of Mr. Hampton this morning."

"Mr. Hampton should just wait his turn, aye?" Sally snapped.

Anne bustled over to set a steaming cup, a full bowl of lump sugar and a brimming creamer on the table. She tapped a finger to the brooch she wore pinned to the neckline of her gray dress. "Good morning, Mr. Hampton."

"Good morning Mrs. Merrick." Up close Jack could see a golden curl of hair encased beneath a crystal and framed with a circle of seed pearls. He gave her a nod, sharing some secret he did not quite understand. "It does me good to see you so fit and happy this morning."

"A good night's sleep works wonders sometimes."

Jack raised a dubious brow to the fare she'd laid out. "This all looks . . . grand."

She smiled. "I prepared everything special for you."

Jack laughed, and dropped two lumps into his cup. "Sally appears a bit out of sorts."

"She grows snippy when worried." Anne let the tray rest on her hip. "While I was out yesterday, an officer came by asking for me by name."

"And?"

"And it bodes ill. She's certain he means to arrest me as a Loyalist and commandeer our home for quartering."

"You're no Loyalist." Jack pointed out the doorway with his spoon. "It says 'liberty' right there on your shingle." His wry comment drew a rare laugh from the widow. "As for quartering, well, I think every citizen who can should be willing to provide room and board for our soldiers."

By the set of her shoulders, and the shift in tone, his comment surely annoyed. "I'll fetch your scones from the kitchen." Anne left him to his coffee.

Jack looked over and found Sally scowling at him from across the room. He tried his best to answer with an equally rude glower, but after a moment, he realized she was not scowling at him at all, but at the Continental officer who had just entered the shop.

Wearing a gray jacket with dark green facings, the young fellow bore the marks of rank—a silver epaulet on his left shoulder and a well-polished saber hanging from the scabbard belted across his chest. He had a friendly, open face.

Jack greeted the man, guessing, "New York regiment?"

The fellow nodded and tucked his cocked hat under his arm. "Third Yorkers." Though an officer, he had the air of an enlisted man—he was no powdered Bob. His chestnut hair was drawn back in a short tail with a rather ragged ribbon. The stockings he wore were home-knit and in dire need of a mending.

Jack kicked at the empty chair across from his. "Here. Have a seat, Captain."

"Thanks, but not just yet." The officer took a few steps, craning his neck as he searched the room.

Anne stepped through the back door with a tray on her arm. She stood briefly, squinting at the man. Her face then blossomed into most beautiful thing Jack had ever seen. Dropping the tray to the counter in a clatter, she squealed and skipped across the shop, throwing herself into the handsome officer's arms.

The big man lifted the widow into the air and swung her round and round—skirts and petticoats rustling. Jack watched the two of them hug and laugh, and hug again, and with all his might, Jack wished he could take a barrel stave to the officer's head.

Hanging on to the soldier's arm, swiping happy tears from her cheeks, Anne called out, "Sally, come meet my little brother!"

Chapter Four

✣

Now is the seedtime of continental union, faith and honor.

THOMAS PAINE, *Common Sense*

June 29, 1776
In the Garret, above the Cup and Quill

SALLY gripped a fistful of fabric at the back of Anne's skirt and braced her other hand against the window frame. "All set."

Anne sat on the sill, snapped the three telescoping brass tubes of Mr. Merrick's spyglass to full open and leaned out the garret window as far as she dared. Squinting her right eye shut, she pressed the glass to her left eye and aimed it beyond the rooftops, eastward, at the dark plume of smoke rising up from the hilltop across the East River. Panning across the horizon, Anne fixed her sight on a lone soldier standing at the crest, waving a pair of small red and blue flags. "Smoke and flags . . ." She hopped from the sill and passed the glass to Sally. "Have a look-see."

Sally took a turn hanging precarious from the window. "Aye, somethin' of import is afoot for sure . . . Maybe Mr. Cuddy knows a thing this time." As part of his morning delivery, Cuddy, the tea-water peddler, passed along news of the British fleet being sighted rounding Sandy Hook.

But one never quite knew what to believe. The series of rumors careening about the town were embellished and altered by each and every person coming through the coffeehouse door.

Only last week, Mr. Cuddy was, as usual, the bearer of shocking news—Washington had been murdered, poisoned by a dish of his favorite green peas. Then just as quickly, the tale turned. The Patriot general was not murdered, but kidnapped by the Loyalists. At the end of the day, Washington was neither murdered nor kidnapped, but over twenty men, including the mayor and several members of Washington's Life Guard, were arrested for organizing an armed Loyalist rebellion. One of the perpetrators had already been tried and hanged.

It was impossible to separate fact from fiction, and lately, what Anne judged to be wild rumor proved to be utter truth. Who would have thought the British Parliament would hire thousands of brutal German mercenaries to fight against their British citizens in the colonies? But hire them they did. Who would have thought their sovereign, King George, would send forth an armada to wage war against his own subjects? But merchant ships and fishermen reported a mighty fleet was on its way.

So many rumors flying fast and furious within the span of a few days forced Anne to ponder a series of scenarios that scrambled her brains and bunched the muscles at the back of her neck. Reason dictated she flee the city and seek refuge in her father's home in Peekskill, so Anne clung desperately to the unreasonable hope that a peaceful resolution was still possible. The sight of the signalman atop Brooklyn Heights surely added another ruffle to her apprehension.

"C'mon, Sally—let's get the wash in . . . It's as hot as Hades up here." The pulley wheels squawked as Anne tugged on the clothesline suspended between the Liberty Coffeehouse and the building across the lane.

Their laundry line resembled pennants strung from the mast of a first-rate frigate—Anne's somber achromatic apparel interspersed with the bright-colored petticoats, aprons and scarves Sally favored. Sitting side by side on the wide sill, Anne and Sally tossed the wooden clothes pegs into a small basket, and folded the dry clothing into the hamper.

Sally sighed. "I wonder if David'll come by tonight—he always knows what's doing. He'd be able to tell us straightaway what those signals mean."

"If he does show, you can be certain it will be to give me an earful on how and why we should pack it all up and leave for Peekskill."

"Shame on ye, Annie." Both women hopped down from the sill, each grabbing hold of a handle on the laundry basket. "Ye ought to thank the stars in heaven for such a brother—so concerned about you, he is."

"You know as well as I, David's visits have far more to do with your pretty make than his concern for my well-being." Anne reached around and pinched blushing Sally on the rear.

Though very busy training his company and working on fortifications, what little free time David did have was spent at his sister's home. Anne was not surprised to see her brother smitten the moment he was introduced to Sally. He had a habit of falling in love, and a weakness for ginger-haired girls. David readily informed Anne he'd graduated from smitten to besotted the moment he found Sally in the kitchenhouse, up to her elbows in dough, reading a copy of *Common Sense* she'd propped open with a wooden spoon. And it did not take a gypsy fortune-teller to discern the feelings were mutual.

David's Third Yorkers had been part of the Patriot Army's disastrous Canadian campaign. It was lucky their mother—a well-read woman and a modern thinker—saw to it that her children were inoculated, for David did not succumb to the smallpox epidemic that decimated his regiment and wiped out half of the Continental Army in Montreal. Good health combined with his avid devotion to the cause served to propel David's army career, and in a few short months he rose in rank from enlisted man to captain. He pursued these new duties with his usual boundless energy.

Sally bustled down the stairs. "I'll go an' fix a little supper—in case your brother shows."

Anne called, "I'm off to the hospital. I promised Dr. Treat I would do some letter writing."

With close to a full third of Washington's soldiers ailing, the makeshift hospital was overflowing with patients. Oppressive summer heat had combined with bad food, tainted water and crowded living conditions to exact a terrible toll on the Patriot troops, so Anne and Sally took turns spending a few hours every evening volunteering.

Anne tied a new straw hat over her mobcap. "I'll be back by curfew!" She grabbed her writing box by the leather handle and was on her way.

⚓ ⚓ ⚓

Dearest Wife,
Though this letter comes to you by another's hand, it is still from my heart.
  Jenny, pray do not suffer any unnecessary worry for my well-being. I have been something unwell, but am feeling better now. I find I am gaining Strength with the passing of every hour and very soon I will be as Hearty as ever before. I hope these lines find you possessed of the same Blessing. I only look to the day when I can enjoy once more the Comfort of your society. Give my duty to all parents and my respect to all friends. I remain your loving husband.

"Can you sign?"

"I'd like to."

The soldier hiked himself up from his straw-stuffed pallet to a sitting position. Perched on her little three-legged stool, Anne swiveled her lap desk around, and facing the sloped surface his way, she offered the man the freshly dipped quill. With a shaky hand, he scratched a sloppy "Levi" at the bottom of the page, and flopped back to lie flat.

Anne was glad Captain Levi Fullshire had survived the worst of his bout with camp fever. The young lawyer from Boston was newly wed, and as he spoke with such loving fondness of his wife, it would have been a terrible shame to write the woman an entirely different sort of letter.

Helping the soldiers write to their families was her favorite hospital duty. Anne gave the captain's letter a final dusting of sandarac to set the ink. Tapping the excess grit back into her pounce pot, she folded the sheet twice, sealed the page with one of the paste wafers from her writing kit and flipped it over to pen the address on the other side. "I'll see to it that your letter leaves with the post rider tomorrow."

"Thank you for your help, Mrs. Merrick." Levi offered a weak smile. The effort expended signing his name seemed to have sapped what little strength he'd lately recovered. "My poor Jenny's bound to worry. It's been a month since I last wrote and my letters were as regular as the tide up until the day I fevered."

"This letter will be a certain relief to her, then." Anne stoppered her inkwell and stored it along with her pounce pot, quill and paper inside the compartment of her lap desk. "Your health is much improved, Captain. The next letter home will be from your own hand." Anne snapped her writing box shut, and bid good evening to all of the patients in the crowded ward.

The Continental Army was sickly. Since a smallpox epidemic nearly doomed the rebel cause during the Canadian campaign, General Washington maintained an overriding concern for the health of his army. Soldiers or citizens showing symptoms of smallpox were immediately quarantined on Montressor's Island. There were a good number of soldiers who suffered with the flux and the itch, but the majority housed in the hospital the army'd set up in King's College Hall were afflicted with the camp fever that was rampaging through all of the regiments. The newly formed medical corps was overwhelmed and hard-pressed to care for so many struck ill with fever. Anne and Sally were among the many New Yorkers who stepped forward to answer the desperate call for help.

Good intentions aside, Anne learned on her first day she did not possess the qualities required to be of service as a nurse. It was not for lack of compassion, or willingness to work hard and give aid. She just could not detach from the patient's discomfort, especially with cases of camp fever, when the cure proved far worse than the ailment.

Try as hard as she could, Anne could not gain control over her

queasy stomach and sensitive nose when it came to administering
the purging emetics and clysters the doctors prescribed to excite the
nervous system and rid a body of fever. These popular treatments
resulted in foul expulsions from one end or the other, and Anne's
first day of duty found her off in a corner, heaving into a chamberpot for the better part of her shift. Having witnessed her unnurse-
like behavior, the physician general had suggested she limit her
volunteerism to working with the recovering patients, who required
a simpler form of nursing that would prove easier on her stomach.

Anne paused after exiting the hospital to draw in a deep breath of
fresh air. Under Dr. Treat's rule, the staff put forth a valiant effort to
maintain cleanliness and discourage the spread of contagion. The
wards were fumigated with smoke from burning brimstone, cham-
berpots were emptied promptly and floors were swabbed every day
with vinegar—but regardless—the malodor of vomit, diarrhea and
death hung in the air, wet and thick as steam from a boiling kettle.
Anne kept a hanky saturated with lavender oil tucked under the seam
at her left shoulder, to allow quick relief with a turn of the head when
the smell became more than she could bear.

She set the writing box down on the stoop. Overlooking the college grounds, Anne removed her straw hat, swiped the mobcap from
her head and used it to blot the sweat from her face and the back
of her neck before stuffing it into her pocket.

There were only a few moments of daylight left to be had and the
shadows cast by the disappearing sun were long and murky. Realiz-
ing she'd been time-tricked by the lengthening summer days into
missing the set curfew, Anne turned back into the building to obtain the requisite pass. She chased after the physician general as he
bustled by with a pair of young medical students in tow.

"Certainly, Mrs. Merrick." Dr. Treat wagged his head at her request, distracted. "Await at the front entry, and I will send 'round a
pass and an escort to see you home safe."

Anne sat on the stair with her writing kit on her lap and watched
as nightfall overcame the last tinge of orange light in the western
sky. The street was deserted—silent but for the passing footfalls of a

stout sentry making his rounds armed with a slim halberd nearly twice his height. After the sentry disappeared, the old lamp warden came moving along Robinson Street in starts and stops. Wielding a long iron hook, one by one, he lifted lanterns from lightposts, filled the wells to the brim with whale oil and lit the wicks.

Dr. Treat must have forgotten about me . . . Anne gathered her skirts, her hat and her writing box to go in search of the busy administrator. Scrambling to her feet, she turned and bumped square into Jack Hampton.

Jack held her at arm's length for a brief instant. "Mrs. Merrick! What are you doing here?" He brightened at their meeting, his dark eyes shining. He was dressed in rough work clothes—brown leather breeches and a linsey shirt open at the frayed collar with sleeves rolled above his elbows—his face and hands were stained with soot. Hatless, and ribbonless, his hair hung sweat-drenched about his shoulders.

Anne waved an exasperated hand toward the open doorway. "I'm waiting for my pass and a promised escort, but I suspect Dr. Treat is so busy he most likely forgot to send both."

"I'm headed home," Jack volunteered. "I can see you to yours."

"If you don't mind . . . I would appreciate it. I hate to be a bother"— Anne glanced once more at the doorway—"but I fear Sally is twirling herself into a redheaded fret on my account."

"No bother at all—the Cup and Quill is on my way." Jack held up a finger. "I'll be right back." Turning back into the hospital, he emerged after a few moments with hands and face washed, shirttails tucked in and wild hair tied back with a scrap of twine.

Anne smiled at the ablutions he'd undergone on her behalf. "You've come to my rescue once again, Mr. Hampton."

"I'd have you call me Jack," he said, taking her writing kit to carry.

"All right . . . Jack . . . and you must call me Anne."

"Well, c'mon then, Annie—we're off!"

She fell in beside him, very much enjoying how he used her familiar name as if they'd been boon companions for years. They strolled along the deserted street—stretches of darkness punctuated by soft ellipses of wavering lantern glow.

"I didn't know you were helping to nurse the infirm," Jack said. "I commend your duty."

"Withhold your commendation, sir, for I'm afraid I am the poorest excuse for a nurse," Anne said, with a shake of her head. "Since I lack the fortitude needed to be of good service to the patients in dire need, Dr. Treat has relegated me to the recovery wards. Today I wrote letters for the men."

"Ol' Treat—he finds use for every willing pair of hands." Jack walked, swinging her case like a lad on his way home from school. "It's no wonder I haven't seen you here, for I'm usually out back in the yard boiling the linen and burning the straw. Although some days, I help out in the upper wards with the lifting and turning."

Anne noticed Jack's shirt was wet around the collar, and she caught a whiff of the lye soap he'd used to wash. "Difficult and grim—the upper wards. You're the one to be commended."

"All for the cause." Jack shrugged. "Since Parker moved his press out of the city, I have the time. I don't mind working with the sick—poor fellows—rather help them than dig a trench any day."

"Sally and I were wondering why we haven't seen you lately with your shovel." Anne winced a little in telling the lie. Sally couldn't give a fig for what happened to Jack Hampton.

Jack noticed the inclusion. "Sally wondered?"

Anne sidestepped his observation. "Well, I'm no fanatic to the cause, but Patriot or Loyalist, the unwell still need to be tended. I have to say, I am surprised by my squeamishness. When my son was so ill, I suffered no such qualms in seeing to his comfort and treatment . . ."

"You have a son?"

Anne swallowed back the painful lump lodged sudden in her throat. "I had a son—Jemmy—such a good boy. He was but six years old when both he and Mr. Merrick succumbed to the smallpox three years ago."

"The brooch . . ." Jack said. "In memory of your son?"

She nodded. "And most precious to me. I keep it safe at home now, and no longer carry it about."

Jack rested a hand between Anne's shoulder blades for a brief moment. "The death of one's child must be the awfullest pain to bear."

"The worst I've ever borne." Anne nodded, shoulders slumping a bit under the burden of her recollections. "Jemmy's gone from me, and I'm left with naught but a lock of his hair and a loneliness about my heart for which I fear there is no cure."

To her relief, Jack did not sweep her grief away with some platitude concerning the ability of time to somehow "heal all wounds," including one as deep and grievous as her own. Instead, he walked a ways in silence before striking up a new tangent.

"Contagion is a vexing problem. With nary a shot being fired, our army lost fourteen men just today. And who knows how many at the other hospitals? I tell you, at this rate, General Washington won't have much of an army left when the fleet invades."

"There may not be an invasion," Anne said. "Didn't you hear? The King is sending Admiral Howe with a peace commission, and maybe . . ."

"Peace commission!" Jack spat the words. "Don't tell me you actually believe that Tory tripe?"

"Of course I believe it," Anne countered. They stepped off the curbstone on Broad Way and crossed the cobbles to the middle of the thoroughfare. "Better to be a fool and hope for peace than a fatalist expecting nothing but mayhem, bloodshed and death."

"Oh, don't be such a noodle. The time for talking peace has long passed. Didn't you hear? Over two hundred ships were sighted rounding Sandy Hook today." Jack stepped over the wide gutter that coursed the center of the street. "The King's 'peace commission' is preceded by enough firepower to lay our city and all within to ashes several times over." He reached out a hand to help Anne across the gutter.

"I'm no noodle!" Anne ignored his hand and traversed the gutter unassisted. Misjudging the span in the dark, her heel slipped the edge, and she lost her balance.

Quick to catch her around the waist—saving Anne from landing bum-end in the feculent trough—Jack took her by the hand. "Best keep close to me, alright?"

Anne was startled by this shift to kindness. Jack's gentle voice and her hand within his engendered a sudden, all-encompassing well-being—a feeling akin to being tucked into pan-warmed sheets on a wintry night—the wonderful, long-missed feeling of being cared for.

It struck Anne right then—from the time it took to travel from the steps of King's College to the gutter on Broad Way, Jack Hampton had shown her more compassion and kindness than Mr. Merrick ever had during a full seven years of marriage.

Anne had never been foolish enough to hope for love from Peter Merrick—not the kind of passionate love she'd read about in novels anyway—but she did hold hope her marriage might at least resemble a comfortable, respectful relationship similar to the one her parents'd had. After the first few weeks, she realized even that minimum would most likely never come to pass.

Merrick wore marriage like a hair shirt—a constant discomfort he bore as a penance in exchange for acquiring the progeny he deemed necessary to fulfill God's will. The handful of times her husband drank enough courage to knock on her bedchamber door, their coupling was at best difficult, awkward and brief. Merrick was most relieved once Anne announced she had conceived, and never again did he cross the threshold into her room. After Jemmy's birth, it became crystal clear she was deemed no more important than any of the other slaves and servants in her husband's employ. Anne only managed to float along in the misery of it all, buoyed by the love she bore for her son.

Anne held tight to Jack's hand as he led her across the Commons toward the Presbyterian church. Looming in the dark, the steeple was an immense black finger stirring the night sky strewn with as many stars as Anne had ever seen. She could count on five fingers the number of times she'd been out walking the streets of New York after nightfall, and never before had she ever seen such a celestial display.

The lamp warden had yet to fire any of the streetlamps on the crooked streets east of Broad Way, and the moonless night painted the narrow lanes a deep blue-black. Every so often faint scraps of laughter and conversation floated down from an open upper-story window. Wavering candle glow emanating from the same windows helped to abate a few of the sinister shadows crossing their path.

"Watch your footing," Jack warned. "There's not a sliver of moonlight to see by tonight." He chucked a stone to disperse a pack of rats swarming at the end of the block.

Anne wished they had thought to bring a light. Marshall law and curfew had emptied the streets of humankind and opened them to all manner of four-legged nocturnal habitants. Moving shadows scurried along the peripheries with gleaming eyes blinking red and gold in the night.

"Oh!" She stopped short, and squeezed Jack's hand. "What was that?"

"What?" Jack checked over his shoulder.

"Listen."

They stood in the center of the lane, motionless.

"There!" Anne clung to Jack's arm. "Did you hear it?"

He didn't answer but to pull Anne up a pair of steps and into the recessed doorway of a shuttered storefront, crowding her into a dark corner.

Anne's straw hat slipped from her head, the knotted ribbons pulled tight to the hollow of her throat, the crown squashed between her back and rough brick. Jack set the writing box down. The stubble on his face scraped a prickly path across her cheek as he leaned in to whisper, "Be very quiet."

Every manner of evil-doer could be on their path, and all the Widow Merrick could think on was the handspan of warm space redolent with lye soap, wood smoke and lavender that separated her body from this man.

The distressing sound that had sent them into hiding drew near and distinct—leather soles slapping along tamped earth. Anne rose on tiptoes to peek over Jack's shoulder as two men marched by, the steel halberds on their shoulders reflecting blue in the starlight.

"Only the sentrymen . . ." Anne sighed, and made to squirm past Jack, out to where she could catch a breath and collect her wits.

"No—wait!" Jack braced both arms against the wall, trapping her in.

"Wait? Wait for what?"

"I don't have a pass."

Off in the distance a dog began to bark, and Jack shuffled in closer to stand a mere thumb's breadth away. His breath caused the loose hairs on the top of her head to flutter. If she but tipped her head slightly, she could rest her cheek on his chest. The wanton thought sent a shudder down her spine.

"Don't be afraid," he said, lips to her ear.

A very warm night, and this whisper raised gooseflesh on her arms "But we don't have a . . ."

"Shhh . . ." Jack pressed a finger to her lips. He leaned in closer—a lock of hair slipped his queue and tickled her forehead. Anne shrank back against the wall, and the sound of the sentries' steps faded away.

Anne gave Jack a two-handed shove. "I thought you had a pass."

"I forgot it."

"You know I have a history . . ." Her whisper was harsh. "I could be arrested . . ."

"Right, and that's why we need to hide whenever the sentries come 'round."

Anne stepped back out into the lane. "Let's hurry, then, before they come around again."

Refusing the hand Jack offered, Anne walked a pace behind, happy for the dark to mask the flush she felt come to her cheeks. Untying the sweaty knot beneath her chin, she used her hat as a fan to cool her temperature, and took several deep breaths to calm her racing heart. Jack Hampton strolled ahead—la-di-da—without a care, and here she was, as fevered and faint as a silly heroine in one of her novels.

They reached the short street on which her shop was located. Sally and Quakenbos had lit the lanterns hanging over their respective doorways, and the little lane seemed friendly and cheerful for the light. "Well," Anne said, fiddling with the brim of her hat. "Here we are. I won't trouble you further. Thank you for . . ."

The writing box landed with a thump in the dirt and Jack grabbed Anne by the wrist. Her hat flew from her hand, and there was no time to retrieve it as he rushed her into the dark gangway between her shop and the Quakenbos Bakery.

"What is it?" Anne asked. "Sentries?"

Jack spun her around to land with her back against the brick. Pinning her wrist against the wall with his left hand, he slipped the right to wrap her rib cage. His actions so fierce and determined, Anne was stunned when he leaned in and kissed her.

Like touching a spark to a stream of gunpowder, Jack's kiss coursed a path through her body that struck at her very core. Rendered senseless, breathless and weak in the knees, Anne braced her free hand to Jack's shoulder, torn as to whether to push him away or draw him closer.

His hand slipped up from her ribs to caress her breast. Inching forward he buried his face in her hair—Anne's eyes snapped open—his every muscle pressed hard against her.

"Anne?!"

She turned to her name. David stood in the lane, dangling a lantern over his head. Sally stood beside him with the forsaken straw hat clutched to her breast.

Anne shoved Jack away, and David moved in, shining a light on Jack. "Who's this?"

Jack stepped into the light, hand extended. "Jack Hampton—I was seeing your sister home . . ."

"Ye were doing a bit more than that!" Sally laughed.

David refused Jack's hand and turned back to his sister. "Where've you been? Sally and I have been worried sick . . . searching for you . . . thinking the worst . . ."

Anne stepped out into the lane, her joints as feeble as a rag doll's. "I-I missed curfew, and had to wait a long while for a pass. Dr. Treat's so busy—and I knew Sally would worry—I said as much, didn't I, Jack?"

Jack nodded. "That she did, Sal."

"—so I accepted Mr. Hampton's kind offer to escort me home—but he'd forgotten his pass . . ." Anne paused. "We had to hide from sentries—because he has no pass, you see?"

David folded his arms across his chest. "All I see is my sister behaving no better than a common dockside whore . . ."

"David!" Sally exclaimed.

"That is harsh, brother." Jack laid a hand to David's shoulder

"We're not brothers." David shrugged Jack off, handed the lantern to Sally and drew his sword from its scabbard. "You are under arrest."

Jack raised his hands. "C'mon, Captain. Naught but a little kiss and cuddle in the shadows . . . nothing to get up in arms about . . ."

"David, *please!*" Anne said. "Put your sword away. There's no need . . ."

"No!" David extended his arm, the point of the blade level with Jack's throat. "Curfew was put in practice to keep the likes of him off the streets and away from decent women. He has no pass and he will be brought to stand before the provost marshall."

Jack glanced at Anne and slipped his hand inside his shirt. "I do have a pass." He handed David a folded note.

"You see—" David waved the paper at Anne. "The rascal had a proper pass all along."

"I don't understand . . ." Anne shook her head.

"You are so gullible, Annie. Father is right. We need to see you married and settled. Tomorrow, I want you to close your shop and pack your things. I'm sending you home to Peekskill." David sheathed his sword and handed the pass back to Jack. "Hiding from sentries—putting your virtue in peril . . ."

"Virtue!" Anne snapped to attention and faced her brother square on. "I would advise you not to waste any worry for my virtue, David, for our father sold that years ago." She marched to where Jack had dropped her writing box, and snatched it up by its handle. "Tomorrow, I will open my shop for business as usual. I love you dearly, *little* brother, but you are neither my husband nor my father. Thank God, no man holds dominion over me." Anne turned on her heel and headed to her door.

"Hoy, Annie!" Sally scurried to catch up. "Wait up!"

"Good night, Anne!" Jack called.

David turned and swept his blade up, laying the tip to Jack's cheek in an instant. "You will stay away from my sister."

"Oh, I don't know about that, Captain," Jack said. "I don't take well to orders—a problem that keeps me from joining you Regulars."

With an expert flick of the wrist, David nicked a small gash just below Jack's left eye.

Jack backhanded the blade aside, thumbed the blood from his cheek and studied it for a moment, rubbing the stickiness between his fingertips. "Your sister has a will of her own and—I'll warn you right now—so do I."

Jack turned his back to David's blade, and headed west, retracing the path back to the room he kept right across from King's College.

ঙ ঙ ঙ

ANNE flopped over to her back, kicked off the bedsheet and tugged at the sweat-damp muslin bunched about her hips. She bolted upright, flipped her pillow and gave it several smart whackets to encourage the feathers, before lying back again. She could not find a wink of sleep—not a wink.

That kiss . . .

She could not shake the memory of it. *Very silly and quite sad,* Anne thought. Here she was, a woman who'd married and birthed a child, and she'd just been given her first real kiss—a kiss more intimate and thrilling than anything that had ever transpired in her bedchamber with Merrick.

Hot as Hades in here . . . Anne plucked at her shift, fanning her legs. Daylight began to keek in through the cracks of the shutters, and there was no point in even trying to fall asleep anymore. Bedropes creaking, Anne rolled up to a sit, swung her feet to the floorboards, stumbled to the window and pushed open the shutters.

A fair dawning. She leaned out over the sill to catch the breeze, and there, bobbing lightly out in the harbor—a thick, dark forest of ships' masts silhouetted against the misty sunrise.

"Bloody hell!" she muttered.

The fleet was in.

CHAPTER FIVE

The sun never shined on a cause of greater worth.

THOMAS PAINE, *Common Sense*

Monday, July 8, 1776
Closing Time at the Sign of the Cup and Quill

TALLY up the points, lads," Sally called out. "It's time t' close it
up."

A groan went up from Titus Gilmore and the group of soldiers
clustered near the dartboard at the front of the shop.

"Sorry, lads, curfew." Sally collected their dirty mugs onto her
tray. "For your own good as well as ours—ye ken we dinna make the
rules here, we just abide by them."

Titus gathered the darts. "You heard the lady! Let's tally up."

One of the soldiers added the marks on the chalkboard and
announced the final score. Titus was declared the winner. Coins
exchanged hands, the men collected their sundry caps, jackets and
weapons and shuffled out onto the lane. Sally shut the door and shot
the three bolts home. She turned to Titus, who dropped a stream of
coins into her outstretched hand.

"Why, I thank ye, sir." Sally bobbed a curtsy.

"The pleasure is all mine, miss." Titus grinned, pocketing the rest of his winnings.

As per agreement, Titus paid Sally a fair share to keep an eagle eye on the chalkboard and to ensure that she announced closing time at an advantageous moment.

"The two of you . . ." Anne came in with a worn birch broom in hand, shaking her head at the wily pair.

"Aw, there's no harm in it, Mrs. Anne." Titus began hoisting chairs and benches up onto the tabletops. "The shop has to close sometime, don't it?"

"I suppose . . ." Anne began sweeping out the dirt and clots of dried muck from beneath the tables. "I just worry you two will get caught one of these days."

"Not by that lot. Backcountry lads every one—they didna have a clue." Sally jingled the coins in her pocket and danced a merry little jig, when a sudden, fearful pounding shook the door she'd only just bolted.

With the front windows boarded, there was no telling who it might be, and Anne urged Sally, "Go on, miss—answer the door."

Sliding back the bolts, Sally cracked the door open a scant and very controlled inch. Quick to issue a terse—"No, not here"—she shut and rebolted the door in almost the same instant. The pounding renewed immediately, but Sally paid no heed, and began to stack dirty plates and mugs onto a tray as if nothing were amiss.

"Who is that, Sally?"

"Only one o' them Virginia lads . . . wonderin' he'd left his hat here."

The pounding did not abate and Titus took steps toward the door. "Don't worry, Mrs. Anne, I'll take care of him."

"No, Titus!" Wide-eyed Sally shook her head to and fro, like a terrier who'd just nabbed a rat. "Dinna bother . . . I mean, I could smell the rum on him, the sot. The man's worse for the drink. No need to court trouble . . ."

"Sally's right." Anne leaned on her broom. "No need to tangle with a drunk—all the noise he's making, the sentries will find him soon enough." And just as she said it, the pounding ceased. "There, you see? All's well."

Anne launched into a vigorous sweeping, moving an ever-growing pile of debris from the front of the shop to the rear. She stepped out the back door to fetch the dustpan from the kitchenhouse.

"Anne! *Pssst!* Anne!" Jack Hampton's head popped up intermittently, above the six-foot-tall stone wall surrounding the garden. "Annie!"

"What in the world?" Anne drew close. "Is that you, Jack?" She had not seen hide nor hair of the man since that night when he'd seen her home from the hospital, and she thought for sure David had succeeded in scaring him away.

Jack leapt up and grabbed ahold of a low-slung peach tree limb, sending dozens of peaches raining down in a thumpety-thump. In another flurry of fruit, Jack swung his long legs up and over to perch atop her garden wall like a self-satisfied tomcat.

Anne looked up at him, her arms akimbo. "I do have a door, you know. A simple device—you step through it."

"I tried your door, but the fierce watchdog you keep would not let me pass."

Sally remained inside the shop scrubbing a tabletop, very intent on avoiding Anne's piercing eye. Titus stepped into the garden, his big arms folded across his chest.

"Do you need any help, Mrs. Anne?"

"It's all right, Titus. This is Mr. Hampton, a friend of mine."

"May I come in, *friend?* I need to speak with you." Jack leapt down at her nod, and began fumbling within his linsey workshirt.

With eyebrows raised, Anne reached out and almost touched the scabrous wound below Jack's left eye. "What's happened there?"

Jack fingered his cheek. "Oh . . . that . . . bumped into a sword." He resumed scrambling inside his shirt, at last pulling forth a folded piece of paper. "Here it is! I have desperate need of your press . . . We have to print as many of these as we can."

"My *press?!* My press was put to ruin . . . You yourself saw to it . . ."

"Now, Anne, don't play coy. There's little enough time as is. Everyone knows Merrick's was always a two-press shop." Jack brushed past, and went inside.

Anne scurried after him. "What is this thing you so need to print?"

"Here . . . read it." He tossed the paper into her hands and stepped in front of the big cabinet where the stacks of wooden treenware used for serving cakes and coffee were now stored.

Anne unfolded the page and carried it over to better light. She read a few lines and looked up. "You either did not read this, or you are quite insane."

"Oh, I am quite insane, but I did read it. Besides *Common Sense*, I think it is the most wonderful thing I've ever read, and so I think everyone should read it. That's why I need your press." Jack dug his fingers between the plaster and the heavy cabinet and began inching it away from the wall.

"Wait!" Anne pinched the bridge of her nose. "To hear of it is one thing, to disseminate this from my press is quite another. This is beyond sedition, Jack." She shook the page in his face. "This is high treason. This work leads straight to the gallows."

"First to the gallows for a little neck stretch, then the executioner's knife for a nice drawing and quartering." Jack laughed and resumed his struggle with the cabinet. "They'd go easy on you, Annie—being a woman and all—treat you to a dance at the end of the noose, and then a nice toasting at the stake."

"*Stop!*" Anne grabbed hold of Jack's arm. "This is not a joking matter . . ."

Jack shrugged her off and the broadside fluttered to the floor. He planted his feet, took firm hold and swung the cabinet away from the wall, exposing the hidden doorway to the storage closet. Sally rescued the broadside from the floor and studied the headline.

"Jack, please—listen to reason." Anne measured her tone. "Even if I agreed to print this, my press is in pieces, and we've not a shred of paper nor a drop of ink . . ."

"There are the makings for ink," Sally announced, handing Titus the broadside. "At least a gallon of varnish and a pound o' lampblack in there, stowed away with the rest of the gear."

Anne shot her friend a look sharp enough to slice through a hard cheese, but Sally didn't seem to care. Opening the door to the storage closet, she dove in and came up with a corked varnish pot. "Near full," she determined with a shake.

Anne fumed. "There's still the small matter of paper . . . We've none of *that* stowed, do we, Sally?"

"Don't fret for paper. I know where I can lay my hands on half a ream at least . . . maybe more." Jack reached into the closet and pulled out a crate stuffed with composing sticks, quoins, leading and gutter sticks—the bits and bobs necessary for typesetting a form.

Titus handed the broadside to Anne. "I can get the press together in no time, Mrs. Anne."

"No." Anne creased the page into quarters. "Nothing is being put together—we will not be printing anything, Titus."

"Goddamn it, Anne!" Jack swore, dropping the heavy crate onto the composing table. "Even Titus and Sally understand. No one need know whose press printed it, the import is in getting it printed . . ."

"Not on my press." Anne shook her head. "I will not risk my neck."

"*Feich!*" Sally threw up her arms. "I never took ye for a coward, Annie."

"Have you three idiots looked out into the harbor lately? The King's Navy *and* Army are on our bloody doorstep! Printing this broadside is complete and utter madness." Anne pressed the folded sheet into Jack's hand. "You've a fire within, Jack, and it burns bright and true for your cause, but I don't share your conviction—not enough to swing for it."

Titus and Sally moved forward to stand beside Jack. Shoulder to shoulder, the odd threesome faced Anne forming a solid phalanx. Jack, Titus and Sally were united in cause—comrades—their faces lit with rebellion and fierce determination.

"Help us, Annie," Jack said, "and we'll do this thing together— otherwise stand aside for I *will* use your press."

Left with but dread and doom for companions, Anne could not

bear to be so forsaken. She closed her eyes, heaved a sigh and held out an open hand. "Let me see it again."

Jack snapped open the broadside and laid it lightly on her up-turned palm. She took several steps toward the door, held the page in the best light and examined the copy.

"It seems I've no choice but to cast my lot with your unlikely fellowship . . ." Anne said at last. She tossed the page onto her work surface and began digging through the crate for her favorite composing stick. "Break out the finest Caslon, Titus. If we're to hang for our work here, it will be for our best."

Jack let out a whoop, lifted Anne from her feet and swung her through the air.

☙ ☙ ☙

ANNE flung off her French heels and stripped down to stays and chemise. For a moment, she considered shedding the stiff, sweat-drenched stays as well, but Jack Hampton waited down the stairs, and only the most shameless slattern would consider going without stays in the presence of a man not her husband. She struck a compromise between decency and ease, loosening the laces a touch.

Hotter than the hinges on the gates of hell, Anne swiped the mobcap from her sweaty head and tossed it onto the bed. The heat of the day tended to collect and hover in the upper stories. She pushed open the shutters to find some relief just as the church bells began to bong the midnight hour.

How the hours fly—

Evening had passed into the wee hours, and but for the bells, she would never have noticed, so intent she had been on her task. One could not expect to be dexterous when setting type by candlelight, but still, she managed to complete the form for the broadside in the same time it took Titus and Jack to bolt the press together and make it ready to print.

Being required to muster for a work detail at daybreak, Titus bid them good night and left for home as soon as the press had been assembled, assuring Jack that Anne was as fine and capable a second as he'd ever worked with. Anne could see Jack was skeptical—for in truth, she was no journeyman—and she was anxious to prove Titus's faith in her ability.

Digging down into her clothespress, she unearthed the utilitarian linsey blouse and brown fustian skirt she wore when working with ink. She changed into her work clothes, slipped her bare feet into a pair of comfortable, flat slippers and skipped down the stairs to help Jack finish printing the job.

To clear the area for the press, tables, chairs and benches had been shoved harum-scarum into a confused tangle toward the dark, front end of the shop. Sally sat slumped over one of those tables, her head on her arms, snoring. Anne saw no reason to wake her, as Sally would not find a more comfortable sleep in her oven of a room up the stairs.

A warm night was made sweltering by six lanterns hanging from the rafters over the press and a dozen near-spent candles lighting the compositing table at the rear of the shop. Both front and back doors were propped open in a vain hope of catching what breeze there was coming in off the river.

Jack had the form in place and locked up fast upon the carriage. A ream of newsprint was stacked wet and ready to print on a tray positioned near the press. Wearing Titus's leather apron with shirt-sleeves rolled to his elbows, Jack worked within the circle of light, sifting soft, powdery lampblack onto the glob of boiled linseed oil he'd poured out onto the ink block. Anne paused on the last stairstep and leaned into the newel post, drawing in the acrid smell that had permeated her life from the very minute she'd been born. For all of her protestations, it was a pleasure to have her press back at work.

"There is something awry with the world indeed," Jack announced, "when a journeyman performs the work of his devil. Best don your apron, lest you spoil your clothes."

Anne joined him at press-side, tying the strings of a bib apron snug at the small of her back as he continued to mix the ink.

"Mind now, Jack, don't stint on the blacking. I cannot abide pale ink."

"Here, then—" Jack handed off the package of lampblack and the slice—a square metal blade attached to a wooden handle used to mix ink. "For the life of me, Annie, it's been so long since I rubbed the black into the varnish, I've quite lost the knack."

Anne took over at the ink block while Jack moved on to knock up the ink balls, tacking the leather covers over wool stuffing. When she was happy with the consistency and color of her mixture, Anne dabbed the balls onto the block, rocking them both to and fro to coat the leather with a thin, even layer of ink.

Starting at the top of the form and moving down-and-up, down-and-up in a steady, deliberate pattern, she beat the balls to the type. An adept and skilled beater, Anne knew exactly how to tap and not drag the leather across the type, to avoid choking the spaces between and within the letterforms with an excess amount of ink. Satisfied with the thoroughness of her coverage, she took a half step back. "There."

Jack positioned paper onto the points. "Let's pull a sheet and see how it pleases us."

Anne nodded, but she could not peel her eyes from the freshly inked form—the raised type glistened and shone like black glass in contrast to the dull gray lead between the letters and lines—even backward, the words caused her heart to lurch, sending a rush of blood pounding in her brain.

In CONGRESS, July 4, 1776

A DECLARATION

By the REPRESENTATIVES of the

UNITED STATES OF AMERICA,

In GENERAL CONGRESS ASSEMBLED

Anne wavered on her feet—the inkballs so heavy in her clenched fists—dizzy with sudden despair. *Oh, these words will cause worlds to collide.*

The tight, ordered bits of lead formed the words and sentences that shattered any hope for peace. The might of the British Empire would no longer float patiently out in the harbor. These words would bring it crashing down upon them like a monstrous wave, to wash away every speck of rebellion, and crush the colonies into complete submission.

"Step aside, Annie." All smiles, Jack snapped Anne back into the moment, pounding his fist to the wooden upright. "This fine press stands ready with paper pinned up and here my second stands, gathering wool."

Anne shuffled aside, allowing Jack to move in. With fluid prowess, he put the press in motion—shutting the tympan and giving the rounce a turn to move the carriage under the platen. With one hard pull at the lever, the screw turned to strike the first impression. A counterclockwise turn of the rounce and flip of the tympan exposed the newly printed page. Jack peeled the damp paper from the press, and Anne followed, as he carried it over to the candlelit table. Side by side, he and Anne admired the work.

"Beautiful." Jack beamed. "Crisp and clean—you have as fine a hand and eye for composition as I've ever seen."

"The United States of America . . ." Anne read aloud, still incredulous she had actually set such treason into type.

"Has a ring to it, no? Ahh . . . you see this?" Jack pointed to the second paragraph. "This here's my favorite bit—*'We hold these truths to be self-evident, that all men are created equal, that they are endowed by their Creator with certain unalienable Rights, that among these are Life, Liberty and the pursuit of Happiness.'*" His eyes bright with hope, Jack threw an arm around Anne's shoulders and gave her a squeeze. "Now those are words to swing from a gibbet for!"

She leaned in to his strong body, and like a scrap of blotting paper, absorbed his courage and conviction for what she always knew to be right and true—letting it seep through skin and sinew, and soak in to strengthen her very bones.

"If all goes well," Jack said, "we'll have at least two hundred fifty copies ready to hand out."

"What do you mean 'if'?" Anne clapped her hands together. "Enough of this twiddle-twaddle—let's get it done!"

ॐ ॐ ॐ

THE fife and drummer boys from each brigade banded together, blowing and beating an exuberant version of "Yankee Doodle," as every Continental Regular posted in and around the city marched up Broad Way from the Battery. Brigade by brigade, the soldiers entered the Commons and lined up in ordered ranks along the perimeter of the green.

By comparison, the remnants of the city's civilian population massed to witness the parade in complete disorder, choking the streets leading up to and bordering the Commons. Jack waited under the portico at St. Paul's with the four young lads he'd enlisted as newsboys.

"After the announcement has been read to the troops, I want you boys to divvy up that lot there." He pointed to the bound-in-string stack of broadsides near the church door. "Pass them out to the crowd, but don't be handing 'em to illiterate sailors, longshoremen and the like. Be selective—and be warned—I'll not cozen any shirkers. I was a newsboy myself, and I know every one of your lazy-arse tricks. If I find pages layin' in the gutter or on the rubbish heap, or anywhere other than in the hands and pockets of Patriots, I will seek out each one of you and deliver a sound box to the ears you'll not soon forget. Understood?"

Pleased with the sincere vigor of their nodding heads, Jack called out to a passing fruit vendor and purchased five apples. Keeping one for himself, he handed the rest out to the smiling boys, and issued a final warning, "Mind, then—wipe your sticky mitts before laying hands on my sheets."

Jack left the newsboys to their treat and wandered to the edge of the stair. From this vantage raised above street level, he scanned the happy chaos swirling around the Commons as the bells began to toll the hour. Anne had promised to meet him under the portico at St. Paul's at six o' clock. He took a bite from his apple and wondered if she would be true to her word.

Food, laundry and sexual favors—Jack prided himself on limiting his need for womankind to those necessaries he could acquire with a charming word or smile, or the simpler inducement of a few shillings. He had never entertained a desire for further entanglement, and avoided any at all cost.

But for some reason he could not yet fathom, Anne Merrick had a hold on his attention. Sparked by the recollection of a long-ago kiss, fueled by a shared taste in literature and fanned by a chance glance down her blouse, the attraction to the young widow began that night he'd put her press to ruin. Jack was quick to deem this interest a "fleeting passion" when it was further fed by anger over her apparent Loyalism, and easily quenched by a comely whore bent over the tousled bedstead at Mother Babcock's bawdy house on Murray Street.

Though Jack claimed it was duty to the cause of liberty driving him to visit the widow's coffeeshop day in and day out, he knew better. Anne Merrick was no true Tory, no threat to the cause, yet he could not control his fascination. He'd never run across a woman who'd confounded him so—at once strong and sad, independent and needy—and though he sensed the danger of digging a hole he'd have difficulty climbing free from, he found he just could not stay away.

What the widow needed—Jack determined, after kissing her in the gangway—what would do her the most good, was a complete and thorough frolic between the sheets. Coincidentally, Jack figured such activity would also relieve the distraction this woman had interjected in his life. So, threatening and well-armed brother notwithstanding, contriving a way under Anne Merrick's skirts and between her legs had now become Jack's driving aim.

Even if she shows, she's bound to be dragging Sally along. Annoyed, he tore one last bite from the apple and tossed the core into the gutter. *Sally* . . .

He may have made some headway in his quest the night before, if not for Sally and her damn snoring. Much to Jack's irritation, his every smooth and subtle attempt at amorous congress was interrupted by a phlegmy, snorty, indrawn breath.

Working the press with Anne Merrick had been both exhilarating and exasperating. Not only was she a skillful compositor, but from mixing the ink, to inking the type, she impressed him greatly with her meticulous attention to detail. As a result, not a single sheet of precious paper was wasted in their endeavor.

But never, in all his days at Parker's Press, did he ever have to deal with such distractions as his second's sweat-wet breasts glistening in lantern light, or the sight of her soft, round rear bent over in reaching to beat the ink to the form. Jack had restrained an awful urge to flip the widow's skirts up and have done with the whole business right then and there.

Jack had envisioned capping off the night's work by trotting hand in hand with the widow up the stairs, but thwarted by Sally's snoring, he only ended up adding, once again, to the jingle in Mother Babcock's purse.

Evening time had not provided any relief from the July heat—the air thick, heavy and still. Jack loosened the sweat-damp knot at the linen cravat he foolishly wore, and stuffed it into his pocket. A deep rumbling drew his eye upward to a swirling, threatening sky, and he was glad for the prospect of rain. Wiping a hand still sticky with apple against the emerald green wool of his weskit, he peered down the busy street, and smiled. For all the hustle and bustle on Broad Way, it was still easy for him to spot the Widow Merrick and Sally Tucker coming arm in arm up the brick walk.

Like flowers on a midden heap, the two women stood distinct amid the male majority. Sally made sure to be noticed, having rigged herself a patriotic red-and-white striped sash draped over one shoulder to meet at the waistband of her bright blue skirt. Jack was happy to see Anne join in on the spirit of the day, enlivening her sedate mourning-wear with a series of red, white and blue ribbon rosettes pinned around the crown of her straw hat.

"Anne! Sal!" Jack called and waved. "Up here!"

The women struggled through the throng and joined him and the growing crowd of onlookers at the top of the church stair.

"I salute you both"—Jack bent his knee in a florid bow—"the prettiest pair of Patriots in all of New York City!" His silliness drew a girlish giggle from the widow.

"Ahh, would ye listen t' him . . ." Sally laughed, giving Anne a poke with her elbow. "A honey-tongued devil if ever I heard one, na?"

Together they watched as the last regiment of foot marched by. Along with the many pennants and banners snapping on the wind, a tangible excitement fluttered though the crowd as a cavalry of mounted officers came clattering up the cobblestones behind the column of infantry, led by a standard not seen before.

"A new flag for a new country!" Jack cheered as the colors passed by. He'd never cared for the flag the Continental Army had adopted at Breed's Hill—a design merging the British Union Jack with the red-and-white striped standard of the Sons of Liberty. This new flag still made use of the rebellious Liberty stripes, but the reviled Union Jack in the corner was replaced with a hopeful constellation of white stars on a field of blue.

"David!" Sally squealed. "I can see David!"

In the same instant, Anne's brother—cutting a fine figure atop a jet-black stallion—noticed the trio on the stair. Anne and Sally bounced up and down, cheering and waving. Jack stepped between the two women, and wrapped his arms around their shoulders. Grinning like a madman, he joined in, shouting, "Huzzah! Huzzah!"

David trotted past, maintaining a soldierly demeanor made even sterner by the irritation of seeing his sister in the company of Jack Hampton. Sally broke away, and ran down the stairs to track alongside David in the parade.

The pleasure derived from rankling Anne's recalcitrant brother and bidding good riddance to Sally was soon eclipsed by the sight of

General George Washington himself. Busked out in blue and buff military splendor and mounted on a lively sorrel gelding, the Commander in Chief cantered by, inducing a raucous cacophony of cheers and huzzahs.

Anne said something, but for all the noise, Jack could not hear her. He leaned down, and she rose up on tiptoes, her mouth to his ear. "The general—he seems sad."

Jack nodded. "The enemy armada in the harbor," he shouted. "No doubt a bit worrisome."

"No doubt."

Jack took Anne by the hand, and they left the portico of St. Paul's to join the citizens following behind the army to the Commons. The general, accompanied by his immediate staff, rode out onto the green, and took a place at the center of the hollow square formed by the infantry ranks. The crowd, the fifes and drums all quieted. A terse order was given, and the officer at the general's left dismounted and stepped forward. Without preamble, he began to read in a booming voice, "The unanimous Declaration of the thirteen united States of America." He paused, taking in a deep breath before launching into the heart of the declaration.

"When in the Course of human events it becomes necessary for one people to dissolve the political bands which have connected them with another . . ."

The words washed over the thousands gathered at the Commons and Jack took note of the people's reaction. Peppered throughout the multitude, a few faces evinced anger or dread, but the vast majority of heads nodded in resolute concordance as each grievance against the King of England was read aloud.

The officer finished reading the last sentence, ". . . And for the support of this Declaration, with firm reliance on the protection of Divine Providence, we mutually pledge to each other our Lives, our Fortunes and our sacred Honor." Folding the Declaration into his pocket, he then announced, "The general hopes this important event will serve as a fresh incentive to every officer and soldier to act with fidelity and courage, as knowing that now, the peace and safety of his country depends solely on the success of our arms: and that every soldier is now in the service of a state possessed of sufficient power to reward his merit, and advance him to the highest honors of a free country."

Caps and hats flew from heads. The intensity of the cheer rising up from the ranks shook the very ground they stood upon. Horses whinnied and stamped and the officers struggled to control their mounts while muskets and pistols were fired haphazard into the air.

The troops were dismissed and the newsboys tore into the crowd. The broadsides Anne and Jack had worked so hard to print the night before were snatched up by eager hands, as if each sheet were wrapped around a sweetcake. Small crowds of soldiers and citizens encircled those lucky enough to grab a copy, rereading the incredulous words they'd just heard, puffed with pride, faces alight, happy to at last officially shed the cumbersome yoke of tyranny.

"There it is, Annie," Jack proclaimed. "The power of ink on paper—"

Anne stood looking up at him, smiling proud, her blue eyes sprung with tears. "Oh, Jack . . ." She squeezed his hand and tipped her head to his shoulder. "Our independence is won as much by lead type as it will be by lead bullets."

Jack gathered Anne Merrick in his arms, and there—in the middle of Broad Way—kissed her most thoroughly on the lips.

ふ ふ ふ

BEFORE Anne knew what he was about, Jack slipped his arms around her waist and pulled her into a crush, his mouth on hers. This bold kiss unfolded with such force and speed as to leave her no recourse but to cling to the bunched muscles at his shoulders, lest she be swept from her feet. Innate modesty was overcome in an instant by the taste of sweet-tart apple coupled with a brazen and wonderful sensation stirring in the warm place between her legs. Anne let escape an unexpected and wanton moan, and she cradled his face with her hand, the day's unshaven stubble rough in the cup of her palm.

Jack released Anne as suddenly as he had embraced her, and she wobbled for a moment to maintain her balance, unsteady on the cobbles. A wild horde of celebrants brushed by, marching back toward the waterfront with a cry of *"T' the Bowlin' Green!"*

Without giving Anne much opportunity to gather her wits, Jack looped his arm through hers, and the couple became part of the human current sweeping down Broad Way, marching in time to the thunder of drums and trilling fifes.

Anne struggled to keep the pace in her French heels, all the while cursing her vain choice of footwear. Taking two steps to Jack's one, she realized she had somehow lost her hat.

"Don't worry—I've got a hold on you, Annie," Jack shouted, holding tight to her arm. His tricorn was cocked at a dashing angle, and he looked down at her with a happy, satisfied face, as if they'd been at play and he'd just won every one of her marbles. All Anne could do was nod and notice how he was made even more handsome for the jubilant smile crinkling the corners of his eyes.

"That's the way, lads!" Jack shouted as they marched past Trinity Church. A tall sailor had mounted atop another's shoulders, and to the cheers of all passersby, the pair tore down the banners hung over the church doors that proclaimed the King's crest.

The fife and drum boys struck up "The British Grenadiers," a familiar tune from the time, not so long ago, when red-coated soldiers would drill on the Commons. The marching Patriot mob began to sing along, substituting the standard lyrics with a popular rebellious refrain:

> *"Vain Britons, boast no longer*
> *With fine indignity,*
> *Your valiant marching legions,*
> *Your matchless strength at sea.*
> *For we, your loyal sons oppressed,*
> *Have girded our swords on.*
> *Huzzah! Huzzah! Huzzah!*
> *For War and Washington!"*

Singing at the top of their lungs, Anne and Jack merged in with the mad tumult congregated on the street around the Bowling Green. Spirits were high—bottles produced and shared, and New Yorkers banded together with soldiers from all the colonies in impromptu song and jig. Anne scanned the confused throng of happy revelers, searching for Sally and David with no luck. The drummer boys began to pound a quick-time march while soldiers and citizens continued to swarm the green.

An impatient crowd of men churned near the locked gates of the green as a burly, red-faced Irishman strained with a crowbar, working the sturdy padlock. At last he broke through, the gates swung open and the six-foot-tall iron fence encircling the elliptical green was breached.

"We better stay out of there . . ." Jack steered an aggressive path to claim a spot outside the enclosure. Grabbing the iron bars with both hands, Anne stepped up onto the curbstone that curved along at the base of the fence, improving her view by a few inches. Jack moved to stand behind Anne, both hands at her waist, planting his feet to defend his ground, and keep from being pushed aside.

"Finest seat in the house," Jack said, his bristly cheek rasping the curve of her ear.

A half a dozen laughing boys ran up with a bulging gunnysack. Bypassing the crowd clogging the open gate to scramble over the fence like a troop of monkeys, the lads entertained the growing crowd, flinging rotten peaches at the statue centered on the green.

Raised up on a massive marble pedestal almost two stories tall, the figure was posed clad in patrician Roman robes astride a noble steed. With head wreathed in triumphant laurels, New York's golden King George III loomed out of reach against an ever-darkening and flashing sky.

A spindly forest of musket barrels, halberds and pikes and upraised fists had sprouted around the pedestal, shaking in happy defiance. Amid a chorus of "Coming through!" and "Let 'em pass!" the crowd parted to allow two men—one carrying several coils of stout rope, the other, a ladder. The ladder was quickly propped against the marble base, scaled, and King George now shared his pedestal with determined men busy securing rope around the horse's withers, middle and rump. The activity garnered the attention of one and all, and a deafening roar went up when the last noose was tossed over the monarch's head.

Jack pressed forward, the dome-shaped buttons on his weskit dimpling a vertical line along her spine, his hot breath tickling her ear. "Can you believe it?" he asked.

The loose lead ends were tossed down to many willing hands. Anne and Jack shouted along, "Heave! HO! Heave! HO!" Muscles and ropes strained, stretched taut as bowstrings, but the King did not budge.

Bright flashes chased behind the thunderheads roiling in the sky and big summer raindrops pattered down, ticking like an erratic mantel clock as they hit the sun-warmed King and his mount.

"Arrah!!!" The same burly Irishman who'd opened the gates charged up the ladder, brandishing his iron pry bar in an upraised fist to rally the crowd. *"Arrah!!!"*

He shoved the flattened end between marble and fore hoof, and called, *"Pull!"* to the men at rope's end. The pullers ground their heels in the turf, and slack rope drew tight. The Irishman scurried back to loose a hind hoof and the chanting began again, "Heave! HO! Heave . . ."

Two of the four hooves popped free from the plinth and the behemoth creaked to one side, canted on a two-legged axis. With the statue balanced at this precarious angle, the tugging men gave one last mighty heave before dropping their ropes and scattering like grapeshot. King and horse arced over and toppled from the pedestal in a clanging crash, brought down by their own ponderous weight.

The figures landed in a broken heap, and the illusion of solid gold was exposed as the thinnest layer of gilding over common lead castings. The crumbled plaster, clay and sand used to fill the castings' hollows spilled from the mutilated figures like entrails from a butchered carcass.

Anne pressed her face between the two iron pickets she clutched, her breath caught in her throat, stunned. The symbol of her Sovereign Lord knocked like so much rubbish to the ground—the same Sovereign she'd taught her child to include in his prayers—the beloved monarch whose health was toasted in homes and taverns throughout the colonies—the King who, not six years before, earned this ornate monument erected in his honor—this man would lose an empire. She was certain of it.

The destroyed figures were at least twice the size of natural man and beast, but the giant proportions did not hinder a pair of prostitutes from running in to wrest the gilded crown of laurels free from the statue's head. A solemn-faced infantryman wearing the blue and buff coat of a Massachusetts regiment marched forward, and to rousing huzzahs, aimed his musket and discharged a ball, embedding it between unblinking regal eyes.

The crowd surged forward with shouts of "Liberty!" and "Freedom!" Jack braced his arms to the iron cross rail, acting as a protective counterforce, providing Anne a shield against the crush. A fierce gust swept in off the water, followed by several deafening thunderclaps and accompanying streaks of lightning. Rain began to fall in earnest.

A hard-muscled man armed with a maul began hacking at the king's thick neck, rousing wave after wave of rebellious cheering with every blow. The severed head was speared upon a sturdy pike and the same man who'd acted as axeman paraded the trophy around the green, out the gate and up Broad Way. The fife and drummer boys struck up the "Rogue's March," fell in step with the most boisterous of the soggy multitude trailing along.

The rain dwindled to a drizzle and the crowd winnowed down to no more than a few score who lingered and watched a young officer direct a handful of men in dragging the statue parts and pieces into a pile outside the gate.

"Hey, Captain," Jack called. "That's a good supply of lead. I hope you plan on running it into musket balls . . ."

The captain smiled, and raised one booted foot to rest on a portion of the torso. "Even though the poor fella's lost his head, King

George here will be making a big impression on more than a few Redcoats."

A carpenter hurrying home stopped, set his toolbox down with a thump and pondered the salvage operation. He folded his arms, shook his head and announced, "You know, it still ain't right." Tugging a tool free from his kit, he stepped up onto the curbstone and proceeded to saw at one of the little cast-iron crowns that decorated the top of every fencepost. After five good strokes of the blade, the carpenter snapped the crown off the post, hurled it to the pavement and moved down the line to the next fencepost.

Hand in hand, Anne and Jack tarried, amused by the determined carpenter as he moved from post to post sawing, then flinging the little crowns to the rain-slicked cobblestones.

"Hey, Jack! Jack Hampton!" a man called from a jovial gang making its way around the green. "We're off to Montagne's to toast the Declaration. Join us for a pint . . ."

"Not tonight, Ezra." Jack laughed. "My pocket won't support one round with you, much less the herd you roam with!"

"Come along, brother—your pretty lady's welcome as well—*I'm* buying!"

"What?!" Jack clutched at his chest, aping a fit of apoplexy to everyone's great amusement.

"Why don't you join your friends?" Anne urged. "I have to get going anyway. David will be sending the cavalry out in search if I'm not home before curfew."

"Alright . . ." Jack's eyes shifted to his fellows waiting on his answer. ". . . but I'll see you home first."

"Don't be ridiculous." Anne pulled her hand free from his. "I'm not helpless—there's still plenty light and home is but two blocks away . . . I'll be fine."

"Alright, then . . ." Jack said, taking several backward steps. "I'll come by tomorrow morning—to break down and stow the press." He turned to circle the green in a brisk half run to catch up with his mates. Suddenly, he pulled up short, bent down to retrieve something from the pavement and ran back to Anne.

"Look . . ." Jack smiled, breathless. In his hand he held one of the discarded crowns that had broken cleanly into two pieces. He dropped one half into his pocket and pressed the other half into Anne's hand. "For us—a token to remember the day by . . ."

Anne grasped Jack by the placket of his weskit, pulled him down to her level. "Oh, I'll not soon forget this day." And before she knew what she was about, she kissed Jack Hampton most brazenly on the lips. Releasing him with a little shove, she took a step back. "Go on . . . off with you now . . ."

"Why, Widow Merrick." Jack grinned, straightening his hat thrown askew by her kiss. "You never fail to surprise."

"Hey, Hampton! You comin'?"

Jack took off up Broad Way. He looked back once and waved, and Anne waved back, watching until he disappeared in the scrum.

A gust of wind off the bay tugged at her damp skirts. Anne's fingers tightened around the little half-crown Jack'd given her—the broken edge biting into her palm as she pressed her closed fist to her heart. Turning toward Whitehall Street, Anne cast a lingering look over her shoulder, at the empty pedestal on the green.

Void of its King, the marble monolith stood desolate in the twilight, facing a storm-tossed sea and the silhouette of the armada menacing the horizon.

CHAPTER SIX

❧❧❧

'Tis not the concern of a day, a year, or an age; posterity are
virtually involved in the contest, and will be more or less affected,
even to the end of time, by the proceedings now.

THOMAS PAINE, *Common Sense*

Friday, July 12, 1776
The Cup and Quill Is Closed for the Day

Wood squawked against wood, and stacks of treenware plates tottered on the shelves, clacking in alarm as Anne and Sally wrestled the unwieldy cabinet away from the wall.

"Heave, Sal! *Heave!*"

Together, the women managed to jerk the heavy cabinet from its comfortable footprint, and push it far enough to make accessible the small door behind it. Swiping mobcaps from heads, Anne and Sally fell back, gasping.

Anne could no longer operate her business with the back end of the shop in total disarray. After waiting two days for Jack Hampton to come as promised and break down the press, she decided to take matters into her own hands. She chased the dregs of her breakfast trade out the front door, and closed her shop for the day.

"It's only but forenoon, and this day's already hotter than the middle pits o' hell." Sally whisked off the kerchief tucked at the neckline of her dress and floated it to hang over the lever handle on the press.

Anne opened the door to the odd-shaped little storage room beneath the stairs, only to be pushed back by a heated cloud of dusty air. "Ullcchh!" she said, scrinching nose and eyes. "Best give it a moment to air out."

"This swelter is no friend to me." Sally unbuttoned her skirt and kicked it off. "I canna bear it—soakin' wet I am."

Anne stepped out of her skirt as well, and pulled her blouse over her head, giggling. "Brazen, but it is just the two of us here. Why should we suffer this heat?"

Barefoot, and considerably cooler stripped down to sleeveless muslin shifts and stays, the women went a step further, pinning their hems at their hips to accommodate a breeze and ease of movement about the legs.

"Well." Anne propped her hands akimbo and took stock of all the printing accoutrement piled upon and around the press. "I suppose we ought first get this lot stowed and out of the way, and then we can figure out how to dismantle the press."

Together the women slid heavy cases of type across the floor, pushing and pulling them to the pitch-black, narrow end of the space.

"Damn that Jack Hampton—he's a canny one, aye?" Sally said. "Leavin' all this work for us . . ."

Anne shook her head. "I don't know . . . He promised to come by on Wednesday morning, and here it is Friday with no word. I confess, I'm a bit worried."

"Och, Annie, dinna waste a smidge o' worry on th' rogue. He's the devil's get, that one—as charming and handsome-dark as he is—the devil's get—I'd lay a wager on it." On the count of three, they lifted a ponderous crate filled with leading strips and quoins, and waddled it in through the door, dropping it with a thud.

"*Whew!* Like to put a hole through the floor." Sally swiped a forearm across her dripping brow and Anne sank down on the crate, taking a moment to catch a breath, when the brass bell tinkled, signaling the shop door had opened and closed.

"*Bugger it!*" Sally's hand flew to her lips. "Ye didna shoot the bolts home!"

"I thought *you* had."

The women poked their heads from the storage room, squinting and blinking at the bright daylight, as two tall figures moved toward the back of the shop.

"Away wi' ye, lads," Sally called. "Cup and Quill is closed for the day. No a drop o' coffee to be had. Away wi' yiz! Come back tomorrow— we'll be offering blaeberry tarts."

"Sally? Mrs. Anne? We've come to lend you a hand . . ."

Anne recognized Titus's voice, and for a moment, the muscles at the back of her neck relaxed. Her eyes adjusted, and as the men drew closer, she could see the "we" in Titus's pronouncement included a grinning and rather disheveled Jack Hampton. The women ducked back into the shadows, fingers fumbling to tug free the hems of their shifts, and at least cover bare legs.

Jack peered inside the storeroom, calling, "Come out, come out, wherever you are!" and Sally burst forth, ablaze in a redheaded ire, backing Jack up to the printing press with a remonstrating finger in his face.

"And where have you been? It's either honey or turd from you, Jack Hampton, na? First ye have us throw our shop topsy-turvy with all yer Patriot palaver—and then ye dinna make good on yer promise t' clean up this mess. Out carousing wi' yer mates, from the smell of ye, while two of us have been trippin' over the press and one another t' git from kitchen to customer . . ." She gave him a rough shove to his shoulder.

Jack leaned back, his arms upraised, laughing. "Sal! I thought we were friends?!"

Titus stood by, shaking his head, smiling. Anne stepped out of the stifling storeroom, arms folded in stern admonition. "We've no need for a friend who cannot keep true to his word." Too aware she was standing there clad in her thinnest summer-weight shift, she managed to dredge up the dignity to dismiss Jack with a wave. "Be on your merry way, Jack Hampton—Sally and I can manage on our own, thank you very much."

"Aw, Annie." Jack brushed past Sally. "I'm sorry. I know I'm a trifle tardy, but I'm here now, aren't I? Ready to make good on my promise—see, I've brought Titus." Though his tone mimicked that of a contrite man, his telling smile was made mischievous by the crinkling at the corners of his bloodshot eyes as he stifled a laugh. Two days' worth of dark stubble added to the devilish cast of his features.

Standing there in naught but her shift, Anne squirmed under his scrutiny. "You don't seem to be very sorry . . ."

"I *am* sorry"—Jack's strangled chortle burst into a guffaw—"but the two of you—so fierce in your petticoats—"

Titus sputtered, "It *is* awful funny, Mrs. Anne."

But Anne was not laughing. She noticed all but one button missing on the same green weskit Jack'd worn when she'd kissed him farewell at the Bowling Green, and she considered the curious crimson smudge tinting the unbuttoned collar of his shirt with a bit of animus. Hatless, most of his hair had escaped the sad, bedraggled ribbon slipping so low on his queue that it threatened to fall away at any moment. He tucked a black tangle behind his ear and she caught the glint of gold.

Anne moved in to get a better look, encountering the cloud of alcohol and cheap perfume emanating from him like piss-reek from a chamberpot. "Is that an earring you're wearing?"

"What?!" Jack fingered his ears, the surprise clear on his face as he discovered the small gold hoop pierced through the lobe of his right ear. "So I am!"

Titus doubled over, hooting and stamping his boots to the floorboards. "Oh, you must have had yourself a *good* time!"

Jack nodded. "I must have!"

"Och, yer as shameless as a whore at a christening! I canna believe yiv th' bollocks to cross this good woman's threshold stinkin' of rum and sluts—feh!" Sally grabbed a broom, and used it to prod Jack toward the door. "Be gone—away with ye."

Jack snatched up a gutter stick and used it to parry Sally's every poke and thrust, fending her off with ridiculous cries of "En garde!" and "Touchè!" They moved in a circle around the printing press.

Titus clapped and cheered, and Anne could not contain her amusement, shouting, "You get him, Sal!"

Jack hooked one of the discarded mobcaps expertly on the end of his "sword," and waved it in Sally's face with a cry of, "Quarter—I beg quarter!" and even Sally yielded to laughter.

Titus plucked the mobcap from Jack's gutterstick and placed it on Sally's head, crowning her the victor, while Jack bowed down on one knee in supplication, his weapon offered on open palms. Giggling, Sally accepted his surrender with a gracious curtsy, and thus peace was restored to the Cup and Quill.

With her things draped over her arm, Sally headed to the kitchen-house to prepare a midday meal for everyone. Anne collected her clothing and Jack said, "Me and Titus will have this press put away in no time."

Arms engulfing a poof of poplin and petticoats, Anne marched up the stairs with Jack smiling up to her and waving from below. It wasn't until he tipped his head at an odd angle that she realized he'd positioned himself to get a good look up her shift.

"*Oh!* You are such a *scoundrel!*"

Anne ran the rest of the way up the stairs to her room. She tossed her clothes and threw herself onto her bed, arms and legs splayed, heart a-thumping. Closing her eyes, she focused on catching her breath and suppressing an overpowering urge to run down, take Jack Hampton by the hand and lead him into her bedchamber.

Her eyes snapped open. Smiling, she stared at the ceiling rafters, fanning her legs with her shift. *What a wicked, wicked notion . . .*

⚓ ⚓ ⚓

AFTER stowing the press and setting the shop to rights, Jack and Titus moved a table and a pair of benches out to the garden, and everyone gathered in the cool shade of the peach trees to enjoy a simple meal.

Titus smeared a hunk of bread with potted cheese, topping it with a slice of cold roast pork and a dollop of Sally's peach relish. "I heard tell General Washington has captured and questioned four of them Redcoats who are camped out on Staten Island."

"I heard the same at the butcher's." Sally set a tray with a pot of coffee, sugar bowl and creamer onto the tabletop.

"Yep." Titus chewed. "They say General Howe has ten thousand soldiers ready to invade."

"Dinna fash, Titus, General Washington has more than ten thousand men at arms ready to defend our liberty . . ."

Jack reached to pour himself a cup of coffee. "But way too many of our boys are laid up with the fever or the flux, Sal—and General Howe's brother is on his way with more ships, each one filled to the brim with Hessians. Parliament paid a pretty penny for those mercenaries. They plan to come down on us hard in trying to squash the life out of our rebellion. You girls really ought to get out of town while the roads are still clear."

"They might not invade." With a steady hand, Anne carved uniform slices from the roast. "Admiral Howe also brings the crown authority to negotiate peace."

"Peace!" Jack jabbed an elbow into Titus's side and rolled his eyes. "Any hope for peace was tossed to the wind when the Congress declared independence. Mark my words, we're in it now—up to our necks—pitted against the most powerful army and navy in the world."

"Such portents of doom and gloom"—Anne forked more meat onto each man's plate—"but I don't see you leaving town, Jack Hampton. Nor you, Titus."

"Well, I can't speak for Titus, but I'm a New Yorker, and I'll be damned if I turn tail and leave my city to Georgie's Germans. I'd sooner burn it to the ground." Jack dropped a lump of sugar into his cup.

"Don't be ridiculous," Anne said.

Jack shrugged. "If we can't hold the city, it would be a mistake to leave it to the Redcoats."

Anne poured herself a cup of coffee. "If the Redcoats sweep across the countryside with overwhelming force and bring us to heel, I argue that it makes no difference where Sally and I go. If I am to cower and quake while war wages around me, I'd rather do so here, under the protection of my own roof, than under my father's mean thumb in Peekskill."

"Aye that!" Sally clunked her mug against Anne's in toast.

"A well-reasoned argument, but a foolish course." Jack tore a hunk of bread from the loaf and used it to wipe up the last of the soft cheese from the crock. "This will be a bloody summer, Annie. We showed the lobsterbacks at Breed's Hill that we're not so easily vanquished."

Titus poured a stream of cream into his coffee. "Why is it you haven't joined the Continentals, Jack? You and that new earring would cut a fine figure in one of them fancy New Yorker jackets."

"Naw." Jack shook his head, and fingered his newly pierced ear. "I know enough to know I'm not one for army life—all that drilling, discipline and taking orders—I'd be flogged on a daily basis for insubordination." He took a sip from his mug. "I'm no Regular, but I do my part."

"I'd join up in a heartbeat, but General Washington don't allow negros in his army—free or slave."

"Now there's another fine example of foolishness—they won't allow a black man to carry a gun or stop a British musket ball when it is clear they need every willing hand. More afraid of slave insurrection than they are of becoming slaves themselves." Jack waved the bowl end of his teaspoon toward Titus. "You're a free man with a trade and no ties that bind. How is it you've not moved on to seek out a friendlier clime?"

Titus smiled and shrugged. "This town's my home, too, and I don't mind doing my part. We all need to pitch in where and how we can." He swung a leg over the bench and stood, patting his midsection. "I thank you, Mrs. Anne . . . Sally . . . that was a fine supper, but speaking on pitching in, I need to get going. They'll be needing my shovel for fortifying the batteries along the Hudson today."

"Hold on, Titus . . ." Jack gulped down his coffee. "I'm with you."

"Wait for us." Anne hopped up and began collecting dishes. "Sally and I can walk with you—now that the press is put away, we can lend a hand at the hospital this afternoon."

Clearing the table in no time, Anne and Sally donned hats. Jack and Titus shouldered their shovels and followed the women as they cut a diagonal course across town, toward King's College.

A sleepy, hot and humid afternoon, the narrow streets were quiet and devoid of much activity. The foursome skirted the barricade surrounding the Commons to cross Broad Way, when a series of shrill whistles reverberated across the cobbles, causing the few souls braving the heat of the day to pause and wonder.

The whistled signals were soon accompanied by erratic drumming, and three boys came racing full speed up dusty Broad Way, pounding the skins of their drums, shouting, *"To arms! To arms!"*

Jack snatched one of the boys by the sleeve. "Where've they landed?"

Struggling to catch a breath, the boy gasped, "All I know is battleships are headin' up the Hudson." And just as he blurted the information, a booming cannonade erupted from the southernmost tip of the island.

Doors flew open and people poured forth from taverns, businesses and homes, tumbling into the street like apples spilling from an overturned bushel basket. Men began to rush about in a pandemonium of shouting, pulling on clothing and shouldering weapons. Like Anne and Sally standing on the curbstone, a few women came out to stand on doorsteps in stunned disbelief.

Jack took off running, shouting over his shoulder to Titus, "You get the girls back home." They watched him cross Broad Way, the handle of his shovel in a two-fisted grip, dodging around the crowd emerging from Montagne's Tavern door to disappear around the corner of Murray Street.

"Go on with Jack, Titus." Anne gave him a shove. "Sal and I can manage on our own."

Titus didn't argue. With a nod, he dashed away to meld in with the stream of men running toward the river.

"C'mon." Anne took Sally by the hand, and instead of heading back to the shop, they crossed Broad Way and joined an ever-rising sea of panic and confusion. Another barrage of cannon thumped and thundered. Everyone's attempt to discern the distance created a momentary pause in the excitement. The noise was definitely drawing closer.

"It sounds as if we're winning," Sally said.

Anne shook her head as they cut across the lawn of King's College. "Those must be the batteries at Paulus Hook—and that means the ships are advancing and returning fire. Look . . ." She pointed to a crowd gathered on a flat rooftop of a three-story building commanding a view of the river. "We'll be able to see from up there."

Neat block letters on the small wooden sign nailed to the right of the front door read: MOTHER BABCOCK'S BOARDINGHOUSE. Anne rapped at the door, and when no one answered she tested the knob. Unlocked. Anne stepped inside and urged Sally to follow.

The heavy drapery on every window was drawn shut, and the house seemed abandoned. They ventured into a paneled parlor filled with upholstered furnishings smelling stuffy with tobacco, calling, "Hello!" to no response.

"They're all on the roof," Anne suggested, looking up the stairway.

Another round of cannon fire caused Anne and Sally to shed their trepidation, and they ran up the stairs. The door at the top of the last flight led onto the rooftop. Anne and Sally joined the chattering crowd of onlookers clustered at a two-foot-high parapet hugging the edge of the roof, facing the Hudson.

Sally grabbed Anne by the arm and whispered in her ear, "We've stumbled into a bawdy house, Annie!"

Anne took a good look at the crowd. They were all women, at least a dozen, and all but one older woman—the procuress, Mother Babcock, no doubt—standing barefoot and in some incongruous stage of undress. A heavy coating of powder and rouge masked most of the faces, a rather garish display in the light of day.

Though Sally tugged relentless at her sleeve, Anne's initial instinct to beat a hasty retreat was overruled by curiosity combined with the smell of gunpowder and an extraordinary view of the drama floating up the Hudson.

A bold naval squadron materialized from the lingering cloud of cannon smoke hovering over the river. Moving at a smart rate on a steady breeze under full canvas, a single, two-masted schooner led a pair of battleships, each frigate accompanied by a nimble ship's tender. From her elevated vantage point, Anne could make out marines and sailors bustling about on decks piled high with sandbags to absorb shot and flying debris.

Along the river's edge, like beetlebugs exposed when a stone is overturned, Continental artillery crews scrambled to reposition and reload their guns. Disorganized companies of infantry wandered the river's edge, wasting lead in firing their muskets to no effect at the passing ships.

To add insult to the display of Royal Naval power, one fearless jack-tar climbed the gallant mast and perched upon the top yard thumbing his nose as the convoy sailed past unscathed, just beyond the range of the ineffectual American batteries.

"The King's Navy is giving our boys a good drubbing, aye?"

Anne turned to the familiar voice and recognized the pretty girl from the tarring and feathering on the Commons. Dressed in an exotic silk dressing gown tied with a sash, the prostitute's dark hair hung loose and disheveled. Her cheek, smooth and untroubled as a bowl of clotted cream, was missing the black heart-shaped patch pointing to her pure blue eyes. Anne managed to cull up the name from more than a year before. "Patsy Quinn?"

Patsy smiled.

An older woman Anne presumed to be Mother Babcock stood beside Patsy watching the engagement through a spyglass. "The ship nearest us is the *Rose* . . . the other—the *Phoenix*. I can't make out the name of the schooner . . ."

"Look! Virginia lads and their long rifles." Sally pointed to a handful of men in their telltale fringed hunting shirts taking up a position on a short promontory that jutted out where Barclay Street met the river.

The guns began to pop and smoke and the riflemen's range and accuracy caused a stir on the decks of the *Rose* and the *Phoenix*. The *Rose* soon replied to the rifle fire with a smart salvo from her starboard guns, sending many a soldier along the shoreline facedown into the dirt. Undeterred, the Virginians continued to pepper the passing ships, and the women on the rooftop burst out in cheer, shouting encouragement, waving bright kerchiefs and scarves.

The *Phoenix* then took a turn discharging her guns. Several well-aimed shots whizzed overhead, close enough to ruffle hair, and silenced the women in an instant.

Mother Babcock was the first to react. "Shooting at defenseless women!" she screeched, shaking a clutched fist. "Sniveling cowards! Boatloads of boy-buggerers!" Her bawds joined in, hooting and shouting a chorus of curses and invectives that would cause an old sailor to blush.

"Let's show the British bastards what we really think of them, ladies." Mother Babcock gathered the hems of her skirts. "Royal Navy mine arse!"

And on that command, hoisting petticoats, shifts and robes, the whores lined up along the parapet and presented their rear ends. Laughing, Sally turned to Anne with eyes flashing, and without hesitation, they both joined the row of giggling women and wriggling bare bottoms, lifting their skirts in mass contemptuous salute.

The *Rose* responded with fourteen of her starboard guns. Solid shot lopped off the top of the chimney no more than twelve paces away, another smoking iron ball tore through the brick a story below. The women took off in a screaming melee, tumbling down the stairs to fall in laughing, breathy heaps onto the furnishings in the parlor on the first floor.

Patsy Quinn caught up with Anne and Sally as they headed for the door. "You can stay with us until the streets are safe."

Anne retied the loose strings of her straw hat. "Those ships are moving upriver and my shop's down near Whitehall Slip—I think we'll be safe enough, Patsy."

"You know, I remember your name as well—Anne Merrick, right?" Patsy leaned against the doorframe. Clutching her dressing gown at her throat with one hand, she smoothed her hair with the other. "I see you sometimes . . . around the college."

Sally fidgeted, peering up and down the street. "Let's be gone, Annie, afore anyone sees us here."

Anne ignored Sally and questioned the prostitute. "So will you all be leaving town now?"

"Not us," Patsy said with a laugh and a shake of her head. "If the Redcoats invade, we'll make do, just as we did when the Continentals took over." Her voice dropped to a whisper. "The ol' bitch is always sayin' how war is nothing but good for business."

"Hmph," Anne muttered. "She's most probably right."

With that exchange, Sally succeeded in pulling Anne out the door and down the stoop.

Anne called out over her shoulder, "Fare well, Patsy!"

Patsy waved and closed the door.

∞ ∞ ∞

THE bombardment of the town set another panic in motion among New York's citizenry. The Royal Navy's foray up the Hudson resulted in hasty packing and many new refugees with bundles and carts heading northward, making their way off of the island.

In an effort to carry on and ignore the dread and uncertainty muttering at every street corner and doorway, Anne and Sally rolled up sleeves to try their hand at producing a batch of peach cordial with the overripe peaches they'd collected over the course of the week.

Sally brought a cauldron of water to a roiling boil in the kitchen, and they began the steamy business of scalding the fruit. The peaches were dropped into the hot bath, then scooped up one by one with a long-handled wire strainer and dumped into a tub of cool water.

Anne transferred the scalded fruit to a large bucket, and the sweat-drenched women decided to move the cordial enterprise to the table in the garden shade. Paring knives in hand, Anne and Sally straddled the bench facing each other, and took up the tedious chore of peeling and slicing. Sally slipped off the fuzzy skin, and rolled the slippery peach into the tin bowl they'd set between them.

"The English surely rubbed our noses in it today, na?"

"That they did." Anne halved the peeled peach and pried the stone out, plunking it into a tin pail. Charred peach pits ground to a powder made a decent pigment for writing ink.

"An' there's surely no doubt now who owns the river," Sally added.

"I expect that is true." Anne dropped the pitted peach halves back into the bowl.

"If Howe can sail about us and land thousands of soldiers where he will, there's no chance Washington will be able to hold this city." Sally peeled and plopped another naked peach into the bowl. "We should think on packing it up for Peekskill, Annie."

"Leave for Peekskill . . ." Saying the words aloud caused Anne to shudder on the hottest day of the year—absurdly, far more frightened by the prospect of losing her own place in the world than by the notion of invading Redcoats and Hessians.

"Leave my home to ruin? Leave Jemmy's grave behind? Become, once again, my father's chattel, at the mercy of his selfish intentions?" Anne shook her head. "No . . . I just can't do it—but if you want to leave, Sally, I wouldn't stop you."

"Annie! Ye know full well I willna go anywhere without ye." Sally's brogue tended to thicken when she was excitable.

Anne could see the tears spring to her friend's eyes. "You know, the British put a scare into everyone today with that run up the river. Maybe now the Congress'll be more amenable to negotiating some sort of peace."

"Aye . . . and maybe the funny wee man with no arms will catch a hare."

Anne laughed and grabbed another peach from the bowl. "As I see it, we have two courses from which to choose. We can panic, become vagabonds on the road and let this war be the ruin of us for certain—" her blade bit into the peach flesh, the sharp edge circumnavigating the pit—"or we can show patience, and see how this game plays out." Twisting the two halves apart, she dug a thumbnail under the stone and tore it free. "Maybe Mother Babcock has the right of it—war *is* good for business—maybe we should look upon the whole situation as an opportunity—"

"Aye . . ." Sally retorted with a snort. "Never underestimate the wisdom of a rich old whore."

The sound of thunder rolling across the eastern horizon caused them both to look up to the cloudless blue sky.

"What on earth . . ."

This thunder was too regular—too rhythmic—too incessant to be the result of a distant storm at sea. Sally and Anne splashed their peach-sticky hands in water. Wiping wet hands on aprons, the women ran through the shop and out onto the lane.

The pounding noise drew the interest of the neighbors. Armed with a long spyglass, Walter Quakenbos was already on the march to the waterfront. Anne and Sally trotted after the baker, and they all scrambled up to join the equally curious gathering along the top of the battery wall at the end of Pearl Street.

Out on the eastern horizon, flashes of fire amid puffs of smoke accompanied the thumping bombardment, and the shouts of men cheering, "Huzzah," carried bright and clear across the still water of the bay. Quakenbos trained his glass on the commotion coming from the fleet of ships anchored around Bedloe's Island.

"Hey, Annie! Sal!" Shovels on shoulders, grimy and sweat-stained Jack, accompanied by Titus, called out from the street. "What do you see up there?"

"Looks like the lobsterbacks are giving salute," Quakenbos answered, waving the men up onto the wall. The baker continued his report, peering through the glass. "A big ship of the line with an immense St. George's Cross flying from the main mast has joined them." He dropped the glass. "I'd wager pounds to pennies that's Black Dick's standard they're cheering—Admiral Howe has arrived. Have a look . . ." The baker handed Jack the spyglass.

"Of course they cheer," Anne said, with a sad shake of her head.

"With the admiral comes a hundred more ships and thousands more soldiers."

"Och . . ." Sally moaned, her apron a twist in her hands. "We'll never win without a navy."

"We don't need ships. This is our country. We have but to stand our ground," Jack said, his eye never leaving the lens, his voice solid and sure. "By cunning, daring and dark of night we will harry them—and we will win."

CHAPTER SEVEN

❧

Nothing but heaven is impregnable to vice.

THOMAS PAINE, *Common Sense*

Thursday, August 15, 1776
Over Darts at the Cup and Quill

CLOSE to curfew, Sally shot the bolts home on the front door, closing the Liberty Coffeehouse for the day. Anne moved from table to table, gathering dirty dishes onto a tray and wiping down the tabletops with a damp rag.

It had been a full month since the *Phoenix* and *Rose* sailed blithely past the Continental batteries and riverfront forts, traveling twenty-five miles upriver to where the Hudson widened and formed a natural lake called the Tappan Zee. The ships dropped anchor near Tarrytown, effectively choking off a major supply route for the people of New York City and the army quartered there.

The British incursion caused many steadfast New Yorkers—including a few of the Widow Merrick's competitors—to close shop and leave the city, and as a result, business at the Cup and Quill flourished. After a long, busy day, Anne poured a tot of rum into her coffee, and dragged a chair over to join Sally watching Jack and Titus embroiled in a serious game of darts.

Jack toed the chalk line that had been paced out and marked on the floorboards. Eye asquint, lower lip caught in his teeth, the wooden barrel of a turkey-feathered barb pinched just so between thumb and forefinger, he let the dart fly, hitting the edge of the smallest center circle.

"Hah!" Jack punched Titus in the upper arm. "Your fate is sealed, my friend. Submit to my superior skill and commence to digging in your pocket—what was our wager? Five dollars?"

"Two dollars . . ." Titus replied. Rubbing his arm, he shot a glance at the score Sally tallied up on the chalkboard. "But it's fine by me if you want to make it five."

"Done." Jack slapped a tabletop. "Five dollars to the winner."

The two men had developed a comfortable camaraderie over the past several weeks, spending most days together on crews building fortifications, and most evenings at the Cup and Quill, over spirits and darts.

Boosted by the accuracy of his last throw and anxious to claim a rare victory, Jack hurried to finish his set. His rushed shot flew wide, missing the board and bouncing off the plaster to fall with a clatter to the floor.

"There's your chance, Titus!" Sally exclaimed.

"No worries." Jack gathered the three darts and handed them off to Titus for his final turn. "My last set was the death knell for ol' Titus."

Titus stepped up to the line, threw his first dart, hitting the board dead center.

"He needs to hit two more of the same to earn a draw," Jack scoffed, pulling a chair up to sit with the girls. "The match is as good as mine."

Titus threw his next dart for a second bull's-eye.

"Ha!" Sally exclaimed. "Ye ken now, don't ye, Jack? Titus's been toying wi' ye all along."

"A lucky throw." Jack folded his hands behind his head and leaned back in his chair, rocking on the rear legs. "The odds are against him hitting three in a row."

Titus took his final throw, and the front legs of Jack's chair thumped to the floorboards as the last dart joined its mates in the center.

"A draw!" the women clapped and cheered.

"You've only managed to prolong your misery, my friend." Jack snatched the offending darts from the board. "One last set to settle the match—three darts each."

Titus grinned and shrugged, stepping back to allow his opponent a position at the line. Jack took his time, making three careful throws, landing one bull's-eye and two very respectable near misses. "Witness the steady application of skill, as opposed to plain dumb luck," Jack proclaimed with a wide wave toward the board.

"You'd best mind your boasting tongue, Jack Hampton," Anne admonished. "Overconfidence can lead to a dangerous fall . . ."

Unfazed by Jack's braggadocio, Titus retrieved the darts and took up his position. With a cool aplomb Sally and Anne had witnessed many times before, he threw two darts in quick succession, landing one bull's-eye and one near miss. Titus let fly his third dart, landing the throw just within the center mark. Turning to Jack with hand outstretched he said, "You owe me five dollars."

Annoyed, Jack rooted about in the pocket of his weskit. He pulled forth a crumpled bit of paper and tossed it onto the tabletop. "There's two dollars—I'll have to owe you the rest."

"Continentals! No, sir—" Titus shook his head, scrunching his nose as if Jack had just served up a turd. "Our wager is in real dollars . . ."

"We wagered 'dollars,' and this is the currency of the realm. It's not only unlawful, but it's unpatriotic to refuse it as payment." Jack snatched up the note to read the fine print. "I don't know why you worry; it says right here—'*This bill entitles the bearer to receive two Spanish milled dollars.*'"

"Dinna bother puttin' thatch on an empty barn, Jack Hampton," Sally snorted. "We all ken the worth of a Continental—next to nil." She made a circle joining thumb and fingers, and peered through the negative space.

Titus held the paper at an angle to catch the light coming in through the back door, noting the shiny mica flecks embedded in the paper stock. "Could be worse, I suppose. At least it's not a counterfeit . . ." He slipped the note into his pocket. "Just don't forget you owe me three."

"Have I ever not made good on one of our wagers? Consider yourself fortunate to have bested me, you lucky bastard." Jack plopped down in a huff to sit beside Anne.

"Will you ever learn?" Anne shook her head. "Vanity and conceit only breed arrogance—and arrogance can be parlayed to your foe's advantage."

Sally joined in on the scolding. "Aye, yer no better than the bloody lobsterbacks out on the bay—certain of victory, and bound to lose it all in the end."

"If I were General Washington, I know what I'd do to beat them Redcoats." Titus straddled a chair backward. "I'd wait for a moon on the wane and send a few small boats across the bay—set some of them Royal Navy ships alight. Those British are packed together tighter than herring in a barrel, and a little fire would go a long way."

Jack perked up, happy to turn the conversation from his character flaws to the flaws in Titus's military strategy. "That would be suicide. Too much water betwixt us and the fleet—any boats crossing the bay would be sighted by the ship's watch and blown out of the water before they could get close enough to do any harm."

Anne joined in the conjecture. "Well then, I'd set fire to those ships moored out on the Tappan Zee—naught but three ships, but they've strangled our trade and supply and do far more harm than the fleet out on the bay."

"You know, she's got something there." Jack hitched his chair to move closer to Titus. "It wouldn't take much to wreak a bit of havoc on the Tappan Zee . . . a pair of fireboats, launched upriver—ride the current—sneak up and burn both the *Phoenix* and the *Rose* to the waterline."

"I'm game." Titus gripped the finial ends on the chairback. "Daring and doing beats worrying and waiting any day."

Jack slapped his friend on the back. "Then let's do it!"

"D'ye hear, Annie?" Sally jeered. "They're ready to take on His Majesty's Royal Navy."

"Fully armed with a bottle of rum and two Continentals . . ." Anne added with a shake of her head.

Jack and Titus ignored the women and put their heads together to hatch a daredevil scheme, making quick work of the rum. With inebriated enthusiasm, they went next door to roust Quakenbos the baker, and tap him for the lend of his big gelding and the funds required to complete their mission.

Anne's futile efforts to persuade the men to wait and reconsider their plan in the sober light of day fell on drunken ears. Unable to dissuade the obstinate pair from their course, and sure she'd find them both on her doorstep come morning, Anne bid the men good-bye and good riddance. Titus and Jack set forth in the dark, riding double, trotting north on Queen Street, toward the Bowery Lane.

When drowsy Titus slipped his seat and tumbled off onto the road just before reaching the King's Bridge, the fellows decided to take advantage of a convenient hayrick and catch a few hours of sleep. At daybreak they woke, discovering neither had bothered to hobble the baker's horse, and they'd lost their mount. Horseless and hungover, but still determined in their quest, they begged two cups of coffee, cheese and a loaf of bread from a kind Dutch farmwife and set off on foot. By noontime they'd reached the town of Sleepy Hollow, on the shore of the Tappan Zee, a few miles north of Tarrytown.

In Sleepy Hollow, Jack reunited with an old friend and Liberty Boy he'd apprenticed with at Parker's Press, a fellow by the name of Joe Bass. Joe helped them locate a pair of decrepit but somewhat seaworthy ships suitable to the purpose—a rickety single-masted sloop and an ancient two-masted schooner. Excited by the fireboat strategy, Bass volunteered to captain the schooner, and he enlisted four local Patriots to bolster the crew.

After purchasing the necessary incendiary supplies, they moved the two ships to anchor at a point two miles upriver from the British convoy. The rest of the long, hot day was spent fashioning the ships into floating bombs.

Yards of old canvas were ripped into strips, saturated in turpentine spirits and draped over the sails and rigging. The local boys set to work assembling foot-long bundles of straw as thick as a man's leg and dipped in molten pitch. The decks of both ships were carpeted with these combustible faggots, leaving a narrow path of exposed decking stretching from stem to stern. Along these paths Jack traced a thick stream of gunpowder leading up to a dozen small kegs filled with flammable pine tar.

Off in the distance, the bell from the old Dutch church in Sleepy Hollow tolled eleven o'clock, and two fireships bobbed on the current, ready for duty.

The men gathered together on the deck of the schooner. Preparing the ships was a thirsty business on a warm August evening. Joe Bass combined a bottle of rum with a bottle of peachy, and concocted a fine punch with which to drink to a fair night's work and the success of their mission.

"To Liberty and the United States!" they toasted, in a knock of wooden cups.

The assault required stealth and surprise to succeed, and fortune smiled further upon their endeavor—a heavy cloud cover masked a good amount of light from a waxing moon.

"Pass me the blacking." Jack scooped up a handful of lard and soot mixed in a tin pail. Stripped down to britches and bare feet, he blacked his torso, arms and face. Other than Titus, who was roundly envied for requiring no additional blacking, the rest of the crew followed suit. Joe Bass went so far as to smear a quantity over his crewmate's head, to dull his blond hair.

"Your fuckin' towhead shines brighter than a spermaceti candle."

Before dousing the ship lights, Joe and Titus each made certain to light the end on a yard-length of match cord, the long, slow-burning fuses being the only fire allowed on board. Leaving Bass and his boys on the schooner with handshakes and shouts of "Good Luck!"

and "Fare Well!" Jack and Titus hopped over the side to man the oars on the sloop.

Anchors lifted and with oars slapping in time to the *ching-ching* of the crickets' chirp, the sloop towed the schooner straight out, about fifty yards before drawing in oars and disconnecting. Jack and Titus sat on the back bench, the rudder between them. Turning south, the fireships coasted silent on the current carrying them toward the British squadron.

Jack shifted forward to sit on the very edge of his seat, gripping tight the tiller. The rough, dry oak, weathered by countless seasons, bit into his palm, giving traction to a hand slippery with lard and sweat. It seemed a bit of a farce—steering the rudder on a night so dark he couldn't even make out the prow of his own boat—but the tiller in his hand at least fostered the illusion of being in control.

Floating through the pitch-black with only the smidge of light cast by the glowing tip of the match cord Titus cupped in his hand caused an eerie unease to tickle up Jack's backbone. He leaned toward his friend and whispered, "Darker than the depths of a papist priest's arsehole . . ."

Titus had to bite on his fist to keep from laughing out loud, and after a moment, he whispered back, "I'll just have to take your word on that . . ."

Jack stifled his snicker, and shot Titus an elbow to his ribs.

Deprivation of sight excited all other senses, and Jack became acutely aware of every sound—the breeze filling the canvas, rigging thumping against the mast, the ancient ship's tired creaks and groans echoing through the hollow hull as water pushed them along. Jack scrubbed his bare feet on the decking, pining for solid ground, and it occurred to him then that he was not one for boats. Regretting his decision to limit his consumption of rum punch to just one cupful, a song came to mind, and he began to sing softly under his breath.

"What do you do with a drunken sailor, earlye in the morning?
"Way hey and . . ."

"Shhhsh!" Titus gave him a shove to the shoulder.

It was hard to gauge how far they had traveled. Jack began to worry that they had somehow sailed past the British ships, when the canvas belled with new wind, and lightning flashed behind the clouds, illuminating, for the briefest instance, the mass of naval vessels, dead ahead.

"D' you see that?" he rasped.

Titus answered by slipping the sloop's anchor over the side to slow their approach. A moment later they heard the reciprocating plop ahead and to their right—Joe Bass dropping anchor on his schooner.

Jack stared ahead at the patch of black where he thought he'd seen the British ships riding at anchor. A single chime rang out from one of the frigates, followed by a voice calling, "All's well!"

"To your left," Titus said, so soft in his ear Jack had a hard time hearing it over his heart hammering in his chest. He gave the rudder a pull and Titus put an oar into the water. Slowly, quietly, they skimmed toward the call.

A loud thump and bump followed by the scraping squeal of wood and iron raised a series of shouts. The area to their right was suddenly hissing and alight with flames leaping up the sails of the schooner in a grapple with the squadron's bomb ketch.

The conflagration cast a brilliant light on the entire scene—and their sloop was no more than ten yards away from the *Phoenix*. The alarm was raised and *Phoenix* beat to quarters.

Titus swung the anchor aboard, yelling, "Take an oar!"

They rowed like mad to put distance between themselves and the inferno overwhelming the bomb ketch, maneuvering the sloop into *Phoenix*'s shadow.

Titus shouted, "Fasten the lines!"

They scrambled with grappling hooks to secure their fireship to the frigate. The *Rose* unleashed a sharp cannonade, and the *Phoenix*, a flurry of musket fire. One iron ball crashed into their hull. Another cut the mast in two.

Ducking and dodging as small shot whizzed by, thunking into wood, dinging off iron fittings and buzzing into the water, they tangled hooks into the rigging along the prow of the *Phoenix*, and pulled the sloop tight to the frigate.

"Fire!" Jack shouted, and Titus touched the glowing end of the match cord to the gray stream of gunpowder.

For moment they stood transfixed, watching the powder burst into a smoky, sizzling serpent, setting the pitched straw and oily canvas alight as it snaked along the deck—the flames leaping up to catch fire to the tarred hull and rigging of the *Phoenix.*

Shouting, *"Jump!"* Titus grabbed Jack by the arm. Jack snatched up their gunnysack and they dove into the river.

∾ ∾ ∾

GOING to breakfast, Anne paused at the top of the stairs. Sally was standing at the open front door, talking with Walter Quakenbos. Vexed by the sight of her neighbor, Anne took a step back, not wanting to be drawn into a conversation with the baker. *The old fool. He could plainly see Jack and Titus were worse for the drink, and yet he gave them money and a horse.*

Sally made her farewells and rebolted the door.

"What did he want?" Anne called.

Sally startled. "Och . . . I didna see ye standin' there . . ." Without answering, Sally headed for the back door.

Anne skipped down the stairs and followed Sally into the kitchen-house.

A steaming pot of coffee hung from a trammel chain over the fire. Sally sat on the hearthstone. Using a long pair of tongs, she arranged embers from the fire into a compact pile. "I'm making pancakes," she said, centering a three-legged griddle over the coals.

The little kitchen was a bright and cheerful place. The sharply pitched ceiling was engineered with thick planks and supported by an exposed structure of sturdy rafters and beams long since aged to a smoky, dark patina. Running just beneath the sills of three diamond-paned windows, a long work surface stretched the length of the whitewashed wall, and a multigenerational accumulation of pottery, brassware and ironware was stored in cupboards below.

The opposite wall was taken up by the large brick fireplace. The raised hearthstone Sally rested on extended into the room a generous two feet. A massive pair of black andirons sat within an arched opening framed with a border of blue-and-white glazed tiles—each tile depicting a different scene featuring windmills, fishing boats and happy peasants wearing wide-brimmed hats, harvesting crops. Anne would often huddle together with Jemmy and Sally in the cozy kitchen on cold winter days with cups of sweet black tea, and buttery shortbread, concocting funny stories to go with each tile.

Anne clattered through a cupboard, fished out a wooden noggin and poured herself some coffee. "So tell me, what did ol' Quakenbos have to say at the break of day?"

Sally plopped a dollop of lard the size of a quail egg to sizzle on the hot iron. "Nothing of consequence. He'd been by the Bear Market yesterday and seen a man selling chicory root there. Knowing we've been stretching our coffee berries, he thought to let me know."

"Chicory root?" Anne said, with a squint to one eye.

"Aye, chicory at the market . . ." Sally repeated, her voice a bit trembly as she ladled batter onto the griddle. "The market, the chicory . . . and the gelding's return . . ."

"What?"

Sally tossed the ladle into the bowl and looked up from her task, eyes brimming. "The gelding! The baker's bloody gelding! He's wandered home with nae rider. I didna want to add to your worry . . ."

"Oh." Anne sank down to sit next to Sally, too stunned to admonish her for cursing like a longshoreman. "A riderless horse—that does not bode well, does it?"

"No, it doesna."

A sudden loud and heavy pounding roused them both to their feet.

Anne brightened. "That's Jack now!"

Sally pushed the griddle off the coals, and they ran to the front of the shop. Fumbling with the bolts, Anne opened the door to find her brother banging on the oak frame with the pommel of his sword.

"David!" The women fell on him in relief with hugs and kisses.

"It's been weeks and weeks," Sally sobbed into his jacket sleeve.

"Weeks and weeks," David mocked with an added dose of melodrama. "Weeks and weeks . . . suffering so terribly . . ."

Sally looked up at him. "Ye suffered?"

"Of course I did." David laughed. "There's not a decent scone or bannock to be had on the whole of Long Island."

"Ye gomerel! So it's my scones ye missed?" Sally took a step back, swiping tears away with the back of her hand.

"Ah . . . you're my favorite redhead," David cajoled, pulling Sally back into his arms. "And you know very well how I've missed you. Why, I fell asleep every night dreaming on your smile."

Appeased by her beau's pretty poetry, Sally settled into his embrace.

Anne was reminded of the poignant letters she'd written home to wives and sweethearts as she watched the couple's happy reunion. Being loved and needed and missed went a long way in tempering a man's inherent reckless spirit.

Truly, the distress she'd suffered since Jack had rode off was a revelation to her. When he had ignored her reasoned entreaties and went on his merry way, she'd said good riddance, and now she so regretted the angry words uttered in bidding Jack farewell. She underestimated how much she had come to care for Jack Hampton, and the thought of him injured or dead was an awful ache tied tight about her heart that could not be loosed. *If Jack returns . . .* Anne gave her head a vigorous shake. *When* Jack returned, she would somehow let him know how much she cared.

Anne shooed Sally and her brother inside to swing the door shut and lock the bolts. "Quite the spectacle, you two—and on the Sabbath to boot . . ."

They gathered together in the kitchenhouse, and while Sally mixed up a batch of currant scones, David enjoyed several cups of coffee and recounted his most recent exploits training troops stationed on Brooklyn Heights.

"How long can you stay this time?" Sally asked him.

"Two days at most—I'm here with Colonel Livingston for a staff meeting at headquarters."

"Do you think, David," Anne questioned, "that there still might be a chance for peace?"

David shook his head. "Surely you are sensible that we have rebelled against our King and declared ourselves a sovereign state? Britain will not stand idly by and allow her richest colonies leave her dominion without a fight. War is inevitable, Annie, and I wish you would give up your fanciful hopes for peace, and go stay with Father in Peekskill . . ."

Once again, there began a brash knocking at the front of the shop. Sally shot Anne a hopeful glance as she ran to undo the latches. The front door slammed open and a powder-wigged, lace-cuffed and cravated Walter Quakenbos barreled past Sally, brandishing his walking stick in his fist, shouting like a madman. "Damn if they didn't do it!"

"What on God's green earth!" Anne and David ran out to meet Quakenbos under the peach tree.

"Forgive me, Widow Merrick." The baker sat down at the table, breathing heavy. "I hurried across town to bring you the good news . . ." Whisking off his wig, he used it to fan his red face, raising a powdery cloud. "They did it—they broke the blockade."

"Who broke the blockade?" David's question went unanswered.

Anne asked, "How do you know this?"

"I saw it!" Quakenbos took a gulp from the glass of cider Sally pressed into his hand. "I saw the ships—the *Rose* and a well-scorched *Phoenix*, heading out into the bay to rejoin the fleet."

Anne sat down next to Quakenbos. The sudden image of a wellscorched Jack Hampton floating facedown in the Hudson caused her knees to go to jelly. "Did you see them . . . speak with them . . . Jack and Titus?"

"Hampton?" David scowled. "And Titus? What's Hampton to do with Titus? What's this all about, Anne?"

Before she could form a response, a lumpy canvas bag came sailing over the garden wall, hitting Walter Quakenbos square on his shaven pate. The peach tree began to tremble, and peaches rained down in a thumpety-thump as Jack and Titus used a low-slung limb to pull up and straddle the wall.

"Lord in heaven!" Anne jumped to her feet.

Sally clapped and squealed.

"The Heroes of the Hudson!" Quakenbos shouted.

"Just what are you raggedy thieves up to?" David demanded.

Jack smoothed a hand over his hair gone wild for lack of ribbon or string. "And a good morning to you, Captain!"

"Sorry, Mrs. Anne." Concern rippled Titus's forehead like a washboard. "Being Sunday, we figured the front door would be bolted . . ."

"Pay my brother no mind, Titus." Anne encouraged them down with a wave. "We've been worried sick for you both."

The pair hit the ground on bare feet, filthy and hatless in muddy shirttails and knee breeches. Sally pointed in alarm to the sleeve covering Titus's left arm, saturated with blood.

Jack said, "Titus caught a ball . . ."

"Looks worse than it is," Titus assured. "Lodged in the meat, not the bone."

"I dug the slug out and he's fit as a fiddle now, aren't you, Titus?"

"Shoes!" the baker quacked, peering inside the sack.

"Wet shoes," Jack said.

"Giving us blisters," Titus added.

"Sit down . . . sit down." Anne's face ached for the smile she sported. Restraining the urge to kiss him welcome, she took Jack by the hand. "Come sit."

Jack and Titus sat to share the bench across from Quakenbos and David. Anne brought a pitcher of cider and Sally set a pot of jam and a plateful of fresh-baked scones on the table. Quakenbos filled everyone's tankard, and called for a toast. "To the Heroes of the Hudson!"

"No heroes here . . ." Titus said, helping himself to a scone. "Just tired and hungry is all we are."

David groaned. "Will someone please tell me what this is all about?"

Anne began the tale, with interjections from Sally and the baker. Titus picked up the story, telling of their adventure from the point when they'd set off on horseback.

"We gave it our best effort," Jack finished. "The bomb ketch Joe

Bass mistook for the *Rose* burned to the waterline, but the *Phoenix* managed to disengage from our fiery sloop. In the time it took us to swim to the riverbank, they'd doused the flames, and we struck out on the long road home." Jack popped the last bite from his third scone into his mouth. "All in all, just as you predicted, Annie, a right dismal failure."

Anne sat beside him. "Then you don't know?"

"Know what?"

"The *Phoenix* and the *Rose* have rejoined the fleet, man," Quakenbos said. "The blockade is broken."

Goggle-eyed, Titus choked out, "What?!"

Jack pulled stunned Titus into a headlock and knuckle-scrubbed his close-cropped hair. Titus jerked free, and the pair shoved and punched each other in elation. "Can you believe it? We broke the blockade!"

"The two of you have struck terror into the very heart of the Royal Navy." David stood and raised his tankard. "Cheers to the Heroes of the Hudson!"

While everyone joined in the toast, and without glancing her way, Jack reached a bold hand under the table to give Anne's knee a squeeze. Rather than brush him away, she slipped her hand over his.

"You know, Hampton . . ." Resting one boot on the bench, David leaned forward, his face so suddenly serious, Anne was certain her brother was aware of the brazen goings-on beneath the table. "This fireboat escapade is the perfect example of the type of stratagem I've been trying to persuade my colonel to . . ." Without completing his thought, David performed an abrupt about-face. He marched into the kitchen, and returned wearing his tricorn, buckling on sword and scabbard.

"You two are coming with me."

⚓ ⚓ ⚓

JACK shifted his weight to his right foot, distracted by the big blister chafed into his left heel by wet shoe leather. He sped through the fifth telling of the fireship escapade, anxious to be out the door and out of his shoes.

". . . after Titus touched fuse to powder, we stayed aboard to assure a good blaze—Titus snatched me by the arm, I snatched up our gear, and it was into the river with us. In the time it took for us to swim ashore, the *Phoenix* managed to cut loose from our sloop. From the riverbank, we could see them douse the fire, and so we took to the road."

In soggy shoes and dirty shirts Jack and Titus stood alongside David Peabody, his commanding officer and an aide-de-camp. They faced a large table draped with a crisp linen sheet and scattered with papers, maps, instruments and writing materials. The cavernous office on the second floor of the City Hall building featured a tall pair of arched windows in the Palladian style, and the room's spartan furnishings were arranged to offer the Commander in Chief a fine view down Wall Street to Trinity Church and the Hudson beyond. General Washington sat in a spindle-back chair behind the table, considering Jack's recounting without a word, availing himself of the view with impassive blue-gray eyes.

Bent over a small writing desk in the corner, a stocky black man in a stark white wig marked diligently in a ledger, leaving Jack to wonder on what he was writing. But for the quill scratchings, everyone waited in silence for the general to react. At last, leaning back in his chair, large hands resting light on the armrests, he asked, "Your occupation, Mr. Hampton?"

"Printer, sir." Jack straightened his shoulders to stand a bit taller, hands clasped behind his back. "Journeymen—both of us."

The answer raised an eyebrow. Washington nodded to Titus. "This man is your slave?"

Titus and Jack exchanged quick, amused grins.

"I am a free man, General, sir," Titus uttered his first words since crossing the threshold of the Continental headquarters. "Jack and me are colleagues and companions."

"Good friends," Jack added.

"Good friends . . ." Washington repeated, the flash of a closed-mouth smile altering his sober countenance for an instant. "Tell me, Mr. Hampton, by this experience, if you were to put forth another effort of this sort, what would you do differently?"

Exhausted, filthy, hungry and having spent the past two hours moving up the chain of command, retelling his story over and over, Jack scratched the three-day stubble on his chin, at a loss for words. "What would I do differently . . ."

"We ought to have paid more mind to the weather . . ." Titus offered. "A stronger wind would have wrought the damage we were hoping for."

Jack nodded in agreement. "True . . . though dark enough to allow a stealthy approach, the night didn't offer any wind to fan the flames up into the sails. With a good wind, the crew on the *Phoenix* would have been hard-pressed to put out a fire."

"An astute assessment—" Washington spoke to Jack, as if Titus didn't even exist. "Our Continental Army could make use of a brave Patriot such as yourself. I hope you might consider joining our ranks, Mr. Hampton."

Irked that the man's slave-owning fears kept good men like Titus Gilmore from bolstering the American ranks, Jack snapped, "I'm afraid me and Titus just aren't suited to army life—both of us being dark men . . ." Glancing over his shoulder to see the pained look on Anne's brother's face, Jack took a breath and tried to temper his response. "Nevertheless, we're in this thing whole heart, sir. We do what we can to fight for our cause—the belief that all men are created equal, that they are endowed by their creator with certain unalienable rights . . ."

"Hampton!" David Peabody took a step forward. "That's enough . . ."

Jack paid him no heed. ". . . that among these are Life, Liberty and the Pursuit of . . ."

"Captain Peabody, Mr. Hampton . . ." The general curtailed David's remonstration and Jack's recitation with a firm tone and an upraised palm. "Although I am aware of the content of the Declaration," he said with a nod to Jack as he turned to David, "I still appreciate the honest and heartfelt viewpoint of our Patriot citizens." Washington called, "Billy—"

The man in the corner laid down his pen, came over and set a bulbous pair of leather pouches onto the desktop. After muttering some instruction into the general's ear, Billy took a position immediately to his left. Astride or afoot, the general's body servant was never far from his side. Always dressed in blue and buff livery to match his master's well-tailored uniform, the slave Billy Lee was almost as famous as Washington himself.

The general rose to his feet and came around his desk. Jack knew Washington for a tall man, but having only seen him on horseback, he was surprised to be bested in height by at least two inches. Washington handed one of the heavy pouches to Jack.

"A small emolument in gratitude for your brave and most valuable service." After passing the other pouch to Titus, the Commander in Chief shook them both by the hand, and they were dismissed.

Running harum-scarum down the wide stairway, leaping the steps three at a time, they tore out of City Hall to skitter around the corner of the building, where they stopped to kick off wet shoes and evaluate the content of their reward.

"Silver!" Titus exclaimed upon opening his pouch.

Jack counted quickly. "Fifty Spanish dollars!"

"He gave me forty!" Titus beamed, wide-eyed. "Forty dollars!"

"That's not right." Jack moved five coins from his pouch into Titus's. "Fair is fair." He then added three more. "And there's what I owe from darts." Jack threw an arm around Titus's broad shoulders. "Now let's go celebrate."

"Phew!" Titus shoved Jack away. "You stink worse than the inside of my musty ol' shoe."

"Well, you're no sweet perfume yourself. Tell you what—" Jack said. "Let's go home and wash up. I'll meet you at the Commons in an hour, and then we can treat ourselves to the best supper offered at Montagne's!"

"Fried oysters." Titus grinned. "And a thick, juicy beefsteak . . ."

"Gravy and Irish potatoes . . ."

"Wash it all down with a bottle of the finest Madeira!"

"A bottle for me, and a bottle for you." Jack raised his pouch to his ear with a shake, the silver jingling a happy song. "As you well know—us being colleagues and companions—money is no object."

CHAPTER EIGHT

❦

The blood of the slain, the weeping voice
of nature cries, 'Tis TIME TO PART

THOMAS PAINE, *Common Sense*

Monday, August 19, 1776
Over Liberty Tea at the Cup and Quill

Waking with the same nagging headache she'd gone to bed with, Anne began her Monday morning in the kitchenhouse, gagging down a double dose of willowbark tea. Sally pushed a plate of day-old scones her way.

"Best eat a little somethin', lest ye exchange a headache for a bellyache."

Though dry and hard to swallow, the scone did help to erase the bitterness of the headache remedy. Sally brewed a pot of lemon balm tea, and poured them each a mugful. Anne doctored her tea with a lump of sugar, leaned back against the counter and heaved a sigh.

"I'm feeling out of sorts . . . Good thing the shop is closed today."

Sally offered a sympathetic smile as she stirred two lumps and a good amount of cream into her cup. "On most days I drink my liberty tea without complaint, but I'll confess, on a day like today, I long for a cup of proper tea—strong and sweet. A good black bohea serves t' put a body right in the morn, na?"

Anne squeezed her eyes shut and pinched the bridge of her nose. "A good night's sleep would serve me well. Between worrying when and where the Redcoats will attack, and being left to wonder where David and Jack have gone off to, I tossed and turned and cursed into my pillow all the long night."

"Aye . . ." Sally sat on the hearthstone, sipping her tea. "D'ye suppose maybe General Washington's sent them off on some sort of mission?"

"I was thinking the same. I suppose it's possible, but even so, I think David would have sent us some word." Anne sat beside Sally, her two brows knit into one. They finished their tea in a long silence, contemplating the bottoms of their empty cups.

At last, Sally hopped to her feet, and plucked two straw hats hanging from hooks on the wall. "Gather your things. I'll lock up the sugar."

"No, Sally . . . not today!"

"On yer feet, Annie," Sally scolded. "No use wasting the day worrying and pining—not when every willing hand can be put to good use at hospital."

"Hospital!" Anne made a face like a hen laying razors.

"On wi' yer bonnet!" Putting on her hat, Sally centered the other on her friend's head and secured the ribbons beneath Anne's chin. "We're a miserable pair, sittin' here . . . There's a pleasure comes from doin' good. If the lads come 'round while we're out, they can sit and wonder where it is we went off to!"

Anne capitulated to Sally's good sense, and she went to find her door key and writing box. The bells tolled eight o'clock when the women set out for the hospital at King's College.

The morning sun beat incessant in a cloudless sky on a breezeless day. Gutters overflowing with human and animal waste percolated up through a filter of rotting garbage. The street stench coalesced with the smell of a low tide, forming the thick blanket of malodor smothering the entire city. With lavender-infused handkerchiefs pressed to their noses, Anne and Sally traversed the narrow streets on their trek across town.

Broad Way was congested with several new regiments from Delaware and Connecticut arriving via the Bloomingdale Road. Anne and Sally had to wait for a thinning in the ranks for a chance to cut over to Robinson Street and the college grounds.

The consequences of impending invasion were most noticeable on a hot day as they hurried past tree stump after tree stump. To supply the timber used to build breastworks, barricades and batteries, the city had been shorn of the beautiful water beech, linden and locust trees once lining the thoroughfares and dotting the Commons and college lawn with cool shade.

As they mounted the stair to the main entrance of the hospital, Sally pointed across Chapel Street. "Isn't that Jack and Titus?"

Anne followed her finger, setting her writing kit down on the landing. "It is!"

Much like a pair of moles just emerged from subterranean depths, Jack and Titus stepped off the stoop in front of Mother Babcock's boardinghouse, their eyes slitted to the bright light of day. Sally shouted and waved.

"Hoy! Lads!"

"Shhhh!" Anne grabbed Sally's flailing hand and pulled her down the stairs to take a stand partially hidden by low-growing shrubbery.

After a brief discussion on the brothel stoop, the men headed north. Jack paused after a few steps, and began a frantic search through his pockets. Titus stretched and yawned, all the while shaking his head. Except for Titus claiming Jack would lose his arse if it weren't attached, Anne could not make out much of what the two were saying to one another.

"Oh, *Tiii*-tus!"

The two men looked up to the melodious voice. A plump and pretty half-caste woman wearing a scarlet turban trimmed with a white ostrich plume called from an open second-story window at

Mother Babcock's. Leaning out, she launched a tricorn hat into the air. It twirled down to the ground like a seedpod from a maple tree, and Titus ran back to retrieve it, shouting, "Ruby, you are truly a gem!"

Ruby answered, "Have your friend wait—he's left something behind as well."

"Libertines!" Sally sputtered, taking Anne by the hand. "'T' think you lost sleep over that whore-mongering bastard! C'mon—we've seen enough."

Anne shook Sally off. The front door of Mother Babcock's opened and Patsy Quinn ran out on bare feet, a black tricorn clasped in her hand.

Sally tugged at Anne's skirt. "Away—"

Anne did not budge. She was fettered to the unfolding scene: Jack, so charming and cavalier—Patsy Quinn so self-assured and completely at ease with him. Anne cringed with thinking how she must compare to this lovely, carefree creature.

Patsy's loose black curls were tied up with a yellow ribbon that matched the silk macquerett trimming the wide sleeves and hem of her bright blue robe. Clean of powder and rouge, the girl's skin was as fair and blush as a new peach. It was not hard for Anne to picture Patsy languid in Jack's arms, and the notion gripped her heart in its burning fist.

Patsy smiled as she rose up on tiptoes to fit the hat onto Jack's head. She then pulled a heavy leather pouch from the bell sleeve of her robe and dangled it, swinging, in front of his eyes. Jack snatched the pouch from her hand and danced a little jig. Titus slapped his leg and let out a happy hoot. Before slipping the pouch into his shirt-front, Jack plucked a silver dollar from it. Taking Patsy by the hand, he pressed the coin in to her open palm, pulled her into an embrace, kissed her on the cheek and called Patsy his angel.

Anne could not find her breath. As if choking on a bite of food, she needed a pounding between the shoulder blades. She turned her back to Jack and his whore, and forced herself to draw in some air. *My angel*, he called her.

"To home with us," Sally ordered, slipping an arm about Anne's shoulders.

They crossed the college grounds and headed south on Broad Way. Anne could not afford to speak. She used every ounce of effort to contain her anger and tears and manage a semblance of composure, nodding and umm-humming as Sally rambled on in a virulent anti–Jack Hampton diatribe all the long way home.

"The rake! He was bound to tread upon yer heart, Annie. Better to ken his true nature now, afore he's had a chance to lay his hands upon yer fortune . . ."

Anne was stunned by the ferocious jealousy swirling like a West Indies hurricane in her head. What a fool she was to think herself the one and only woman Jack Hampton wrapped his arms about. The sight of Jack with his beautiful lover caused Anne to envisage further, more intimate scenes so painful to her mind's eye, she ground a knuckle into her temple to eradicate the images. She felt as if she might retch.

". . . I had a knowance he was no' th' man for you. Recall how he did not hesitate to ruin yer books? And th' night when he claimed not to have a pass? A practiced and artful deceiver is he—aye, the devil's get . . ."

They cut across Broad Way, past the Bowling Green, and Anne stared miserably at the iron fence, recalling Jack's handsome smile when he had pressed the little half-crown keepsake into her hand. He shared that exact smile with Patsy Quinn today.

His angel.

". . . he is a pretty man—I will give him that. A charmer. Did ye see the sack of coin the whore give him? Och, yer not the first woman to fall under his spell, Annie, and ye willna be the last; tha's a certainty . . ."

Anne struggled to fit the key in the lock. Once the door was opened, Sally took Anne by the hand. "Come along, my honey. We'll put the kettle on the boil, and have a good cry over a nice cup of tea."

Anne nodded, her voice small. "I could use a cup of tea."

The two of them shuffled about in the kitchen. Sally brought the fire to life, and Anne readied a tray with cups and spoons. Sally poured boiled water over the clump of herbs she added to the china teapot. "Linden flower," she said. "Good for the melancholy. 'Twill lift our spirits."

Just as Anne and Sally settled to have their tea at the table under the peach tree, a black tricorn hat came flying into the garden. A moment later, Jack pulled himself up to perch atop the wall.

"Morning, ladies!"

"Blackguard!" Sally ran over, grabbed the hat and flung it back over the wall.

Jack looked back to where his hat landed in the alley. "Now why did you go and do that?"

"Off with ye, spawn!" Sally threatened with clenched fist. "Back to hell from whence ye came!"

"Though I always look forward to your welcome, Sal"—Jack jumped down, brushing the dirt from his breeches—"it's your mistress I've come to see."

"She wants nothing to do with you." Sally grabbed Jack by the arm and proceeded to propel him toward the front door.

Jack dug his heels in and shook Sally off, dark brows hooding his eyes. "I have no quarrel with you, Sally, but sometimes you annoy me . . ."

"Off wi' ye, hear?" Sally gave Jack a shove.

"Sally!" Anne stood up, smoothing her skirt. "Why don't you go on upstairs and bring in the laundry?"

Sally took a step back. "Are ye certain?"

"I am."

"Awright . . . but be wary, Annie—he is a canny devil. Dinna succumb to any o' his nicknackery." Sally gave Jack a gimlet-eyed glare as she backed away and left the pair alone in the garden.

"There is a mad bee in her Scots bonnet today." Jack put on a big smile and took a few steps Anne's way, pulling the same leather pouch Patsy had given him from his weskit pocket. "Look—an 'emolument'— and I want you to share in my good fortune. Come out walking with me. Let's buy a basket supper at Fraunces's and have ourselves a picnic . . ."

"Please, don't come any closer." Anne held up both hands as if to ward off an attack, stopping Jack in his tracks. Taking a breath, she lowered her hands and knotted them into a clench at her waistline. "I will not walk with you today—nor any day—not after seeing you this morning . . ."

"This morning? Where?"

"I was at hospital." She gave her head a little shake to dispel the awful image that rushed to her brain. "Sally and I saw you and Titus leaving Mother Babcock's."

"Ohhh . . . well . . . I can explain that . . ." Jack reclaimed his charming smile, and jingled the pouch in his hand. "Washington dropped a sack of silver on me and Titus—a reward for the fireboating—so of course, we celebrated . . ."

"At a brothel?"

"We started with dinner at Montagne's." He shrugged. "Mother Babcock's, well, that's the result of high spirits and a bit too much to drink."

But for the pink patches that sprung to her cheeks, Anne's face was as pale as porcelain paste. "There is nothing I regret more than trusting you as a friend."

"Now, Annie, what happened last night doesn't have anything to do with you . . ."

"Do you even hear yourself?" Anne laughed, incredulous. "Imagine you chance to see me happy in the embrace of another man. How would that make you feel? Would my actions have nothing to do with you?"

"Well . . ." Jack nodded, moving closer. "When you put it like that, I can allow how you might be angry, and I am truly sorry for making you so." He took her by the hand. "I care for you, Anne—you know I have a great affection for you. I see now that I made a foolish mistake, and caused you some pain. I promise I'll not repeat it. I ask you to forgive and forget this last, thoughtless transgression."

"Forgive and forget?!" Anne jerked her hand away. She could feel her voice going shrill, but she could not stop herself. "You are possessed of an unconstant character, Jack Hampton, and I will not keep company with a man of such low moral standards—a man with such a lewd and licentious nature. I ask that you leave here and not return."

"Quite a high-handed dismissal from a widow who was more than warm to my lewd and licentious nature on several occasions." Jack smiled. He slipped one hand to the small of Anne's back, and pulled her close. "C'mon, Annie, to be human is to make mistakes—and it is human kindness to forgive." He leaned in and whispered, "Be kind to me, Annie . . ."

His plea delivered soft and tender to her ear hammered a deep dent in her resolve. Reaching up, she trailed fingers along his dark, stubbly jaw.

He hasn't shaved . . . having spent the night in a brothel . . . with a prostitute . . .

The image of Jack and Patsy entangled in each other's arms slammed to the forefront of Anne's mind. She twirled from his grasp and skittered away, her back pressed up against the garden wall.

"No! I don't believe you can regulate your libertine inclinations—and I will not be made a constant fool. I *saw* you with that woman."

Jack towered over her, his dark eyes a sudden fury. "If there is no forgiveness to be found in that cold, hard heart of yours, then perhaps I was no fool to find comfort with a sporting wench. I have offered a sincere apology for the error in my behavior, but you are mistaken if you seek to have me grovel at your feet."

"Please leave, Jack."

"With pleasure, madam." Jack bent in a florid bow. "Good day to you, Widow Merrick." Steps pounding on the floorboards, he stormed through the shop, the resound of the door slam accompanied by the raucous peal of the doorbell.

Anne leaned back against the garden wall, the plain gray poplin of her skirt clutched in each white-knuckled fist. Blinking her tears back, she heaved a ragged sigh.

"He is mistaken, if he thinks that I will cry."

ඉ ඉ ඉ

JACK marched straight to Fraunces's Tavern. He waved at Titus behind the bar and plopped down at an empty table. Titus pulled two pints of stout and came around to sit with Jack.

"No picnic today?"

"Not today . . . not any day! The widow has bid me to never darken her door again." Jack took a deep slug from his beer. "Unknown to you and me, it seems she happened upon the scene at Mother Babcock's this morning. The sight of me with Patsy inflicted a deep wound on what I have learned is a very jealous heart."

"She's a wise woman, and deserves better than you anyway."

"Thank you, Titus. You're a fine friend."

"Mrs. Anne's been my friend longer than you." Titus savored his brew. "I'll never forget the day mean old Merrick passed on—all of us feigning sorrow, but every once in a while she and I'd exchange a quick smile, for by his dying, we were both of us set free."

Jack shifted in his seat, a sharp something jabbing his upper leg. He dug into his breeches pocket and came up with the broken bit from the Bowling Green fencepost. He set the piece on the table, and studied it for a long moment. Tracing a finger around the half-crown he said, "Believe it or not, Titus, I really do care for the widow."

"Says you after a night of drinking and whoring."

"I *do* care for her." Jack looked up. "But I'll not beg—that I will not."

"You surely have no ken of womankind. She doesn't need or want you to beg." Titus rose to his feet and finished the rest of his cup in one long pull. "What she needs is for you to be true."

Titus left to serve a group of Continental officers who'd wandered in for a drink at the bar. After collecting the coin for the round, he came back to sit with Jack.

"Those fellows"—he said with a jerk of his head—"they tell me the

Redcoats are on the move. Washington's spies on Staten Island have reported Howe has given orders for all regiments to prepare three days' worth of provisions. Transport ships crowded with troops have begun to embark."

Jack sat up. "Where to?"

Titus shrugged. "Looks like Long Island. No one knows for certain."

"Can you find someone to take over for you here?"

Titus nodded.

Jack downed the remains of his pint. Leaning back in his chair, he shoved the cast-iron piece back into his pocket and buttoned the flap. "Let's gather our gear and get to Long Island."

cb cb cb

ANNE sat in the garden, her ledgers spread out on the tabletop. As a ruse to avoid Sally's never-ending derision of Jack Hampton, she pretended to work on the accounts. When Sally answered a knock at the door to find David had come to pay a visit, Anne was happy for the diversion. Sally must have said something to David, for they shared a pleasant supper under the peach tree without a single mention of Jack Hampton.

"I'm going back to my regiment in the morning," David announced as he poured himself a glass of cider. "We have word that British ships are heading toward Long Island."

"They're invading Long Island?" Anne asked.

"All we know is the British are provisioned and on the move. The general suspects it might be a feint to draw attention away from the true invasion," David said. "As yet, we just don't have enough information."

Sally's woeful expression compelled Anne to leave the couple their last few hours together in private. Though early in the evening and still light out, Anne pled exhaustion. Taking a candle and a copy of *Gulliver's Travels* along, she dragged her sad, tired bones up the stairs. She squeezed the candledish and her reading material onto the cluttered night table beside her four-posted bed.

Much like a knight shedding heavy armor after an arduous battle, Anne peeled off her clothes and stiff stays, and stripped down to the light freedom of her shift. She opened the shutters on her window facing the river to allow the fresh eastling wind to wash through her bedchamber.

A dark and heavy cloud moving in with the wind began to cast a pall over a fair evening. Anne protected the flickering candle flame with a chimney glass, and climbed up to sit tailor-style on her bed. She removed pins and ribbons, and ran her fingers to loosen the tight braids wound around her head all day. Anne raked a brush through her sweat-damp hair, the boar bristles digging in to scourge her scalp. She found this nightly ritual calming, as if she were brushing her cares away—scattering them into tiny particles to be borne away on the breeze.

Anne scooted forward to sit on the edge of the bed, legs dangling, her toes brushing floorboards. She squeezed the hairbrush onto her night table—between *Gulliver's* and the candle—tipping over a half-full bottle of lavender water and knocking the keepsake Jack had given her to the floor. The little broken crown bounced and skittered about, finally settling like a ragged black wound on the timeworn oak right beneath her feet. Anne stared at the cast-iron piece for a moment, then with a swipe of her bare foot, she sent it hurtling to bang into the far corner.

I'm better off alone.

Lightning flashed, and rain began to tick on the clay roof tiles. A gust of wind—strong enough to pound the shutters closed and open again—whipped around the room. Anne ran to the window, and leaned over the sill, turning her face up to fat drops of warm rain.

The sky became an inky, swirling cauldron, stirred by an invisible spoon. The air was soon charged with the smell of sulfur, and with flashes of lightning so numerous and incessant, the corresponding thunderclaps became a rolling, constant din, like that of a hundred drummers beating wild on a hundred bass drums. She held tight to the wooden sill through it all, cleansed by the cathartic wind and rain.

The view from her storm-darkened bedchamber presented an uncommon picture. Across the dusky East River churning with whitecaps, the hills of Brooklyn Heights were bathed in golden twilight. Anne ran to retrieve her spyglass from the night table. She extended the glass and scanned the horizon. In the flashing yellow cast by lightning bolts, Anne noted two men pulling oars on a skiff caught out in midriver.

"Lord in heaven!"

Anne fixed her scope to the scene. She could not believe her eyes. Jack and Titus manned the oars of the little boat struggling against the wind and rain.

"Reckless fools!"

Anne kept a long and fearful vigil at her window as the violent storm over Manhattan progressed without let up, and she tracked the boat's progress until at last it disappeared into the smudge along the opposite shore, just beneath the Brooklyn Heights.

With relief, she collapsed her spyglass in three snaps and moved out of the puddle collected beneath the window. Slipping weary arms through sleeve holes, she stepped out of her rain-drenched shift and kicked it to the side. She dried her skin and scrubbed her wet hair with a towel from her linen chest, and pulled on a dry chemise.

I think he's safe.

The hope came unbidden to her brain, along with a stinging onslaught of tears. Anne curled onto her bed. Shoulders shaking, bedcords quaking, she cried for Jack—mourned his kisses—and grieved, once again, for the happy life she imagined just beyond her grasp. At last heaving a great sigh, she flopped onto her back, threw her arms up over her head and stared at the flickering shadows dancing along the ceiling rafters.

"What kind of an idiot am I, to think I wouldn't cry?"

CHAPTER NINE

Cannon are the barristers of Crowns;
and the sword, not of justice,
but of war, decides the suit.

THOMAS PAINE, *Common Sense*

Thursday, August 22, 1776
A Hilltop on Long Island

JACK and Titus stood at the crest of a wooded hill on a bright, blue-sky morning after another stormy night. With southward-aimed spyglasses trained on Gravesend Bay and the British landing operation on the beach, they did not stray from the cover provided by the shade of the treeline.

"By God, what order!" Jack admitted with grudging admiration.

"Now that is discipline." Titus whistled low. "Reminds me of working a well-tuned press with an able crew—people, parts and pieces all moving in accord . . ."

Sails unfurled, flags and ensigns floating on a soft breeze, the transport ships sat at anchor just beyond the shoals with broadsides parallel to the shoreline, their massive firepower serving to discourage any opposing force. Besides the scattering of rifle fire that drew

Jack and Titus from the road to the hilltop, there was not a Continental in sight.

"Their flatboats are very clever," Jack said. "That's what they've been up to all this time—building those boats."

The wide landing craft were built with flat bows designed to hinge open and serve as ramps upon beaching, efficiently discharging cargo after cargo of soldiers, horses, ordnance, munitions and supplies. The oared flatboats ferried to and fro between the troop transports and the beach, oars dipping into the sparkling water with frightening unison.

"One moves away, and the next moves in . . ." Titus noted. "They've at least a hundred of those flatboats, and nary a tussle."

"Their spies serve them well. This bay and beach could not be better suited to their purpose—and with good access to the roads." Jack took a few steps back and sank down to sit on the trunk of a sweet gum tree uprooted by the recent storms. "Between flatboats and transports, I tally close to four hundred vessels swimming around out there."

Titus tucked his spyglass under his arm. From his pocket he produced a folded square of paper and a stubby graphite stick wrapped in jute string. After scribbling "400 vessels," he took a seat next to Jack. Titus divided the blank side of his sheet with three vertical lines and four headings titled "red," "black," "green" and "blue." He alternated between peering through the spyglass and scratching numbers for every formed regiment, categorizing his count by uniform color.

"Break off a piece of your writing stick, and give me a scrap of that paper," Jack said. "You count the foot soldiers, I'll count cannon and cavalry."

Emptied transports moved away and were replaced by a new line of transport ships, their decks crowded with red coats. Hours passed and wave upon wave of flatboats moved between the shoals and the shore, unchallenged. When the flatboats were beached and the last man waded to shore, formed battalions with artillery in tow began marching from the plain toward the road. Jack tracked along, peering through his glass. "They're heading to Flatbush." He snapped his glass into its most compact form. "Let's go."

Titus rolled the scraps of paper into a tight tube, slipping it and his pencil through a tear in the lining of his waistcoat. Shouldering muskets and gathering bedrolls and knapsacks, they turned back into the woods.

db db db

To impede forage opportunities for the British Army, Captain David Peabody spent a long day in the saddle, gathering cattle, horses and sheep from the nearby countryside to be driven to pasture under armed guard.

David dismounted and tethered his mount to the paddock post. By his own estimation, Black Bill was one of the finest horses in the Continental Army, and no matter how saddle sore he was, David always saw to his stallion's comfort before his own. After Bill was curried, fed and watered, David hoisted saddle to shoulder and slogged back to his tent pitched among the many on the outskirts of the village of Brooklyn.

It was past the dinner hour, and with stomach rumbling, David hoped his messmates thought to save him a portion. On the whole, provisions available on Long Island proved fresh and varied, but these past two days—since Howe had landed his army—meals in camp had become a very haphazard affair. His heart sank a bit, spotting the pot simmering over the fire in front of his tent.

Standard soldier's fare tonight—boiled salt meat no doubt accompanied by wheat cakes burned on a hot iron.

"Peabody!"

David turned to his name, and to his surprise, he saw Jack Hampton and Titus Gilmore headed his way, waving and smiling. Taller than most men, the odd pairing was made even more incongruous by the musket on Titus's shoulder, and the full-on beard Jack sported. David was surprised at how pleased he was to see them.

But for his being in company with Titus Gilmore, David would not have recognized bearded Jack Hampton. The city dweller looked every bit the country yeoman dressed in a green hunting shirt and soft cowhide boots. Both Jack and Titus were fully accoutered with painted canvas packs and rolled blankets. In accordance with the general's latest order that all soldiers without uniform distinguish themselves with a bough of greenery on their hats, these two wore holly leaf sprigs tucked into the cockades on their tricorns. Coming to a stand before him, they saluted properly, bringing their muskets to shoulder firelock position.

David dropped his saddle and returned the salute with a sweep of his hat. "Don't tell me you two have joined the militia!"

Titus laughed and Jack said, "Nah! The greens and salutes just make it easier to get around on this side of the heights."

"*This* side of the heights—" David noted the distinction as he hoisted his saddle back to his shoulder. "It sounds like your army of two might be causing the British some mischief."

"Might be." Titus grinned.

"Come along with us to the Ferry House Inn for dinner," Jack said, "and we'll tell you all about it."

"The Ferry House!" David snorted. "I'm afraid my meager pay will not support a meal there."

"Did you forget the emolument?" Jack reached inside his shirt and pulled forth a plump purse. "C'mon, lobster dinner all around."

David looked over to his tent as one of his messmates pulled a steaming gray lump from the simmering pot. "Let me stow my saddle and shed my spurs."

The three men marched down to the gable-roofed inn flanking the ferry landing, and they were seated around a comfortable table with a fine view of the East River. Once a round of pints was pulled and dinner ordered, David asked, "So how long have you two miscreants been on the island?"

"Six days now," Titus answered.

Jack added, "We came over on Monday night."

David unbuttoned his jacket. "Monday night? After the storm?"

"During the storm." Jack smiled.

"We were halfway across the river when the storm blew in." Titus scowled. "Took us some doing—getting across—soaked to the bone we were."

"That was the worse storm I've ever seen," David said. "The next day we found three officers lightning-struck on Cortlandt Street. Roasted to a black crisp they were—the tips of their swords and the coin in their pockets melted."

"Bad omen, that," Titus said.

"Pish," Jack scoffed. "Just a bad storm is all."

A pair of tavern maids brought over a platter piled high with steamed lobster and clams, a bowl of buttered and parsleyed potatoes in their jackets, and a fresh green salad of spinach and cress dressed with oil and vinegar. The hungry trio fell into silence, concentrated on wresting every bit of sweet meat from the shells, calling for seconds on the potatoes and salad. Sated, they finished the meal off with glasses of rye whiskey and stubby cigars.

David blew a cloud of smoke up to mingle with the ceiling rafters. "A grand meal. Thank you, Jack—Titus." He savored a sip of his whiskey. "You two really ought consider joining up for the fight. We are about to give the lobsterbacks a sound drubbing—just like we did at Breed's Hill."

"We lost at Breed's Hill," Jack reminded.

David ignored him. "Our lines are solid and well situated—naturally fortified by the heights—and the passes through the high ground are guarded by our best troops."

"The King's army has might." Titus puffed on his cigar. "They can barrel right through one of those passes—crash through and lay siege to your works from landside *and* from warships on the riverside."

"They can try and get through." David nodded. "And be severely bloodied in the process."

Jack reached into his shirtfront and handed David a folded sheet of paper. "Have you seen one of these?"

David unfolded the page, smoothing it on the tabletop. He moved the oil lamp centered on their table a little closer, and read:

A PROCLAMATION

Notice is hereby given to all Persons forced into Rebellion, that on
delivering themselves up at the HEAD QUARTERS of the Army, they
will be received as faithful Subjects; have Permits to return peaceably
to their respective Dwellings, and meet with full
Protection for their Persons and Property.
All those who choose to take up arms for the Restoration of Order
and good Government within this Island, shall be disposed of in the
Best Manner, and have every
Encouragement that can be expected.
GIVEN under my HAND, at Head Quarters on Long Island,
this 23rd Day of August, 1776.   WILLIAM HOWE
By His Excellency's Command.

"Are many answering this call?" David asked.

"We'll find out. Titus and I intend to join up."

"Join the Redcoats? You're mad!" David pushed back from the table. "Both of you!"

Jack stroked his beard. "There's no madness in a Loyal citizen and his slave volunteering to help restore order."

"It is madness when the Loyal citizen is truly a most ardent rebel, and his slave is in truth a free man."

Jack and Titus sat puffing their cigars, grinning like boys on school holiday.

David shook his head. "You're bound to be caught and strung up as spies."

"We've already been to Flatbush—fifteen thousand soldiers camped there, and not one gave us any trouble but to hand us that broadside . . ." Titus said, pointing to the page.

"Fifteen thousand?" Beetle-browed, David stubbed his cigar out on the table. "What do you mean fifteen thousand? Our scouts reported eight thousand landed."

"Your scouts are dead wrong." Jack threw back the last of his rye, and signaled the barman for another. "We were there at the landing, watching and counting to the very last man. They've fifteen thousand camped at Flatbush. Maybe more now with this proclamation. We have our tally from two days ago. Show him, Titus."

After a few moments, Titus worked the tiny paper scrolls back out through the hole in the lining of his waistcoat. He pushed the notes across the table.

David studied the writing. "What does this mean—red, black, green, blue?"

"Redcoats," Titus said, pointing to the first column. "Foot, grenadiers and dragoons."

"And the black are Highlanders—" Jack added. "Dark caps and plaids."

"Green jackets are those Jäger riflemen," Titus said. "And blue is for the other German mercenaries—Hessians, Waldeckers and the like."

"I need to get this information to General Putnam." David stuffed the papers into his pocket. "With the report of eight thousand landed, General Washington is of a mind that the army here on Long Island is a feint to distract our attention from a true invasion force at King's Bridge. He's been holding back troops . . ." David misbuttoned his gray jacket and seated his hat crooked on his head. "Fifteen thousand! With so many of our lads fever-stricken—we're lucky if we have six thousand fit for duty." With that David stomped off. Halfway to the door, he halted, turned and called, "When are you leaving for Flatbush?"

"Now." Jack tossed the butt of his cigar to the floor and crushed it underfoot. "We aim to be back by Monday—Tuesday at the latest. We'll find you."

With a nod and a wave, David all but ran out the tavern door.

ↂ ↂ ↂ

NEAR the town hall serving as General Howe's headquarters in the tiny village of Flatbush, Titus and Jack hooked onto the tail end of a long, slow queue of men and boys formed in front of a trestle table set up near the shade of a white oak tree. A few of these locals were interested in joining the British Army as colonial irregulars. Most waited in the hot sun to register as Loyalists, and obtain the requisite permits as per Howe's proclamation.

When Jack and Titus were yet two dozen places away from a turn with the sergeant, a pair of farmers—father and son by the look of them—walked opposite, newly issued permits in hand, all the while staring boldly at Jack.

Titus was becoming accustomed to the stares Jack engendered by wearing a full beard, and he took to claiming that Jack might ride through the heart of New York City on the back of an African elephant, and draw less attention. Jack still insisted on the need to alter his appearance. Titus was only glad that he was able to talk him into removing the earring.

When the farmers drew parallel to Jack, the elder gawker stopped in his tracks, cocked his head to the side and asked, "Jackie, is that you?"

"Charlie!" All smiles, Jack stepped forward and embraced the man. Looking over to the younger man, Jack exclaimed, "This can't be Billy!"

"It is." Charles pulled his son forward. "Give your uncle Jack a kiss."

"When last I saw you, lad, you were wearing leading strings and bouncing on my knee." Jack wrapped his nephew in a bear hug. "Titus! Meet my brother Charles, and my nephew William."

The family resemblance was suddenly plain to Titus. Charles Hampton was a stockier, graying version of Jack. Not more than fifteen years, and not yet reached his full height, young Billy was blessed with his forbear's dark, good looks.

It was also plain Charles Hampton did not know what to make of his younger brother or his negro companion. Glancing from Titus, then back to the group of red-coated officers hovering behind the table in the shade of the big oak tree, he muttered, "What kind of mischief are you up to now, Jack?"

Jack took his brother by the arm. "Let's walk a bit."

The four of them strolled down the street, away from Loyalist ears. After a brief exchange of family news, Jack told Charles of his intent to join the British Army and scout out information for Washington's Continentals.

"You are a brave heart for the cause and I'm very proud of you, Jackie," Charles said. "I only wish I could do something to help, but with eight mouths to feed, I have to be very careful to husband my resources. Very careful indeed."

"Eight mouths!" Jack slapped his brother on the back.

"Aye, Bess is newly delivered—a girl, at last—so you see how I just can't afford to mix in this mess," Charles said, with an apologetic wave of the permit in his hand. "Between the Continentals confiscating our provender and cattle, and British foraging, there's little left to us. I expect it will be a lean, hard winter."

Jack dug inside his shirtfront, and handed his brother the leather sack given to him by Washington. "Here—there's at least twenty Spanish dollars there—to help get our family through the winter."

"No, Jack . . . you have done more than your share for the family." Charles pushed the purse back into his brother's hand.

"Don't be an idiot. Take the money and my love to Bess and the new baby," Jack insisted, slipping the pouch into his brother's coat pocket.

Charles clasped Jack's hand in his two. "Just promise me you'll be very careful, Jackie."

Jack nodded. "Go on home now, before young Bill here catches the recruiting sergeant's eye."

As they watched Charles and his son disappear down the road, Jack rubbed the beard on his jaw. "Try as I might, I never could fool Charles."

"A family man, your brother," Titus said. "The eldest?"

"Of six boys—no more than eighteen years Charlie was, when our folks died of the bloody pox. He took care of us, and our farm— more father than brother to me, what with me being the youngest. He suffered so when I left to be bound out to Parker . . . always wanting to keep us brothers together . . ." Jack swiped at the corner of his eye. "It was good to see him."

They rejoined the queue, which began to move along at a brisker pace, and soon they found themselves at the head of the line. The beleaguered sergeant in charge of dispensing permits sat back in his chair dabbing face and neck with a kerchief, mopping rivulets of white powder-tinged sweat. "Foh! What have we here?"

Jack paid no mind to the disdainful tone and glare. Throwing back his shoulders, he announced in a strong, clear voice, "I've come to volunteer my services, along with those of my slave, to help restore the Proper Order."

Years of service in the British Army had not quite obliterated the Irish brogue from the sergeant's speech. "Are ye some sort of foreigner?"

Titus was sure the irony of this question coming from a man who'd recently traveled three thousand miles to get to the American shore tickled Jack's rebel heart as much as it did his own, but they both managed to maintain a stern countenance.

"Just like yourself, I'm a good Englishman, sir," Jack replied. "Come to do my duty for King and country."

"Away with the likes of you. A good Englishman kens the worth of strop and razor," the sergeant growled. "British soldiers are clean-shaven."

"I am aware, sir." Jack did not budge. Squaring his shoulders he loudly proclaimed, "Though I may not be fit for the serious business of soldiering, surely I can be put to some use. If not me, then perhaps my slave . . ."

One of the officers wandered from the shade to stand just beyond the sergeant's shoulder. Titus was developing an appreciation for uniforms, and the one worn by this captain was by far the most splendid he'd ever laid eyes on.

Titus figured the captain for a cavalryman by the buckskin breeches he wore tucked into gleaming black topboots. His red coat was faced in dazzling white and fastened with silver buttons—real silver, not pewter—each embossed with the number *17*, twinkling in the sunlight. Most impressive was the helmet. Fashioned of jacked leather and golden brass, it was crested with a flowing plume of madder-dyed horsehair to match his red coat. A black-lacquered plate rising up from the brow of the helmet was decorated with a white skull and crossed bones painted above the words "OR GLORY."

Death or glory—Titus imagined that mounted, these dragoons at a full gallop must present an awesome sight.

"Shove off, ye hairy bastard!" The sergeant waved Jack away. "Come back after you've scraped them whiskers."

Ignoring the sergeant, the splendid officer spoke directly to Jack. "Your name?"

"Jack Stapleton, sir."

"You are a local man?"

Jack said, "Born and bred to this island, before being sent to the city as apprentice . . . I know my way around."

Good boy, Titus thought. Stick to the truth as much as possible— the course they'd both agreed upon to avoid blunders and detection by suspicious minds.

The officer rattled off another question. "Apprenticed? At what trade?"

"Printer, sir. A thriving business, at least up until my press was put to ruin by them bastard Liberty Boys."

The mention of the Sons of Liberty struck a chord, and both captain and sergeant instantly shifted into more amenable attitudes.

"Captain Blankenship, your farrier has been complaining of being shorthanded, sir . . ." the sergeant suggested. "This slave looks to be a fit fellow. He'd do as an ostler, at least."

"Yes, send the negro to work with the horses," Blankenship agreed. "I will escort our bearded friend to headquarters. He might serve as a guide."

Jack shouldered his musket, and left with the captain.

"Give this to the farrier-major—" The sergeant scribbled off a note and directed Titus to the horse paddock. "An easy one to find— dressed all in black, he is, with a horseshoe insignia on his sleeve."

ርቴ ርቴ ርቴ

Titus looked up from the tin plate balanced on his lap. "There's my master, sir," he explained, pointing to Jack crossing the pasture. "He serves as a guide with the Seventeenth. Might I have permission to go to speak with him?"

"Yer master?" The farrier looked up, squinting, to where Titus pointed. "Aye—g'won, ye poor bugger."

Titus ran out to meet Jack, and they sat together under a big tulip tree. "I hope you brought something to eat. The horses are fed better rations than what we were just given for our supper—a hunk of pickled beef so rusty with rot I wouldn't feed it to a dying dog. And the biscuits—squirming with weevils . . ."

"From what I can tell, the regulars don't fare any better, which is why I went foraging." Jack unloaded his sack, laying out an oblong loaf of dark bread, four wizened sausages, a waxed cheese and half a dozen apples. "Plain fare—but fresh," he said, handing over a sausage.

Titus broke the sausage in two. After a quick visual inspection and a good sniff, he took a bite. "Where'd you sleep last night?"

"I made a bed in a tent with three other guides—Tory farmers from hereabouts." Jack pulled out a folding knife and sliced a chunk from the cheese. "Spent the whole evening listening to their Loyalist mouthings, and thereby, I learned less than nothing. How about you?"

"Dragoons have been coming all morning, checking their horses and gear, and the smiths have been running from horse to horse repairing shoes and tack. The farrier-major gave me orders to fill fifty feed sacks. He says the Seventeenth is moving camp to a village called Flatlands." Titus tore off a fist-sized hunk from the loaf.

Jack leaned back against the tree trunk. "That's odd—moving south to Flatlands, when the Continental lines are to the north . . ."

"I thought it odd as well. Do you remember Blankenship? The officer from yesterday? He was among a bunch seeing to their mounts, and I heard him tell another that 'Clinton would turn their flank.'" Titus reached for another sausage. "At first I figured he was yammering horse-talk, as they are all wont to do . . . but later on, when a little fellow came around wanting *General* Clinton's mount saddled, I got to thinking there might be something more to what Blankenship said."

A sudden drum call resounded from the main encampment—three long rolls punctuated with two hard beats. With a groan, the farriers and ostlers shoveled down the last of their suppers as the rhythmic drum sequence was repeated over and over.

One of Titus's fellow ostlers waved him in. "C'mon, Titus! They're beating Assembly!"

Jack and Titus rose to their feet, sausages in hand.

"Repair to your colors!" the farrier-major shouted at Jack.

Titus shoved the sausage, the rest of the cheese and a few apples into his shirtfront. "Looks like we're on the march. You better go and join your company. I'll find you in Flatlands!"

Chapter Ten

❧❧❧

Of more worth is one honest man to society and in the sight of God,
than all the crowned ruffians that ever lived.

THOMAS PAINE, *Common Sense*

Monday, August 26, 1776
On the Way to Fetch Water for the Cup and Quill

ANNE clattered from the kitchenhouse, carrying four empty
wooden buckets by the handles—two in each fist, fitting the
buckets onto the pushcart parked near the back door of the shop.
Originally designed for delivering printed materials and paper supplies, the square barrow with its two wide wheels and high wooden
sides was the perfect cart for conveying water from the pump in
Chatham Square.

Anne pulled down the skirt hems tucked into her apron strings
and secured her mobcap with a T-shaped silver pin. "I'm off!"

Sally popped out the kitchenhouse door, her head turbaned in a
linen towel, a smudge of flour dimming the freckles on her cheek.
With a wave she said, "Hurry back!"

Anne steered the barrow through the shop, down Dock Street
and onto the bumpetty cobbles of Queen Street. The city was bus-
ier than usual for a Sunday afternoon, and the unexpected traffic

hampered her plan for a quick forth-and-back to the pump. Anne gauged the time of day by the length of the shadows her cart rolled over as she headed uptown to the tea-water pump, sorely missing the hourly music of the city bells. General Washington had ordered all of the bells stripped from the church towers, and the plundered metal was recast into artillery.

Still a few hours till nightfall . . . Anne sighed, and slowed her pace, calming her inclination to crash along at full speed with long strides.

After spending her day roiling over Cup and Quill concerns, wondering for the well-being of her brother, and anxious over how and where the British might strike an invasion, Anne found she craved the solace of her pillow more than ever. But try as she might to encourage a good night's rest by working hard, drinking cups of chamomile tea and stuffing sprigs of lavender into her pillowslip, deep sleep proved elusive. Most of her bedtime hours were wasted in rigorous tossing and turning, accompanied by vigorous pillow thumping.

Though she pointed to hot weather and worries as reasons for her restlessness, she knew the true cause. Anne was bedeviled by shameful, uncontrollable yearnings and fevered imaginings. Night after night, she lay in the tangle of her bed linen, reliving over and over the few moments spent enveloped in Jack Hampton's embrace . . . *against the wall, lips crushed to his . . . one of his work-rough hands on her breast, the other reaching up under skirts . . .*

The sudden trill of fife and the rattle of drum disturbed her reverie. Anne tightened her grip on the crossbar handle and leaned in to push the cart across a rough patch in the cobbles. Up ahead she could see the source of the military music—the intersection at Maiden Lane was blocked by a soldier's parade. She pushed her cart to the side and continued unencumbered to watch the regiment march by.

Delaware Blues . . .

These soldiers in their short blue jackets and neat leather hats had been crowding into the Cup and Quill of late. Hailing from one of the smallest colonies, they were the largest and—by most estimation—

the best equipped of all the Continental regiments. Carrying full packs and shouldering new, polished muskets, the Delaware Blues presented a fine military display, marching three abreast.

She tapped an elderly pipe smoker observing the parade. "What's going on?"

"Reinforcements shipping out," he said. "Howe's landed his entire force on Long Island—twenty thousand Redcoats! There will be a mighty push on Brooklyn for certain."

"Brooklyn! Not the city?"

"Never you fear, miss, our shores are safe." A thin man in rolled sleeves and leather apron joined the conversation. "Our lads will push those Redcoats off of Long Island and into the ocean. Right makes might."

Twenty thousand . . . The news fanned her constant glowing ember of worry and it burst into flames. Anne rose up on tiptoes, scanning the even files stretching down and forming ranks two blocks away at the Fly Market Square, and she caught a glimpse of a familiar green weskit moving through the gathering crowd of observers.

"Jack!"

He did not hear her call over the hubbub and marching music. Weaving a course along the fringes, he headed toward the square.

"Jack!" Keeping her eye on the flash of emerald green bobbing in and out of her view, Anne sailed after him. Whipping through and around the onlookers at full speed, she managed to catch up when he came to a standstill near the stairs leading down to the ferry landing on Water Street.

"Jack!" At once breathless, elated and relieved, she reached out and took hold of his shoulder.

All the wind was sucked from her canvas the moment she touched the man, suddenly aware this man was not tall enough—this man was too broad in girth and had gray streaks mixed with the dark hair drawn into the bedraggled ribbon at his neck.

"Madam?" he quizzed her through a pair of spectacles perched at the end of his nose. Anne snatched her hand back, her mumblings tangled on the square knot lodged in her throat. Blinking back tears she stammered, "B-beg pardon, sir . . . I-I've mistook you for someone else." With a nod, the man turned his attention back to the parade, and Anne shuffled back to brace her hand against the railing.

How could I have taken that man for Jack?

Her true colors were just revealed. The mere glimpse of a certain shade of green sent her flying into a heart-thumping tizzy—and the mistaken identity just as quickly consigned her with a thud to the depths of disappointment.

Made a fool by a green weskit . . .

"Widow Merrick? Are you ill?"

Anne startled. She looked up to see a familiar young officer dressed in the same gray and green regimental coat David wore. She shook her head, and forced a smile. "The heat . . . I just needed to take some air away from the crowd. But thank you for your concern, Lieutenant . . . ?"

"Collins . . . John Collins." The young lieutenant shook her proffered hand. "I've frequented the Cup and Quill. Your brother is a friend of mine."

"Of course! Have you any news to share, Lieutenant? Does David fare well?"

"He's anxious, as we all are, what with the bloodybacks on our doorstep." Collins shrugged. "But since David is such a cheerful fellow, I'd say he fares better than most. Why, I last saw him Friday night when I shipped over—at the Ferry House he was—smoking cigars and drinking whiskey with a Spaniard and a negro man."

"A Spaniard?" Anne squinted.

"A foreign-looking fellow—tall—with a heavy dark beard."

"No!" Anne laughed. "Don't tell me he's grown a beard!"

"You know the man?"

"I know both the Spaniard and the negro man—friends of our family."

"*Collins!*" an officer shouted up from the landing.

"I have to go." The lieutenant flipped a haversack over one shoulder.

"Good luck to you, Lieutenant."

"I'll tell your brother of our meeting."

"Tell David he is a constant in our thoughts and prayers."

John Collins skittered down the stairs, taking a seat and an oar in a flat-bottom scow.

Anne leaned over the railing. "Mr. Collins! If you should happen to see the other two—the Spaniard and the negro man—tell them Anne Merrick bids them both to take care!"

ᴔ ᴔ ᴔ

As the sun drew close to the horizon, an unseasonable chill crept in from the east to settle over the British encampment at Flatlands. The cool temperature combined with wood smoke from the many campfires to end the summer day with an aspect more akin to October than to August.

With a gunnysack full of foraged foods thrown over his shoulder, Jack meandered past row after row—hundreds of wedge tents—in search of the one he shared with his fellow guides and three British regulars.

After his midday meal with Titus was interrupted by the call to assemble, the 17th and all of General Cornwallis's units struck camp at Flatbush and marched two miles south to encamp with General Clinton's forces at the old Dutch village called Flatlands.

Jack puzzled over it, but he could make no sense of this move away from the rebel lines. And though no one seemed to understand the why or wherefore of the orders, it was plain these seasoned soldiers recognized the movement as a meaningful portent, and the camp buzzed with industry in preparation for the inevitable.

Jack strolled past men with wood-framed mirrors propped, wielding lather and razor, shaving while there was still good light to see by. Others were busy seeing to their uniforms, mending tears, and applying fresh coats of pipe clay to mask the grime and stains on white crossbelts, breeches and waistcoats. Boots, shoes, cartridge boxes and canvas gaiters were also being attended to, receiving a good rub with brush and blackball.

The colonial guides were housed in the third tent beyond a neat pyramid of regimental drums, right next to a group of small conical tents used to shelter the racks filled with barrel-end-up muskets.

"Ahoy!" he shouted to his fellow guides busy building a campfire in front of his tent. He was at once greeted with a rousing cheer from his Tory messmates. To Jack's surprise, the three surly troopers, who had complained so bitterly to their sergeant over having to share tent and mess with "colonial bastards," cheered as well—all prejudice overcome by the full gunnysack slung over his shoulder.

"I hiked to the bay and met with some luck . . ." Jack dumped the contents of his sack: Three large flounder, a dozen ears of corn and at least two dozen not-quite-ripe yellow pippins all spilled onto the tamped-down grass.

"I can clean those fish," volunteered the small, pointy-faced trooper putting a fresh edge to his bayonet with a honing stone. "Afore I made the mistake of taking the King's shilling, I worked as a fishmonger in Swansea."

Pointy-face made quick work of the fish, and in no time they were threading chunks of sweet flounder meat onto bayonets to broil over the flames, and ears of corn were roasting in their husks on a bed of embers. One of the Tory guides passed a bottle of rum around their circle, and though he was sharing food, drink and conversation within the bosom of the enemy, Jack managed to enjoy his dinner, and the company.

The bottle had made several rounds when a pimply faced ensign approached with orders for colonial guides to gather their gear and report to General Clinton's marquee "at once." Jack and his cohorts scrambled to shoulder packs and weapons, and fell in, marching along with the ensign to the opposite side of the camp, where the officer marquees were located.

A pair of fox terriers stood guard at the tied-open door flaps, barking a friendly welcome as the ensign ushered them inside. The large tent was empty, save for one fubsy fellow—plump and squat—with a clean-shaven pate. Dressed in waistcoat and shirtsleeves, the man hunkered over a big table centered between two tent poles.

The ensign removed his tricorn. "General Clinton, sir."

The major general looked up, prominent dark brows raised. "Ah! The guides!" With a wave he urged, "Come forward . . ."

A negro servant boy followed in on their heels and hung a pair of lanterns from hooks screwed into the tent poles, casting needed light onto the detailed map of Long Island spread across the table-top.

"I plan to turn the enemy position by means of this gorge . . ." General Clinton pointed to the Jamaica Pass, located at the eastern end of the Gowanus Heights. The British Army needed to somehow penetrate this densely wooded ridge in order to reach the Patriot forces entrenched behind the Brooklyn Heights. "Our informants tell us this pass is little used and ill-guarded.

"While Grant's brigades and von Heister's Hessians divert our rebel friends, keeping them busy here, here and here"—the general tapped his finger to the heavily guarded Bedford Pass, Flatbush Pass and Martense Lane—"my flanking force will come around the rebel left and crush them from behind." Clinton swept his palm across the parchment and brought his fist down with a thump.

Astounded, Jack stared at the map with newborn clarity, restraining a strong urge to knock knuckles to his skull. *Thick. Thick. Thick.* He had been too stupid to comprehend the import of the words Titus overheard at the stable. *Clinton would turn their flank* . . . He should have gone to Washington with those words alone. His eyes leapt from point to point on the map, and Jack could find no flaw in the brilliant stratagem. "A perfect trap . . ." he muttered.

The general acknowledged the praise with a nod. "You local men will join me in guiding a swift vanguard of light cavalry and foot to take control of the gorge. Generals Howe and Cornwallis will follow us with the main body and artillery. We will move ten thousand men and twenty-eight guns through that pass."

I have to find Titus. His brain awhir fathoming the consequences of Clinton's strategy, Jack studied the map anew, calculating the quickest route to take to warn the Continental forces. *After dark . . . steal horses . . . travel through the night and cross the heights before the Redcoat vanguard gains an inch . . .*

The servant came to stand beside the general, a freshly powdered wig in hand. The negro boy held a looking glass steady, and the general contemplated his reflection as he dressed his bald head. "I have ordered mounts readied for the four of you. We leave at nightfall. The troops are forming now."

Nightfall! Forming now! Rocked, Jack sucked in a breath and leaned over the map on both hands, trying to think over the desperate clamor ringing between his ears. He studied the map, floundering— searching for something—some reason to cause Clinton to put a halt to the plan.

One of the Flatbush farmers spoke up. "A company of rebel riflemen patrol regularly along the road here . . ." He dragged a finger along a stretch of the Jamaica Road. "Pennsylvania sharpshooters."

"We are aware—and thus require your services to guide us a path through the *countryside*"—Clinton drew a line parallel to the Jamaica Road—"avoiding the main road and evading any enemy patrols that might discern our intent."

Jack pictured the terrain the general proposed they lead an army through by night, and referred to the map. "The off-road path will necessitate a very narrow column, sir," he said. "Your forces will be stretched thin for miles"—he pushed his finger from the position at Flatlands, tracing the six-mile span to Jamaica Pass—"vulnerable to attack—at risk every inch of the way—especially at the gorge."

General Clinton slipped his arms into the coat his servant held ready, and contemplated Jack with a furrowed brow. "Your name, yeoman?"

Jack stood upright. "Stapleton, sir."

"Your outlandish beard does little to disguise a keen eye and an artful mind. I will enjoy riding with you, Mr. Stapleton." The general buckled the strap of his sword sling across his chest, and zinged a shiny brass-hilted saber into the scabbard at his hip. "No plan is invincible, but with utmost attention to secrecy, silence and under cover of dark, our force will be as stealthy as a viper, and I am confident we will be sinking fangs into Mr. Washington and his ilk come daybreak." Clinton took up a bicorn hat trimmed with gold tape to match the fringed epaulettes and lacing on his red coat, and he fit it square to his face. "Let us go and possess this island."

The general led them on a brisk march, across camp, to an open field where, without benefit of a drum call, a full brigade of light infantry stood assembled into ranks, and a regiment of dragoons waited in open file array, standing beside their mounts. To Jack's great relief, he saw Titus Gilmore among the ostlers leading rider-less horses to the fore.

"There are your mounts." Clinton pointed. "Secure your gear and stand ready to depart." With those orders the general turned on his heel and joined two tall officers in conversation—one corpulent, one slim—both bedecked and festooned in gold fringe and trim.

Cornwallis and Howe . . . Jack thought as he claimed the horse Titus was tending. They pulled several yards away from the forma-tion and any prying ears.

"You see the three of them with their heads together?" Titus whispered. "No one knows where they are taking us—not even the officers."

"Well, I know. Clinton means to sneak up on the Continental left flank by way of the Jamaica Pass," Jack said through gritted teeth, sliding his musket into the gunsling suspended from the saddle. "Ten thousand men—twenty-eight guns—on the march now."

"Clinton would turn their flank . . ." Titus remembered in an ominous tone. "We have to go, Jack . . . give warning . . ."

"I know . . . I know . . ." Jack settled his knapsack and bedroll onto his mount's rear, lashing the straps through a loop at the back of the saddle. "But I'm caught in the eye of this storm—expected to ride alongside the major general himself."

Together, he and Titus turned to see Clinton swing himself up onto his saddle, and on this quiet signal hundreds of dragoons fol-lowed suit.

Titus fiddled with the saddle blanket. "This march could mean the end of our army—the end of our country . . ."

"I know"—Jack sidled next to Titus, making a pretense of adjust-ing the stirrup length—"and I will be leading the Redcoats to it."

Titus whispered, "I'm on foot with the farriers, at the rear of the horse ranks. No one pays me much mind. I think I can steal away . . ."

"Ho! Jack!" One of the guides, already mounted, called him back to the line with a wide wave. "It's time."

Jack took the reins. "Do it, Titus. Break away as soon as you can—get through with all speed. This column must be stopped before it breaches the pass."

Titus clapped Jack on the back and took off running to the rear of the light horse, where he rejoined the ostlers.

"There you are!" the farrier-major scolded as he loaded heavy churns filled with smithing and horse-leechery equipment onto the back of a sturdy gelding. "Gather up yer gear and fall in line. Can ye not see the Seventeenth is on the move?"

Titus shouldered the musket and knapsack he'd left lying off to the side. Holding up his bedroll he said, "I'm ordered to bring my master this blanket . . . he's a guide, riding in the lead with the major general."

"With the major general!" The grizzled campaigner shooed Titus with a dismissive flick of his fingers. "Off wi' ye, then, ye poor black bugger—go to yer master's bidding."

The column began to move forward, at first lurching in starts and stops, then shifting into a smooth, rhythmic pace. No one stopped to question Titus as to his destination or his intent as he sprinted by the slow-moving stream of horse soldiers, toward the head of the column.

Titus reached the lead of the vanguard just as it turned onto a narrow, woodland path. General Clinton was with the guides, riding alongside Jack. "Master!" he shouted, and reaching out, he grabbed ahold of Jack's stirrup.

Jack looked down in surprise.

Titus trotted alongside, offering up his bedroll. "Here you go . . . a warm blanket."

Flashing a smile, Jack took the proffered bundle. "You are most thoughtful, Titus."

Breathless, Titus said, "So I'll find you . . . beyond the heights."

"Or maybe I'll find you."

Titus laughed. "Fare well, then, till we meet again!" He sent Jack's bay along with a slap on the rump, and then slowed his pace to a gradual halt. None of the dragoons cantering past paid him a scant bit of notice as he stepped off the narrow path to make way for the column. And no one seemed to notice as he inched backward, blending into the black shadows under the dense canopy of trees.

Jack glanced over his shoulder, and squinting, he could barely make out the gray linen of Titus's shirt moving against the dark backdrop, away from the path.

"There *is* an uncommon chill in the air." General Clinton drew on the cloak he had bunched behind his saddle. "Your servant is most devoted, Mr. Stapleton."

"Yes . . ." Jack said, twisting around—craning—searching the trees to see his friend disappear. "Titus is most devoted to our cause."

With a wry smile, Jack unfurled the blanket Titus had brought, and pulled it over his shoulders. Relieved that at least one of them was tearing pell-mell through the trees toward the Patriot lines, he sank into his saddle and put his mind to a new task. Like a hungry snake on the prowl, the double file of cavalry and infantry moved forward—relentless—and Jack must somehow prevent this red viper from slithering through the Jamaica Pass.

At the onset of the march, orders prohibiting conversation were passed along and strictly observed by troops armed with a sharpened sense of vulnerability. But no order could stifle random equine snorts and huffs, the thud of hoof and boot, and the creak and clank of leather and metal carried by a multitude on the move.

In keeping with the need for stealth, the vanguard advanced without the aid of lantern and torch. The first mile saw a near-full moon rise in a cloudless sky to illuminate the way, and the Redcoats were not overly hampered by the lack of light—another testament to Clinton's good planning. *Or good fortune . . .* Jack thought, glancing to his right at the major general.

I should put an end to the bastard's good fortune . . . Cut the head from the snake . . . Jack leaned forward and touched fingers to the hilt of the dagger kept ready in his left boot, considering a quick lunge and slash at the good general's windpipe. The ensuing confusion might cause the flanking force to falter. *Not for long though* . . . Jack discarded the idea. *The hydra would quickly grow another head, what with Cornwallis and Howe not far behind.*

The vanguard moved forward in the night, unchallenged.

About an hour into the march, the company met with a salty, rotten-egg breeze wafting inland from the fetid wetlands bordering Jamaica Bay. The cadaverine smell and the chirping marsh frogs gave way to the fresh scent of dew-soaked meadow and the owl's hoot as the vanguard moved inland and closer to the pass. Jack judged their position to be less than three miles away from the mark. These dragoons moved with greater speed than he'd anticipated, and Jack worried whether Titus got through to rouse some sort of attack or defense.

I make for a poor dragoon . . . Jack winced, shifting his weight forward in the saddle.

After two solid hours on horseback, he was decidedly saddle sore. Riding at the head of the column, with only three Tory guides between him and the open road, the tantalizing urge to simply dig heels into his mount and bolt was tempered by his rather middling horsemanship, and the three hundred dragoons on his heels.

A familiar pain jabbed his leg, and Jack mined his pocket for the little cast-iron crown he carried. He closed his fist on the rough metal. It seemed a lifetime ago when he and Anne Merrick worked the press together, printing the wonderful words read aloud and cheered on the Commons. It seemed far longer than seven weeks since the happy mob had torn down the King's statue—since his nation was born in the hope and dream of liberty.

Jack smiled, remembering how he'd kissed the widow most thoroughly on that happy day. He could recall exact the softness of her lips, and how she'd laid her small hand light to his cheek. *Lavender* . . . Her neck, her hair—she always smelled of lavender. *She lost her hat* . . .

Jack worried the metal fragment between his thumb and forefinger, wondering what had ever possessed him to leave her behind at the Bowling Green. *I should have stayed with her that night . . . with her wrapped in my arms that one night . . .*

Shifting in his saddle, Jack stole a glance at the stern-faced general riding alongside him.

I have to stop them.

A sudden sadness coiled tight around his heart. Not used to having regrets, Jack Hampton found himself beset by them—regretting having nothing more than a few stolen kisses with Anne Merrick—regretting most of all that he would never know what pleasure and happiness would have been found in sharing a life with her.

Nevers and evers of one man are not of much consequence when weighed against the hopes and dreams of many who will die if these Redcoats breach Jamaica Pass.

Jack pushed the broken crown back into his pocket, his jaw set.

A wild tear down the road. Lead the bloody bastards on a merry chase . . .

He would cause a rumpus—ride off hooting and hollering. Jack thought he might get off at least one shot with his musket.

Draw the attention of those Pennsylvania sharpshooters . . .

Jack took the reins in two hands. He rose up in his stirrups, putting air between his hindquarters and the horse's, twisting around to contemplate the grim faces trotting behind.

Time to make some noise . . .

"Come to a halt," General Clinton suddenly ordered. The column shuffled and creaked to a full stop. Jack slumped back into his saddle.

"You know, Stapleton," Clinton said, as he swung his leg over to dismount. "I am accustomed to long hours in the saddle, but your fidgetry reminds me the men might need to take their ease."

A low-register, communal groan echoed down the line as cavalrymen dismounted, and rushed to relieve themselves along the side of the road.

Jack relished a surge of new confidence with his feet landing on solid ground. Though still a dire risk, taking flight on foot better suited his abilities and his purpose. Dashing through the dark woodlands, he might actually be able to make good his escape. He wandered a ways down the path from the clump of men and horses—casually unbuttoning the flap on his breeches, edging into the thick woodland, all the while his heart beating a mad gallop.

A hand gripped him by the shoulder. "Hold there."

Jack turned to Captain Blankenship—the death's-head on the dragoon's helmet grinning toothless in the moonlight. He jerked free from the grasp.

"The major general would have a word with you," Blankenship insisted.

"The major general will have to wait until I've had my piss." Jack shrugged his member free and arced a steamy stream, causing the captain to leap back to save himself a boot-wetting.

Jack shook off the last drops and heaved a deep breath, taking his time to settle his business and button up. The dragoon marched him back to the column, where he half expected to meet with a company of hangmen—noose in hand.

Much to his relief, Jack was led to the guides and the general, all down on their hunkers. Dropping to one knee, he joined them, encircling a patch of smoothed earth lit by moonlight.

"Ah . . . there you are, Stapleton . . ." In low tones, dagger in hand, Clinton began to draw a diagram in the dirt. "Thus far, we have been traveling parallel to the Jamaica Road." He scratched two lines close together. "The rebels guarding the pass no doubt expect an attack to come from this direction." He marked an X for the pass. "As we are uncertain of the level of force and fortification we may encounter, I propose we veer away from this straightforward route, and come upon them from behind." He scraped a large bump on the line. "I'm not one for contending with the vagaries of chance, and I do not want to risk another Breed's Hill in gaining this pass."

While the other guides grunted and nodded in agreement, Jack studied the general's scratchings. The detour Clinton proposed and the mention of Breed's Hill—where the Redcoats lost over one thousand men—exposed a weakness Jack knew he must try to exploit.

"I know this road." Jack pointed to Clinton's suggested detour. "Your army, sir, will have to cross a very narrow bridge over a saltwater creek here . . ." He added a squiggling line to intersect Clinton's proposed detour, and met the general square in the eye. "Schoonmaker's Bridge—a bottleneck—the perfect spot for a rebel ambush. Riflemen posted in these woods"—Jack swept a finger over either side of the bridge—"would wreak havoc on our line—another Breed's Hill—only worse."

"Aye," one of the Tory farmers agreed. "That's a choke point, that bridge."

Clinton rose to his feet, arms folded, tapping the tip of his dagger to his chin. "We will proceed with caution. Before crossing the bridge I will send skirmishing parties to sweep the woods for any rebels lying in wait."

"A wise and prudent course, General." Jack tried very hard not to smile.

಄ ಄ ಄

"*Up with your arms!*"

The terse order, accompanied by the hammer clacking back on a flintlock, caused Titus to halt in his steps. He raised his arms and turned slow to the commanding voice. Two figures stepped out from the shadows and onto the road.

"Get his gun." The larger man stood with his musket trained while the smaller of the two—a young boy, no older than fourteen or fifteen—ran up to wrest the weapon from Titus's shoulder.

"He's a black fella, Dad . . ." the boy said, giving the Brown Bess to his father.

"Keep your gun on him, Jimmy." The father shouldered his weapon, and took a moment to examine Titus's loaded musket, then he asked, "Where're you headed in such a hurry this time of night?"

Titus squinted in the dark. These two wore no uniform. He could not discern any greenery in their hats. If they were Patriots or Loyalists, he couldn't tell by looking at them.

"I asked you a question, nigger. Whose business has you skulking on this road with a loaded weapon?"

Titus heaved a breath—not wanting to implicate himself as either a Patriot or a Loyalist, he said nothing.

The man stepped close. "Answer me! Who gave you this gun?"

Arms still raised, Titus only shook his head.

The man swung the butt end of the musket up, hitting Titus square on the temple, knocking him to the ground. "Black bastard! Are you scouting for the Redcoats? Who do you work for?"

Patriots... Dazed, Titus smeared a finger through blood dripping down his cheek. He tried to rise up on legs suddenly gone to pudding, working hard to make words, he said, "Redcoats are mar..."

The man didn't wait to hear the rest. Using the musket like a club, he dealt yet another vicious blow to the head, and laid Titus flat on his back.

"Jamaica Road..." Titus uttered as he blinked at the show of bright stars dancing in the night sky. Twirling and swirling, the stars whirled off into a sea of crimson black.

ф ф ф

GENERAL Clinton's vanguard dawdled for at least two hours waiting for search parties to finish combing the woods on either side of Schoonmaker's Bridge. Once the skirmishers gave the all clear, the vanguard proceeded in slow single file across the bridge, and Jack could only hope the fruitless exercise bought time for the Continentals to mount a strong defense at Jamaica Pass. With only a few hours left until daybreak, and the vanguard less than half mile away from the pass, Jack commenced another plan to further delay the Redcoats, and enable his escape back to the American lines.

"Howard's Tavern is just up the road, and it is no more than one hundred yards from the pass," he said, riding alongside General Clinton. "The tavern is most likely filled with rebel soldiers and sympathizers. It would only take one man, swift of foot, to raise an alarm, and the pass would be lost to us. Make another brief halt, and I'll ride ahead to scout the situation."

Clinton pondered Jack's proposal before turning in his saddle. "Blankenship! Stuart! Wemyss!" he beckoned to three of his aides-de-camp. "Form a patrol of twelve to accompany Stapleton and take control of the tavern ahead—sweep up any locals you run across and report back once the area is secured."

Instead of galloping off alone, through the pass, and to the Patriot lines as he'd planned, Jack adapted to the situation, and took the lead in a party of twelve dragoons. Once at Howard's Tavern, the soldiers broke in, stirring the sleeping Howard family from their beds, and herding the frightened innkeeper, his wife and children by tip of bayonet into the barroom for questioning by the officers.

Jack felt bound to make good his escape, if only to justify having put these hapless folk into a dangerous situation. "Captain Blankenship," he said, "I'll ride back and give the general the all clear."

"I've already sent Lieutenant Wemyss," Blankenship said. "Our friend Mr. Howard is very kind and generous. He tells me we can reconnoiter the pass by means of a secret path."

"The Rockaway Path—" Howard added. "An old Indian trail—not much more than a bridle path—it runs along the rim of the gorge." The innkeeper looked especially pale and miserable standing in the huddle of his wife and children, all of them barefoot in their nightshirts. Jack could hardly blame the man for wanting to appease these Redcoats.

As they waited for Howard and his eldest boy to dress, Jack helped himself, along with the other officers, to a bottle of spirits. He sipped a glass of rye, wondering if he would ever be able to get shed of these persistent Redcoats. There would be little opportunity for escape on a rough ridge path. Daybreak was drawing near and Jack came to believe the best hope for raising an alarm was bound up with Titus Gilmore making it through to the Continental lines.

The party mounted horses and left the inn just after the wall clock chimed the three-o'clock hour. Howard and his son led Jack,

Blankenship and eight dragoons up a steep and difficult path, ducking low-hanging branches all the way. They skirted along the length of the gorge, and in the moonlight could not discern any motion or fortifications.

No artillery—not one single gun—in evidence. No troops—no soldiers of any kind. *The Continental lines will crumble like a day-old scone if Clinton succeeds in getting ten thousand through this pass.*

"That way will take you down to the other end of the pass," Howard said as they reached the point where the bridle path transitioned onto a proper road.

"Continue forward, innkeeper," Blankenship urged.

In strict obedience with Clinton's original order for stealth on the march, the disciplined dragoons rode in complete silence, which made it all the easier to discern the undisciplined chatter and laughter coming from the road ahead. Blankenship's patrol picked up speed.

Soldiers or citizens, the Redcoats had orders to sweep up anyone crossing their path. The captain used hand signals to organize his men into a double-file formation. Jack and the two Howards hung back as the efficient dragoons rode forward as of one mind to encircle and capture a party of five American horsemen, as neat and quiet as you please.

New Yorkers . . . Jack recognized their jackets, and the sight of the Continental officers—though captured and disarmed—gave him hope.

Maybe all is not lost . . . Maybe Titus got through and a strong guard is in place.

The rebel prisoners were led bound and gagged back to the tavern. Jack and his fellow guides were ordered to wait out in the dooryard while the general interrogated the prisoners.

Jack hovered on the stoop landing, itching to know what was going on behind the closed door. Nearby, a pair of dragoons kept a group of soldiers in thrall with the retelling of the rebel capture, but the majority of Clinton's vanguard seized the opportunity to catch a few winks of precious sleep on a handy hayrick or a smooth patch of ground.

Mr. Howard came up with two cups of coffee, and handed one to Jack. "I am quite certain your Redcoats have just captured the entirety of the Patriot force defending our little pass," he said with a snort.

"The other passes are all heavily fortified—why would this pass be any different?"

Howard shrugged. "They never seemed to pay much mind to it. They considered our pass unimportant—too narrow—too out-of-the-way for this lot to bother with." He indicated with a sweep of incredulity the soldiers crowded onto his property. "I can tell you this much, the Continentals will pay dearly for their folly come morning—dearly, indeed." Shoulders slumped, he gulped the last of his coffee and trudged back to his family.

Jack crossed the wide stoop to sit on the stair steps. Propping elbows on his knees, he cradled his head, closed his eyes and pictured the map spread out on the general's table under the big marquee tent hours before. He envisioned the fortified Patriot lines at Brooklyn Heights sandwiched between a British invasion force twenty thousand strong, and the power of a naval armada riding anchor on the East River.

This awful viper is poised to strike, and when it gains the pass, Washington's ragtag numbers will not only be bitten, they will be swallowed whole.

The door banged open, and a dozen officers stomped down the steps, fitting on helmets, girding on swords, and rousting their companies to assemble and form.

Jack jumped to his feet and caught up with Blankenship collecting his mount. "What's happened?"

Blankenship turned, his handsome face alight, his voice tinged with more than a little bravura. "The pass is absolutely undefended! The rebels admitted as much when put to the question."

"I don't believe it!" Jack gripped Blankenship by the arm.

"Believe it—it's true! The pass is ours! I'm taking a party through to affirm what the rebels have reported, and the vanguard will follow forthwith. You best get ready." The captain swung up onto his horse. "Mark my words, Stapleton—I will be standing you a pint in a pub on Broad Way before the week is out!"

The dooryard was a tumult of horses and men as dragoons and troopers bumped about in the dark to create semblance from disorder. In the confusion, Jack claimed his horse, and led it around to the back of the tavern.

Clinton has yet to breach this pass . . . He struggled with the knots he'd tied in securing his pack to his saddle . . . *He still needs to get ten thousand encumbered with heavy artillery and baggage through that gorge* . . . "Bloody hell!" Jack cursed and pulled the knife from his boot to cut his pack free. He might not be able to prevent the British incursion, but he could certainly still warn his brothers-in-arms and get them to fall back to the Brooklyn works, and avoid total annihilation.

Pack on back, musket on shoulder, Jack skirted along the woodlands until he found the trailhead to the Rockaway Path. For not having slept in almost twenty-four hours, Jack was energized with new determination, and he climbed up the overgrown trail in the dark with some speed. Pausing when he reached the crest of the ridge, he scanned the valley view.

The eastern sky was imbued with a velvety blue, presaging the dawn. The waxing moon, sitting low on the western horizon, cast deep purple shadows on a patchwork landscape sewn of gray and black scraps. To the southeast, toward the Bedford Pass, he could see the flicker of campfires—yellow flashes amid the shadowed woodlands—like fireflies signaling to each other in a hedgerow.

Our forces guarding the Bedford Pass . . . Jack marked the position and his course. He launched into a trot and made for those fires.

Jack raced with the rising sun and reached the encampment in the woods in less than half an hour. A sleepy-eyed picket wearing a dark hunting shirt and a sprig of oak leaves in his tricorn leaned on a long rifle, contemplating the few stars in the western sky. Jack snapped a branchlet from a nearby oak, and decorated his own hat accordingly. He gave the picket a wide berth and wound around, making his way into the camp pitched within a woody grove of white oak trees.

A lone drummer sat near one campfire—practicing, tapping out a soft call. Two men coaxing a fire under a simmering pot of water barely shot Jack a glance as he strode past with a tip of his hat, heading for the largest tent, as if he knew exactly what he was about. He swept a door panel aside and poked his head in.

A slim man with a hawkish nose stood bare-chested and barefoot in breeches, positioning a small mirror to best advantage, the light coming from a single candle set on a cluttered desk. His momentary puzzlement at Jack's appearance caused him pause.

"Are you the commanding officer here?" Jack asked.

"I am," the man answered, his eye turned wary. "Colonel Samuel Miles, Fourth Pennsylvania Riflemen. And you are . . . ?"

Jack entered. He moved into the light, sweeping off his tricorn in salute. "Jack Hampton, sir, bringing you urgent intelligence."

The crowded tent was further disordered with a disheveled camp bed, a small table desk and a single folding chair. Colonel Miles found a badger-bristle brush and a wooden cup amid the melee scattered on the desktop, and nodded to the chair. Jack shrugged off his gear and settled into the canvas sling.

Miles dipped his shaving brush into a bowl of steamy water and began beating up a soapy froth, the brush handle clacking merry against the sides of the cup. "What regiment do you serve with, sir?"

"Well . . ." Jack scratched his beard. "These past two days, I've served as a scout in the King's Army . . ." and he proceeded to tell his story as a concise series of facts and events as they pertained to the British advance, including Titus's escape from the line. The colonel lathered his face, and hurried to scrape his whiskers during the telling, interrupting twice for clarification, and nicking his chin once.

"I had a feeling the bloodybacks had their eye on the Jamaica Road." Miles freed a frock shirt from the tangle on his bed. The colonel poked his head out the tent and shouted, "Drummer—beat the long roll—muster the battalions."

After pulling the shirt over his head, he tugged on a pair of boots, rifled a hand across the desktop and snatched up a ring of keys. "Come with me."

In contrast to the aligned rows and precise order of the British camp at Flatlands, American tents were scarce and strewn through the woods like dice tumbled from a cup. Jack followed the colonel on an erratic path weaving through trees, tents and between soldiers, who slept curled with blanket and gun under the open sky, just waking to the call to arms.

Miles pulled to a halt in front of such a slouched figure propped against a sapling. Leaning in, he gave the man's shoulder a shake. "On your feet."

A heavy chain rattled a rusty tune. The man grasped the tree trunk and rose slow. Legs shackled, he stumbled forward into the mottled dawnlight filtering down through the canopy.

"Titus!" Jack lurched and caught his friend around the waist. "Unfetter him at once!" he demanded, helping his friend to lower back to a sit.

Miles already worked the padlock on the shackles. "A pair of farmers brought him to us bleeding and unconscious . . . They said he was a Tory spy."

"Knocked me out cold afore I could convince 'em otherwise." Wincing with a halfhearted smile, Titus fingered the gash on his head, his speech and appearance distorted by considerable swelling on the left side of his face. "Did the Redcoats get through?"

Jack hoisted Titus back up to his feet. "I'm afraid they did. Can you walk? We need to get back behind the works at Brooklyn."

"I can walk." Titus pulled away from Jack and looked around. "I guess them two took my gun and my pack?"

"They must have kept the gun. I have your pack." Miles fell in leading Jack and Titus back to his tent. The thud of artillery sounded from the west—followed by a series of six more reports. With a glance over his shoulder, Miles said, "Hessians on the Flatbush Road."

The guns continued to thud dully in the distance, and three more drummers joined in beating the troops to assemble. The rhythmic rat-a-tat cast a spell in the ghosted morning light, and the waking riflemen were drawn to the camp center like hungry boys to the dinner bell, to be herded by shouting, sword-wielding officers into order.

The colonel ducked into his tent and came out wearing a tricorn decorated with a white ostrich feather and carrying a sword in scabbard. He dropped Titus's pack at Jack's feet. "So, Hampton, will you be joining our effort?"

"What effort?"

"I'm mustering my battalions to march south to those guns."

Jack blinked, and he gave his tired brain a shake, certain he must have misheard. "You're what?"

"Do you not hear those guns? We have standing orders to engage when the enemy begins its advance at the Bedford Pass."

"Orders be damned! There are ten thousand Redcoats and Hessians on your front and another ten thousand on your rear—sound the warning to fall back to the works at Brooklyn, before you are trapped between the two!"

Miles buckled on his sword belt. "Pennsylvanians are not cowards and will not run from a fight. We are marching south to engage the enemy, as ordered."

Jack's brows met in a fierce scowl. He reached out and grabbed Miles by the shirtfront, pulling the shorter man up onto his toes, knocking his fine plumage into the duff at his feet.

"You best heed my advice, Colonel, or your courageous Pennsylvanians will be slaughtered in a useless endeavor." Jack pushed the colonel back and slipped the strap of Titus's pack over his shoulder. "Let's go, Titus—away from this madness."

Chapter Eleven

✿❧✿

Arms, as the last resource, decide the contest;
the appeal was the choice of the king, and the
continent hath accepted the challenge.

THOMAS PAINE, *Common Sense*

Thursday, August 29, 1776
Twilight at the Works on the Brooklyn Heights

LIEUTENANT David Peabody recited the order to the commander in charge. "Fresh troops are arriving and General Washington proposes to make a change in situation. Be prepared to parade your regiment to the head of your encampment at seven o'clock, with all arms, accoutrements and knapsacks."

Except for the five regiments manning the extreme front trenches with a constant watch, the order to prepare was being sent to every regiment on the lines. David passed by a huddle of sodden, desultory soldiers eating—for lack of dry firewood—a dreadful supper of hard biscuit and raw salt pork. It had been difficult for these exhausted men to keep their spirits up, their powder dry, and their muskets in working order without any or shelter from the rain. The troops were worn down, and David prayed Washington's new orders did not foretell a night attack on the British, as most of his fellow officers predicted.

Swinging up onto his stallion, David rode to the front line, to survey the scant mile and a half separating the British encampment and the American works. The scene was serene for the moment. As daylight faded, the squeal of cannonshot along with the sporadic pop and buzz of exchanged musketfire gave way to the thud of pick and scrape of shovel. In only two days, working through the night, the diligent British sappers had advanced their zigzag trenches to less than six hundred yards away. David peered through his spyglass.

By this time tomorrow, the Redcoats will have us in musket range . . . hordes of Hessians with their merciless bayonets storming the works . . .

He pocketed his glass, gave his horse a nudge and a tug to the left, and they trudged back to the stable. Leaving Black Bill watered, fed and curried, he headed toward camp with his saddle on his shoulder, slogging through an ankle-deep morass of mud and puddles.

At least it's stopped raining . . .

He looked to his tent, and for the first time in three days a smile crossed his face. A good-sized campfire was blazing away, and one of his tentmates, Duncan MacBryde, sat on a campstool with bare feet stretched to the flames, his empty boots draped with wet socks set close to the fire, steaming.

"Saint MacBryde, you've wrought a miracle! Where did you come upon dry wood in this muddy hellhole?"

"Och . . ." Duncan's blue eyes bore a devilish gleam. "I only made do . . ."

David went inside to dump his gear, and immediately noted the canvas roof and walls were a bit cockeyed and saggy. Every tent pole had been replaced with hewn birch trunks still in the bark.

The bastard's a genius!

David hurried to join Duncan, to dry out a bit and scribble a quick letter home. He shed his damp wool coat and soggy hat, and dug pen, ink and journal from his pack. Sitting down at the campfire, he stripped off soaking wet boots and socks and extended his feet. "Fie on foot rot!"

"Aye, the bane of every soldier!" Duncan tossed a chunk of firewood onto the pyre.

A merry swarm of sparks soared up into the twilight, and David leaned inward, the wood hissing and popping, his damp skin and linen awash in the wonderful, dry heat. Setting his inkpot to one side, he opened his journal on his lap, thumbed to the first blank page and began to write:

> *Thursday Evening, Aug. 29th*
> *My Dear Sally, it has been too many days since last I wrote, and now I must tell you the enemy has dealt us a severe flogging here on Long Island. The Redcoats and Hessians surrounded a large portion of our Army guarding the passes, and many are dead and captured before they could get behind the safety of our intrenchment. Some say more than a thousand of our men are worse for the actions of the enemy—and among those thousand are two generals and many good officers. The British Army sits in full array on the plateau directly in front of us and we watch and wait for them to storm our works—as they must.*
>
> *Oh, Sal! Our cause is so Just, and I cannot fathom how we did not succeed—how we have come to such Dire Straits. I am extraordinary wet with the steady torrent poured down upon us these past two days, wherein it was often difficult to tell thunder and lightning from the clap and flash of cannon. For all the misery the rain has inflicted, it has kept the Redcoats from our lines, and its strong wind keeps the Navy from entering the river at our backs. We are caught in a dangerous position. Share this news with Anne. I strongly urge you both to leave the city for Peekskill at once. I think on you often with a very Fond Heart, and I live to be together with you once again.*
>
> *With the most Tender and Great Affection, I am, dearest Sally, Truly Yours—David Peabody*

David reread the lines he'd written, tapping the ink from his quill, wiping the tip with the hem of his shirt.

A severe flogging . . . He winced at his choice of words. By all accounts the soldiers had at first fought bravely, protecting their positions against superior numbers and arms—but once the British flanking forces swept down on their rear, the Patriot army disintegrated in a scattered, disorderly retreat.

He watched from the works as Patriot soldiers ran for their lives pursued by merciless Hessian and Scots grenadiers who showed no quarter with bayonets fixed. In flight, hundreds crossing the plain were surrounded and trapped by mounted dragoons. David heard many were mired in the bogs, crossing the marshlands under a hail of fire, only to be drowned or captured.

As the vanquished soldiers tumbled behind the safety of the fortifications at Brooklyn, they braced to repulse a massive assault. But Howe did not press his advantage. To everyone's amazement, he pulled his troops back, and began a formal siege.

Lucky for us . . . In total disarray, panic-stricken and outnumbered, David doubted they would have survived. Careful in tearing the page loose from the book, he waved the letter about to dry the ink, folded the sheet in thirds, sealed it shut with a paste wafer and addressed it:

To: Miss Sally Tucker at the sign of the Cup and Quill, New York City

Leaving his boots to dry, David ran barefoot to the boat landing, hoping it was not too late to get his letter aboard the last ferry to the city.

Not only was the ferryboat still at the dock, the harbor was oddly crowded with all manner of boats—flatboats, sloops, whale boats, pettiaugers, dories, sailboats—with General Washington himself surveying the assembled vessels astride his sorrel, Nelson.

David spotted Mr. Gourley, one of the regular boatmen, leaning against the pilings smoking a long stem pipe, and he greeted the man with a handshake.

"I'm happy to find you're still here . . ." he said, handing over the letter and a coin for the man's trouble. "If you could deliver this, I'd appreciate it."

The ferryman slipped both letter and coin into the pocket of his oilcloth jacket. "We're waiting to evacuate the sick and wounded to the city."

"That's an awful lot of boats . . ."

Gourley puffed and shrugged.

David pointed to men in tarred trousers, wrapping the iron oar-locks on every ship with rags and strips of old canvas. "Are they muffling the oars?"

"A-yup . . ." The ferryman squinted at the darkening sky and worried the graying stubble on his chin. "You know, this nor'easter's been keeping navy shipping from the river. There are warships anchored in the Narrows waiting for the wind to shift." Gourley chewed on the stem of his pipe. "King's Army advancing on the front, King's Navy advancing on the rear. Think on it lad, if you were Washington, what would you do?"

Walking back to his tent, he pondered Gourley's question and the unusual activity at the landing. The vast collection of boats with muffled oars, coupled with the order to parade pointed to a design— to a plan—

Escape the island?

A crazy notion, that—nighttime retreat over water—improbable as it seemed, the idea put some steam in his step, and he sprinted the rest of the way to the tent.

"We have new orders from General MacDougall." Duncan MacBryde tossed their gear into a pile. "We're to strike the tent and report mounted at the ferry landing."

At the landing, MacDougall set David, Duncan and six other officers to the task of assembling the sick and wounded, along with two militia regiments for evacuation to the city. There were to be no drum calls or shouting of any sort. Orders were passed from officer to officer, and whispered from man to man. Though the sky had darkened to a cloud-shrouded black, lights were not allowed. Each and every clandestine action further cemented the theory David shared in a whisper with Duncan: Washington meant to move the entire nine-thousand-man army over the mile of rapid-running East River separating Brooklyn and New York under cover of night.

As they rode alongside the militia regiments parading to the landing, Duncan pointed to an artilleryman who was rendering a cannon mired in the mud useless by driving a spike into the touch hole. "There does seem to be some skullduggery afoot. You might not be as daft as I first thought."

"Skullduggery is paramount to the success of such a maneuver," David said. "If the British discern a retreat, they'll spill over our works like a swarm of bees—a seventeen-inch steel stinger affixed to the barrels of every musket."

Duncan leaned in his saddle, muttering. "Wise to keep the secret from our own lads as well. So miserably trounced, they are—they'd likely trample each other in gaining a seat aboard one of those boats if they knew a retreat was in order."

The reprieve from wet weather was short-lived. The same northeast wind keeping the British ships from entering the river carried in another gusty rainstorm. Up on Black Bill, David stuffed his tricorn into his saddlebag so as not to sacrifice his hat to the bluster.

By nine o'clock the storm clouds blew over, but the fierce wind did not abate. The boatmen and General MacDougall deliberated. High winds combined with the ebb tide to make the river too rough to cross. Troops ready to embark were ordered to stand down and wait out the wind in silence.

Just when it seemed MacDougall would call a halt to the entire endeavor, Mother Nature took pity on their predicament. The wind died as rapidly as it had sprung up, and the churning river became as calm and smooth as satin.

The first detachments were loaded onto the boats, and mounted officers were dispatched to the lines to organize the next regiments for embarkation. Though no one made mention of the word retreat, there was a definite sense of the night's true purpose, and all worked in furious accord to see it carried through.

When a regiment was led from the lines to the ferry landing, the remaining troops extended to the left or right, filling the void, maintaining the illusion for any Redcoat who might be paying close attention. Artillery and wagons filled with baggage were pulled to the waterfront on well-greased wheels, and loaded onto flatboats. Horses and cattle were coaxed aboard. Barrels of the much-despised hard biscuit and salt pork were rolled onto sailboats to such a capacity the gunwales rode but three or four inches above the waterline. Nothing of value was being left behind for the enemy.

And so it proceeded through the night. For more than six hours, with as much order and organization as could be scrubbed up when working in the quiet dark, the boats were loaded, and the hardy mariners rowed with little pause, silently shuttling back and forth across the East River.

In the midst of such industry, David began the night's work happily thinking he would reach Sally before his letter did. But as the hours wore on, and the sky began to brighten on the eastern horizon, he gauged the number of soldiers yet waiting to withdraw. Trepidation began a slow creep up his backbone. "We're quick running out of nighttime . . ."

"Aye." Duncan nodded. "Now that the wind's shifted, the English warships will fetch up into the river along with the daylight."

As the sun inched above the horizon, the same realization dawned on every waiting soldier. Mass desperation welled up like a monstrous wave, washing over the troops assembled at the landing with a tidal force. Strict order dissolved into chaos, and the next empty boat to pull up to the dock was swamped in a mad rush of frantic men climbing over one another to gain passage.

All the officers on duty jumped in trying to staunch the riot with little effect. General Washington himself drove through the pandemonium, shouting, *"Put an end to this mayhem at once, or I will sink this boat to hell!"*

The rioters calmed in the face of their Commander in Chief's imposing presence. Washington's harsh invective served to quell the panic, and the officers were able to reorder the lines so the exodus to the city resumed a hectic but methodical pace.

David and Duncan rode out to the front line to fetch the last remaining regiments. "There're hundreds still on duty. We'll never be able to get them all across."

"When day breaks in earnest, the Redcoats will see our line has more holes than a nunnery—they will not tarry in storming our works," Duncan predicted, checking through the cartridge box belted at his waist. "I have four dry cartridges. How many have you?"

"Three, last I checked."

In the time it took to ride from the landing to the front line, fortune smiled once again on the Patriot cause. A heavy fog came down over the island, clinging to the earth like tufts of sheep's wool to a briar—a fog so dense, David could not see his fellow officer riding a horse no more than five yards ahead.

The fog represented new hope for the soldiers who bore the burden of holding the front line through the long night. David held a true admiration for these brave men who stood their posts as regiment after regiment left the lines, and he was happy to whisper, "Bid a fond farewell to these trenches, Colonel; it's time to parade your men to the landing."

The providential fog lingered, providing cover during the daylight hours of the retreat. As the last vessels were loaded, it became apparent they must leave a few good horses behind. David waited till the very last moment before taking his turn to board. With much regret, he stripped Bill of his saddle and hitched the stallion to the post in front of the ferry house. Right ahead of General Washington, David jumped onto the last boat to leave Long Island.

"I canna believe he did it—but do it he did!" Duncan nodded to General Washington at the prow. "Moved an entire army right out from under the nose of the British high command—with nary a shot being fired."

"And we live to fight another day . . ." David heaved a sigh of relief, sharing his friend's admiration of Washington. Heavy in the water, the boat lurched across the river. Black Bill . . . the ferry landing . . . Long Island . . . all disappearing into thick mist.

I'll never have another horse as fine as my Bill.

The more David thought about it, the more he could not bear the idea of his stallion falling into enemy hands. When they pulled into the sunny ferry landing at the end of Maiden Lane, he rushed to find General MacDougall.

"General, sir," he said, pointing to the opposite shore, shrouded in fog. "We've time for one last run. If I muster volunteers, might I have permission to go back and fetch my horse?"

MacDougall eyed the mouth of the river for enemy warships. "Aye—g'won, then—find your volunteers, but do so with speed, lad."

Old Gourley was game, and Duncan was willing. By offering a hot breakfast courtesy of the Cup and Quill as an inducement, David was also able to coerce four of the Marblehead mariners to join in on the rescue mission.

Carrying a light load, and with strong muscles behind the oars, the flat-bottom scow cut across the water as if pushed along by a great invisible hand. The fog was beginning to lift, patches of mist swirling to open up in clear expanses. With no time to waste, David leapt from the boat as it bumped to the landing, and ran up to the ferry house where Black Bill waited just as he was left, hitched to the post with a short lead.

No sooner did David set foot on Long Island, did he want off again. After so much hubbub and confusion earlier, the ferry landing was now a forlorn place, made even more desolate in the eerie fog. An inexplicable dread congested in his chest, and he cursed his own stupidity, fumbling with the complicated knot he'd used to hitch his horse to the post. Impatient, Bill tossed his angry head, snorting and stamping his hooves in chastisement.

"Goddamn this knot . . ."

Tail swishing back and forth, Bill stiffened his neck, his ears pivoting back.

David heard it, too—the clank-clank of armed soldiers on the prowl. He looked down to the landing. Duncan, Gourley and the

Marbleheaders, all standing in the scow—all waving their hands wildly. He turned to see a row of bright specters emerging from the swirling mist—red figures crisscrossed in white, moving with stealth toward the landing.

What a fine mark to shoot at ... he thought ... *and my musket's on the boat.*

The soldiers came into full view—grenadiers in furry, peaked hats. With a shout, they began running toward the landing. Gourley gave a shout, and the others scrambled to the oars. pushing away from the dock. The Redcoats broached a stand, flintlocks clacking back, and laid several rounds upon the scow as it disappeared into the fog.

"*Shhhh ... Billy ... shhhh ...*" David ducked down and slipped around, putting the skittish horse between himself and the soldiers. He unbuckled the stallion's halter, disengaging Bill from the post. Grabbing a fistful of mane, he pulled up onto Bill's bare back.

The movement caught an eye.

"Halt!"

Kicking and jabbing his heels, David yanked hard on handfuls of mane in a struggle to direct the bridleless stallion. A single shot sounded, and the ball whizzed past, plinking off the iron ring on the hitching post with a high-pitched ding.

Bill reared up. David squeezed tight to his mount, clinging to the mane, clenching his every muscle to stay astride. More shots flashed in the fog, sharp sulfur smoke mingling with the mist. Nostrils flaring, eyes gone wide and wild, Bill wheeled to the left, and then swerved to the right, going nowhere in a mad circle.

David was jerked one way and then the other, barely able to keep his seat, feeling as if he'd been slapped hard on the shoulder—then the leg—with a wet leather strop. Heart thumping in his brain, he hunched over his stallion's withers. On this signal Black Bill at last gave in to his instinct to flee. Taking off in full gallop, he raced inland.

David shot a glance over his shoulder. Muskets a-crackle, the Redcoats gave good chase, but on foot they were no match for his stallion. Black Bill continued to run hard, and as the gunfire faded in the distance, the stallion slowed to a canter, then to a gentle trot.

Drawing upright, David tottered. Head swimming round and round, he groped at a burning ache in his left shoulder. His fingers came up sticky and scarlet. Try as he might, he could not make a fist with his left hand and Bill's mane slipped through his fingers. Dizzy, David slumped down and wrapped his right arm around the stallion's strong neck.

"I'm shot, Bill . . ."

As if understanding the dilemma, the horse came to a complete standstill. Blowing short puffs through his nostrils, Bill twisted round and nuzzled David at the knee.

With Redcoats not too far on his heels, David tried to urge Black Bill forward, and noticed his right leg buzzing with biting pain from ankle to knee as if being stung by a hundred wasps at once. Suddenly thrown off-kilter and at odds to keep his balance, he slipped to the left, flailing at air. Keeling over, David landed hard.

Pain screwed through his shoulder and into his gut like a white-hot auger, fastening him helpless to the ground. His leg felt as if it were being crushed between the grinding maws of a jagged vise. Eyes rolling back in his head, David gagged and coughed up the mouthful of sour bile rushing to his throat.

Lying with one cheek in the sick, the world slowly blinked back into focus—and he could make out four stamping black hooves in the fog. He drew in a deep breath. Blowing it out slow, he struggled to regain control of his wits. Bill bent and whuffled concern in his ear. The stallion nosed David's good hand, the wiry horse whiskers tickling the pads of his palm, his gritty tongue licking the salt from David's curled fingers.

"Run, Bill . . ." David stroked the soft velvet nose. "You run—I'm dead."

"Oh no, Captain . . . you're not dead yet."

Hands carefully rolled David onto his back, and he stared up at a fuzzy black face framed in filmy white and asked, "That you, Bill?"

A different yet familiar voice said, "My God, Titus—his leg's a bloody mess—"

"He's shoulder shot as well." Brown wool floated down beside him. "We'll have to carry him in the blanket . . ."

"On three," Jack said. "One . . . two . . ."

In a mercifully quick but still painful up-and-down, David was moved onto the makeshift litter.

"They're coming . . ." David gasped. "Redcoats . . ."

"Be more worried about your redhead than Redcoats," Titus said, taking hold of the two blanket corners. "Miss Sally will be none too pleased when she sees that leg . . ."

Strapping his musket across his back, Jack hunkered hear David's head, wrapping each fist in a good clutch of wool. "Are you ready, brother? This will be a rough ride . . ."

David nodded. "I'm ready."

Jack and Titus hoisted the blanket, and with David cradled in its sling, they ran into the fogbank.

෯ ෯ ෯

"We'll never find the rebel bastard—not in this fog," Lieutenant Wemyss grumbled.

Stuart chimed in. "The blasted rebel retreat would never have succeeded if not for this damnable fog . . ."

Edward Blankenship cantered alongside the pair of young lieutenants, part of the dragoon detachment following the trail of the lone rebel officer who managed to gallop away from a whole company of grenadiers.

Wemyss picked up the rant. "If those grenadiers bloodied the bastard as they claim, you might think we'd see some sign of it— drop of blood or two—or perhaps a corpse . . ."

Stuart laughed, and Wemyss's sarcasm drew an understanding smile from Blankenship. At last given the order to storm the Brooklyn works, only to find that their miserable foes had vanished in an artful evacuation—it rubbed everyone raw. That the grenadiers had allowed the lone rebel left behind to escape was in the least inexcusable.

"Running away—the cowards—they are becoming expert at it," Wemyss huffed. "We had them by the short hairs . . . By all rights, Captain, you have to admit, we should have crushed this rebellion days ago . . ."

"Aye." Stuart nodded. "Now the traitors live to bedevil us another day."

Why Howe had not allowed them to completely crush their enemy upon breaching the Jamaica Pass and executing the flawless flanking maneuver was a rankling mystery being pondered by officers and enlisted men alike. Edward refused to join in the muttered discontent, and he would not rise to the bait Wemyss dangled.

"What lies behind our commander's judgment is—as it should be—beyond our ken. We are soldiers, Wemyss. We have but to do our duty . . ." Blankenship pulled his horse to a halt. "What's this?"

Traveling through a rocky, shrubby field, they had come upon a torn-up patch of mud, with faint horseshoe tracks leading away from it to the northwest. They dismounted, and leaving the horses tethered to a birch, the men traced the trail on foot until the tracks grew even less distinct and disappeared.

After reaching the dead end, Stuart uncorked his canteen, and took a deep swallow. "This fellow's long gone—most likely at home by now, making a bonfire of his regimental uniform. He'll be among those waiting to sign Howe's oath of loyalty."

"Colonials!" Wemyss snorted. "Curse every one of them to . . ."

"Shhhh . . ." Blankenship put his fingers to his lips, and cocked his head. "Hoofbeats . . ."

The rhythmic *thud-duh-dump, thud-duh-dump* grew louder and louder, until piercing through the veil, about ten yards distant, a jet-black horse burst through in a swirling mist. With a nicker, the stallion cantered up, and bold as you please began jostling and nibbling at one of the mares tethered to the tree.

Secure within the herd, the stallion allowed the officers to approach. Stuart took a spare halter from his saddlebag and slipped it over the horse's nose.

"He is a beautiful animal," Wemyss noted. "Well tended."

"He's bleeding." Stuart point to a patch of dark red blood smeared across the stallion's right flank.

Blankenship examined the spot. "A lot of blood here, but no wound." He showed his palm, red and sticky from the effort. "It seems the grenadiers did manage to sink a ball into the rebel."

"Bleeding, escaping upon a stallion without a bridle or saddle—the devil must be dead or dying in the brush somewhere," Stuart surmised. "The grenadiers will have better luck finding him on foot with dogs than we will on horseback."

"Quite right, Lieutenant." Blankenship fashioned a long lead with a length of rope, and attached it to the stallion's halter. "Let's head back."

Chapter Twelve

We fight neither for revenge nor conquest; neither from pride nor passion; we are not insulting the world with our fleets and armies, not ravaging the globe for plunder. Beneath the shade of our own vines are we attacked; in our own houses, and on our own lands, is the violence committed against us.

THOMAS PAINE, *Common Sense*

Saturday, September 14, 1776
Midmorning at the Sign of the Cup and Quill

A doleful harbinger, the wool-stuffed mattress thump, thump, thumped, from step to step to step as Anne dragged it down the stairs. "Like moving a dead body," she complained, tugging the unwieldy thing the last few yards across the floor.

"I dinna think it'll fit." Sally eyed the mattress as she finagled the sugar chest into the storage closet beneath the stairs. "There is not a square inch to spare in here."

The women managed to squash the mattress in nonetheless. Sally put her weight against the door so Anne could thread a padlock through the hasp and lock it with the corresponding key on her ring. They pushed the big cabinet back into its spot, concealing the door's existence.

"If we're lucky," Sally said, wiping her hands on her apron, "the lobsterbacks willna think to look behind the cabinet."

"If we're lucky," Anne said, "Washington won't order the whole city put to the torch, as they say he is wont to do, rather than leave it for the British."

Sally sighed. "I'll put a lock on the kitchen door anyway, for whatever good it might do."

Anne spun in a slow circle on one heel, going over the checklist in her mind. All linens and valuable furnishings were stowed under lock and key. All the doors and shutters were latched secure. The pushcart and two rucksacks were packed and waiting by the front door.

"I suppose we're ready." Anne flopped down in a chair, scrunching her nose upon viewing her shoes poking out from her hems.

It was a fifteen-mile trek on the Post Road to cross over to the mainland by King's Bridge. Boats willing to take passengers upriver were few and far between these days, and they might well have to foot the additional thirty-five miles all the way to Peekskill. Anne packed her pretty French heels away, and borrowed a sensible pair of brown shoes from Sally—low flat heels with squared toes, secured with a wide strap and buckle.

"Blech!"

Sally tossed their straw hats on the tabletop, and pulled up a chair. "The baker's boy just popped his head over the fence. Quakenbos will be by within the hour to fetch us along."

Anne nodded. "Then we will have to bid farewell to the Cup and Quill . . ."

The days since the army's retreat from Long Island had whipped by faster than a hurricane wind. The coffeehouse had been filled to capacity morning, noon and night with vanquished, exhausted soldiers in need of a hot meal, and some respite from defeat and the wet weather. Anne and Sally flung open the doors to all comers, and without charge offered cups of chicory coffee and liberty tea, bowlfuls of porridge and heartfelt smiles. Even penny-pinching Quakenbos handed out loaves of fresh-baked bread—everyone doing their part to bolster the sad wreck of an army that had stumbled up from the ferry landing.

"I still dinna see why we have to leave," Sally grumbled. "Washington's made a mess of it. Our soldiers are deserting in droves, our army is in shambles, and the English have all but won the war anyway."

"I don't want to go to Peekskill any more than you do, Sally, but it is just too dangerous for us to stay here. David would want for us to go."

Sally pursed her lips. Digging in her pocket, she produced David's last letter. Unfolding it on the tabletop, she traced a fingertip across the words, as if she would be able to divine her man's whereabouts and his well-being by some magical transmission. *"I live to be together with you once again . . ."* her voice wavering a bit as she read the line aloud for the hundredth time.

It verily broke Anne's heart to see her friend in such despair. Sally seemed to fight tears every minute of every day since Mr. Gourley had delivered the letter and the horrible telling of David's being marooned in enemy territory.

Sally moved easily from tears to rage. She scooped the page up and shoved the letter back into her pocket, saying for about the thousandth time, "The stupid gowk—risking all for the sake of that damn horse!"

Like a china plate balanced on the sharp point of a needle, Sally teetered from worry, to anger, to desolation, and back to worry— ready to fall and shatter into shards at any moment. Anne tried to be a strong shoulder for Sally to lean on, but as each day wore on, without any word of her brother's fate, she, too, found it difficult to maintain her stoic optimism.

General Washington had ordered all New York citizens to evacuate two days before, but Anne and Sally did not join the latest exodus. Holding out hope that David might yet show up among the soldiers coming through their door, they kept on brewing coffee and baking scones, denying the reality of their tenuous situation. The endless work served a dual purpose—a welcome distraction from wondering and worrying, and as an excuse to avoid heeding the order to evacuate.

Anne knew the situation had become untenable the moment she heard Walter Quakenbos pounding on their door that morning. The Continental Army was abandoning the city, and the baker allowed them three hours to gather their things, if they meant to travel along with him. Anne felt she had no choice. She and Sally prepared for the trip they had for so long resisted.

"Duncan MacBryde stopped by, and I tolt him we were off to Peekskill."

"Good," Anne said. "When David rejoins his regiment, Duncan will pass on the word and he will know that we are safe."

There was a knock at the door.

"There's Quakenbos . . ."

Anne glanced around her shop. "Time to bid farewell to the Cup and Quill."

Both women were slow to their feet. Anne reached for her hat.

A second round of knocking threw Sally into a snit. "We hear ye, auld man, we're comin', aye?" She slid the bolts, and swung open the door. "My God!" she shrieked, taking a step back, her mouth formed a perfect *O*.

Hunched together, Jack and Titus pushed past her. With hands linked to form a seat, they carried David straight up the stairs. "We're putting him in the old master's bedchamber!" Titus called over his shoulder.

The women scrambled after them. Anne skirted around with the key to unlock the door to the room. "Set him on the floor for now— we'll have to bring up a mattress and bed linen . . ."

"He's taken a ball to his leg and shoulder," Titus explained as he and Jack lowered their charge to the floor with much gentleness, helping him to sit propped in the corner. Sally dropped to David's side, her eyes brimming. Brows knit, she pressed the back of her hand to his forehead, then to his cheek.

"He's been fevering." Jack rubbed the circulation back into his arms. "I wish we could have brought him home sooner, but British warships kept us from the river."

"The trip was not an easy one," Titus added. "I'm afraid David's worse for it."

"I'm fine . . ." David said, with a weak smile. "Happy to be home, thanks to these two miscreants."

His right calf was wrapped in a rusty bandage stained bright and wet with red, and his left arm tied up in a sling fashioned with wide strips torn from Jack's green weskit. Anne judged David had lost at least a stone in weight, if not more. The sight of her younger brother so ill and damaged caused her heart to wither. *He is so very pale and wan . . .* Reminding her of her Jemmy in those last, terrible days.

Sally took David's hand and pressed it to her heart. She was smiling.

"Take a good look, Jack," Titus said. "Miss Sally Tucker is struck dumb."

Jack laughed. "I never thought to see the day."

"How did you find him?" Anne asked. "Where . . . ?"

"David can tell you himself, for we've not the time to linger," Jack said, with a wave. "Fare thee well, Captain. We leave you in the best of hands."

Titus and Jack ran down the stairs, and Anne followed after them. "Wait . . . how can we thank you . . ."

Ever-practical Titus asked, "Do you have any food?"

She pulled a covered basket from the goods piled in the pushcart, offering the food Sally had prepared for their trip. "Picnic fare— bread . . . dried beef . . ."

"Ah! This is perfect, Mrs. Anne."

"I wish we could stay"—Jack shoved the loaf of bread inside his shirt—"but the British have landed at Kip's Bay and routed our forces once again."

Anne nodded. "So the Redcoats *are* on our doorstep . . ."

Jack pointed to the cart. "You'll have to postpone your trip until we can figure a way to get your brother back to his regiment."

"The army is pulling back to the high ground at Harlem. We have to catch up before we're cut off." Titus took a bite from a chunk of shortbread, rewrapped it in newsprint and stuffed it into his pocket. "And there are a few of them Redcoat officers I'd rather not bump into."

"Wait. Just wait—please . . ." Anne ran back to unlock the kitchenhouse door. She returned, offering Titus a bottle. "Take it . . . I wish there was more I could do . . ."

"West Indies Rum!" Titus waggled his brows and showed the bottle to Jack.

Jack slapped his friend on the back. "Let's go . . ."

Like a nor'easter wind, the two of them blew out as swiftly as they had blown in. Anne stood tottering in the wake of their departure, waving and watching from the doorway as they disappeared around the corner.

She heaved a sigh and leaned back against the wide doorframe, reeling. In mere minutes her world was once again turned upside down—but she had to admit, she was filled with joy for it. Her brother was rescued from the enemy's grasp, and was brought home to where he could be cared for properly, and they had Jack Hampton and Titus Gilmore to thank for it.

Just as she was about to shut the door, Jack came pounding back down the lane. Skittering to a halt, he pressed a hand to the doorframe above her head, leaning in to catch his wind.

The Spaniard beard she'd heard tell of must have been recently shorn, the lower half of his face a shade lighter than the rest. Hatless, with dark hair loose and tangled, wearing a belted shirt and boots, he looked ready for adventure. She wanted to reach up and brush fingertips to his stubble-rough cheek—she wanted to go with him.

"Annie—I don't know when I'll see you next . . . and though you consider me of no account and a rogue—I need you to know this . . ." He fiddled at his collar and pulled forth his half-crown from the Bowling Green fence—with a hole bored through it fastened to a leather thong tied around his neck. "I am always your true and constant friend."

Anne laughed. Digging into her pocket, she showed him the matching half she carried.

"I am your friend as well . . ."

Jack took her by the hands, and kissed her most tenderly on the lips.

"Hey! Jack!" Titus whistled and shouted from the end of the lane. "Will you come on?"

Jack grasped her by the shoulders. "Listen to me, Annie . . ." Two furrows creased the bridge of his nose, his eye intent. "When the Redcoats occupy the city, you must be very careful to keep your brother hidden and secret—the nature of his wounds will betray him at once as a Patriot. I have seen how they take care of their prisoners, and David will not survive it."

With one last, quick kiss and squeeze, Jack ran to catch up with Titus. At the corner he turned and shouted. "Be very careful, Annie! *Be a Tory!*"

ಧಿ ಧಿ ಧಿ

"Widow Merrick! *Widow Merrick!*"

Anne flung open the shutters and leaned out the window. Walter Quakenbos and an overladen, horse-drawn cart filled the narrow lane in front of her shop.

Looking up, the baker waved and shouted, "Come and join us, Mrs. Merrick. We are ready to depart!"

"I'm afraid we aren't able to travel with you today, Mr. Quakenbos."

"Don't be foolish now, there's no time to waste . . ."

"Fare well on your journey, Mr. Quakenbos." She waved. "Sally and I are staying put."

"But, Mrs. Merrick, the city is deserted. Only the most scurrilous and desperate remain. And you will be at their mercy . . ."

"All the same, sir, we will not leave the Cup and Quill. Best of luck to you on your journey!" She closed the shutters, and went back to help Sally make up the bed for David.

"Why did ye not tell the man our David's been returned?"

Anne stuffed a pillow into a slip. "We do not need to broadcast our business to the street."

"Aye . . ." Sally nodded. "Yer a wise woman, Annie."

Anne built a fire in the stove and heated what was left of their water supply. Between the two of them, they were able to settle David onto the bed. They gave him a sponge bath, a good dose of willowbark tea for his fever, and re-dressed his wounds. Comfortable in clean linen and a soft mattress, an exhausted David dozed off.

"His wounds dinna seem to be festering," Sally said, as they walked down the stairs. "The lads took good care of him, but we must be mindful of that fever. Who's to know what manner of poison the English monsters dip their bullets into?"

The women evaluated the food supply and decided to use dried beef and root vegetables from the garden to cook a fortifying broth. Anne emptied the cart they'd only just packed, and with her empty buckets left for the tea-water pump.

She pushed the cart up Queen Street, feeling as if she'd been transported to some strange and foreign city. Every single shop and business concern along the way was locked up tight with windows shuttered. Usually crowded with fluttering laundry, the empty clotheslines strung from building to building crisscrossed overhead like the rigging on an anchored brigantine.

It was the oddest sensation—broad daylight, and Anne Merrick traveled over a mile to the pump, not once crossing paths with another living soul. Without any of the other city sounds to blend in with, wooden wheels clattering on the cobbles resounded like a hard stick dragged along a picket fence. The city was deserted, but Anne had never felt so exposed.

She worked the pump handle in a hurry, the shrill squawk of it echoing in empty Chatham Square, alerting anyone within earshot to her presence. A little spotted hound with funny, floppy ears was drawn by the sound, running up to lap at the puddle collected under the faucet. Anne filled all six of her buckets to the brim. Wasting no time, she hoisted them into the cart and headed back home at a right smart clip.

As she rattled along, toward the crossing at Maiden Lane, her ears perked to something heard over the noise of her wheels. Anne slowed to a halt—

A hammer?

Not exactly a hammer, but before she could define it, the pounding ceased, and she could hear indistinct voices mingled with the sound of shattering glass.

Be careful, Annie . . .

She took a deep breath, putting the initial, visceral desire to take off running like a mad woman in check. Up ahead, what looked to be white rabbits hopped across the intersection. Squinting, she raised a hand to shade her eyes . . .

Kerchiefs?

It was—five handkerchiefs, caught on a breeze, tumbling along the cobbles toward the Fly Market. As quietly as she could, Anne wheeled her cart into a narrow gangway between two buildings and went to peek around the corner, down Maiden Lane.

Land pirates!

Anne's heart jammed into her throat. Three doors down, a gang of brigands had broken into Van De Meer's Dry Goods. Four boys ran in and out of the shop with armloads of plundered goods—bolts of fabric, reels of ribbon, towels and handkerchiefs—dumping their ill-gotten gains into a brewer's wagon waiting in the middle of the street, and guarded by three older men wearing swords and pistols.

"Gorblimey!" one of the men swore and flailed his arms as a gust of wind sent his tricorn tumbling down the street.

Greedyguts!

Her stomach churned at the sight of the ugly pink scars on his head—the very same foul man who would have left her murdered months before.

"Move yer arse, ye wee shit-sack, and fetch my hat." Greedyguts gave one of the boys a shove and a none-too-gentle kick in the pants.

"Why fret fer that auld hat with the hatter's shop right 'round the corner on Queen Street?" one of his cohorts questioned.

"Heigh-ho, me matey, right you are!" Greedyguts brightened.

"It's off to the hatter with us!" He joined the other two, pulling at the harness yoke like human draft animals, to roll the heavy wagon down the street.

Anne looked up at the wooden sign swaying overhead. DIBBLEE'S FINE HATS, it read on one side, a black cocked hat with flowing red feather painted on the other. Heart pounding, she ran back to the gangway where she'd stashed her cart. Pulling the barrow deeper into the shadows, she ducked down to hide behind it just as the marauders turned the corner.

Crouched hugging knees, with her back pressed up to the brick wall of the hatter's shop, Anne concentrated on making herself small. There was no need to risk raising her head a few inches above the buckets in her cart to check on the progress of Greedyguts and his thievish band of rascals. Her ears told her everything she needed to know. The brigands made no secret of their nasty business. They moved up Queen Street toward Chatham Square, breaking into shops and businesses all along the way.

Driven into hiding by the noisy plunderers, the same little dog she'd met at the tea-water pump came scrabbling under her cart, a lovely handkerchief edged in Brussels lace clenched in his teeth, which he relinquished in exchange for sanctuary.

"*You little bandit!*" Anne whispered, stuffing the hanky into her pocket. She settled to sit tailor style, and the dog required no coercion to curl up on her lap. Alternately tracing her finger around the black and brown patches on the dog's white coat, and toying with his floppy black ears, she was happy to have company as she waited the time it took for the thieves' noise to dissipate into silence.

Deeming it safe, Anne set the dog on his feet and ventured out from her hiding place. The marauders had indeed traveled out of sight.

"Time for us to go . . ."

With her cart bounding on the cobblestones, buckets sloshing to and fro, heedless of losing half the water she'd collected, Anne ran full speed the rest of the way home, her newfound friend behind her all the way.

Careening around the corner onto her lane, she slowed to a trot and turned into the open doorway, bumping the cart up and over the threshold. Shooing the dog inside, Anne kicked aside the tin of lead slugs propping the door open, and slammed the door shut, snapping the brass bolts home.

Sally stepped from the kitchenhouse, swiping hair back from her eyes. "Hoy, Annie! I was beginning to worry fer ye . . ."

The dog scurried through the shop, ears flapping, tail wagging, making straight for Sal.

Dropping to her knees, Sally gathered the little dog in her arms, accepting a thorough face licking in the process. "Such a fine wee doggy . . ." She laughed. "Who does she belong to?"

"*He* belongs to us. And he's called Bandit." Anne emptied the buckets of water into the stone-lined cistern built onto the side the kitchenhouse wall. She puzzled the wooden lid into place, eyeing the plume of smoke trailing east from the kitchen chimney. "We'd best put out that fire. I saw a band of brigands tearing up the shops along Queen Street. We do not want to draw their attention."

Sally's smiling face turned grim in an instant. She immediately pulled the kettle cooking over the fire and scattered the embers with a poker. "Ye ken, Annie, if there's one band of evildoers, there are bound to be others."

"We have to be prepared to protect ourselves." Anne went into the shop and swung open the doors on the big cabinet. Standing on a chair, she dug to the back of the topmost shelf, muttering, "I thought I saw . . . ah! Here it is!" She jumped from the chair and carried a flat rectangular box to the nearest table, wiping the dust from the mahogany and brass corner fittings with her apron.

"Old Merrick's pistols," Anne said, flipping the latch to open the case.

The interior was lined with rich green wool. A pair of brass barrel pistols and their necessary accoutrements lay in compartments designed to fit each piece exactly. "He sent to England for these—paid a pretty penny for them, I recall." Anne took up one pistol, surprised by the weight of it.

"It's hard to believe the auld pinchpenny parted with the coin for such lovely things." Sally examined the other gun, admiring the smooth walnut stocks decorated with elaborate silver mounts worked with a pattern of twisting acanthus leaves. "What do ye mean t' do with these?"

"Shoot marauders."

"Yer jokin'!"

"Until the British get here, we are isolated in a lawless city, and we have to be prepared to defend ourselves. David will show us how to use these." Anne replaced the pistols and snapped the case shut. "Tonight we'll lock everything up, bring food and drink upstairs and sequester ourselves in David's room for the night. Hopefully, no one will even notice we're here."

When David woke, they propped him up with pillows, and sitting together on Peter Merrick's big bed, all three of them enjoyed a picnic supper of brown bread, cheese, pickle and a drink of cold rosehip tea. Bandit hopped up and lay with his muzzle across David's lap, and they took turns feeding the dog bits of bread and cheese.

Though feverish, David was rested, fed and in good spirits, and he agreed it might be useful for both women to know their way around a gun. "Bring those pistols over, Anne, time for a lesson."

She laid the open case across David's lap and he examined the weapons. "Dueling pistols—very clean—I'd wager Merrick never once fired them."

Anne and Sally had a giggle at the notion of Peter Merrick engaged in a duel.

David flipped the lid on the kidney-shaped gunpowder flask and held it to his nose. "Powder's still good . . ." He raised the hammer on the pistol and shaved a curl from his thumbnail on the flint, satisfied with the quality of the edge.

"There's a supply of lead balls in this box." Anne pointed to one of two compartments built into the case.

"And wee greasy bits of cloth in the other," Sally volunteered.

"Patches," David corrected, setting the gun down. "I can't do much with one hand—you both must follow instructions. This is the charger—" He pried a small brass tube up and handed it to Anne. "It holds the proper measure for these guns. Fill it with powder."

Sally helped Anne pour a gray stream to the top of the measure.

"Bring the hammer back to half-cock—hear how it clicked once? Now pour it down the barrel—good, good—center one of those greased patches over the muzzle of the gun and press a ball to it, pushing it into the barrel with your finger." David handed his sister the brass-tipped walnut rod. "Use the ramrod and seat the ball firm to the powder."

"That's a tight fit," Anne complained, jamming the load down the barrel.

"Store your ramrod—without it, your gun is useless. Now flip open the frizzen."

Anne thumbed open the brass plate covering the shallow pan.

David handed Anne the powder flask. "Tap just three or four grains into the pan. Mind not to overcharge your pistol, or you'll end up blowing your own hand off. Close the pan and your pistol is loaded. When you want to shoot it, pull the hammer back to full cock, aim and pull the trigger."

"I never knew it was so simple." Sally filled the charger, and began to load the other pistol.

David sank back into his pillows, his face flush with fever. "Pistols have a short range. If you want to put a hole in someone, you'd better be within several yards."

Anne took the loaded pistol to the window. Extending her arm, she aimed at the building across the way. "Oh, Lord! Come, Sally— grab hold of my skirt." She set the gun down on the bedside table and ran back to the window, climbing up to stand on the sill to better her view.

"What is it, Annie? Brigands?"

"Of a sort—" She hopped down. "A Union Jack flying from the staff at Fort George. The British are here."

꿁 꿁 꿁

SALLY carried a pierced tin lantern to light their way through the shop as they lugged the ladder from the garden to the front door. Setting her end down to unlatch the door, Sally peered up and down the lane.

"All clear . . ."

The ladder thumped loud as they propped it against the face of the building, causing both women to hunch their shoulders and wince.

"I'll go up—I'm stronger." Sally pushed Anne out of the way and climbed the angled steps.

Sporadic gunfire popped in the distance. "That's close by." Shifting from one foot to the other, Anne kept a hand on the pistol weighing heavy her pocket, the bulge a comfort while keeping a look out as Sally fiddled with the hooks and chains.

"Och, it's all a bloody tangle—I need some light . . ."

Anne opened the door on the lantern and held it over her head, aiming the beam at the shop sign. "Does that help?"

"Aye . . ."

More shots rang out—accompanied by shouting and shoe leather pounding on cobblestones.

"Hurry, Sal . . ."

"Quit yer jiggling . . . I'm almost . . . ah!"

Sally succeeded in disengaging the chains from the iron bracket. Anne set the lantern aside to take the unwieldy round placard from Sally and roll it inside the doorway. Sally scrambled down, and they slid the ladder into the shop and locked the door.

Sally heaved a breath. "Och, it's a good thing ye remembered th' sign."

"Um-hmm . . ." Anne aimed the light on the shop sign, the word *liberty* even larger and more conspicuous at such a close proximity. "Not exactly what we want to advertise these days, is it?"

CHAPTER THIRTEEN

❧❧

*The laying a Country desolate with Fire and Sword, declaring
War against the natural rights of all Mankind, and extirpating the
Defenders thereof from the Face of the Earth, is the Concern of every
Man to whom Nature hath given the Power of feeling . . .*

THOMAS PAINE, *Common Sense*

Friday, September 20, 1776
On the Way Home from the Bear Market

THEIR meager pantry had been depleted over the course of the past week, and when she heard tell of traders at the market, Anne exhumed the strongbox from under her bed. Tossing a wad of useless Continental currency into the box, she pocketed a handful of guineas and shillings she'd stashed away when Washington's Army had come to town.

Bandit joined her on the long trek across town to the Bear Market on the Hudson, to find the stalls filled with upstate and cross-river farmers and merchants hawking their wares. Droves of eager customers paying in good old British coin crowded the aisles. A great variety of provisions were on exhibit—an abundance of riches Anne had not witnessed since before the Patriot army was in command of the city.

Commerce is lured by silver and gold . . .

So many hungry customers with ready coin drove market prices high, but Anne did not stint. She was more than willing to pay the price for best quality, for Jack would be coming soon to rescue them all, and David must be fit and ready to travel.

She pushed a full cart back home, more than pleased with her acquisitions. Cornmeal, wheat flour, salt pork, coffee berries, sausages, eggs, cheese and butter—the kind of fresh food her brother needed to recover his health. Anne suffered a small pang of guilt for the pound sack of black bohea in her cart, but it had been so long since she'd had a proper cup of tea, she could not resist the aroma wafting from the tea merchant's stand.

Very Torylike, drinking tea . . .

That morning, when British dragoons came marching down the lane, knocking on her door with the pommels of their swords, Anne tried not to panic, but she was quite terrified David would be arrested and carried off to some awful prison. She envisioned herself and Sally set upon the street, their home and possessions confiscated by order of the King.

Armed with pistols, Sally and David waited upstairs, while Anne answered the door with a gentle widow's countenance, and an offer of refreshment.

Be a Tory, she thought, knees quaking, as she invited the Redcoat officers inside to take a seat at a table.

Bemoaning the lack of tea, she offered cups of chicory coffee and coarse corn muffins with peach preserves, and proceeded to weave a Tory tale of woe designed to tug at any Englishman's heartstrings. Beginning with a homily to her dearly departed, staunch Loyalist husband, she gave a dramatic recitation of the harm she'd endured at the hands of the demon Liberty Boys—the blackguard rebels who put her livelihood to ruin, and destroyed the very press and types she used to extol the King's Majesty, and defend Crown interests.

Quite a performance . . .

Not only did Captain Blankenship praise her bravery and her fortitude, he told Anne about the Bear Market in progress, and gave her a length of red ribbon to wear. "To show your loyalty to our King," he said. The Redcoats bid her good day, never knowing an armed rebel officer lay in a bed situated just above their heads, and they moved on without painting the dreaded "G.R." on her door, indicating her property confiscated by the King for service to the Crown.

Anne found great wisdom in Jack's command to "Be a Tory." In truth, women had it far easier when it came to shifting loyalties. No oath or promise of service demanded—only a few inches of red ribbon and a pin required for a total transformation.

An instant Tory.

Like a figure carved on the prow of a ship, Bandit sat at the head of the cart, proudly perched upon the firkin of cider she'd purchased. Nose to the wind, silly ears flapping, he sported a red ribbon collar matching the red ribbon rosette Anne pinned to her straw hat.

"Tory doggy," Anne teased, when she tied the collar to his neck. Bandit growled, and spun round and round, making himself dizzy trying to tear it off.

She pulled her cart to a stop at Broad Way. The street was choked with a reverse exodus—wagons hauling supplies, furnishings and many Loyalist New Yorkers driven from their homes now returning in happy triumph. Loyalists seeking sanctuary from rebellious strongholds like Boston and Philadelphia also flocked to the city for protection.

"Surrounded we are . . ." Anne muttered. Bandit agreed, beating a tune on the little keg with his tail.

She dove into the fray, wriggling her cart through the tangle to travel down Fair Street.

The city had also transformed in an instant. In the seven days since the British began their occupation, people poured in on the Post Road, and ferried in from the hundreds of boats anchored in the harbors. A whole new influx of sailors and soldiers roamed about in packs defined by uniforms different from those she'd become accustomed to, and Anne was learning a whole new set of distinctions.

Crowding the sidewalks along with the multitude of British Redcoats were Scots Highlanders in dark tartan kilts, green-jacketed Brunswickers wearing upright plumes on their caps, and mustachioed Hessian grenadiers in blue jackets and mitered brass helmets topped with a fuzzy red wool ball—the sight of which always sent Bandit into a barking frenzy.

The forlorn clotheslines bridging streets and alleyways were now filled with coats of red, blue and green wool flapping alongside petticoats and nappies. These new occupiers came with families in tow. The nomadic wives and children of officers and enlisted men took up residence in dwellings confiscated by the Crown, and the women now collecting water at the tea-water pump spoke in accents and languages foreign to Anne's ear.

With the population burgeoning, lodgings were quick becoming a scarce commodity, and Anne was beleaguered daily by newcomers in search of rooms to rent. The probability of being forced to quarter British soldiers in her home was high, and the stuff of her most recent nightmare.

Jack will be here soon . . . and then all will be well . . .

Smiling, she turned the corner onto her little lane between Duke and Dock Streets, and skittered to an abrupt halt, causing Bandit to lose his seat and leap from the cart.

She had seen many a G.R. painted on the houses and businesses she passed along the way, but the G.R. on the Quakenbos Bakery door stopped her dead in her tracks.

G.R.—George Rex.

Anne touched her fingertip to the wet black paint.

A few strokes of a brush, and the hard-earned rewards of one man's toil and sweat become the property of another . . .

Anne pulled her cart the few steps to her door, pondering the paint on her finger.

It's not going to be easy, being a Tory.

❧ ❧ ❧

ANNE bolted upright with an indrawn gasp—eyes wide-open.

In two staccato leaps, Bandit bounded from bed to floor, then to the chair she'd left beside the open window. Front paws resting on the sill, he joined the enthusiastic barking and howling chorus disturbing her sleep.

"Shush that noise," Anne moaned and slapped the mattress. "*Come.*"

Bandit continued to bark without even suffering her a sideways glance.

Anne rubbed her eyes and blinked—the portion of sky visible though the window flashed in shades of gold, blue and green. Amber light flickered on her whitewashed walls.

Sally appeared in the doorway with a stubby candle sputtering in a dish, her sleepy-eyed face squashed in squint. "D'ye smell smoke?"

Anne threw back the sheets and ran to the window.

Bandit stopped barking. Sally squeezed in, and the three of them leaned out over the sill.

"What's happening?" David stood with his right shoulder bolstered against the doorframe, his left arm in its sling.

"Whitehall Slip is on fire." Anne pointed toward the East River.

"It looks like the Fighting Cocks Tavern is in flames." Sally pointed straight ahead to the battery.

Anne boosted up to stand on the sill. "Take hold . . ."

Sally grabbed two fistfuls of muslin nightgown.

Bracing one hand to the window frame, toes curled to the edge, Anne leaned way out, straining for a better view to the east. "Something on Cruger's Wharf is alight . . ."

"Three separate fires?" Hopping on one foot, David traveled from doorway to bedstead to chair.

Sally stared out the window, chewing her thumbnail. "D'ye think Washington's spies are putting the whole city to the torch?"

"No." David plopped down in the chair. "Congress expressly forbid it, and the general would never disobey the rule of Congress." Twisting around he pulled up onto one knee to view the scene. "Like most fires, I'd wager these were begat by drunkenness or carelessness."

Anne nodded. "And spread by wind—not spies—look . . ."

Large flaming embers floated up from the fire at the Fighting Cocks. Borne on the breeze from the harbor, they scattered onto the neighboring rooftops. In the blink of an eye, six more buildings were alight.

David shook his head. "This is dangerous. Without a drop of rain in days, cedar roof shakes are as dry as a nun's gusset . . ."

"Brother!" Anne chastised.

"David's right, Annie. The rooftops are so much tinder. This fire's movin' onward with every blast of th' westlin' wind."

David pounded the sill. "Why does no one ring the alarm?"

"Washington took the bells—for cannon." Anne jumped down from her perch.

"Aye, and who's t' know what's become of our lovely fire pumps—gone the way of the bells, no doubt."

Anne shrugged. "The neighborhood men like Quakenbos, who manned the fire brigades and knew to work the pumps, are long gone as well."

The three of them stood in nightclothes, mesmerized by exploding showers of sparks and the growing wall of flames leaping and moving in tall spires. David whistled when the fire swirled in like a flood tide, flowing across Broad Way. "It's a good thing the wind is in our favor . . ."

The silhouetted figures battling the blaze had no success containing it. The breeze drove the fire northwest, and running blocks of property along the tip of the island were engulfed in roaring flames.

Anne left David and Sally at the window, and threw open the lid to the chest at the foot of her bed.

"What are ye about?"

Anne tugged a brown skirt over her nightshift. "I'm going to help."

David said, "Don't be foolish. What can you do to help?"

"Well—I can pass a bucket of water. I can do that."

Sally snatched up her candle. "I'm comin' wi' ye."

David threw up his one good hand. "You're both a pair of idiots."

"You stay with David, Sally." Anne pulled her ink-stained linsey blouse over her head, tucking it into her waistband. "Keep an eye on the fire. If the wind shifts, you may need to evacuate . . ."

David rose on one good foot and hopped to grab hold of the bed-post. "Promise you'll be careful, sister . . ."

"I will."

Anne took a bucket from the kitchen. She heard the mantel clock chime once as Sally bolted the door behind her. One o'clock in the morning, and the southern sky was lit up brighter than a papist church on Christmas Eve. Anne ran parallel to the wall of fire that curved along Broad Street, slowing to a stop when she reached Broad Way. Empty bucket in her fist swinging, she was immobilized by the confused scene, not certain where to go or what to do.

British soldiers were everywhere, forming bucket brigades, evac-uating buildings, herding huddles of stricken women and children dressed in nightclothes and bed caps to the periphery. One company of marines armed with axes and crowbars worked at demolishing a whole row of combustible tenements to create a firebreak. Others worked as litter bearers for the injured.

"Come with me, Mrs. Merrick." A hand slapped her on the back, and the familiar voice added, "They're calling for hands to fill the pumps."

Anne followed Patsy Quinn all the way to where Wall Street met Broad Way. She joined the line transferring water twenty yards from the well on the corner of Wall Street to the fire engine positioned in front of a burning mansion.

A man stood on the top of the engine and aimed the protruding copper tube like a cannon at the uppermost story. Buckets and buckets of water were passed up the line and poured into the reser-voir at the back end of the engine. Six strong-armed men flanking each side moved the crossbar handles up and down, working the pump.

Something was not right. For all the hands and muscle power, they only managed to produce a feeble spurting stream, half the water never even reaching the target.

"Like spitting on a bonfire," Anne said.

Patsy leaned in, passing a bucket. "Be better off pulling out their pizzles and pissing on the fire."

Timbers popped like musket shot, and the structure began to collapse. Brick walls crumbled inward, and in one giant sucking roar the house imploded in a ball of smoke and dust. A great golden plume of embers swirled up into the air, and everyone scattered, running as flaming brands and burning chunks rained down like the storms of hell, bouncing off the cobblestones in miniature glittering explosions.

Bucket in hand, Patsy grabbed Anne by the arm and they ran in a crouch across Broad Way, coughing and choking, raising arms to shield their faces from the intense heat, and the cinders and ash roiling through the air.

Flakes of fire alighted on the pitched roof of neighboring Trinity Church. In no time, flames crawled up toward the tall steeple, gobbling up the cedar shake skin like a swarm of locusts. Anne could not believe the tallest structure in the city was burning like a pine pitch torch. Soon the old stone walls supported a fiery skeleton of beams and rafters, looking much like a burning fist pointing one bony finger to the heavens.

All efforts came to a halt, and all eyes transfixed with a collective indrawn breath on the steeple moving in a slow, graceful list to the west—snapping and cracking—hitting the earth in a booming iridescent puff of debris.

"It's hopeless." Anne fell back against the wall.

A mass of men and women with a gang of children tagging along came bouncing down Broad Way, shouting and shaking fists. At the forefront, pinioned between two large grenadiers, a slight, shirtless man was dragged along, sobbing, "Christ Almighty, it wasn't me! I swear it wasn't me."

The throng fell back as the Redcoats made straight for the burning church. Like watching a macabre shadow play in silhouette, one soldier drove the suspected arsonist to his knees with a brutal musket butt to the head. Taking the stunned man by the limbs, swinging once—twice—they tossed him into the heart of the fire.

To the shrieks of those watching, the man emerged from the fire—a stumbling, howling, keening apparition—smoke rising from the top of his head and from his right leg in flames. Arms outstretched, he lurched forward, steam wafting from the seared flesh covering his shoulders and back. With their relentless bayonets, the Redcoats herded him back, poking and prodding the wailing wretch, forcing him back into the conflagration.

Gagging, Anne could not find a breath. Choking on sick, she hunkered down over the bucket of water Patsy had carried away from the line, splashing the brackish well water on her face. She sucked a mouthful from her cupped hands to wash the sharp taste of burnt hair and scorched flesh from her mouth.

"Feels like I swallowed a spoonful of sand." Patsy squatted down beside Anne, and took a drink. Tearing two wide strips from the hem of her petticoat, she doused them in the bucket, and handed one to Anne. "Tie it on—over your mouth and nose."

A passing Redcoat gave them each a shove with his boot. "Up off yer arses, bawds, and back to the buckets!"

Anne bristled, and rose to give the man a good piece of her mind, but Patsy snatched her by the hand. "Not this night, Mrs. Merrick. Not after how they did that poor fellow."

The west wind swept the fire into the dense maze of wooden tenements behind the churchyard. Anne and Patsy ran past the graveyard and joined the bucket brigades trying to keep the fire from jumping over to Lumber Street.

All nearby buildings were being evacuated, and Anne passed buckets to Patsy, watching several hundred rebel prisoners stumble out from Van Cortlandt's Sugar House to be hustled into a double-file column by several companies of armed guards.

"There are some customers of mine in those lines . . ." Anne whispered, with a nod, swinging a heavy leather bucket into Patsy's hand.

"I know some of 'em as well . . ." Patsy waggled her brow. "Customers."

Anne stiffened. This woman *knows* Jack.

Sordid images flashed through her mind, knocking the wind from her as if she'd fallen from a great height. She tugged at the swath of fabric stifling her breath. In the chaos, it was easy to forget this friendly, helpful girl with soot smudged across her forehead was the same exotic temptress she saw Jack kiss so dearly—the cause of much heartache.

In a sudden tumult, a prisoner broke free from the column, running in a mad tear toward the Hudson. Muskets propped to shoulders in an instant, and before the escapee could put twenty yards between himself and his captors, he was shot down.

"Tim!" a voice cried in anguish.

A company of Redcoats rushed in to help the guards struggling to keep the agitated prisoners in check. Patsy took off running to help the fallen man lying facedown in the dirt road, and Anne chased after her. Patsy fell to her knees and turned him over.

Anne groaned, dropping down beside Patsy. "Naught but a boy . . ."

A gaping tear in his neck pulsed a red river of blood. Like the trout Anne's father would pull from his hook and toss onto the shore, the boy stared up with round eyes, mouth opening and closing. Gulping for air, he was drowning on blood flooding into his broken windpipe.

"Oh, Tim . . ." Patsy crooned, brushing the hair from his forehead. She stroked his freckled cheek once—twice—and he died.

The sergeant of the guards stood over them and prodded Patsy with the bayonet fixed to his musket. "On yer feet."

She stood, tottering in the dancing light from the fire, her soot-smudged face muddy with tears.

"Do you know this boy?" The sergeant was joined by a grim cohort of regulars, jostling into a ragged circle around Patsy, Anne and the dead boy. "Speak up—what's he to you?"

A hawk-nosed corporal with a face terribly pitted by the pox grabbed Patsy by the arm and gave her a shake. "Answer, you rebel bitch whore!"

Still on her knees, Anne cried out, "I beg of you, Sergeant—the girl meant only to—"

"And you"—the sergeant turned his musket toward Anne, lifting her chin with the tip of his bayonet—"you speak when spoken to . . ."

"Sergeant Frye! Put by your weapon at once!"

Edward Blankenship pushed into the circle, and the company snapped to attention. The captain rushed to help Anne to her feet. "Have you been harmed, Widow Merrick?"

"No, but who's to know what our fates might have been if you hadn't come along." Anne glared at the sergeant in righteous Tory indignation. "I never expected to suffer by the hands of the King's men, as I've suffered by the rule of the Liberty Boys . . ."

The captain turned on Frye. "What purpose is served here, Sergeant?"

"They was giving succor and aid to the enemy, sir."

"Blubberin' over him," the corporal added.

Anne looked down and heaved a sigh, not even trying to control her tears. "This 'enemy,'" she said, "is but a boy—brought down and dying when the girl and I acted on the instinct of soft hearts. Truly, our only thought was to ease a poor soul onward, as good Christians are wont to do. I will allow we shed tears, for we are unused to schoolboys dying before our very eyes."

"Soft hearts . . ." Blankenship repeated, and it was as if he just noticed the dead body lying in a pool of blood, "a luxury soldiers can ill afford. I'm afraid hearts hardened by battle view the world in a different light. These men have seen the damage wrought by rifles in the hands of schoolboys such as this."

There was an earnestness in his speech Anne did not expect, and the soldiers all nodded in appreciation of his words.

"Though I deplore how you have been treated here, it saddens me to hear you equate my men with rebels of any sort. I know them to be exemplary soldiers—solid and true to the service of our King, and I know they regret their actions in this instance."

"Captain's right—we're sorry, mum." Frye volunteered an apology, and the rest of the men mumbled the same.

Anne nodded in acceptance.

"Back to your posts—move those prisoners to the Commons," Blankenship ordered. "And Frye—see to the boy's proper burial." The captain turned and bowed to Anne. "If you will permit me, Widow Merrick, I will see you to your door."

Anne looked to Patsy. "Will you be alright?"

"I'm fine." She nodded. "Shaken, but still whole."

Patsy lingered, watching Anne take the handsome captain's arm, and stroll away from the fire, turning the corner to Broad Way.

The sergeant set to barking out orders. "Pennyman! Kirby! Ye heard the captain—proper burial for this rebel." Spotting Patsy still dawdling, he jerked his musket and growled, "Off with you, imp— caused us enough trouble this night, ye have. Off with you, now."

Ambling away, Patsy untied the mask from her neck, and used it to wipe her face. After a few steps, she did an about turn to see two soldiers carry poor Tim across the road, and heave him into the flames.

᭡ ᭡ ᭡

ANNE woke the next day as filthy as she'd ever been in her entire life.

The washbasin in her room was definitely not up to the herculean task she required of it. Down to the kitchenhouse she went. Standing in the tin laundry tub, she gave herself an all-over sudsing using a scrub brush and her last bar of French lavender soap. Sally emptied three pails of water over her head to rinse her clean.

With fresh clothes, a splash of lavender water and damp braids wrapped in a crown around her head, Anne claimed, "I am fit to face the world again, and I'm off to see what's left of it."

"Yer brother will be spittin' tacks when he finds yer gone after being out all night long," Sally warned.

"The baker is no longer here to bring us the news. We need to know what's happening."

"Who'd have thought we'd ever miss auld Quakenbos?" Sally looped a market basket over Anne's arm. "Haste ye back."

Anne walked along Broad Street, shaking a head at the one short city block separating the Cup and Quill from utter carnage. The devastation was epic—from Broad Way west to the Hudson, and from the Bowling Green, north, all the way to the lawn of King's College—a full quarter of the city destroyed. Anne wandered in a parade of people bewildered by the vast landscape of charred ruins, crumbling masonry walls and chimneys.

Incidences pointing to the fickle vagaries of the wind were made evident in the light of day. The mansions at #1 and #3 Broad Way were intact. Diverted by the graveyard at Trinity Church, the fire passed over Van Cortlandt's Sugar House and a group of nearby tenements was also spared. St. Paul's Chapel and many of the houses facing Broad Way along the more northerly stretch survived the holocaust untouched.

Anne joined a small crowd gathered at the corner of Wall Street, pondering both the void in the patch of sky Trinity Church used to occupy, and the neighboring unscathed oasis of green grass and peaceful tombstones still surrounded by white pickets.

"These devils certainly considered the weather in deciding when and how to fire the city . . ." a stout gentleman opined, waving around his silver-tipped cane. "The wind was a friend to the rebels who wrought this havoc . . ."

Anne interrupted. "Has arson been proven, sir?"

"Madam . . ." The man looked down his nose at her. "The fire originated in three separate locations taking best advantage of an opportune wind. The city's bells were removed. The fire engines had all been tampered with and rendered useless. That villain there was apprehended for cutting the handles from buckets . . ." He pointed with his cane to a lamppost ahead where a dark-haired man with wrists bound back was hung by his heels—throat slashed. "Others were found with incendiary materials. I have it on good account that arrests have been made. A spy who's admitted to working for Mr. Washington has already been sentenced and is due to hang at the Commons this morning."

Hanky pressed to nose, Anne trailed after the curious crowd going to ogle the body at the lamppost. It was impossible to identify the face caked in coagulated blood and writhing with green blowflies. A boy ran up on a dare and gave the corpse a poke, sending the mass of shiny flies buzzing into the air, and the corpse swinging. Relieved the face did not belong to Jack Hampton, Anne stumbled from the sight, gagging from the putrid stink.

Another spy due to hang this morning . . . She gripped tight the handle of her basket. A sick thunderhead of dread began to roll up from her gut and pound in her head with every step to the Commons.

Barricades and cannon had been cleared away, and a row of marquee tents was erected across the wide end of the green. She had not participated in the most recent Loyalist celebration when the Redcoats cut down the hated Liberty Pole. Like missing Trinity's steeple, there was something unsettling about the Commons without the pole.

No more than a stone's throw from where the Liberty Pole once stood, a new gallows—the timbers pale and raw—loomed, almost centered on the green. The jutting limb of the gibbet was wound around with a hempen rope, dangling in a noose. She skirted along the scattering of soldiers and citizens watching a mulatto man position a horse-drawn cart beneath the noose. Steering toward two friendly looking starched linen caps, Anne took a stand beside a chubby Dutch *vrouw* and her skinny daughter.

Two men emerged from one of the marquee tents—a thin man in a brown frock coat leading a prisoner by the tether bound about his wrists.

Not Jack. She heaved a sigh. Anne did not know the spy, but the brown-coated man was familiar, and she asked the Dutch woman, "Who is that?"

"Ze new provost marshall—Cunningham."

A pinheaded, pinched-faced Tory sniveler, Patsy had called him—the same man they'd seen tarred and feathered beneath the Liberty Pole, and beaten to within an inch of his life for refusing to damn the King.

The captured spy was led to the gallows. The mulatto climbed onto the cart and hoisted the bound man up to stand on it. After threading the noose over the prisoner's head, the mulatto jumped down, took up a stiff riding quirt and waited, muscular arms folded across his burly chest.

The condemned man stood tall and proud—sun shining on his golden hair—and nary a glimmer of fear or doubt in his bright blue eyes. This man was a convicted Patriot spy, but watching him face death, Anne was somehow reminded of Captain Blankenship. The two were very alike in looks and spirit. *They could be mistaken for brothers.*

"For crimes of High Treason . . ." Cunningham continued to read the sentencing order in a stumbling, mumbling monotone. "Sentenced to suffer death and be hanged without mercy . . ." When finished, he folded the sheet into his pocket and said, "If you've any last words, speak 'em now."

The brave man looked out on the congregation. With gentle dignity, and in a fine, clear voice he said, "I only regret that I have but one life to lose for my country."

Cunningham's face screwed into a scowl. He waved his hand in disgust and barked, "Richmond!"

His assistant whipped the horse with a snap of the quirt.

The cart lurched forward.

Mercifully, the man's neck snapped at the drop, and there was no awful dance at the end of the rope, no strangled, prolonged suffering. And oddly, there were no cheers or sneers.

Anne stood stunned by this brave Patriot's eloquent last words. The short, simple sentence struck like an arrow to her heart—delving deep—piercing her very core. Squeezing the handle of her basket in both hands, and wavering to and fro in unison with the gentle sway of the Patriot's body against the blue sky, she sent up a prayer for the keeping of his everlasting soul.

A short queue formed at the right of the gibbet. The Dutch woman pulled her daughter to the fore. Snatching up the dead man's hand, she rubbed it over the large goiter protruding from her girl's throat. The touch of a hanged man's hand was said to cure growths, tumors and sores of the skin, and desperate, afflicted people paid in good silver for such a miracle.

Cunningham will reap a tidy profit.

Anne hurried away from the Commons. She could not allow the memory of the man's sacrifice to his country to be marred by such irreverent spectacle. So inspired by the unnamed Patriot's bravery and the words he spoke, Anne felt fortunate to have borne witness to his death.

He will receive the attention of angels . . .

Turning onto Duke Street, Anne saw Sally careening down the lane, dodging around startled people and pigs, her cap askew, skirts clutched in fists.

Breaking into a run, Anne met Sally midway. She tossed aside the empty basket, and clasped her friend by the arms. "Is it David?"

"Na . . ." Sally gasped, trying to catch her wind. She leaned in and whispered, "It's Jack!"

ॐ ॐ ॐ

With Sally and Bandit fast on her heels, Anne took the stairs two at a time and skittered to a stop at the doorway of her room.

"You've come!"

Jack and Titus were both on their knees helping David fit his injured leg into a boot. Jack looked up and flashed a smile. Bandit ran round in circles barking as Jack swept Anne up in a wild, laughing embrace that lifted her from the floor, swinging her around twice before setting her back on her feet.

"I'm so happy to see you." Breathless, Anne beamed. "Even if you smell like fish . . ."

"I'm supposed to smell like fish—" Jack pounded his chest. "I'm a fisherman."

Sally laughed. "Tha's the disguise, Annie—the three of them—smelly fishermen!"

The men were all dressed alike—stained, coarse linen shirts and baggy, striped trousers tucked into cuffed seaboots. There was a red knitted cap for Titus, a blue one for David, and a grimy checked kerchief tied round Jack's neck.

"Practice with boots on and take a turn around the room." Titus helped David to stand, and walked with him for every step with an encouraging, "That's the way, Captain . . ."

David braved what Anne knew to be excruciating pain, and pulled his bad leg along in a faltering, uneven stride. With Titus's support, he stumbled from one side of the room to the other, and then fell onto the chair in a heap.

Jack exclaimed, "Perfect!"

"The brace inside the boot helps." David forced a smile.

Anne sank down on the bed. "Are you all mad? He's nowhere near ready—look at him . . . eight steps and he's as pale as a sheet . . ."

"Too soon to be puttin' any weight on yer leg . . ." Sally said, with a shake of her head. "Stumblin' around like a drunk . . ."

"Three *drunken* fishermen to be exact." Jack sat beside Anne. "David only has to walk a single block to our dory moored at the Fishmarket Wharf. Once we get him in the boat, he has but to sit back and watch us pull oars."

"I can do it." David nodded. "I have to do it—I'm a danger to us all if I stay here."

Sally stood beside David, stroking his hair. "But why not just wait until dark and be carried down to the boat?"

"The roads and waterways are heavily patrolled. There are hundreds of navy ships in the East River ready to blow any odd boat skulking around out of the water—especially after dark. There's no way around it," Jack said, with a shake of his head. "We have to travel by day, and have some good reason for being on the river."

Titus pulled his cap over his head. "Now's our best chance to get your brother to safe ground, Mrs. Anne. The fire last night has the Redcoats tying the city up tighter than old Merrick's purse strings."

Sally cocked her head, and gave Jack the gimlet eye. "Did th' pair o' ye start the fire?"

Titus laughed. "Naw, Sal, we didn't start it . . ."

"Only because someone beat us to it," Jack added.

"We have to get going . . ." Titus said, pulling his cap on. "It's a long, roundabout course we have to row, and we'll need every bit of daylight."

"Right you are. Time's a-wasting." Jack plucked up a gunnysack, and stuffed David's clothing and shoes into it.

Anne rose to her feet, giving Sally a nudge. "Better gather our things . . ."

"We're not goin' with 'em, lass. Not this time."

"What!?" Anne looked to Jack, blinking fast to allay her welling tears.

"Sorry, Annie." Jack dropped the sack and took her by the hands. "Our little dory is just too small—"

"Oh . . ." Anne chewed her bottom lip.

"You'll be safe enough here once I'm gone," David said.

"Right . . ." She gave Jack's hands a squeeze and shake, and dove under the bed to fish out the strongbox. Scooping up a handful of coins and notes, she shoved them into her brother's hand. "Take it . . . you'll need it . . ."

"No, Annie . . . you and Sally need it . . ."

"Take it." Anne rumpled his hair like she used to when he was a boy. "Sally and I will earn more . . ."

Sally popped to her feet. "I'll go fix a parcel of food . . ." Bandit scrambled after her.

Titus helped David to his feet. "Let's get you down the stairs now, Captain."

"There's been a chill in the air—he'll need something to keep warm . . ." Anne flipped open the lid to the chest at the foot of the bed and dug out a woolen blanket.

"Give us a moment." Jack waved Titus and David on. "We'll be right down—"

Anne tied several rolls of linen bandages, a small pot of unguent and a packet of willowbark powder into a kerchief and handed the bundle to Jack. "See that he keeps his wounds clean and dressed . . ."

Jack stuffed the blanket and the medicaments into his gunnysack. "You understand, don't you, Anne? It's just too dangerous for you to keep David here any longer . . . if there was a way for us all . . ."

"I know . . . I know . . ." Heaving a sigh, she turned and leaned in, pressing her forehead to his breastbone. "The world's gone upside down, hasn't it?"

Jack rested his chin on the top of her head, and pulled Anne into a bear hug. "I *hate* leaving you behind . . ."

Rocking back and forth, Anne slipped her arms around his waist and turned her head to listen as his heart beat in time with the squeak of the floorboards.

"*C'mon, Jack!*" Titus shouted up from the bottom of the stair.

Anne looked up at Jack with sad eyes. "You'd better go . . ."

Jack buried his nose in her hair, drew a long, deep breath. "My sweet Annie—I'll come back for you. I promise."

"Only promise me you'll be careful . . ." Anne rose up on tiptoes to press a tender, farewell kiss to his lips.

Jack groaned, and the quiet kiss exploded like a sail unfurled in a hurricane wind. Pulling Anne tight, he bent her back in the kind of kiss she'd been dreaming about for weeks. Off balance, feet tangled on the gunnysack, they stumbled, tripped and toppled onto the bed. Anne found herself under Jack, pressed into a froth of petticoats and bed linen.

"*Jaaaaack!*" Titus shouted once again. "*Let's go!*"

"Another promise—" Jack said, a merry sparkle in his brown eyes. "One day, we'll finish this kiss properly." Planting a quick peck on her lips, he leapt to his feet, took Anne by the hand and they raced down to meet the others at the foot of the stairs.

"What were you two up to?" Sally teased, tucking a bundle of food into Jack's gunnysack.

"Not enough," Jack replied.

Titus passed small flask around, each man taking a good swallow and splashing a bit around the ears. "That's the last of your rum, Mrs. Anne."

"Good friend Titus, I don't know how I'll ever repay you." Anne gave him a hug, then turned to kiss her brother on the cheek. "Take care of yourself—and don't be a ninny—give yourself time to heal . . ."

Sally threw her arms around David's neck for one last kiss. "Mind what yer sister just said . . . and send us word, when ye can." She stepped back, sniffing, wiping her eyes on her sleeve. "Take care, lads."

"Listen . . ." Jack grabbed Anne by the shoulders. "A man by the name of Mulligan keeps a tailor shop on Queen Street—call on him for help, should you need it. He's a friend of mine."

Anne nodded, pulled the hanky from her bosom and pressed it to Jack's hand, with a quick kiss. "Till next we meet."

Jack put the hanky to his nose, smiled and tucked the favor inside his shirt.

Sally peeked out the door to make certain there were no Redcoats lurking about. With the all clear, she swung the door full open and the threesome spilled out into the lane, arms about each other's shoulders, stumbling toward the wharf.

Anne and Sally ducked back into the shop and shut the door.

"Well," Anne said, putting fists to hips. "We have our work cut out for us, don't we?"

☙ ☙ ☙

KI-KI-RI-KU-DOO. A five-toed rooster flew up to perch on the ladder leaning up against the shop front, and crow up the sun with great gusto.

The front door swung open and Sally propped it with the tin of lead slugs. "Off wi' ye, noisy creature," she said, shooing the cockerel away with a flap of her apron.

Anne lugged the unwieldy sign by the chains. "You climb up first—then I'll hand it to you." She muscled the sign up, and Sally hooked the chains onto the iron bracket jutting out at a right angle into the lane.

Sally scrambled down, and they took a few steps back to stand with arms folded, admiring the new sign. The words ROYAL COFFEE-HOUSE encircled the image of a gray goose quill curved over a golden crown.

"Sign of the Crown and Quill . . ." Sally said with a wicked smile, "open for business."

"Come right in, Captain." Anne waved a pair of grenadiers across the threshold. "Welcome to the finest cup of coffee and tea in all of New York City . . ."

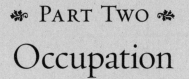

PART TWO

Occupation

Not gold but only men can make
A people great and strong;
Men who for truth and honor's sake
Stand fast and suffer long.
Brave men who work while others sleep,
Who dare while others fly . . .
They build a nation's pillars deep
And lift them to the sky.

RALPH WALDO EMERSON

No longer a part of the United States, New York City is the
home to British Headquarters, a safe haven for Loyalists, and
for some brave Patriots, a fertile ground for gathering intelli-
gence useful to the Revolutionary cause.

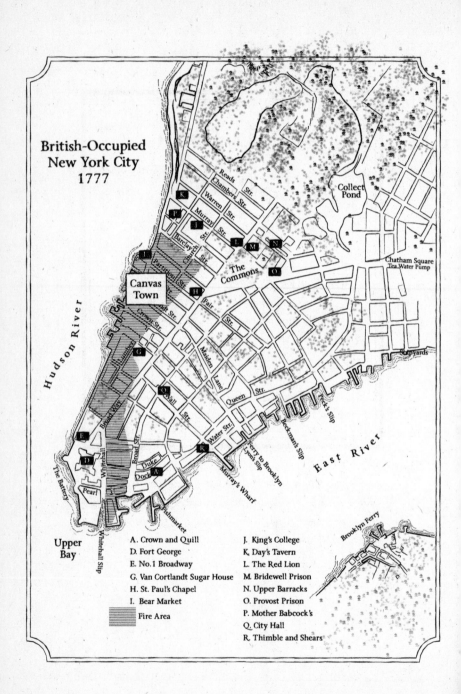

British-Occupied
New York City
1777

Hudson River

Collect
Pond

Reads Str.
Chambers Str.
Warren Str.
Murray Str.
Barclay Str.

K
P
J
L
M
N
O

I

Canvas
Town

H

The
Commons

Chatham Square
Tea Water Pump

Greenwich Str.
Cortland Str.
Fair Str.

Broad Str.

Stanyards

G

Maiden Lane

Q

Queen Str.

Peck's Slip

East River

Water Str.

Beekman's Slip

Hall Str.

R

Murray's Wharf

Ferry to Brooklyn
Lyon Slip

E

Whitehall

Broad Str.

Duke
Dock

A

Brooklyn Ferry

The Battery

D

Pearl

Fishmarket

Upper
Bay

Whitehall Slip

A. Crown and Quill
D. Fort George
E. No.1 Broadway
G. Van Cortlandt Sugar House
H. St. Paul's Chapel
I. Bear Market

　　　Fire Area

J. King's College
K. Day's Tavern
L. The Red Lion
M. Bridewell Prison
N. Upper Barracks
O. Provost Prison
P. Mother Babcock's
Q. City Hall
R. Thimble and Shears

CHAPTER FOURTEEN

❦

Resolution is our inherent character,
and courage hath never yet forsaken us.

THOMAS PAINE, *Common Sense*

Friday, May 30, 1777
At the Sign of the Crown and Quill

ANNE stepped out from the sweltering kitchenhouse and drew a pail from the cistern. She splashed cool water on her face and neck, and ran wet fingers over hair swept up in loose curls at the back of her head. Removing her stained apron, Anne smoothed and admired the skirts of her new day dress—very pleased with her choice of fabric—the twining leaves and tiny forget-me-nots on a pale ivory background seemed especially lighthearted in the morning light.

Sally followed Anne into the garden, a clean, pressed apron in hand. "Ye should wear an apron—ye dinna want to dirty yer pretty dress, do ye?" Arms raised, Anne turned around and Sally tied the apron sashes into a sprightly bow. "There ye go, madam!" she said, giving Anne a pat on the bum. "Bring out the trays and ready the teapots. I'll go pull the drapes and open the door."

Dust motes danced along the gleaming shafts streaming in

through the diamond-shaped windowpanes, along with customers through the open door. Bandit barked a greeting as regulars bustled in to take their usual seats, and the sleepy shop was suddenly awake with manly laughter, cheery voices and the scrape and squawk of chairs and benches being dragged across the floorboards.

Anne placed three trays filled with the day's baking on the compositor's table at the back of the shop, covering each with a large napkin to protect the muffins and scones from flies. She brought out a wicker hamper filled with two dozen small pewter teapots, all rinsed and polished for the day's use. After arranging the pear-shaped pots in rows of four on the countertop, she scooped a generous amount of black tea into each one.

Sally set two heavy urns onto the counter—one filled with hot coffee, the other, boiled water. Hands at hips, she turned to glare once again at the half-assembled printing press and clutter of tools occupying a good amount of floor space between the compositor's table and the front end of the shop.

"Can it be so bloody difficult to assemble a press? The lazy-arse grubshites ye hired have accomplished less in three days than Jack and Titus did in three hours."

"I know . . . I know . . . I've already decided to give them the sack—if they bother to show up—the drunkards."

"Och!" Sally groaned. "An' what are we to do with all this mess?"

"I'm posting another notice today." Anne pulled a folded sheet from her pocket and showed it to Sally. Written in her best hand in neat block letters:

WANTED IMMEDIATELY
Sober and Skilled
JOURNEYMEN PRINTERS
who Can and Will work
Apply to Mrs. Merrick
at the sign of the Crown and Quill

Sally eyed the advert with no little scorn, whispering through clenched teeth. "It's bad enough havin' t' smile and scrape t' these Redcoat bastards always lurking about, aye—without havin' to press ink to paper promoting their Loyalist treachery."

Anne slipped the notice back into her pocket. "I'd be a fool not to take Mr. Rivington up on his offer." She began pouring hot water into each teapot. "What with publishing the *Royal Gazette* and printing all the Crown business, Rivington has more than he can handle, and he is kind enough to direct some work our way."

Sally came up behind Anne and hissed in her ear. "Rivington prints th' most vile Tory swill, and I for one wouldna wipe a shitten arse with the *Gazette* for fear of offending the arsehole. *I* wouldna have *anything* to do with him or his disgustin' rag, not for all the gold in Christendom." Feathers in a ruff, she strutted off to slam an assortment of cups and saucers onto her tray.

Anne grabbed Sally by the arm, and dragged her out into the garden. "You think I don't know Rivington is a tool of the Crown?" she scolded, her brows meeting in a bump above her nose. "Yes— reviving the press and stationery will add to our pocketbook—but that is not our aim, as you should ken. Doing business with the likes of James Rivington lends us a great measure of protection, and will provide opportunities . . . protection and opportunities that will aid us in our *important* business."

"I'm sorry, Annie." Sally puffed out a breath, rubbing her arm. "I sometimes canna bear the loud smell that rises from some of what we do . . ."

"It will help if you try to remember there are others who, for the same cause, bear far worse than we."

Mutual feathers somewhat smoothed over, Anne and Sally went about the business of distributing tea, coffee, scones and muffins to a full house of customers.

"Good morning, Mrs. Merrick," Captain Blankenship called as he came trotting down the stairs with red jacket thrown over one shoulder and helmet cradled in his arm.

"Tea and scones today, Captain?" Anne smiled up to him. "I saved you some clotted cream . . . and we've strawberry jam . . ."

"You know me too well, Mrs. Merrick. Tea and scones it is."

Edward Blankenship took a seat at a table near a front window, joining lieutenants Wemyss and Stuart, the other two British officers Anne had been forced to quarter.

Exactly three days after Jack and Titus spirited David away, Edward Blankenship showed up on her doorstep—most apologetic—in possession of a writ commandeering three rooms in her home in service to the Crown.

"It was bound to happen—we are not alone in being forced to quarter soldiers," Anne had said to Sally as they made the many trips up and down the narrow stairs, moving all of their things to the two garret rooms. "Blankenship has done us a favor, actually. I'd rather quarter three agreeable British officers than house a whole horde of Hessian grenadiers and their cabbage-cooking wives."

"Lobster scoundrels! Soddin', thievin', bloodyback bastards!" Sally did not hesitate to pile on the adjectives as they bumped Anne's heavy chest up the stairs. "I'm only glad the lads took our David safe away—just in the nick, too."

Safe away . . . Anne mused as she arranged little covered glass pots of jam and clotted cream on the tea service she prepared for Captain Blankenship.

Not a note, not a message passed . . . No word in the eight long months since the three drunken fishermen went lurching down the lane—nothing to indicate whether or not Jack and Titus had succeeded in getting themselves and David out of harm's way.

After Washington ordered the evacuation from the works at Brooklyn Heights, the Patriot army moved in an almost constant retreat. From Long Island to New York City, stretching up the entire length of Manhattan, across King's Bridge and then across the Hudson to the southern half of New Jersey—the British gaining ground with very little effort or loss.

Patriots were left to bemoan the sad, sorry state of Washington's draggle-tail army. With thousands of soldiers and militiamen either captured, deserted or unfit for duty, most considered Washington's defeat and surrender to be impending and inevitable.

But cautious General Howe failed to deliver the felling blow before the campaign ended with the approach of winter. Washington performed a miracle and managed to somehow keep his dwindling army intact. The Continental forces slunk across the Delaware to regroup, and General Howe settled in New York City to enjoy the whirl of gaieties Loyalist society had to offer, and seemed more than happy to remain there through the spring as well.

Using a pair of sharp nippers, Anne clipped chunks from the cone-shaped loaf of fine white sugar, telling herself for the hundredth time it must be nigh on impossible and very dangerous for Jack to get a message delivered.

Oh, dear Lord, please, please let that be the reason for this long, awful silence. For the heinous alternatives sidling into her head, nipping and nibbling at her best hopes and wishes, were much too horrible to contemplate.

Anne closed her eyes. Reaching into her pocket she wrapped her fingers around the cast-iron token Jack had given her at the Bowling Green, the rough, ragged edge biting into her skin a comfort.

No.

They are safe.

They just have to be . . .

Anne blinked open her eyes and studied the display of china and silver on the tray, and added an additional cup and saucer to it. Forcing a smile on her face, she carried the service over to Blankenship's table.

"I hope you don't mind, gentlemen, if I join you for morning tea . . ."

The three soldiers scrambled to their feet, and Lieutenant Wemyss offered a chair to Anne, draping his jacket over his arm. "I couldn't think of a more delightful way to start the day, Mrs. Merrick, but I am off to find a tailor." He showed Anne a huge rent in the seam under the right sleeve of his regimental coat.

"I recommend Mulligan's—at the sign of the Thimble and Shears on Queen Street." Anne smoothed her skirts under as she sat. "An Irishman, but he does excellent work for a very fair price. Make sure you mention my name."

"Aye, Wemyss—" Stuart teased. "Have the tailor put a few gussets in your breeches as well. I swear you've gained at least two stone in the time we've been quartered above the Crown and Quill."

Good-natured Wemyss gave his growing middle a pat as he headed toward the door. "Evidence of my penchant for Miss Sally and her sumptuous shortbread."

Once Wemyss disappeared out the door, Stuart excused himself. Mumbling something about lending Sally "a helping hand," he made a beeline for the back of the shop.

"My men are both smitten with your maid." Blankenship dropped a lump of sugar into the tea Anne poured for him. "In this contest, I predict Stuart will prevail—he is the more cunning of the two."

"I would not wager on it." Anne watched Sally going about her business clearing tables and collecting coins, offering Stuart nothing other than the coldest of cold shoulders.

"I'm glad to have a moment alone with you, Anne, there is something I want to ask." Edward Blankenship had taken to falling into the familiar when they spoke privately. "I was wondering if you would be willing to accompany me to the ball being held for the King's birthday, a little more than a week from today? There will be music and merrymaking . . ."

"I would be most happy to attend, Edward. Thank you for inviting me." Anne beamed.

"Wonderful! It is predicted by some to be the last grand event for the summer . . ."

"The last . . . but why? Is the army leaving?" Eyes wide, Anne touched a finger to her lips. "Don't tell me the city's to be abandoned to the rebels once again!"

"Poor Anne." Blankenship leaned forward. Reaching across the table, he took hold of her hand. "I wish you wouldn't worry so. What can I do to assure you there are no plans to abandon the city?"

"You are a great comfort to me, Edward." Anne shifted forward in her chair. "It is so wearisome—the uncertainty—I only wish General Howe would put an end to this war."

"The end is in sight." Edward's voice dropped. "To your ears alone I can tell this—General Clinton is on his way from London after being knighted by the King, and he has been assigned to a post here in New York City. I'm certain he will present plans to Howe and we will soon move against the rebels—at last."

Anne put on a pout and gave his hand a squeeze. "Are you so anxious to leave us, Captain?"

"It's just I'm afraid our army is becoming a bit too fat and happy in New York. And though I am most anxious to crush this rebellion once and for all, I always regret having to leave you, dearest Anne, as I must now." Blankenship brought Anne's hand up and brushed her fingers to his lips. "Off to headquarters with me." He rose to don his jacket and headgear, the glaring death's-head on his helmet's crown lending his boyish good looks a level of fierceness. "Good day to you, Mrs. Merrick."

"Good day, Captain."

Anne gathered all the dirty cups and teaspoons onto the tray and carried it back to the kitchenhouse. "Do you have any laundry ready for the line, Sal?"

"Aye." Sally smiled. "There's a full basket ready near the cistern."

Anne hitched the laundry basket onto one hip, and carried it up the two long flights of stairs to the garret. Sitting on the windowsill in Sally's room, facing the street, Anne pinned the wet laundry to the clothesline strung across the lane between the two buildings— two white petticoats, one red petticoat, followed by three more white petticoats. The wooden pulleys squeaked a merry tune as she tugged on the line, centering the petticoat array over the lane— the signal to her unknown accomplice, indicating she had intelligence to deliver.

cb cb cb

TRAVELING with the current, Jack and Titus moved fast, sculling tight to the Manhattan shore, careful to keep cover within the deepening shadows cast by the setting sun. A lone night heron barked a call as they streamed past, adding a noisy voice to the rhythmic *ching-chinging* crickets and katydid buzz.

No matter the type of craft, or time of day, Jack was never at ease when riding on water, and manning the oars of a broad-beamed pettiauger conveying fifty barrels of contraband along a waterway patrolled by the Royal Navy put a definite edge on a pleasant spring evening.

Jack paused in his rowing, and pointed. "Just ahead there . . ."

Titus drew in his oars and took up the tiller. With a keen eye and a deft touch, he knifed the sharp end of the boat through a barely discernable and very narrow defile in a barrier of tumbled mica-flecked stones. The natural divide sheltered a rocky river edging, where two dark figures hovered near a laden flatboat beached in the shadow of steep, craggy cliffs.

"Watch and ward now . . ." Jack muttered over his shoulder, tugging an oar from the lock.

Titus let loose the tiller, and pulled a pair of pistols free from the red sash tied around his waist, his face settling into a fearsome scowl.

Jack used an oar to pole the boat through the shallow water, running it aground on the riverbank in a crunch of wood to gravel. Jumping over the side, he secured a line to a jutting stone.

As the figures moved from the shadows, Titus leveled his pistols, clacking back the hammers, and Jack zinged his knife from his boot.

Two large, broad men in loose oilcloth jackets and patched-over canvas trousers stepped into the dwindling twilight. The shorter of the two missed several teeth in his grin, and sported a brown-and-white-striped quail feather in his wooly knit cap. Tucking a stout oaken cudgel back into his belt, he approached with arms outstretched. "Titus! M' heart's broken, you black bastard! It's me—Dodd!"

A permanent squint in the taller man's left eye put a surly twist to his square face. He slung the short-barreled blunderbuss in his hands to his shoulder, and called in a familiar rasp, sounding as if his throat'd been scoured with lye, "Sheath that stinger, Hampton! Dontcha recognize your ol' friend Tully?"

Jack and Titus relaxed, put by their weapons, and greeted the smugglers with smiles, handshakes and pats on the back. Tully was a Liberty Boy, bred from the days of the Stamp Act, and Jack recognized Dodd as one of the men who huddled near the dartboard at the Cup and Quill, often trounced by Titus.

"Can't be too careful doing business these days, eh?" Jack gave Tully's blunderbuss a tap.

Tully laughed. "When we come out light on details, we're heavy with ammunition."

"Aye, that—especially with the bloodybacks as close as a wet cunt to a whore's arse." Feather bobbing, Dodd nodded to the pettiauger. "Best get to it. What've ye brought us, lads?"

Titus whisked back the tarpaulin covering their cargo. "Thirty barrels of beef, and twenty of wheaten flour, ten barrels of pickled cabbage."

"Meat and flour? I dunno . . ." Dodd scrubbed his bristly chin. "Cabbage? I s'pose we can take it all off your hands . . . me and Tully being friends to the cause and all . . ."

"Quit shitting through your teeth, Dodd," Titus warned.

Jack bristled. "We know full well meat and flour are going for eight times the price in the city. You'd best make a fair reckoning here, Dodd . . . for the cause and all."

Aggrieved, Dodd put a hand to his heart, a practiced, pained expression furrowing his forehead. "Jack . . . Titus . . ."

"Ah, now . . ." Tully stepped in. "Doddsy just can't help himself, Jack—drawn to the swindle like a pig to mud, he is. O' course we'll make a fair trade. Our stock for yours." Tully waved them over to the flatboat piled high with goods draped in old sailcloth. They gathered around as Tully pulled the cover away.

"We picked and chose our goods with the cause in mind," Dodd offered, in appeasement.

Tully recited the inventory. "Forty-five casks of black powder, nine dozen rose blankets, ten cases of port wine and"—prying up the lid on a wooden crate, he displayed row upon row of flints knapped to size for musket or rifle, packed in sawdust—"a thousand Brandon black gunflints."

"A very good trade, Tully." Titus plucked a handful of flints from the case and deposited them into his pocket.

"We don't have room enough for the wine, but we'll take the rest." Jacked unfurled one of the big woolen blankets. "Good quality this—thieved from British military stores?"

"Ah, now, Jack, *thieved* is a bit harsh." Tully grinned, his squinty eye squashed to a crease. "*Diverted* is the more accurate term."

Dodd chuckled. "Aye, mate—that's what we are—*die-verters.*"

Tully drew his wooden-handled lading hook from his belt. "Let's get to work, lads."

They propped a pair of long, thick planks against the prow, forming a ramp of sorts leading to dry land. Plying their stevedore hooks with practiced expertise, Tully and Dodd hefted the heavy barrels of beef and flour onto the ramp. Jack and Titus rolled the barrels down into a neat stack on the beach.

Once the craft was emptied of its cargo, they rolled the gunpowder casks up the plank ramp for Tully and Dodd to arrange with a mind for weight and balance.

Jack dumped two bales of blankets inside the boat. "So, Tully, how are you faring under Redcoat rule?"

"Plenty of work for the likes of us at least." Tully swiveled a cask into position. "British shipping backed up at every pier—coming in faster than we can unload 'em . . ."

"Aye. The docks are fair groaning with trade goods and military stores—more tea and sugar than anyone knows what to do with—"

"Good opportunities for you boys, eh?" Titus winked.

"Getting rough, the diverting business," Dodd said. "Ye can't fart on the docks these days but for having Cunningham's nose hard up your arse."

"Tory bugger," Tully added.

Titus heaved a crate of flints into the boat, and shoved it under the cross thwart near the tiller. "Who's Cunningham?"

"The provost marshall . . ." Dodd said. "And a nasty piece of work, he is, too."

"Mean and nasty," Tully added.

Dodd hefted a cask of powder into position and fit it snug between two others. "Y'know Molly? Over at Mother Babcock's? Well, she told me the bastard wields a one-inch prick . . ."

"Must be some truth to it," Tully affirmed. "I heard Suzy say the bastard's shot pouch was longer than the barrel of his gun."

Titus dropped the last of the blankets into the boat. "Make any man mean—havin' a little bitty prick . . ."

"I don't know about that . . ." Jack threw his arm around Titus. "After all, you're a nice enough fellow . . ."

Dodd and Tully laughed, and Titus pushed his friend off, shaking a finger in his face. "Not a joking matter, Jack . . ."

"Ah, lads, all jests aside, this provost will hang you as soon as look at you. Hates rebels with a fury, and his gallows is doing a brisk business by it." Tully leaned against the gunwale, finagling his lading hook down the back of his collar, giving himself a good scratch. "You know this fella Cunningham, Jack—from a tar and feather couple years back—the spitting snake of a Tory who wouldn't damn the King even after we beat the living shite from him—"

"*No!* That bollocks is the provost?"

"One and the same." Tully buried his hook into a bale of blankets and tossed it toward the bow. "The city's much changed."

Once all the cargo was transferred, packed tight and secured, Jack and Titus sat down on a flat rock by the water's edge and shared a supper of smoked fish, biscuit and cheese with the smugglers before getting under way.

"Doddsy—why don't you go and fetch a couple of them bottles,

and we can have a sip of port after our meal like the fancy folk do."
As soon as Dodd was out of earshot, Tully grabbed Jack by the arm,
his raspy voice low and slow in his ear. "Stitch says there's a delivery
waiting at the orchard—over three and up six."

Jack nodded just as Dodd returned with two bottles and a tin of
"diverted" almond comfits. The men waited out the last scraps of
twilight, watching the stars pop onto a night sky clear of clouds,
passing bottles and sweetmeats and catching up on the news.

Dodd piped up. "D'ye hear, Titus? The Redcoats captured Sam
Fraunces in New Jersey, and put him back in his tavern to cook and
pull pints for 'em."

"Better than rotting in a prison hulk, I guess," Titus said.

"Here's to our poor brothers behind bars . . ." Tully took a deep
slug from the bottle.

"Say, Tully, is the Cup and Quill still in business?" Jack asked.

"A-yup . . . reopened as the *Royal* Coffeehouse . . ."

"And crawlin' with bloodybacks it is," Dodd added. "As much as
I miss Sally's scones, I don't go near the place."

"A-yup," Tully agreed. "The widow's turned Tory again."

"Naw." Titus shook his head. "Mrs. Anne's only getting by in
hard times."

"Believe it, lads. A Tory-come-lately she is." Dodd munched on a
handful of almonds. "I've seen her strolling along Broad Way in her
fancy dresses, face rouged, hanging on to her handsome dragoon's
arm, batting her eyelashes, all a-giggle."

"Fancy dresses?" Jack repeated.

"All a-giggle?" Titus snorted.

"Aye." Dodd shagged his head up and down. "Ye wouldn't know
her."

Tully passed the port along. "The world's turned upside down,
it is."

Jack upended the bottle, gulping every last drop. Quiet for a few
moments, tossing the empty bottle from one palm to the other, he
jumped up a sudden, and hurled it against the rocks. The explosion
of shattered glass echoed up and down the river, sending a great

flock of snowy egrets and night herons croaking and flapping up into the sky.

Tully gave Jack a shove. "Are you bloody mad?"

"D'ye mean t' bring the bleedin' fleet down upon our heads?" Dodd hissed.

"C'mon—help us shove off," Jack growled and marched off to the boat, taking his seat at the front of the pettiauger. Titus climbed into his seat by the tiller. The smugglers put their shoulders to the prow and sent the boat off into a river spangled with the light of countless stars.

Throwing every muscle in his body into propelling the boat forward, Jack dug the oars into the water to the beat of his heart pounding in his head, the cast-iron token hanging by a thong around his neck thumping to his chest with every motion forward and back. He thought he could feel steam rise from the top of his head.

Face painted.

Fancy dresses.

Handsome dragoon.

"Dodd is an idiot," Titus said.

Jack dropped the oars onto his lap, twirled around and snapped, "What about Tully?"

"You left her there for eight months." Titus shrugged. "Mrs. Anne is doing what she must to survive, but she's no Tory."

Jack heaved a sigh. "You're probably right—as usual." He turned back to his oars. Still with the current, their pettiauger cruised south at a fast clip, hugging the coast. "Take the turn just beyond this bend, Titus . . ."

Titus pulled in his oars, and steered the boat up a wide marshy creek bordered by tall sedge grass, maneuvering the boat to travel up the center of the shallow waterway.

Jack pulled to a stop at the first sound of the pettiauger scraping along the muddy streambed, and he tugged off his boots and stockings. "I'll be right back." Hopping over the side, he sloshed through knee-high water, and scrambled up the soft riverbank.

Running across the spongy ground, Jack cut across the marsh to the apple orchard, crawling in long, even rows up and over the crest of a low, rolling hill. He followed the third row over from the right, counting six trees up, and fell to his knees.

A soft breeze rustled through the tree leaves, and a cowbell clunked in the distance. Jack reached into a natural cleft at the base of the tree trunk and pulled out a small leather-wrapped bundle. Tucking it under his arm, he jogged back to the creek. Holding it above his head as he sloshed through the water, he put the delivery into Titus's hands, turned the boat around to face the river and pulled himself back into it. Titus unwrapped the package.

"Why do you bother? I suspect it's the same as always." Jack pulled an oar from the lock, and used it to push off the creek bottom.

"Yep." Titus affirmed. Within the leather wrapping he uncovered a ream of foolscap paper, wrapped in brown paper, bundled with a length of inch-wide grosgrain ribbon tied in a pert bow. As per usual, Titus pulled the bow loose and flipped through every page. "Nothing. The same as always. An awful lot of risk and bother—if you ask me—for us to pick up and deliver a stack of blank paper."

Jack continued to pole the craft into deeper water. "No one's asking you."

Titus retied the ribbon, rewrapped the ream in its leather cover, stuffed the bundle into his gunnysack and took up the tiller.

The pettiauger accomplished the wide turn north up the East River. Titus hoisted their sail, and they skimmed along on the wind. Jack straddled the cross-thwart and laid back on it, taking a moment to catch a breath and watch the constellations roll by. Groping inside his shirtfront, he found the favor Anne had given him, and draped the lace-edged linen over his face. The vestiges of lavender combined with the sweat from her soft breasts to send Jack to a place where he lay in the dark curled against Anne's back, his nose buried in her hair . . .

. . . *Her handsome dragoon.* Jack jerked to a sit. Crumpling the hanky into a tight wad in his fist, he pounded the side of his leg. That's what Dodd had said. *Her* handsome dragoon.

"I've been thinking, Titus—after we deliver this cargo, I'm going into the city to fetch Anne . . ."

"I don't know, Jack," Titus pondered. "You heard what Tully and Dodd had to say about the provost—I think it's still too dangerous for you to go there . . ."

"No, Titus . . ." Jack stuffed the crumpled handkerchief back inside his shirt. "It's too dangerous to leave her there."

⚓ ⚓ ⚓

ENCAPSULATED within a small sphere of candlelight illuminating his desktop, William Cunningham hunched over in shirtsleeves, sharp shoulders pinched up to his ears, scratching his pen across a sheet of foolscap with a precise hand.

The thick bayberry candle sputtered, and the annoying flicker bounced in the corner of his eye. The provost marshall set his quill down and poked with a ragged fingernail to raise the slumping wick foundering in a pool of melted wax. Burning bayberry helped to mitigate the malignant odor endemic to the Provost Prison, but it made for poor light—not as bright or lasting as a whale oil lamp for doing book work after dark.

Cunningham scrubbed the stubbly hair on the back of his head, took a long drink from the bottle of rum and eyed the sum total at the bottom of the second column on the page. He was required to submit a weekly report to General Howe, an accounting of the prisoners under his charge, and he was always prompt in delivering it first thing Friday mornings.

Rations and supplies for the prisoners were allocated based on Cunningham's "meticulous" figures. He traced a finger along the list of prisons under his purview. Most of the rebel soldiers captured on Long Island and in the taking of Manhattan were held in makeshift prisons—three sugarhouses, four dissenter churches and King's College. The only facilities designed and built as jails—New Bridewell and the Provost Prison, where he kept his quarters—housed officers, some enlisted men, common criminals and anyone suspected of treason. He had recently shifted several hundred landmen to the three prison hulks moored on Wallabout Bay, originally intended for the incarceration of smugglers and seamen from captured privateers.

"Waterborne rebel scum," he muttered, sucking another gulp from his bottle.

Under the second column headed *Living*, the provost claimed a total of 3,896 prisoners. The column headed *Arrivals* totaled eighty-six. He studied the empty column headed *Mortality* for a moment, fingering the bumpy scar curving from the nape of his neck to just above his left temple.

He always kept a very accurate count of new arrivals—but there was no wringing of hands over the death count. The provost picked up his quill and filled in the blank spaces with a series of arbitrary numbers off the top of his head, totaling twenty-two.

Cunningham smirked, leaning back in his chair. Twenty-two dead—plausible, but not alarming—that was the kind of paper and ink mortality number he aimed for. Lacing fingers, he stretched his long arms over his head, eliciting a satisfying crackle from his knuckles. He had no idea how many prisoners had died over the course of the week, and neither did he care.

The standard allotment provided by the Crown for the keeping of prisoners was calculated at two pounds each of hardtack and pork per prisoner, per week. He scribbled some figures on a scrap of rough paper and smiled. Taking into account the bribes necessary in order to accommodate the sale, plus the ever-inflating market prices, he and Loring, the commissary, stood to share at minimum a tidy two-hundred-pound profit by selling off half of the next week's rations. He was very pleased.

Cunningham drew the watch from the pocket on his weskit and checked the hour—half past eleven. "Sergeant O'Keefe!" he shouted. "*O'Keefe!* Get in here now, you fuckin' miserable bog trotter!"

His deputy came bumbling from quarters across the hall, in shirt-tails and stockinged feet. The barrel-chested Irishman misjudged the doorway, and though his protruding belly absorbed the brunt of the collision, he still managed to give his forehead a good knock against the jamb.

"It's the likes of you what give us Irish a black name—drunken sot!"

"Not drunk . . ." Michael O'Keefe wavered on his feet, greasy hair swaying in limp hanks about his face. He belched. "Just fell asleep is all."

"Drunken *lying* bastard—look at you—standing there with a face the color of the devil's nutbag . . ." Cunningham stood and leaned over his desk, the nostrils on his sharp nose flaring in disgust. "*Feh!* You're wearing sick all over your shirt . . ."

The deputy smeared a thumb over the suspicious substance, and shrugged.

The provost shook his head and fell back into his chair. "I want you to go and fetch a few necks to stretch, from"—he referred to his list—"Van Cortlandt's Sugar House."

"What time is it?" O'Keefe ground the heel of his palm into his eye. "Ye know we get complaints from the neighbor women when we scragg 'em this late."

"Never mind the time . . ." Cunningham's Adam's apple jerked up and down the shaft of his neck, as if he had swallowed a thing yet alive. "I am of a mind to see some rebels dangle and dance."

"Aye . . . awright . . ." O'Keefe raked his hair back. "Where's Richmond?"

Cunningham pushed the candledish to the far left edge of the desk, sending light to shine on Richmond sitting in a chair. Staring with watery eyes, mouth slightly agape, his hands lay loose, palms up in his lap. The half-caste slave was dressed in baggy tow trousers and shirt, his waist-length hair twisted by neglect into a dozen snakelike locks, almost as thick as the hangman's rope he liked to wear draped over his shoulder.

"Jaysus!" O'Keefe startled. "Bloody unnerving—him sittin' there in the dark like that." The sergeant's eye darted to the bottle on the provost's desk. Sweeping a furry tongue over fleshy lips, he asked,

"How about givin' yer fellow countryman a scoof—a little hair of the dog, eh?"

"How about I give you a big boot up your arse?" Cunningham growled, and waved him off. "Get going. I'll finish up here and meet you at the gallows behind Bridewell."

O'Keefe herded Richmond toward the door and Cunningham snatched up his quill and called after them, "Put each to the test—I don't want any stoic bastards on my gallows, aye?"

"Aye . . ." The sergeant dragged Richmond along by the sleeve. "We know full well how ye like 'em."

The provost double-checked his tallies and scrawled a signature across the bottom of his report. He dusted the whole document with a sprinkle from his pounce pot, and set it aside. Propping his boots on the desktop, he upended the bottle of rum, gulping and swallowing until his eyes watered and his throat stung, sucking the bottle dry of every drop.

Leaning over in his chair, he set the bottle on its side, and sent it rolling with a gentle push. Like faraway thunder, the bottle rumbled over the seams and knots in the floorboards, ending its long, slow roll with a dead thunk against the wall. Cunningham closed his eyes and fingered the smooth patch of scar tissue above his right ear, lips hardly moving, his whisper barely audible.

"Repay in kind . . . and then some."

CHAPTER FIFTEEN

❦❧

*How trifling, how ridiculous, do the little,
paltry cavellings, of a few weak or interested men appear,
when weighed against the business of a world.*

THOMAS PAINE, *Common Sense*

Wednesday, June 4, 1777
Up in the Garret, Making Ready for the Ball

STARTING with a knot at the top, Sally looped the cording from eyelet to eyelet, tugging up the slack, and lacing Anne into her stays with a firm double bow at the small of her waist.

"Now where's our bum roll gone to?" Hands to hips, she glanced around the room.

Though it was the larger of the two garret rooms, her mistress's bedchamber was overcrowded with furnishings, and so it seemed much smaller than Sally's spartan quarters. She cast about for the errant roll, rifling through the mayhem of petticoats, kerchiefs, stockings and ribbons strewn over the servant-sized bed pushed into the corner.

"There it is, Sal." Anne pointed to the floor near the Dutch stove where Bandit lay, tongue lolling, his head resting comfortably on the moon-shaped pillow.

"Imp! Off wi' ye!" Sally rousted the dog with her toe, and sent Bandit scurrying across the room. He bounded onto the padded chair squeezed into the corner near the open window, and hopped up to sit on the wide sill, surveying the garden. Spongy black nose set a-twitch by the aroma of the beef stew wafting up from the chimney, it seemed he seriously pondered the six-foot leap from the garret window to the kitchenhouse roof.

"Down, Bandit!" Sally lurched forward and shooed the dog back onto the chair. After nosing through the clutter of books, teacups and saucers on the side table, Bandit huffed, and settled into a compact curl, muzzle to tail.

Sally pried the jaws of the bum roll apart like a pair of calipers, and caught Anne's waist within the opening, settling the bulk of the padding on her rear end, centering the crescent tips to point to her navel.

"Yer such a skinny-malink as it is, maybe no one will notice ye lack panniers."

"I couldn't give a fig whether anyone notices," Anne replied, tying the two ends together.

Loath to invest thought, effort or money in attire suitable for attending a gala to honor King George, Anne resisted preparing a wardrobe for the event, so Sally shouldered the burden. Over the course of the week they spit and argued over every trifling detail.

"It's not a proper ball gown without hoops . . ." Sally insisted.

Annie would not relent. "I absolutely forbid you to waste good silver on such fribbles and geegaws. Panniers indeed! Make do with what we have."

Earlier, when Sally tried to dress her mistress's hair to a fashionable height, Annie snatched the hairbrush from her hand and would have none of it. After a bitter exchange, they compromised on a modest upsweep with a few long curls draping down over one shoulder. The ostrich plume adornment Sally offered was rejected out of hand.

Anne stepped into the new petticoat Sally'd sewn of a cerulean blue tissue silk. Pulling it over the bum roll, she secured the drawstring at her waist. Sally held the overdress like a coat and Anne slipped her arms into the sleeve holes, groaning and shifting from one bare foot to the other as Sally struggled to join the front edges of the bodice with a series of straight pins.

"Hold still!"

Sal bumped her head on one of the sloping ceiling rafters as she scrambled back a few steps to put a critical eye to her creation. Anne stood inspection with a sullen slump to her shoulders, her brows meeting in an angry *V*.

"Hmmmm . . ." Sally never laid claim to owning exemplary sewing skills, but she had done her best to refashion an old dress she'd found lingering at the very bottom of the bottom chest. The rich violet-blue figured silk had an excellent hand, and the bright new petticoat and matching silk ribbon trimming the edges of the square neckline enlivened the overall tone. The colors complemented Annie's fair skin and chestnut hair and Sally was pleased with the results. Gesturing with a twirl of an index finger she said, "Turn about—so I can see if the hem is even."

Anne did not budge. "The hem is fine."

Sally cocked her head. "How about ye reach in and plump up yer bubbies a bit?"

"How about you shut your gob?" Anne flounced onto the bed.

Sally bustled about the room, scooping odds and ends into the chests—slamming the lids shut—first one, then the other. "Aye, ye can snap my head off at will, Anne Merrick, but yid best mind that sharp tongue among the Tories, eh?" She hefted the chests up to sit atop the other at the foot of the bed. "A bad-tempered, ill-dressed, ugly bitch willna make a single friend nor uncover the information useful to the cause ye claim t' be willing t' risk all for."

"Ha! There's the pot calling the kettle black! Two British officers trail after you wagging their tails like lovesick puppies—Wemyss willing to sell his soul for a piece of your shortbread—and you won't even give them the time of day." Anne threw herself back on the mattress, eyes shut, fingers laced over her belly. She struck a death pose.

"Yer right." Sally sank down to sit beside Anne. "I canna keep a civil tongue with the Redcoat bastards, much less wheedle any information from them . . ."

"It wears on me so . . ." Anne intoned to the ceiling over her bed. "Wears me thin as a razor's edge . . ."

Sally draped a pair of white silk stockings over her friend's face. "What wears on ye? The lying or the sneakin' about?"

"I don't know . . ." Anne sat up. She bunched a stocking down to the toe and slipped it up over her leg, following suit with the second. "Jack is out there somewhere—alive, dead, imprisoned—and here I sit, primping with bows and feathers to encourage the ardent attention of other men."

Sally cut two lengths from a reel of one-inch-wide grosgrain ribbon. "If we were men, we'd shoulder our muskets and answer the call to arms. Women have no such luxury, aye?"

"No . . . we plump up our bubbies instead." Anne wound the ribbon twice tight above her knee, tying the garters with a knot and a neat bow.

"I give ye much credit, lass. Yiv devised a clever means to aid the cause and our country—I think Jack will be proud of ye."

"I hope you're right." Fluffing the delicate Mechlin lace flounce at her sleeves, she went to stand before the wall mirror. "This is nice, Sally. The old ruffle was very sad and tired." She studied her reflection a moment, and then went in search of her rouge pot. Swiping a fluff of damp wool over the red cake, Anne rubbed a little color into her cheeks, and applied a touch of lip pomade with a pinky finger.

"D'ye think we might add the bows, Annie?" Sally ventured.

"Alright . . ." Anne laughed, throwing her hands up in surrender. "Fetch the blasted bows."

Sally produced from her pocket the three puffed ribbon bows Annie had discarded with much disdain as "silly fribbles." After Sally pinned them in a row centered down the front of the bodice, Anne slipped on her best black leather French heels.

"Wait!" Sally fished a pink-and-white-striped silk bag from behind the writing desk and handed the package to Anne. "Frippery and geegaws. G'won—open it up."

Anne loosened the drawstring, peered inside the sack and gasped, "Oh my!" as she drew out a pair of carmine red brocade pumps, the silver buckles encrusted with rhinestones.

"Put them on! Put them on!" Sally bounced and clapped her hands.

Anne slipped her feet into the slippers, hiked her skirts to admire her new footwear, then threw her arms around Sally and nearly squeezed the stuffings from her. "What in the world would I do without you, dearest friend?"

"Let's have a look." Sally spun Anne around by the shoulders and they contemplated the mirror. "Th' slippers are brilliant . . ."

Anne touched fingers to her throat. "Maybe I should wear something round the neck?"

"How about tha' pinchbeck and paste pendant ol' mumblecrust Merrick give ye?"

"Ulch!" Anne shuddered. "I'd rather string a dead fish about my neck."

"How about a simple ribbon necklet t' match yer dress? There's a bit of the blue ribbon left in my room . . ."

"I know!" Anne snatched something from her bedside table, and ran across the hall. Back with silk ribbon in hand, she sat down on the bed and artfully tied it to the broken bit of cast-iron Jack had given her.

"Och! Nooo . . ." Sally moaned.

Anne rushed to the mirror, her eyes alight. "Help me tie it on."

Knowing there would be no dissuading her mistress, Sally tied the ribbon in a pretty bow at the back of her neck, allowing enough slack for the little half-crown—now half wrapped in ribbon—to lie flat, just below the hollow of her throat.

They both studied the mirror, and Sally had to admit she liked the black crown slightly askew against Anne's pale skin—the contrast of hard metal supported in a delicate cradle of blue silk, ironic, and curiously beautiful. "It suits," she approved with a nod.

"I love it!" Anne proclaimed. "And it gives me a good story to tell." Clasping the necklet in one fist she declaimed, *"One small remnant of our precious Monarchy—rescued from the hands of the ruinous Rebels!"*

The women giggled in delight.

"Miss Sally!" Lieutenant Stuart's voice called from the garden.

Sally leaned out the window, her mobcap instantly swept up in a gust of wind off the bay. A riot of fiery curls tumbled free as her cap danced away on the rooftops.

Stuart cupped a hand to his mouth. "Please inform your mistress: Captain Blankenship awaits the pleasure of her company down the stairs."

Struggling to contain her loose hair in the breeze, Sally snapped, "Well, ye can tell yer captain he can bloody well . . ." She stopped and took a deep breath. Pressing her hands to the sill, she leaned way over and let her hair blow wild.

"Inform Captain Blankenship my mistress will be down in a tick—and, Lieutenant . . ." Sally called up a saucy smile. Dropping down to rest on her elbows, she tucked a curl behind her ear. "Maybe efter, if yer hungry, ye can join me for a bite to eat in the garden."

ↁ ↁ ↁ

BENEATH a massive white marble mantelpiece, two plump cherubs hovered on minuscule wings, sharing a bunch of grapes. Anne pretended to contemplate the hungry angels as she waited for Edward Blankenship to return from braving the mob at the punchbowl.

Several hundred warm bodies crowded into the ballroom, adding to the heat of several hundred candles burning bright in wall sconces, floorstands and brass chandeliers. Anne slipped around to stand beside one of the Greek columns supporting the mantelpiece, and pressed her hand to the smooth marble. She opened her fan—the thin wooden slats painted with a cool blue-green landscape of rolling hills and cypress trees—and she imitated the artful fan flutter on display in the room.

Anne was surprised the abandoned Kennedy Mansion at #1

Broad Way had survived the exchange of armies with its magnificent appointments intact. As designed, the two enormous parlor rooms on the first floor converted into one long ballroom by means of an ingenious set of folding panels. Gilded acanthus leaves twisting up from skirting board to cornice framed a series of enormous mirrored panels that by trick of the eye added to the glitter and size of the room.

Women were far outnumbered by men at this gathering, and men in splendid regimentals far outnumbered the more soberly clad Loyalist citizens who were important enough to garner an invitation. Least in number, but highest in demand, a coterie of young unmarried women giggled and whispered behind fans unfurled, thrilled and eager for the opportunity to mingle with dashing British officers.

How different her life was in comparison to the privileged ones led by these cosseted daughters of New York's Loyalist society. While Anne had learned to set type and mix ink, these women were schooled in the arts of social seduction—taught to play the harp and spinet, and master the latest dance steps.

At the far end of the ballroom, a tall, slender negro man in a yellow silk turban settled a violin beneath his chin, and the band of string and wind musicians struck up a lively gigue. The crowd fell back and couples paired up for the first dance of the evening.

She could see Captain Blankenship holding two silver cups high above his head, plowing a path through a sea of red coats and navy jackets, smiling and pardoning the whole long way. Her escort drew much attention among the husband hunters in attendance. A handsome man, Edward cut a dashing figure in the cropped regimental jacket worn by dragoons, and Anne liked how he'd tied his hair back in a simple black ribbon, without the powder, puffs and curls his fellow officers favored.

"I couldn't get near the punchbowl," he said, offering Anne both cups. "But I was lucky to snatch these from a tray on its way to the sweet table—hurry and choose before they melt."

One cup held a portion of pink ice cream molded in the shape of an open lily—the other, a pale yellow lemon adorned with a green silken leaf. Anne chose the lily. Edward handed her a small spoon from his pocket.

"Mmmm . . . strawberry!" Anne offered her cup to the captain for a taste. "Years back, I saved my pennies and took my son to the ice-cream shop on Nassau Street—the shopkeeper was from Italy—Jemmy chose vanilla. That was my first ice cream—this is my second."

"An ice-cream shop! We must go there and I will treat you to your third."

"I'm afraid when Mr. Washington quit the town, so did Mr. Bosio and his ice cream."

"Here, then—you must try some of mine." Blankenship fed Anne a generous spoonful of lemon flavor, and they finished the treat in an exchange of smiles and tiny grunts of pleasure.

Edward set the empty cups on the mantel. "Let's dance!"

"I don't know the steps," Anne explained with an apologetic shrug. "Feel free to choose another partner—I can amuse myself . . ."

"Don't be ridiculous." He took Anne by the hand. "Come along— I'd like for you to meet some of my friends." Blankenship led her through the throng, across the entry hall to the withdrawing room. Music from the ballroom filtered into the comfortable salon. Much less crowded, the room faced the bay, its windows thrown open to a refreshing sea breeze.

Anne swam in a thick soup of regret as they approached Edward's fellow officers and their wives, suddenly aware she should have paid heed to Sally's good instincts. The wives were all dressed in the latest pastel silk and painted floral frocks, hooped and trimmed with all manner of ribbons, ruching and furbelows. Rather than melt into the background by wearing a dress so dark and sadly unadorned, Anne stood out like a crow pecking at a snowdrift.

"I would like for you all to meet my dear friend Mrs. Anne Merrick . . ." Edward made the round of introductions. She could see disapproval in the female eyes coursing the tops of elaborate fans—their men uncomfortable and filled with pity for their friend to have brought such a drab bird into their midst.

The conversation turned immediately to a not-very-subtle discussion of the latest London fashions, and Anne knew right then the evening would be a wasted effort. Nothing of value could be gained by congress with these callow beings. Anne feigned interest in their meaningless babble about horse-racing on Long Island, and cricket matches at the ropewalk, and she squelched an overwhelming desire to shout, "My God, but we are at war!"

Drawing out her fan, she mumbled, "I feel the need for a breath of fresh air . . . Please forgive me . . ." And she went to stand by an open window.

Edward followed after, his forehead ruffled with true concern. "Are you unwell?"

"I'm fine." Anne sighed. "But I am sorry to be such an embarrassment for you . . ." She plucked at one of the bows on her dress. "I've been in mourning-wear for so long, this actually seemed rather gay to me."

"Anne"—Blankenship placed a hand at the small of her back and bent to her ear—"I think you are quite the most beautiful woman here."

Anne smiled. "You are very kind, Edward . . ."

"Excuse me, Captain, sir," a young cornet squeaked and tapped Edward on the shoulder. "General Howe invites you and the lady to join him for a glass of wine . . ." The cornet indicated an older officer in powdered wig and a uniform heavy with galloon trim and military decoration engaged in conversation with a group at the opposite end of the withdrawing room.

Blankenship dismissed the messenger and turned to Anne. "General Howe!" With eyebrows raised, he proffered an elbow. "Are you ready to advance, Mrs. Merrick?"

Anne wove her hand through the crook. "Sally forth, Captain . . ."

Opportunity! Anne's heart raced, and she used her fan to flutter the flush from her cheeks as they covered the length of the room. The man standing to General Howe's right, wearing the uniform of the Loyalist Brigade, she knew to be Oliver De Lancey—a most wealthy and prominent New Yorker. De Lancey had once been a customer at

Merrick Press. Anne whispered from behind her fan, "Who is the very tall naval officer?"

"Admiral Richard Howe, the general's brother."

"The fat fellow?"

"General Grant."

"And the blonde in pink?"

"The Sultana."

The High Command and the general's mistress. Senses tuned and ready, Anne composed her features and folded her fan into her pocket.

Blankenship met his superior's nod with a simple bow at the waist. "Gentlemen, Mrs. Loring—I would like to introduce Mrs. Anne Merrick, proprietress of the Royal Coffeehouse and a citizen of this city." He plucked two glasses of chilled white wine offered from a waiter's tray, and handed one to Anne. "Mrs. Merrick is one of a mere handful who not only suffered persecution at the hands of the Liberty Boys, but also withstood the occupation of the rebel army."

"Widow Merrick." Oliver De Lancey nodded. "I recall your husband—a good man—fiercely loyal to His Majesty."

Anne adopted the sad widow visage she'd perfected years before in dealing with her creditors. "Yes . . . Mr. Merrick was a devoted subject and supporter of the Commonwealth."

Elizabeth Loring raised her glass. "Then we have a thing in common, Mrs. Merrick . . . I, too, have a husband most willing to sacrifice to the Commonwealth."

The brash toast drew a hearty chuckle from the brothers Howe— Mr. Loring being famous throughout the colonies for trading his conjugal rights to William Howe in exchange for the lucrative position as commissary of prisons. Anne could not resist being amused by the woman's bold and clever dig at her awful husband.

Unprincipled as she might be, Howe's mistress was by any standard a striking beauty. Provincial sensibilities were shocked by the arrangement the general had come to in procuring his bed and gambling companion. But wagging tongues did not stop Mrs. Loring from fully enjoying her position as consort to the most powerful man on the continent.

Muttering, "Damn gout," General Grant pulled up a parlor chair and sat. Anne thought it a testament to its maker that the chair did not crumple under his enormous weight. "Might I ask, Mrs. Merrick," he asked, fleshy wattles animated with every word, "with the coming of the rebel army, and loyal citizens abandoning the city in droves—among them our friend De Lancey here—why did you choose to remain?"

"To be honest, sir, after my husband's demise, I had become accustomed to leading an independent life." Anne decided to keep to the truth as much as she could. "The notion of leaving my wherewithal and returning to that tight place beneath my father's thumb was more fearsome to me than any threat posed by rebel marauders."

"Bravo!" Mrs. Loring raised her glass once again.

"I bore witness to a few rebel mobs, Mrs. Merrick," De Lancey said. "It must have been a frightening time in our fair city."

Anne nodded. "By far the worst day was when the rebels evacuated the city. We were left with only the most desperate criminals and murderers pillaging up and down the streets . . . My maid and I forted up on the second story and kept a vigil with pistols at the ready. I would have done some damage to any scoundrels trespassing on my property."

"Pistols at the ready." Mrs. Loring was impressed. "And here I thought you such a delicate creature . . ."

"Oh, I freely admit to being most relieved when the Union Jack was run up the flagpole at Fort George that evening."

"De Lancey!" General Grant shot an elbow into his friend's ribs. "You should enlist Mrs. Merrick into your Loyalist Brigade, aye?"

"I can't help but notice this unusual necklet . . ." Mrs. Loring touched a manicured finger to the ribbon at Anne's neck.

"It is an oddment, I admit, but of more value to me than any gold or diamonds." Anne laid her hand over the little half-heart. "A token from the day the rebels destroyed the statue of the King."

"You stood witness to that perfidy?" General Grant blustered, his face as bright as a beet. Anne feared the man was about to pop like a boil.

"I did not dare to protest, sir; the mob was most wild and rabid—but I managed to salvage this broken shard. Part of a crown, you see?" She held the necklet up for inspection, and with complete sincerity said, "In my darkest hours, this scrap of iron has given me much comfort."

The brooding admiral spoke for the first time. "You are very brave, Mrs. Merrick. A credit to all Englishwomen."

Anne was glad of the response, and she drove to her purpose. "Do not credit me with more than stubbornness, sir. By my experience, I have learned I am most happy with the security provided by our good men at arms." She turned to General Howe. "I hear the officers talk in my shop, and my greatest fear is that the army will once again leave the city . . ."

"Hmmph," the admiral grunted. "There's a turn—most are complaining that the army does *not* leave the city . . ."

William Howe took the bottle from the wine chiller, and refilled everyone's glass. "Be at ease, Mrs. Merrick, my strategy to crush this rebellion includes maintaining a strong garrison force in New York." Stuffing the bottle back into the bucket of shaved ice, he raised Mrs. Loring's hand to his lips. "Show Mrs. Merrick to the observatory, my dear. We will join you there shortly for the *feu de joie*."

Anne watched over her shoulder as Howe led Blankenship and the others into the adjoining study, closing the door. *The captain will be a fountain of information . . .*

"Soldier's talk—nothing more boring." Betsey Loring rolled her eyes as she dragged Anne up a sweeping broad stair to the second floor. Skirts in one hand, glasses in the other, the women mounted a straight staircase to the third floor, and then climbed a cast-iron spiral stair to the rooftop balcony. A sturdy whitewashed balustrade surrounded the small area, with lit glass-paned lanterns resting on posts at either end. The Kennedy Mansion sat at the very tip of Manhattan, and the observatory faced a glorious purple and pink twilight view of the fleet on the bay and twinkling islands beyond.

"Oh, Mrs. Loring! Isn't it breathtaking?" Anne had never been so high off the ground. She leaned out over the rail, and could see the rooftop of the Cup and Quill.

"You must call me Betsey, and I shall call you Anne." Mrs. Loring put her back to the view, and leaned against the balustrade. Pulling a handkerchief and an enameled snuffbox from her pocket, she tapped her finger three times to the lid. "Do you imbibe?"

"No . . . thank you," Anne demurred.

Betsey flipped the lid open and scooped up a pinch with a tiny silver spoon she wore on a long chain about her neck. She placed spoon to nose and after one quick intake produced the requisite sneeze into the handkerchief. "Ah! Try some—clears the head of superfluous humors." She handed Anne the box.

Anne admired the finely wrought image of a nightingale on a blossoming branch decorating the cover of the snuffbox. "What a pretty thing."

"A naughty gift from William. Look—" Betsey took the box back, and she revealed a secret inner lid, illustrated with a very detailed and lewd pose of a man and woman copulating.

Perhaps it was the wine—for she was unused to spirits. Or perhaps it was Mrs. Loring's frank presentation, but the image caused Anne to burst into giggling.

Betsey Loring laughed as well and snapped the snuffbox shut. "You are a kindred spirit, Anne, of which I have few. Promise you will come visit me when we move to Philadelphia."

"Philadelphia?" Anne grew solemn. "When are you going to Philadelphia?"

"William tells me he and Richard will take the fleet there in July." Howe's mistress fluffed the flounces at each elbow.

What day? Which regiments? How many ships? How many troops? Swallowing back a hundred questions, Anne trod lightly fishing for specifics. "As soon as July? It is sad, then, that we didn't meet earlier . . ." She sighed. "Though June is only just beginning . . ."

Betsey brightened. "That's true. William won't be ready to leave until mid-July, so I will probably join him after the rebel capital is secured—sometime in August, no doubt. Johnny Burgoyne will take Albany, and then Washington will be thoroughly trounced! Oh, I foresee a winter season in Philadelphia to rival that in London." She looped her arm through Anne's. "You must visit."

Philadelphia and Albany. Anne's head spun with the news.

"Oh, my dear!" Betsy cocked her head, her brow puckered. "You mustn't fret for your handsome captain!" She put her arm around Anne's shoulder and gave her a squeeze. "I know for a fact William plans for him to stay in New York as a member of Clinton's garrison."

Heavy boots clanging on the spiral stair heralded the men arriving to view the salute in honor of the King's birthday. Mrs. Loring latched onto the general's arm, and Edward Blankenship came to stand beside Anne on the crowded balcony. He smelled of strong spirits and she could see the slight residue of snuff caught on his upper lip.

Admiral Howe determined the sky suitably dark, and he waved one of the lanterns over his head. Three big warships were anchored separate from the main fleet, and moments after the admiral's signal their guns exploded in a series of deafening salutes, and were immediately answered by a resounding cannonade from Fort George. Celebrants poured out onto the terraces below. The band struck up "God Save the King," and proud voices rose up in chorus.

A crew set up on a barge not too distant from the shoreline ignited a firework display. Rockets zipped up into the air, careening overhead, bursting into silver and gold flowers and stars trailing showers of glimmering sparks.

Feu de joie. Fire of joy.

Anne turned her smiling face to the flashing light and in her mind composed the missive she would write in the morning.

Chapter Sixteen

We are endeavoring, and will steadily continue
to endeavor, to separate and dissolve a connection which
hath already filled our land with blood.

THOMAS PAINE, *Common Sense*

Wednesday, June 4, 1777
At Lyon's Slip, Near the Fly Market

YELLOW fuzz sprouted along the horizon, and like a slab of wet slate, the East River rippled blue-gray, glossy in the tinge of light. Daylight crept up into the sky, reaching out to graze the city's steeple points as Jack worked the oars—and Titus the tiller— crossing the water from Long Island to Manhattan.

They muscled into the slip, knocking the pettiauger through a crowd of market boats jostling for a place at the dock like chickens flocking to strewn grain. Standing at the edge, a barefoot boy with ill-cropped hair and a dirty face shouted, "Throw a line!"

Jack tossed him the bowline. With wiry muscles as taut as the rope he tugged on, the boy pulled them in, hitching the boat with a dexterous knot to an iron cleat.

Always eager to set his feet on something solid, and anxious to see

Anne, Jack climbed out of the boat and stood the dock impatient, with hands on hips. "Quit dawdling, Titus. Let's get her unloaded."

The boy said, "I can fetch yiz an ox cartman."

"Find us a good-sized cart—" Jack tossed the enterprising boy a penny. "We've got twenty-five barrels of cabbage here."

"Pickled cabbage?"

"Yup—now cut mud and fetch us a cart."

The boy was in no hurry. "Like water to a dying man, cabbage is to them Hessians." He tucked the coin into the pocket of his grubby trousers. "For a shilling, sir, I can fetch you a Hessian who'll buy every bit of cabbage you have."

Very interested in a speedy discharge of their cargo, and impressed with the boy's business acumen, Jack asked, "What's your name, monkey?"

"Joe Birdsong."

"I tell you what, Master Birdsong—bring me a Hessian and I'll give you a shilling." Jack scrubbed the boy's head with his knuckles. "Be quick about it, and I'll add a sixpence."

Joe tore off, running up the earthen ramp to Maiden Lane.

Titus grabbed the sorry gray-horsehair wig Jack had left on his seat, and flipped it up onto the dock. "Keep your hair on!"

Jack made a face, but plopped the disheveled thing onto his head, stuffing his queue and stray wisps of black hair under it. "Hot and itchy . . ." he complained. "I don't see how anyone can stand to wear one of these things."

He and Titus were dressed in farmer's garb—smock shirts and leather breeches with coarse, worsted-wool stockings. To avoid being recognized as bearded Jack Stapleton, errant scout to the 17th Light Dragoons, Jack kept his face so close-shaven Titus had taken to calling him "baby boy." Besides changing into very humble attire, Titus altered his appearance by shaving his head completely bald, earning himself the name of "flap ears."

"And wear your hat . . ." Titus scolded, as he donned a linen skullcap.

Jack set a wide-brimmed felt hat over the wig. "There! You happy, flap ears?"

"I am."

Titus rolled the thirty-gallon barrels up the planks and onto the dock, then Jack took over, and rolled them to stand upright in two rows along the dock's edge. They had just finished off-loading the cargo when Joe Birdsong returned with a green-coated German officer in tow, announcing, "Couldn't find a Hessian—but this Brunswicker is just as good—worth a shilling, and I was quick."

"He is, and you were," Jack agreed, dropping one and six in Joe's cupped hand.

A big, sturdy fellow—as were all members of the elite Jäger Rifle Corps—the German was ready to do business. He slapped his hand down on a barrel and proclaimed, "*Sechzehn schilling.*" Sweeping a hand to indicate the entire cargo, he jerked his square chin up and said, "*Alles dieses—zwanzig pfund.* Twenty pount."

Twenty pounds was double the price they'd expected for this cargo, carried as a ruse to get into the city. Jack looked at Titus for a confirming nod, and to the stern-jawed Jäger's surprise, without issuing a counteroffer, Jack said, "Sold!"

"Yer sech a jingle brain," Joe Birdsong groaned. "I bet ye could have got eighteen a keg . . ."

Having struck such a good bargain, the happy German hurried off to hire a cart. After the barrels were loaded onto it, he tore two ten-pound banknotes from a bound booklet, and handed them to Jack in final payment.

"No." Jack waved his hands in refusal. "No paper. I want coin."

The German offered the notes again. "*Ya.* You take."

"That's good money, sir," Joe Birdsong piped up. "You *have* to take it."

"*Ya. Ya.*" The Brunswicker shagged his big head up and down, and waved the notes in Jack's face. "*Ist gut. Ist gut.* You take. Twenty pount. You take."

"Listen, Johann—good money is made from silver or gold . . ."

Jack pulled a guinea from his pocket as an example. "I want coin. No coin—no cabbage. You understand?"

The Brunswicker took a step forward and tried to put the cash into Jack's hand. "You must take . . ."

Jack shook the German off, and grabbed ahold of one of the barrels on the cart. "C'mon, Titus, help me unload . . ."

"*Nein!*" The Brunswicker tossed the money to the dock, and sent Jack flying backward with an angry two-handed shove. The German banged his hand to the wagon boards, and shouted at the drayman, "Go . . . *go!*"

Jack threw off the hat and wig. Eyes hooded in rage, he lunged at the German. The two men thumped against the cart in a fierce grapple.

"*Godammit!*" Titus took off chasing after the banknotes, blown over the edge of the dock into the pettiauger.

Joe Birdsong scrambled up to the top of the cabbage barrels and together with the drayman shouted, "*Fight! Fight!*"

Dockworkers, farmers, porters and draymen abandoned their business and rushed to form a ring of onlookers, cheering and laying wagers.

"Tuppence on the green-jacket . . ."

"I'll take that bet—that dark fella has a mean eye . . ."

Like a pair of rams with horns locked, Jack and the German planted their feet in a contest of strength and will, breaking apart for a moment, only to collide again with growling full force. In a shuffle of feet—each man trying to throw the other down—both men tottered off balance, falling to the deck in a great thud and grunt.

Wincing, groaning and cheering with every blow, the crowd shifted from one edge of the dock to the other as the fighters rolled in a tangle of swinging fists and elbows.

"The provost!" Joe Birdsong warned from his raised perch. "The provost is comin'!"

A shrill whistle screamed out in three sharp blasts, silencing the crowd in an instant. The fighters separated—Jack rolled onto his back, panting. The Brunswicker struggled up to his feet, hands propped to knees, and coughed up a wad of red-tinged sputum. Titus rushed in and pulled Jack upright.

Preceded by Sergeant O'Keefe and his silver whistle, the provost marshall made his way into the circle. Though his pinhead and prodigious ears were somewhat disguised by a very good-quality queued wig of brown hair, Jack was still able to recognize Cunningham as the man they'd tried to tar and feather beneath the Liberty Pole years before.

Tall and lank as the shank of a soupspoon, the provost wore an austere suit of dark worsted wool and heavy jackboots. A stiff, black leather stock was buckled tight around a neck too long for his narrow shoulders. Suspended by a red ribbon, a silver gorget engraved with the Royal Arms provided him a badge of office, a scrap of color and a little light reflected on his gaunt, pox-pitted face. He carried a cane—a rigid malacca shaft, the knob end a hissing serpent's head wrought in chaste silver.

Catching his wind, and swiping the blood trickling from his nose with the kerchief Titus provided, Jack thought if death were a man, he would look exactly like William Cunningham.

Cunningham tapped the cart with his cane. "What do we have here?"

The Brunswicker began barking out a tirade. Casting many a glare Jack's way, he let loose with a long string of guttural syllables, alternately waving his arms, pounding a fist to his palm and pointing at Jack and the cartload of pickled cabbage.

Jack could not understand a single word, but the tone was enough to get him shouting in defense. "He's the one what started it—the madman attacked me! I'd rather feed it to the dogs than sell this twat-lick a shred of my cabbage!"

"*Desist!*" Cunningham ordered, pounded his walking stick to the dock, the tendons on his neck corded. "Or I will have you brought to reason with the aid of nine cattails!"

Titus pulled Jack back and handed him his hat, muttering, "*Don't be an idiot!*" through gritted teeth.

A mustachioed Hessian appeared and in clipped and precise English offered to translate for the Brunswicker. After the two Germans finished a brief, head-nodding conversation, the Hessian pointed at Jack. "This peasant refused to accept banknotes in exchange for his cabbage. The peasant has broken the law and must be punished."

Cunningham turned to Jack and demanded, "Your name and permit, sir."

Jack put his hat on, the brim low over his brow, and he dug a folded paper from his pocket. "A peaceful man, I am, sir"—he offered the page to the provost—"but I defend myself when attacked, as anyone would."

"Aye, the green-jacket started the fight," the drayman concurred. "I saw the whole thing. Gave this farmer a right rough shove when he refused the banknotes."

Titus swept his hat off, and handed the provost the two ten-pound notes. "The German threw these to the ground, sir, afore he went mad and attacked my master."

Cunningham studied the permit. "Charles Hampton of Flatlands, Long Island—farmer."

"Aye, sir." Jack tugged at the brim of his hat in salute, pulling it down to cast a deeper shadow over his features.

The provost took a step forward—a slight cock to his head. "Have we ever chanced to meet before?"

Resisting a strong urge to look away, Jack replied, "Not that I recall, sir. It has been some years since I've come to the city."

"Well, Mr. Hampton, the Germans are correct," Cunningham announced. "It is unlawful to refuse the currency of the realm—as it is unlawful to brawl in the streets."

"I was not aware, sir—about the currency." Jack shrugged. "I was taught from a lad to trade our produce for silver, rather than risk being duped by counterfeit bills."

"In this case your caution is unwarranted. These bills are quite genuine." Cunningham handed back the permit and the banknotes. "Take the money, Mr. Hampton . . . Let the German have his cabbage, and put an end to this unfortunate misunderstanding—or I will act."

"Of course, sir—and I thank you, sir." Jack folded the papers into his pocket, noting the Irish burr in the provost's not-so-veiled threat. "My temper often gets the better of me. I apologize for having disturbed the peace."

"Good man, now be about your business . . ." Cunningham tapped the dock twice with his walking stick. ". . . *All of you! About your business.*"

Sergeant O'Keefe and Cunningham went to stand on the quay and watch the crowd disperse—O'Keefe with arms folded, glaring with beady pig eyes, and Cunningham in a casual but somehow malicious stance—legs apart—both hands resting on his cane.

The happy Germans followed the cabbage cart up the ramp to Maiden Lane. Titus tossed one gunny to Jack, and swung the other over his shoulder. "Let's go."

Joe Birdsong ran after Jack, waving the gray wig. "Hey, mister! Ye left yer wig behind!"

Jack's eye darted to the ratty wig, and to Cunningham observing the entire exchange with that squint to his eye. "Not my wig, lad. You can see I wear my own." He raised his hat, showing off his thick black hair, and in a softer voice said, "But if you fail to find the owner, the wig-maker might give you a sixpence for it . . ."

"I got ye . . ." Joe winked, and stuffed the wig inside his shirt.

Jack didn't need to look back. He could feel Cunningham's eyes sizzling holes in the back of his head as he hurried up the ramp to Maiden Lane. He and Titus both heaved a sigh when at last they turned the corner out of sight.

Titus gave Jack a hard punch on the arm. "So you just had to have coin, eh?"

"I know . . ." Jack rubbed his arm. "I am such an ass—but I never figured the German to lose his wits . . . He went mad, he did."

"Crazy for pickled cabbage, they are," Titus agreed, shaking his head.

They traipsed down Queen Street toward the Cup and Quill, and Titus nudged Jack. "Does everything seem off-kilter to you?"

Jack nodded. "I don't like it."

The shops were burgeoning with the wrong sorts of goods—like tea and woolen fabric—and the clotheslines were filled with the wrong sorts of laundry. The women gathered in clutches, gossiping in the wrong language, and the soldiers all wore the wrong uniforms. Jack loved his New York, but this New York made him anxious to be back on the pettiauger, rowing away.

They turned onto Anne's lane, and grabbing each other by the arm, Titus and Jack skittered back around the corner onto Dock Street.

"Damn! Right in front of the Cup and Quill . . . you can spot those helmets a mile away."

"The *Crown* and Quill—" Titus corrected. Peering casually around the corner he muttered, "On guard. Three dragoons coming this way."

They dropped down to hunkers. Jack pulled the brim of his hat down low, and they pretended to search through a gunnysack. Rising upright after the Redcoats passed them by, Titus said, "Wait here—I'll go on a scout."

Jack took a step out and watched Titus, one hand in his pocket, the other gripping the gunnysack on his shoulder in a happy-go-lucky stroll down the lane. He stopped beneath the sign of the Crown and Quill, and after tying both shoes, turned and strolled back. Taking Jack by the arm, he steered a path toward the Battery.

"Crawling with Redcoats. And that captain—the one who signed us up in Flatbush? He's sitting in the front window with two others from the Seventeenth."

"The front window?"

"Yep. New glass."

"Hmmph . . . Did you see Anne?"

"Nope . . ." Titus shook his head. "Caught a glimpse of Sally, though—serving *tea!*"

"I guess we'd better come back after closing time." Jack slapped

Titus on the shoulder. "C'mon. We can get a cup of coffee at Montagne's."

"I hope so," Titus mumbled. "I don't care much for tea."

∞ ∞ ∞

"I think we're through the worst of the morning rush." Anne untied her apron and hung it on the peg behind the kitchenhouse door. She filled a ewer with water, lit a beeswax taper and screwed it into a candledish. "I'm going upstairs to get my book work done . . ."

Sally put on a crafty smile. "There's a basket of laundry in my room. Would you be a honey and hang it out on the line?"

"I can do that!" Anne carried the water and the candle up to her room and set it on her desk. She opened the shuttered window, and a pleasant breeze blew in along with bright sunlight. She shut and bolted her door.

A puff of violet and cerulean silk sat in the middle of the room—a perfect circle—as if the woman who'd worn the dress had melted away. Anne gathered up the fabric and tossed it onto her rumpled bed, and eyed the rouge smudges on her pillowslip.

She and Edward had returned to the Crown and Quill just past midnight the night before. Unused to keeping such late hours, Anne did not need to feign exhaustion. All she wanted was to be up the stairs, in her room, out of her stays and into her bed.

A gentleman sees a lady to her door—

The captain insisted. She had no choice but to allow a slightly worse-for-the-drink Edward Blankenship to escort her all the way up to her garret room door. It was a relief to see Sally at the ready, peeking through a crack in her door, ready to leap out and bludgeon the man with the iron poker she'd taken to keeping at her bedside ever since the Redcoats moved in. But Blankenship made no untoward advances. He bid Anne good night with a chaste kiss on the cheek, and a courtly bow. Even Sally had to agree, the captain was a gentleman.

Anne cleared the mess of rouge pots, pins and ribbons from her writing desk and sat down with pencil and paper to draft a simple letter listing the information she had learned from Mrs. Loring the night before—that Howe planned to take the fleet to Philadelphia sometime in mid-July, and that Burgoyne was marching his troops to Albany.

Anne proofed her draft to make certain she'd worded the intelligence correctly, and her heart began to thump in her head. Pushing away from the desk, she stared at the words she'd just scrawled across the page. She had not foreseen becoming a conduit to the British High Command months before, when she sought out Hercules Mulligan in his tailor shop on Queen Street. These words were no mumbled rumors overheard while pouring tea and serving scones—this letter was by far the most important and valid intelligence she had ever passed along.

These are words to swing from a gibbet for . . .

Anne smiled, and set about making her ink. Her mother had taught her how to mix all manner of ink—writing inks, colored inks, India ink and as a lark—invisible ink.

She kept her supplies in the desk drawer—a tin measure, a clear glass tumbler, a silver butter knife and a quart jar filled with salt of hartshorn. Anne poured a stream of water into the tumbler, up to the mark she'd scratched in the glass with a sharp awl. She scooped up a measure of hartshorn, and cut the knife across the top, carefully scraping the excess back into the jar. She dumped the coarse powder into the water. With the blade ringing bright against the glass, she stirred and stirred, holding the concoction to the light, to make sure every last grain of hartshorn was completely dissolved. Once the ink was mixed, she conducted a test, to be certain the mixture worked.

Five reams of rose-colored foolscap wrapped in brown paper were stacked beside her desk. Anne opened one package, and peeled off a sheet. Dipping her quill into the tumbler, she thought for a moment, and wrote "Jack" across the top of the page. As the clear liquid dried, the word disappeared. Anne held the page close to the heat of the candle flame. Like magic, "Jack" appeared, as if written with thick black ink.

Anne took a fresh sheet and copied her draft exact. It had taken some getting used to—writing with clear liquid. She had found through trial and error that the invisible ink worked best on English-made tinted paper. Once the missive was thoroughly dry, the writing was undetectable, and the page looked no different than any other blank page in the ream.

She inserted her secret writing exactly thirty-six pages from the top of the pile, rewrapped the ream in brown paper, secured the package in a crisscross of the same blue grosgrain ribbon she used for her garters and tied it off in a pretty bow. "There!"

Anne burned the draft copy, and stowed her ink-making supplies. Three of Sally's blue petticoats and six plain white petticoats were sent flapping over the lane. She tucked the ribbon-wrapped package under her arm and skipped down the stairs.

♣ ♣ ♣

"CANVAS Town they call it." Mrs. Day poured them each a cup of coffee, and pulled up a chair. "A desperate place—the poorest of the poor live in those crumbled ruins, on cinders under canvas stretched over charred beams. Their children roam the streets in packs, competing with dogs for the meanest scraps."

Mr. Day dropped a large lump of sugar into his cup. "By night Canvas Town's a haven for thieves, whores and the most wicked and depraved—not a morning goes by but they don't find some poor sot with his head stove in, stripped clean of valuables—"

"—or some poor unfortunate woman ravaged with her throat slit," Mrs. Day added with a sad shake of her head. "The Watch won't even patrol there."

"I don't blame them. Not when Canvas Towners will murder a Redcoat in a trice for his buttons alone! You mind what I say." Mr. Day shook a knobby finger. "Stay far away from there, lads. It's a desperate place."

"The reek of it's enough to keep me away," Titus said. "I never in my life smelt anything as awful."

"Like burnt hair, fly-blown corpse and pigpen all rolled into one."

Jack made a face like he'd been force-fed a spoonful of manure, and shuddered. "We only walked down Broad Way, and I still can't get the stench to leave my nose."

Mrs. Day nodded. "When the wind's wrong, the smell from Canvas Town poisons the entire city."

Jack and Titus had spent the morning wandering up Broad Way from the Battery, unable to believe their eyes or their noses. Montagne's—once a home to the Liberty Boys, and one of Jack's favorite haunts—had become the Red Lion, and was overrun with Redcoats.

Day's Tavern proved to be an oasis in a desert of depression and disappointment. Mrs. Day was famous for her soups and stews, and Jack used to frequent the tavern at the end of Murray Street back when he kept a room on Barclay Street. There were only a few customers left from the midday crowd—none of them British military—but because "you never know who's who these days," the Days led Jack and Titus to a very private table in the garden.

Mr. Day leaned forward. "You know, there's a handful of us stalwarts left behind, and like you lads, we do what we can for the cause—keep our eyes and ears open, we do."

"Sometimes I wish we hadn't stayed." Mrs. Day laid her hand upon her husband's shoulder. "The city is that much changed."

The Liberty Pole on the Commons had been torn down, and a gallows, ironically, erected in its stead. "I knew the pole would not stand once the Redcoats marched in," Mr. Day said. "But the very day after the fire, a man was hanged for a spy on the new gallows, and the devil Cunningham left the body to swing for three full days."

"A fearful, disturbing warning . . ." Mrs. Day brought a full tray to the table.

The hospital at King's College and the sugarhouses were converted into inhumane prisons, from where emaciated bodies were collected daily and stacked like cordwood in wagons heading up the Post Road.

"Starved to death, they are—and not given any kind of a burial, our poor lads. Cunningham's henchmen dump the bodies into ditches and ravines." Mrs. Day ladled a fish stew into four bowls, and set out a basket filled with chewy brown bread and a crock of sweet butter.

"And with Canvas Town—a full quarter of the city, mind you— reduced to misery, filth and abject squalor, the British bastards hold horse races, cricket matches and gala dancing parties with ice creams and fireworks!" Day banged his fist to the table. "Why it took us this long to revolt, I don't know."

"Mr. Day! You are too loud," his wife admonished.

The door adjoining the tavern room to the garden opened and Patsy Quinn popped her head around. "It *is* you!" She came over to the table, talking very fast. "Hildie said she saw you in Day's, and at first I said, 'You're a daft old purse,' but then I ran over to see if she might be telling true. Oh, Jack!" Patsy threw her arms around him and pressed a cheek to his. "It does my heart good to see you!"

"It's good to see you, too, Pats." In daylight, with her fresh-washed face framed by a straw hat, and wearing a modest dress, Patsy Quinn might be anyone's sister out for an afternoon stroll, in-stead of an "unfortunate woman" employed by Mother Babcock.

"Sit down, Patsy," Mrs. Day urged. "Have a bite to eat—I swan, you are as thin as a rail."

Mr. Day brought a chair and Patsy sat beside Jack and latched onto his arm. Not able to endure Titus's withering glare, Jack extri-cated his arm from Patsy's grip. "I suppose Mother Babcock's was spared by the flames."

"You should come and see for yourself." Patsy winked.

"Ah, no . . . we're only here for the day—on business—right, Ti-tus?"

"Yup." Titus dug into his bowl.

Patsy took a piece of bread, and used Jack's knife to smooth a thick layer of butter over it. "Business with the Stitch, right?"

Jack grabbed a spoon. "This stew looks delicious, Mrs. Day."

"You're among friends here." Patsy leaned toward Jack, dropping her voice. "We all work with the Stitch—tell 'em, Mr. Day."

"Eyes and ears," Mr. Day said.

"I know!" Patsy clapped. "You're working with the engraver, right?"

"Engraver?" Titus hitched his chair in closer.

Jack took a bite from his bread. "Patsy." He chewed. "I don't know what you are talking about."

"Don't play coy." Patsy gave Jack a nudge. "The Stitch said he might bring you in on it."

"Honest, Patsy, I haven't heard from him . . ."

"We only came in for the day," Titus added. "To fetch the widow."

Jack shot Titus a look that could cleave stone. Poor Patsy looked as if her bread had just fallen buttered side to the ground. "What widow?"

Jack locked eyes on his bowl, stirring his stew.

Patsy turned to Titus. "What widow?"

Titus grinned. "The Widow Merrick, from the Cup and Quill. Jack fancies her."

Patsy spun around. "You *fancy* that Tory bitch?"

"Keep that evil tongue within your teeth, Patsy Quinn," Mrs. Day warned. "You know I don't like that kind of talk in my place."

"She's as much a Tory as you are." Jack bristled. "Not that it's any of your business, but yes—I care for Anne Merrick—and I am here to get her out of the city."

Patsy sat back in her chair. "You'll first have to pry her off that handsome dragoon she lives with." She broke off a little bit of bread and popped it into her mouth. "Oh, you didn't know about him? A big man—a full-handed man, by the look of him . . ."

Jack slammed his hand to the table. "That's enough!"

". . . I'll wager he gives the widow a good hard ride on his sugar stick."

"Good lack, have you no sense?" Mrs. Day took Patsy by the arm. "It's time for you to go."

Patsy waved as she was led away. "I know I'll see you soon, Jack!"

Jack sat with half-hooded eyes, fists balled in his lap.

Mr. Day broke the silence. "Everyone is forced to quarter soldiers these days."

"Pay no mind to Patsy," Titus said with a flip of his hand. "I always thought she was head over heels for you, and there's the proof. Hell hath no fury like a woman scorned."

"Handsome dragoon," Jack repeated. "Dodd said as much—Tully, too."

"You know, Jack," Mr. Day said. "You can sit here and stew in a dark cloud, iffing and wondering over the whore's gossip, or you can go to your woman and find out the truth."

"How am I supposed to go to her?" Jack slumped in his chair. "The Cup and Quill is crawling with Redcoats. They *live* there."

"Write a note—arrange a meeting place—talk to her," Mrs. Day suggested.

Mr. Day agreed. "Titus can deliver the note. No one pays any mind to black folk . . ."

"That's a plan." Titus stood and swung his gunny over his shoulder. "Write the note."

ᑫ ᑫ ᑫ

THE Crown and Quill did a brisk business all day, and the afternoon flew by. No one came by to purchase paper.

Anne and Sally worked around the handful of customers still finishing their tea—sweeping and wiping down tables, making ready to close up shop for the day, when an odd little man wearing blue glass spectacles began to hover near the open doorway. Anne grabbed Sally by the arm before she could shoo him away.

"Wait . . . that might be him . . ."

The man seemed at a loss. He finally stepped inside, turning one way, then another, going back out to check the sign. He finally settled in a seat near the window, and commenced to drumming his fingers on the table's edge.

"Naw, Annie . . ." Sally said. "That one doesna seem right in the head." The women leaned on their brooms, scrutinizing the strange customer from a distance.

But for a fringe of brown hair running around the back of his head from ear to ear, the man's pate was as hairless and smooth as an ostrich egg. In combination with the round-colored lenses masking his eyes, he looked like some kind of queer bug. He wore plain wool and linen, and Anne thought he might be a Quaker. She went to take his order.

"Coffee, sir? Or perhaps a pot of black bohea?"

He deliberated longer than most, vacillating. At last he decided on tea, adding with a guilty smile, "It's been quite some time since I've had a cup, you know."

He drank his tea heavy with cream and sugar, chuckling and sighing aloud with every bite of Sally's shortbread. Anne decided she must be demented for thinking this eccentric little man would have anything to do with delivering intelligence to General Washington.

The man paid for his tea, and as Anne handed over his change, he said in a voice very loud, "I'd like to purchase a ream of writing paper, madam!"

"You would?" Anne squeaked. "An entire ream?"

"Yes. I—I'm going to pen my memoirs." He puffed out his chest and almost shouted, "I'd like to purchase a ream of writing paper, madam—and a quill!"

"Of course—just a moment."

Except for the mention of memoirs, the signal was exact and correct. Making a "can you believe it" face at Sally, Anne retrieved the ribbon-wrapped packet of paper and one goose-feather quill from the big cabinet where she kept her inventory of stationery supplies. She set the items on his table, and said with emphasis, "That will be *three and six.*"

Fumbling with his coin purse, he held every shilling an inch from his eye before snapping it down to the tabletop, muttering the price over and over, "Three and six. Three shillings sixpence. Three and six . . ." At last, he slid the four coins her way, and tapped the lens on his spectacles. "Blue—like the petticoats you put out. You know, they say blue will improve the eyesight, but I don't . . ."

"We thank you for your custom, sir." Anne put his purchase in his hands and hustled him out the door before he could blurt out anything else of import. "Please, don't forget—writing bond sold for the very reasonable price of *three and six*."

With the quill tucked behind one ear, and the paper under one arm, he was sent down the lane. Sally came to stand beside Anne, and they watched him turn and smile and wave every few steps. Anne waved back and worried, "I don't know . . ."

"Dinna fash." Sally stood waving beside Anne. "The Stitch knows what he's about. Even a wee mouse can creep under a great corn stack. Nobody would suspect tha' oddling for a courier, na?"

Just as the little man disappeared around the corner onto Dock Street, Edward Blankenship turned onto the lane. Upon seeing the women in the doorway, he swung a green glass bottle over his head and called, "Anne!" Speeding down the lane in a trot, he swept her up into his arms. Spinning around twice, the captain bent her back in an exuberant kiss.

Anne squealed and sputtered, "Oh my!" when set aright.

"You must congratulate me! You too, Sally!" His face was shining like a boy who'd just won a foot race. "I've been promoted! I am General Clinton's *First* Aide-de-Camp. A lieutenant colonelcy is not far behind, and perhaps soon, my own brigade!"

Anne straightened her mobcap. "Why, congratulations, of course!"

"Aye," Sally muttered. "Congratulations."

Blankenship showed Anne the bottle. "The finest Canary money could buy! We celebrate tonight with a toast. Have you seen Wemyss?"

"No sign of him yet, but Stuart is reading in the garden."

"Stuart!" The captain barreled past, shouting, "Good news . . ."

ಞ ಞ ಞ

"You told her to be a Tory . . . I heard you myself." Titus and Jack marched a quickstep down Duke Street. "That Patsy—she's nothing but a jealous and spiteful whore. Hell hath no fury—"

"—like a woman scorned," Jack finished. "I know. You've told me it at least a dozen times already."

Titus threw an arm around his friend's shoulders. "You know, Mrs. Anne is a good woman—she can't help it if the British quartered a soldier in her place. You heard Mr. Day—almost everyone is forced to quarter soldiers . . ." Breathing hard, Titus had a hard time talking and keeping pace with Jack. "Once I deliver this note, Mrs. Anne and Sally will meet us down at the slip, and we can be away from this stink."

Turning the corner onto the little lane between Duke and Dock streets, Jack pulled Titus to a halt.

Anne and Sally were waiting under the sign, waving to Captain Edward Blankenship of the 17th Light Dragoons. The captain ran up, swept Anne Merrick into his arms and kissed her full on the mouth.

Titus grabbed Jack by both arms, and dragged him away.

CHAPTER SEVENTEEN

❧❧

The object, contended for, ought always to bear
some just proportion to the expense.

THOMAS PAINE, *Common Sense*

Friday, June 6, 1777
At the Sign of the Thimble and Shears

JACK lay on his left side, his face squashed against something slick and slimy. His shoulder and hip bone shifted of their own accord, trying to find comfort on a hard surface. Brushing away whatever was tickling the top of his head, Jack concentrated on opening his right eye, sustaining the effort for the briefest moment—long enough to see a flash of daylight.

"Unghh . . ." His mouth was sour and furred, as if he'd licked the inside of a musty old pickle barrel clean. Nearby, a pig snorted loud, and pixies giggled.

Jack forced his eye open again. An arm's length away, Titus Gilmore lay hugging a bolt of red Genoa velvet—emitting a phlegmy snore that would raise Lazarus from the dead. Jack blinked his one eye several times, but the pink ribbon tied in a bow around Titus's hairless head would not disappear.

"Unghh . . ." Jack pushed aside the drooled-upon bolt of blue satin he was using as a pillow and rolled onto his back. With the aid of index finger and thumb, he pried both eyes open and studied the ceiling rafters for clues to his whereabouts. Eyelids thus propped, Jack turned his head right, to see the pixies.

A pair of curly-headed freckle-faces stood beside the table he was lying upon, peering at him with merry blue eyes, giggling into their fingers. Jack struggled up to a sit, and sent the girls on a shrieking run. "Dad! Dad! One's awake, Dad! One's awake!"

"Unghh . . ." Jack cupped his ears.

Bearing a tray, Hercules Mulligan shooed the two squealers from the room. "Out, out, my honeys—away to your mother . . ." Setting his tray at the foot of the long, wide cutting table where Jack and Titus had made their bed, the tailor drew open the heavy curtains on the shop front window.

"*Unnghhhh* . . ." Jack's hands went from ears to eyes. The recollection of whiskey consumed, and the reason for consuming it in great quantity, pierced his brain like lightning sent from the heavens.

Mulligan was the burly sort of Irishman—not very tall, but broad in girth and thick about the shoulders and neck—his build and voice more suited to a rough and ready stevedore than to a fashion-conscious tailor. "Rise and shine, lads—rise and shine! My stitchers need to get to their work."

"Get up . . ." Jack grunted, giving Titus a shove. "The tailor needs his table."

Titus curled to the bolt of velvet as if it were a six-shilling whore. "Go . . . *away* . . ."

Jack scooted on his rump to sit with his stockinged feet dangling over the side of the table. His head weighed fifty pounds at least, and felt as if it were made of baked pumpkin held together with twine. He poked a finger to his brow, relieved to meet with hard skull.

"Hot coffee will make a human being of you." With an apple-cheeked grin, Mulligan slid a steaming mugful across the varnished oak.

Jack took up the stoneware cup with both hands. "Thanks, Hercules."

Persuaded by the aroma to abandon his velvet bedmate for a cup of coffee, Titus slid down to sit beside Jack, and he burst out laughing and pointing.

"What?" Jack patted his head—his hair had been arranged in a topknot and trussed with a blue satin ribbon. Tugging it free, Jack reached over and pulled at the ribbon tied about Titus's head. "Your noggin's been bedizened as well . . ."

"Young Mulligans up to no good." The laughing tailor shrugged. "Take your coffee, grab your gear and come to my office—my table monkeys need to be at their stitching."

The large cutting table was positioned at the front window to take best advantage of the natural light. Jack and Titus abdicated their bed to two lithe young men in linen caps with armfuls of fabric, and a third stitcher carrying a stack of wooden boxes filled with thread, needles, thimbles and bodkins. The tailors scrambled onto the tabletop to sit cross-legged in the good light, their work up off the dirty floor and close in their laps.

Hercules led the way through the small shop crowded with fabrics and imported goods. Rows of clothing in various stages of completion and repair hung from pegs mounted along the back wall. Titus noted the abundance of red wool on display.

"Doing a brisk trade among the lobsterbacks, eh?"

"My bread and butter, in more ways than one." Hercules opened the door to his office. "If you lads require a piss, the privy is out the back door . . ."

Both Jack and Titus dumped their gear and hurried to make use of the facilities before joining the Irishman in his office.

The pleasant room had a big window open to the garden, where a noisy array of ginger-headed Mulligans of assorted sex and size sat around a table eating bowls full of porridge. The tailor leaned over the table desk beneath the window and drew the muslin curtains shut. "Get the door," he said to Titus.

Compared to the cluttered shop, the tailor's office was an ordered and sparsely furnished haven—a tall cabinet occupied the whitewashed wall perpendicular to the desk beneath the window. An upholstered bench sat against the wall opposite the desk, and in the corner, a fruit-bearing lemon tree grew in a large earthenware pot.

Jack and Titus sank down on the bench, backs buttressed by the wall. Mulligan uncorked the bottle of whiskey on his desk, bringing it and a chair over to join them.

"Hair of the dog," Hercules said, adding a splash to their mugs. He hoisted his cup. "Here's to women's kisses, and to whiskey, amber clear—not as sweet as a woman's kiss, perhaps, but a damn sight more sincere."

"Hear, hear!" Titus bumped his mug to the tailor's.

Jack stared into his cup. "I'm through with talking about her."

"Mmm-hmm . . . and I don't blame you. Mrs. Anne kissing the dragoon that way—I still can't believe it." Bemused, Titus smoothed his hands over his head. "Still, there must be some explanation . . ."

"I'll explain it to you, Titus." Mulligan settled back in his chair. "Mrs. Anne is a Loyalist whore who fucks Redcoat officers."

"Harsh." Titus scowled. "Everyone takes you for a Loyalist, Hercules. Mrs. Anne might well be doing like you do—cozying up to the British to garner information."

"Jaysus, Titus." The Irishman shook his head. "If she were working for the cause, I'd be the first to know it. Jack gave her my name—didn't you, Jack?"

Head hanging low, Jack spoke through a ratty tangle of black hair. "Don't want to talk about her anymore."

Titus set his cup to the side. "Mrs. Anne could be working on her own. She is a clever and strong-willed woman, isn't she, Jack?"

Jack shrugged, hands wringing the coffee mug as if it were the Christmas goose.

"Titus, Titus, Titus . . ." Mulligan clucked. "The widow serving the British bastards their tea in her shop is one thing—the widow sucking the Redcoat cock quartered up the stairs is quite another . . ."

Jack leapt to his feet and whipped his mug across the room, hitting the potted plant in the corner. The crash silenced the chatter of children in an instant, and sent a half a dozen lemons thumping onto the floorboards. Face pinched and glaring, he growled through clenched teeth, "Not another word about that turncoat bitch—you hear? *Not another word!*" Reaching inside his shirt, he ripped the iron medallion from his neck and flung it to the floor.

Mulligan held his cup in the air. "Huzzah and hallelujah! Good to see you have a pair of bollocks after all . . ."

Titus bent to pick the half-crown from the floor, and Jack fell back into his seat, snarling, "Leave it lie!"

Hercules kicked the token to the wall and retrieved the mug— surprisingly still in one piece. Pouring more whiskey into it, he passed it back to Jack. "It is ill-advised for a man of your stamp to encumber himself with weighty matters of the heart—especially when I need you to work a job for me, a dangerous job. Are you up to it?"

Jack swallowed his whiskey in one gulp and met Mulligan's eye. "Counterfeiting?"

The tailor laughed. "You, my friend, are a rogue's rogue, to be sure."

"Not too hard to puzzle it out after Patsy made mention of an engraver." Jack jerked his head toward Titus. "Him and me often toy with the notion."

"Print a pile of notes and flood the market with 'em," Titus said. "The British wrecked the value of the Continental dollar with their counterfeits; we could do the same to them."

"Ahh, now, Titus . . . our own Congress had a hand in that mess as well. Counterfeiting in quantities to devalue the currency is a major operation—a grand scheme, to be sure"—Mulligan tossed down his whiskey and blinked—"but I'm just looking for a little pocket money."

Titus snorted. "Not worth risking a neck stretching for pocket money."

"A figure of speech—although I plan to change a few of our notes into coin to pay informants and couriers . . ." Mulligan straddled his chair, resting his forearms on the back. "We'll be trolling for bigger fish." The tailor shuffled forward a few inches. "Patsy has a quartermaster dangling on her line—one of His Majesty's bad bargains—the bastard commandeers trade goods for *military use*, then turns 'em for a profit on the black market. With a supply of British currency, we could purchase the goods and deliver to Washington necessary accoutrements like shoes, blankets, canvas . . ."

"I don't know, Hercules," Titus said. "Doesn't smell right to me . . ."

Jack nodded. "Won't the quartermaster suspect the buyers of such goods for rebels?"

"Rest assured, lads—plenty of Loyalist merchants are thriving on black market trade in this city. How do you think I stock my shop? This shit-sack will sell to anyone paying in pounds." Hercules sat up and laced his fingers behind his head. "The lobster scoundrels are a corrupt lot—especially the type who've worked their way up from the ranks, like our quartermaster. According to Patsy, he is anxious to line his pockets before the war ends, which he fancies will be soon."

Jack put elbow to knee and chin to fist. "We'll need to age the notes, make 'em look like they've been in circulation."

"Aye." Mulligan nodded. "Now you've got your finger on it."

"You're getting ahead of yourself, Jack." Titus slipped into his shoes and tied the laces. "Above all, we need a good plate."

"A quality plate . . ." Jack sat up. "This engraver of yours—he any good?"

"I'm counting on you to tell me." Mulligan fished a ring of keys from his weskit pocket and unlocked the doors to the tall cabinet. "The engraver came to me unbidden—a Quaker—an odd little duck he is, too." He drew out a flat packet wrapped in velvet, and set it and a magnifying lens on the desk.

Jack flipped open the wrapping. Titus pulled the curtain a few inches, casting a beam of light on a bright copper plate. They both bent close.

Perhaps five inches wide by four inches high, the plate was engraved with intricate scrollwork, fancy script writing and a very detailed crest of the Bank of England—the devices used to thwart counterfeiters.

"Excellent work." Titus ran his fingers over the fine lines incised in the copper. "I think we could do something with this plate . . ."

Jack put Mulligan's magnifier to use. "This is the work of a master engraver." He pulled a ten-pound note the German had given him from his pocket and compared it to its reverse image on the plate. "We'll need to find someone who can mimic the cashier's signature . . ."

Mulligan said, "The master engraver has informed me that he is also quite the forger . . ."

Titus took the note and rubbed it between his forefinger and thumb. "We'll need to match this paper stock, and lay hands on some English-made ink . . ."

Jack gave Titus a nudge. "We'll talk to Tully . . ."

Titus put his cap on. "You think Tully will know where we can find a decent press?"

"If he doesn't"—Jack pulled the string on his gunny tight, and tossed it over his shoulder—"we both know where there's a fine press to be had, don't we?"

"Arrah, lads! A toast! Here's to men of action"—Hercules Mulligan raised his cup—"to men who dare to be free!"

ॐ ॐ ॐ

Off to market, Sally marched her empty cart down Murray Street, taking a very roundabout route to avoid Canvas Town. It had become a habit—a ritual performed every Monday—going out of her way to purchase at the Bear Market across town the same sort of goods easy to obtain at the Fly Market closer to home.

Annie advocated positive thinking and hard work as measures to keep from fretting over the lads. But as the weeks and months passed, Sally's unuttered doubts and fears became like a canker on the roof of her mouth—painful and hard to ignore.

She slowed to a halt as she came to the college-turned-prison, tying a thick kerchief doused with lavender water over mouth and nose to mask the awful odor emanating from inside. She gripped the cart handle tight and rolled forward. Fighting an urge to gag, she studied the groups of prisoners crowded at the open upper-story windows, searching the faces.

Sally was aware many of the inmates were too ill to take a turn at the windows. She was also sensible that thousands of patriots were imprisoned elsewhere, but those realities did nothing to diminish the relief infusing her from within, upon seeing David Peabody was not among the filthy, gaunt faces jostling for a breath of air.

"Move along," a guard ordered, as he always did when she lingered too long. Sally averted her eyes to straight ahead, pushing her cart past the prison.

"I-God!"

Straight ahead—not more than twenty yards away—Jack Hampton, Titus Gilmore and a longshoreman crossed Murray Street, heading south.

"Jack! Titus!"

They did not hear her call, muffled as it was by the damp cloth she'd tied tight over her mouth. Hiking her skirts in one hand, she broke into a run, the cart clattering over the cobbles. Less than a block away the men stepped onto the stoop at Mother Babcock's Boardinghouse, and knocked at the red door. Sally slowed to a stop, forcing the mask down into a bunch at her throat. She took a few steps, squinting in the sun. "Tha's not Jack . . ." she muttered.

Similar in build, the farmer she mistook for Jack was wearing a wide-brimmed hat, and stood in a terrible slouch. The black man had his back to her, and she could see he was bald, with ears that stuck out like the handles on a soup bowl. The longshoreman looked familiar—she'd served him before at the Crown and Quill, but not to know his name. "Na . . ." she muttered, surprised by the tears that sprung to her eyes. So desperate for news, she was seeing phantoms among farmers.

All three men swiped off their hats when the whore Patsy Quinn came to the door. Sally moved closer, blinking.

"Oh, Jack . . ." The whore sighed as she pulled him inside. The longshoreman and hairless Titus shuffled in after.

Sally pounded the brass ring to the plate and bowled past the poor girl who answered the door, drawing attention from a few of the red-coated customers at cards in the parlor room. She caught sight of Jack disappearing up the stairs hand in hand with Patsy, and managed to nab Titus by the sleeve just as he was about to mount the stairs.

"*Sally!* You shouldn't be in *here* . . ." Titus pulled her very quickly through the open door, glancing over his shoulder. "I can't talk right now . . ."

"Just tell me . . ." She clutched him by the wrist. "Is David dead? Is that why yiz havena come for us?"

"No need to start blubbering. We delivered David alive and well to his father's care in Peekskill . . ." he whispered. "That's all I can say."

"Thank God he's safe . . ." She loosened the grip on his arm. "Why is it yiv not come for us? What's Jack doing . . . ?"

Titus backed her out of the bawdy house. "I have to go, Sal. I'm sorry . . ." And he swung the door shut.

♋ ♋ ♋

ANNE gave the wash boiling in the copper a poke with the paddle. "You actually spoke with Titus?"

Sally stood in the kitchenhouse doorway. "Aye—direct."

A little muscle set to twitching above Anne's left eye. She touched a finger to it. "And you're absolutely certain it was Jack you saw?"

"Hands over heart, Annie, may mine eyes drop out of my head if I'm not tellin' ye true," Sally said. "I saw the devil skipping hand in hand with his trull, straight up the whorehouse stair—"

Anne swiped the mobcap from her head, befevered a-sudden, with a lump in her throat as if she'd just swallowed a toad whole. Pressing the flat of her fist to her heart, she dropped to a sit on the raised hearth, her voice very small. "He promised to come back for us . . ."

Sally sat beside Anne and threaded an arm around her friend's shoulder. "If that rotten scunner has the bollocks to come for ye now, Annie, he'll be comin' straight from another woman's warm bed."

Anne flinched. Leaning forward, she gripped the edge of the hearth and tried to catch a breath, the wind knocked from her as if she'd been thwacked across the back with a thick strop. The image of Jack with Patsy in wanton embrace cut through her mind's eye like a well-honed razor—severing her heartstrings in one swipe.

Slipping her hand inside her pocket, Anne held up the iron half-crown still bound in ribbon. She set it to swinging with a flick of her finger, and imagined its counterpart strung around Jack's neck, swinging to and fro as he moved in and out of Patsy Quinn.

"God *damn* him!" With a snap of her wrist, Anne sent her token flying through the door, into the garden.

Sally gave Anne a squeeze. "Well . . . how about a nice cup of tea?"

"I don't want any tea." Anne shrugged Sally off and stood up. Wavering a bit on weak knees, she smoothed her hair back, and released a breath in a big *whoosh*. Without a word, she took up the laundry paddle and resumed stirring the wash in the copper.

Sally moved in and tried to take over the chore. "Let me . . ."

"Leave off, Sal!" Anne snapped, maintaining firm control of the laundry paddle with a white-knuckled, two-fisted grip.

"Yiv had a heartbreak, Annie," Sally crooned and rubbed small circles in the space between her friend's shoulder blades. "Ye need to go lie down and rest."

"What I need . . ." Anne dug into the wet laundry in the cauldron, agitating the wet linen with a ferocious vigor. The effort and rising steam coated her face with sweat to mingle with the tears streaming down her cheeks. "What I truly need is to put that bastard from my thoughts—and I assure you, it is a thing not accomplished lying flat on my back in the middle of the day."

Sally surrendered. Palms upraised, she backed away. "Aye, lass, maybe yiv the right of it. It's strength of mind what defeats a thing."

"Don't you fret over me, Sally." Anne hefted a steaming mass of wet linen aloft on her paddle, letting it drain and dribble hot water back into the wash copper. "I have already lived through the worst heartache any woman can suffer . . ." She dumped the wet cloth into the tin rinsing tub. "I'll survive being betrayed by the likes of Jack Hampton."

CHAPTER EIGHTEEN

*It is not in numbers, but in unity, that our
great strength lies; yet our present numbers are sufficient
to repel the force of all the world.*

THOMAS PAINE, *Common Sense*

Friday, June 13, 1777
After Curfew, at the Sign of the Thimble and Shears

HERCULES Mulligan paced the length of his office. Edging close
to the oil lamp on the desk, he thumbed open the case of his
pocket watch and checked the time once again.

"Pacing like a cat in a cage will not speed their arrival, Stitch."
Patsy Quinn lay propped on one elbow, languid on the bench pushed
up against the wall. "You are goin' to wear a rut in the floor. Take a
seat and follow the example set by the Quaker."

They'd all taken to calling the engraver "the Quaker"—a moniker he
initially protested, proclaiming, "But I'm really a Deist," to no avail.

Mulligan eyed the strange little fellow sitting upright in the ladderback desk chair, serene as a broody hen, contemplating the lamp-
light through a pair of blue glass spectacles. The Quaker startled
violently at the sudden *thumpety-thump* on the window shutters, and
Mulligan hurried to open the back door.

"You're late."

"Would you have us arrested for curfew?" Jack pushed past the tailor. Titus and Tully filed in behind—all three of them dressed in dark clothes—Tully with a knit cap pulled over his graying hair.

"We had to wait for the streets to clear," Titus said. "Too many Redcoats about."

"As thick as fleas on a fat old dog," Tully added.

"I forgot." Mulligan knocked fist to forehead. "Mrs. Loring is hosting an evening of drink and cards . . ."

"Hey, Jack!" Patsy sat up, and patted the empty spot beside her. "Come sit next to me . . ."

Jack made straight for the big cabinet and the bottle of rye the Stitch kept there. After taking a good gulp, he banged the bottle to the desktop. "Paper—" Tugging a folded page from the pocket of his britches, he handed it to the engraver. "A close match—but we only have one ream."

"Excellent." The Quaker pushed his spectacles to the top of his bald head and held the paper sample close to the light, worrying the page between finger and thumb. "I must say, lads, I was not expecting anything this fine. This is near exact."

Titus made himself comfortable on the floor, sitting tailor-style beside the lemon tree. "Tully's also diverted a gallon of ink to the cause—best quality—English manufacture."

"Ahoy, Jack! Mind yer pocket," Tully warned with a wave of his finger. "Yer about t' lose yer kerchief . . ."

Along with the paper sample, Jack'd dragged up a lace-edged handkerchief from the depths of his pocket. It dangled precarious by one corner—the lone relic from the last time he had held Anne Merrick in his arms. Snatching the linen up, Jack was ready to toss the thing out the window when a puff of lavender wafted up. Without forethought to the consequence, Jack brought the handkerchief to his nose.

Underlying the lavender, the scent of Anne Merrick sent him back a step—pushed him against the wall. The taut cord connecting his wits to his stones drew tight as a bowstring, sapping all strength from his limbs. Arms dropping to his sides, Jack slid down to sit in the crease where the floorboards met the wall plaster, legs splayed, the lace-edged linen held loose in his hand. No one seemed to notice his plight.

Mulligan clapped his hands. "All well and good. We are fixed for paper and ink. Any luck finding an engraving press?"

The grizzled longshoreman sat down beside Patsy and swiped the cap from his head, his gravelly voice well suited to clandestine talk in the night. "I've spoken with a sailor who claims there is an engraving press working in the belly of the *Rose*, printing out counterfeit Continentals . . ."

"Fiddle-faddle." Mulligan dismissed the rumor as if waving away a bad smell. "Even if it were a fact proven, a press on a ship does us here on land little good."

"True enough," Tully rasped. "There's some credible noise on the docks having to do with Rivington expecting a press from England, but no one knows if it's an engraving press. If a new press shows, we might divert its delivery."

"No telling when, though?" Mulligan asked.

"No tellin' when."

Jack could resist no longer. He crumpled the kerchief into a ball and brought his fist to his face. Eyes closed, he drew in another breath. The scent bonded to the linen threads evoked a moment of pure bliss—respite and relief from the constant, twanging heartache sorely plaguing him the past days.

Mulligan pinched the bridge of his nose, pacing the width of the room. "I fear we're running out of time. Signs point to Howe shipping out the bulk of his forces in an effort to take Philadelphia. Patsy's greedy quartermaster will most likely soon be gone. We need a press *now*—right, Jack?"

Jack managed to nod his head in agreement and smoothed the handkerchief out on his thigh. The farewell token Anne had given him was much worse for traveling all these months in his pocket—very wrinkled—the lace tattered and frayed on one corner, much like the state of his heart. He folded the linen square into quarters.

Those last hurried moments with Anne wrapped in his arms suddenly so vivid, bright and happy, the notion of his woman giving herself to another was utterly unbelievable. *The world's gone upside down, she'd said.* And maybe it had—but for Jack, there was one constant: He *wanted* Anne Merrick.

Titus piped up. "There is an old engraving press stowed way back in the closet at Merrick's. Over twenty years ago, the old man tried his hand at book printing—one of my first chores when I was bought as a slave was to drag them parts into the closet. I doubt the widow even knows it's in there. Though I can't vouch for its condition—and we'd have to dig through a mess to get to it . . ."

Tully said, "Rivington has an engraving press working in his shop . . ."

"Then what are you waiting for?" Patsy gave Tully a jab. "Break into Rivington's and steal the damn press."

"A tricky business, this . . ." Tully's squinty eye disappeared in a clutch of wrinkles. "Not as simple as filching a coin from a drunk's pocket whilst yer givin' him a three-penny upright, missy. Whichever press we go after, we need to form a plan and find a trusty crew."

Hercules Mulligan pulled a copy of Rivington's newspaper from his coat pocket. "We certainly did the Tory a favor when we ran him out of town. He's been richly rewarded for his loyalty—'Printer to the King's Most Excellent Majesty,'" the tailor read from the masthead of the *Royal Gazette*. "Betwixt his monopoly on Crown work, and this Loyalist rag he prints, he has his devils working his presses both day and night . . ."

"Getting in and out of Rivington's without being seen will be nigh on impossible," Titus said. "His shop's front door faces Queen Street, and the back entry faces Wall—two of the most patrolled streets in the city. Ain't that right, Jack?"

Jack slipped the handkerchief inside his shirt. "What?"

"Impossible to get at Rivington's press, I was saying . . ."

Jack drew focus. "Nothing's impossible."

The Quaker piped up. "The press at Merrick's seems to be the better choice, even if it requires repairs. But I'm concerned—thievery of such a large item risks calling attention to our little project, gentlemen. Could we not gather funds and make an offer to purchase the widow's press?"

"We don't have any *funds*, dafty." Patsy giggled. "Why d'you think we're about printing banknotes?"

Mulligan laughed and gave the Quaker's shiny head a good-natured knuckle scrub.

Tully leaned forward, resting elbows on knees. Lacing his fingers, he began to twiddle his thumbs. "Breakin' into the Crown and Quill would be a simple operation—cut the glass out of the back window and drop a skinny boy through to open the back door for the rest of us. Very clean and quietlike."

"You'll have to contend with getting the press parts over the garden wall . . ." Titus reminded.

"No worries," Tully said. "The alleyway is good and dark—patrolled by naught but rats and pigs."

"Still risky," Patsy said. "I don't like it—breaking in with three armed British officers up the stairs . . ."

"Sometimes we have to cut a coat according to the cloth at hand." Mulligan banged a fist down on the desktop. "Merrick's it is. Put your crew together, Tully. Keep in mind, the officers are housed on the second floor—the widow and her maid reside in the garret rooms, but they often stay late in the kitchenhouse to see to the next day's baking. It's probably best to lift the press on a night like this one, when the Tory bitch and her dragoons are out at play."

Jack pulled up to his feet, dark eyes hooded. "How is it, Hercules, you are so privy to the widow's particulars?"

"Don't be about getting your nutmegs in a grind, Jack." Mulligan took a step back, palms out. "I make it my business to be privy to many particulars. One of the young lieutenants quartered there is a customer of mine, and prone to yammering. He tells me the widow and Mrs. Loring have become fast friends." Mulligan snatched the bottle from the desk, and took a sip. "The widow has become quite the Tory gadfly these days. I've no doubt we'll have our press by the end of the week."

Once the meeting was adjourned, Jack and Titus walked Patsy back to Mother Babcock's. Titus went in to pay a visit to Ruby, and Patsy tried to get Jack to cross the threshold as well. "C'mon," she cajoled. "There's a bottle of rum and a soft shoulder to cry on up there—no charge."

"I'm wrung out, Pats." Jack shook his head. "Mrs. Day's fixed a nice pallet for me in her kitchenhouse, and I'm just going to go and sink into my pillow."

"I really hate seeing you so down-gone." Patsy cupped his face in her hands. "You need to remember, nothin' is so bad that couldn't be worse."

"I'll be fine, Pats. You'll see a new man in the morning."

When the door closed behind Patsy, Jack took off in a direction opposite to Day's Tavern, back across town to Lyon's Slip, where the pettiauger was moored. Stowed beneath the cross-thwart, Jack found what he had come for—a thick coil of strong rope and a grappling hook. Slinging the rope over one shoulder, he tied the hook to one end with a solid knot.

Keeping to the shadows, Jack wound a stealthy path toward the Crown and Quill, avoiding the Watch and noisy groups of drunken Redcoat officers. He turned up the narrow alleyway, sending a bevy of rats feeding on windfall peaches into a squeaky scurry. Pulling himself up with the aid of the low-slung tree limb, he perched atop the garden wall.

Jack brushed the hair back from his face, and under the starlit sky, contemplated the distance from the kitchenhouse roof to the garret window.

ꗊ ꗊ ꗊ

ANNE accepted Edward Blankenship's proffered arm, and he escorted her over to the crowd gathered around the faro table. "Stuart and I are hoping your presence might change our luck."

Squeezing in between Edward and Lieutenant Stuart at the short side of the table, the blue taffeta of her new polonaise gown was instantly crushed—the basket panniers sent askew. She plucked the ostrich plumes adorning her hair so as not to torment her neighbors with every turn of her head.

The faro table was a long and narrow rectangle, positioned beneath a brilliant chandelier at the far end of the ballroom. One side of the table was furnished with an indentation at the center where the game's banker, William Cunningham, sat dealing cards, collecting wagers and disbursing winnings. The sight of the provost marshall triggered a recollection of the hanging on the green, and Anne suppressed a shudder. Cunningham had ordered the brave young Patriot's body left to dangle from the gallows for three days—a brutal warning to traitors who dared spy on the King's Army.

The provost was a sharp contrast in a room filled with pastel silks and red wool, dressed as he was in a dour brown suit and a plain linen shirt. He wore a stiff black leather stock buckled tight about his scrawny neck like a brace, as if to support the weight of the elaborate powdered wig he'd plopped upon his pinhead. Contrary to what Anne supposed was its wearer's intent, the unfortunate cauliflower wig served to make the provost's pox-pitted face appear even more oddly proportioned.

Faro was the Sultana's favorite game of chance, and Mrs. Loring and General Howe occupied the preeminent table position just opposite the banker. Anne and the Sultana exchanged smiles and nods across the table, and Betsey mouthed, "Good luck."

Mrs. Loring had proved to be a fount of information, and she'd once again provided the fodder for Anne's pen. During an earlier arm-in-arm stroll in the garden to "take some air"—Betsey's euphemism for using snuff—she revealed her "Billy" was only just beginning to gather provisions for the voyage to Philadelphia. Betsey happily reported her lover did not plan to leave her side for at least another month.

"Hold out your hand." Blankenship handed Anne a dozen clay disks. Some were colored blue with a white bull's-eye, the others were painted red and marked with a white diamond. "This is the last of our checks—mine and Stuart's. You will place our bet."

Anne turned her attention to the faro table. The surface was up-holstered in buff leather. Running from left to right in two rows, oversized images representing the complete suit of spades were rendered in black and gilt paint. "I've no idea . . ."

"It's a simple game of chance," Stuart explained. "You put the checks on one of the painted cards. If your choice matches the winning card drawn by the banker from his wee box, he must pay you a check for a check."

"But before the winning card is drawn, the dealer reveals the losing card," Edward added. "Any checks placed on the losing card revert to the bank."

"What is the purpose of that device?" Anne pointed her fan at a wooden frame lying flat on the table to the left of the banker. A plaque painted with card images matching the layout on the table ran down the center of the frame. A dowel rod jutting out from each card was affixed in the frame. Similar to an abacus, each rod had four red beads riding upon it.

"The case keeper—to keep track of the cards—the beads account for the four suits," Stuart said. "By studying the case, a player can determine the odds." He drew her attention to the jack, with all four of its beads at the far end of the rod. "Jacks have yet to be played. This deep in the deck, odds are high for a jack to show."

"Odds are nil on the king." Blankenship pointed to the four beads pushed up against the king. "All four kings have already been played."

One hand resting on the banking box, Cunningham toyed with a stack of checks, his countenance drawn into a permanent scowl by a crescent-shaped scar dragging the corner of his mouth down to his chin. "Punters, place your bets!"

The command incited a flurry of activity. Anne observed Mrs. Loring and the general placing multiple tall stacks of checks on the jack, and the majority of players followed their lead.

"I have an aversion to jacks." Leaning forward, she placed all of the checks in her hand on the ace—the card in closest proximity.

Stuart groaned. "Three aces have already been played, Mrs. Merrick. Odds favor the jack."

"Odds equally favor the jack to be drawn as the losing card," Anne countered.

Cunningham put his hands on the card-dealing box and called a close to the wagering.

Blankenship leaned in, resting his hand at her waist, his breath hot where her neck met her shoulder. "The top card is called the soda—it's a dead card. The card the provost will soon reveal is the losing card."

The brass dealing box was spring-loaded and contained all the cards yet to be played. The six of clubs—the soda—showed faceup through the opening at the top of the box. Cunningham slid the soda out of the box, revealing the jack of hearts to a loud chorus of groans. "Losing card—jack," he intoned, snaking a long arm across the table to pull a veritable mountain of checks to his side, adding them to his bank.

Mrs. Loring snapped her fan open, angry blue eyes a-dart. Many players abandoned the table in disgust. Cunningham slipped the jack from the box and revealed the winning card—the nine of diamonds, a card no one had wagered upon. A very profitable round for the banker.

"We didn't win." Anne put on a pretty pout and flipped open her fan.

"Ah, but we didn't lose either"—Blankenship gave her a little squeeze—"and we live to wager on."

"Punters place your bets!" Cunningham called.

The dragoons decided the time was ripe to move their checks to the jack. When the provost revealed another jack as the losing card, Edward and Stuart watched the last of their checks swept into the burgeoning bank.

Anne fluttered her fan. "I warned you both—jacks bring bad luck."

The three of them left the faro table and found a very tipsy Wemyss stationed in close proximity to the punch bowl.

"You are wise, Mr. Wemyss, to avoid games of chance." Not having much tolerance for hard spirits, Anne refused the cup of punch he offered.

"You give Wemyss more credit than he deserves," Blankenship said, gulping down the iced blend of lime juice, sugar and rum.

"Aye." Stuart gave his mate a shove. "Wemyss *loves* faro."

"Oh, I *do* so love to play, Mrs. Merrick," Wemyss asserted, wavering on his feet. He'd slicked his hair back into a disciplined queue with a healthy dollop of pomatum, but a few defiant curls had sprung free to frame his plump, ruddy face. "But the provost marshall banks his game with funds earned from the inhumane policies he's instituted, and I, for one, will not gamble with carrion who feed off the misery of starving soldiers."

Anne was not shocked by what tenderhearted Wemyss said, for the provost's inhumane policies were no secret, but she was surprised to hear the lieutenant proclaim his principled stand aloud, among such company.

"*Wheesht* . . ." Stuart gave his friend a poke. "Keep your voice down, ninny."

"That bastard is starving soldiers to death, Stuart . . ."

"They are rebels, Wemyss," Blankenship reminded. "Enemy soldiers."

"Soldiers nonetheless." Wemyss belched—as drunk as Anne had ever seen him—his voice increasing in volume. "There are standards of conduct we must abide by, even when at war. By turning a blind eye, and condoning prisoner abuse, General Howe invites the rebels to treat our poor captured lads in a like manner."

Captain Blankenship grabbed Wemyss firm by the shoulder. "Mind your tongue and tone, Lieutenant," he warned. "General Howe has higher priorities than the disposition of treasonous rebel prisoners."

Wemyss jerked away. "What a load of old bollocks, Edward! You know as well as I, Howe's priorities are determined by the swing of his cock." He turned to Anne, with an ungainly bow. "Please excuse my strong language, madam. Passion and punch rule the tongue."

"We'd better get him out of here." Blankenship grabbed Wemyss by one arm.

Stuart grabbed the other. "Aye, afore he begins to singing."

Anne scurried after the dragoons as they rushed their drunken friend out the door onto Broad Way, and as predicted, Wemyss began singing one of the clever ditties making the rounds at the top of his lungs:

> *"Awake, arouse Sir Billy.*
> *There's forage on the plain.*
> *Ah, leave your little filly,*
> *And open the campaign."*

"Shhh . . . softly, Wemyss, lest you disturb our neighbors," Blankenship cajoled. Wemyss cooperated with his captain by singing the second stanza in a loud whisper.

> *"Heed not a woman's prattle,*
> *Which tickles in the ear.*
> *But give the word for battle,*
> *And grasp the warlike spear."*

They skirted the Bowling Green and turned onto Whitehall, stopping once to allow Wemyss a piss in a doorway.

Anne opened the front door with her key. The candle Sally had left burning in a dish on the newel post had burned down to a stubby inch. Anne led the way, lighting the three dragoons up the stairs. Edward and Stuart deposited Wemyss with an *oof* onto the bed in Jemmy's old room. She lit the lamp on the bedside table. Stuart loosened his drunken friend's neckstock and tugged his boots off, while Wemyss declaimed to the ceiling:

> *"Sir William he, as snug as a flea,*
> *Lay all this time a-snoring.*
> *Nor dreamed of harm, as he lay warm,*
> *In bed with Mrs. Loring."*

"Stuart will see to Wemyss." Edward took Anne by the hand. "I will see you to your door, Mrs. Merrick."

♌ ♌ ♌

JACK stood on the pitched kitchenhouse roof, careful to maintain his precarious footing on the clay roof tiles. Swinging the grappling hook over his head in three whooshing arcs, he released it to land with a satisfying thunk, right on target. He gave the rope a good hard jerk to seat the iron tines firm into the wooden sill, and kicked off—flying across the ten-foot span—feet and legs extended to absorb the brunt of the collision when man met wall.

Arm over arm, boot soles braced to the brick, Jack climbed several yards to the garret window. Giving the shutters a gentle shove, relieved to find them unlatched, he hoisted himself up over the sill, and slipped inside, quiet as a church mouse.

Squeezing between an upholstered chair and a cluttered secretary, Jack was careful to keep from banging his noggin on the low-sloping ceilings, winding a path on soft foot past an open clothing chest, its gaping jaw regurgitating mounds of silk and lace.

Taking a seat on the bed in the corner, Jack heaved a sigh, drumming fingers on his knees. *Biding my time in Anne Merrick's bedchamber—accessed with stealth via upper-story window.* "Oh, but you are indeed a sorely afflicted bastard," he muttered.

Jack fell back on the mattress. Swinging his legs up, he folded his hands behind his head, and crossed his ankles. The garret room felt close, crowded and messy—very different from the spacious, neat bedchamber the widow had kept on the second floor. He bolted upright and snatched the bed pillow, scrunching it to his face. *Anne's, for certain.*

Satisfied he'd trespassed into the correct room, Jack put the pillow aside and began sorting through the items on the crowded bedside table. He tidied a strewn mess of T-shaped pins, gathering them into a shallow pewter dish. While making a halfhearted attempt to drag Anne's boar bristle brush through his hair, he opened the copy of *Gulliver's Travels* to the page marked with a length of silk ribbon, but it was too dark to discern her place in the story. A small lacquered box caught his eye, and Jack flipped opened the lid.

"Most precious," she called it . . . Jack held the gold and pearl memento containing a lock of Jemmy's hair up to the starlight. *Nearly lost to thieves,* Jack thought, careful to put the brooch back exactly as he had found it.

A year and a half ago, he had followed the widow into the alley near the sugarhouse, quite certain of her Tory sympathies. He hoped with all his heart the Loyalism she exhibited of late was of the same ilk—a pretense—a ruse adopted in order to survive in a world turned upside down. *Be a Tory,* he had told her, and he could not fault Anne Merrick for taking his advice.

A cool breeze blew in off the bay, refreshing the stuffy room. In his delight gaining entry with such ease, not only had he left the shutters ajar, he'd left his climbing gear suspended from the open window for the world to see. Tully would have delivered a well-deserved cuff to the head to anyone on his crew exhibiting such amateur ineptitude.

The way in is the way out. Jack pried the hook from the sill and drew the rope in, using his forearm as a windlass to form a neat coil. Piling his climbing apparatus convenient to the window, Jack spied a stack of familiar, paper-wrapped packages, sitting on the floor near the secretary.

Four reams of foolscap—two thousand sheets. An awful lot of paper for personal correspondence—the widow must be accumulating stock for the printing business she meant to rejuvenate. Shoving aside the sundry rouge pots, patch boxes and scent bottles cluttering the surface, Jack set a ream of paper on the desk, knocking a reel of ribbon to the floor.

The ribbon careened away, unspooling. Jack followed the inch-wide trail, retrieved the spent reel and set to rewinding the grosgrain ribbon—the sort of ribbon women used to secure their stockings, or to bind a package. Jack glanced back at the ream of paper he'd set on the desk.

A loud thud issued from the lower story—followed in an instant by manic barking. Jack shoved the ribbon inside his shirtfront. In three long strides, he was at the door, cracking it open, peering out into the dark hallway.

Bandit barked and scratched from behind the door across the hall as hard-soled boots clomped up stair treads, and laughter accompanied by a man's voice rising in song was shushed into silence. The bolt on the door across the hall slid back, and pale Sally emerged in her ghostly shift, moving like a frazzle-headed banshee to peer down the stair, Bandit writhing in her arms.

"*Sha*—ye can see, hellion—it's only Annie and her lobster backs returned." Bandit calmed and ceased his yapping. Sally scuttled back to her room, rebolting the lock.

The garret stairs squeaked and creaked with climbers, and like daylight breaking, an ascending light brightened the hallway. Captain Blankenship appeared at the top of the stair holding a candle-dish aloft, lighting the way for Anne, whose hands were busy managing voluminous skirts as she climbed the steep and narrow staircase.

Jack nudged the door, widening his view by a fraction. Dressed in the most drab grays and browns, with her hair pulled back into a utilitarian knot, Anne Merrick was a beautiful woman. Wearing a gown of cornflower blue silk, matching her eyes exact, with her chestnut curls pinned up to leave two locks trailing over her pale shoulder, Anne Merrick was stunning. She and the British dragoon in his splendid regimentals made for a very attractive couple.

Blankenship stepped forward and planted a rather stiff and sedate kiss on her lips, which Anne seemed to accept as a matter of course. Jack fought an overwhelming urge to charge out with a roar and send the golden-haired captain tumbling down the steep staircase. The thought of whisking Anne into his arms and pledging undying love to the tune of the dragoon's skull bone *thud-thud-thudding* on the treads brought a smile to his face.

Anne reached for the doorknob. "Thank you, Edward, for another lovely evening . . ."

Handing her the candle, Blankenship took her free hand and held it to his heart. In a provocative tone he recited,

> *"Come away, come, sweet love,*
> *The golden morning breaks,*
> *All the earth, all the air*
> *of love and pleasure speaks,*
> *Teach thine arms to embrace,*
> *And sweet rosy lips to kiss,*
> *And mix our souls in mutual bliss . . ."*

Blankenship brought Anne's fingertips to his lips. "Let me share your bed tonight . . ."

Fucking poetry . . . Jack drew the dagger he kept in his left boot.

Before Anne could reply, the bolt to Sally's door clacked open. Anne broke away from her suitor, awkward and flustered. Bandit rushed out, barking and leaping at the dragoon, with Sally not far behind, brandishing the fireplace poker in a two-fisted grip. "Blackguards!"

"Sally! No!" Anne cried.

"Megstie Me!" Sally lowered her weapon. "I mistook yiz fer rovers . . ."

Blankenship kicked at the dog growling at his heels. "Your Scots she-devil and her minion require tethering."

"Shush, puppy. The captain means us no harm." Anne scooped up Bandit, and gave him a kiss. "You must forgive Sally. Her imagination tends to run wild when she's left overlong to her own devices."

Sally stood swaying, toying with the poker, an evil smile on her impish face. "I apologize, Captain, if I frightened ye."

Blankenship shot Sally a look that would freeze water.

"As to your request . . ." Anne gave her captain a little shove toward the stair with a covertly whispered, "Soon, Edward . . ."

"I bid you good night, then, Mrs. Merrick." Mollified somewhat by Anne's whispered assurance, the dragoon smiled, bowed and retreated down the stairs.

Cocksucker . . . look at him—grinning like a cat with a cream-flavored arsehole . . . Dagger in hand, Jack's fingers tightened to the haft, sorely tempted to bury the blade between Blankenship's retreating shoulder blades.

Anne plopped Bandit into Sally's arms.

"Did ye have a fruitful evening, Annie? Was it worth the effort?"

"Mmm-hmm." Anne nodded. "Correspondence in the morning . . ."

"I'll ready the petticoats."

"Good night, Sal."

"Sweet dreams, Annie."

Soon, Edward. Two words from Anne Merrick's smiling lips hit him like a cannon shot to the chest. Moving with the swing of the door as Anne entered her room, he fell back and hunkered down against the knee wall, hiding in deep shadows.

As he was loath to have the widow privy to what a pathetic fool he had proven himself to be, he was forced to hunch like a rat in the corner until the treacherous hydra snuffed out the light and fell asleep—this final humiliation a cruel afterclap to his entire misadventure. Jack returned his dagger to his boot, wishing he could turn the blade on his heart and eviscerate the awful pain lodged there. *Anne Merrick might not be a Tory, but she was a whore for certain.*

He settled in to wait for a chance to sneak away, dropping into an uncomfortable crouch onto something hard and lumpy digging into his seat. Slow and careful, Jack extracted the annoyance—Anne's half of the little crown token he'd given her, all tangled in a length of silk ribbon, forgotten and discarded in the corner like the rubbish it was.

Jack clenched his fist around the broken bit of cast iron, and watched the widow set the stubby little candle on her bed table. Kicking off slippers, she removed the pins fastening her gown, dropping them with a *ting, ting, ting* into the dish. She peeled free from the heavy silk dress and multiple petticoats, draping the garments over the open chest.

She struggled like a bird trapped in a cage, trying to untie the complicated strings securing the panniers that supplied her with fashionable wide hips. At last she took a pair of shears to the strings, and let the entire ridiculous contrivance drop to the ground, stepping out of the whalebone structure dressed in naught but a thin shift and tight stays.

Illuminated by the dancing flame of the diminishing candle, the widow raised the hem of her lace-edged shift, and braced one foot to the mattress, exposing a shapely leg encased in white silk. She loosed the garter bow tied above her knee, and rolled her stocking down to her toes.

On his haunches, in the shadows, Jack's heart beat a fiercesome call to action, and the fine line drawn between pride and desire blurred as the second garter was loosed and the corresponding stocking slipped off and tossed over the bedpost. Jack considered the pleasure that could be had by bending the widow over the bedstead, his knife at her throat . . . *More pleasure than she deserves,* he decided.

Anne freed her hair from pins, scrubbing her scalp, combing fingers through the wavy length glinting copper as she moved closer to the light. Starting at the bottom, she undid the front hooks on her stays—skin glowing golden in the candlelight—breasts quaking with every pop of every hook.

Released from her stays, Anne heaved a breathy sigh. And with what seemed like malicious intent to torture, she turned, stretching her arms over her head, arching her back and striking a pose where Jack could clearly discern through the thin gauze of her shift a pair of choice nipples and an enticing dark patch between her legs. He bit down on his fist.

A cool gust of wind blew in off the bay, nearly dousing the candle and drawing the shutters closed with a slam. Bandit began to bark and Sally was at the door in no time, calling, "Alright, Annie?"

"Just the wind, Sal—I'm fine, go back to sleep." Anne squeezed between the desk and the chair to reopen the shutters, and tripped over the coiled rope. She brought the grappling hook up—examining it—trailing fingertips along the windowsill, she began to call out, "Sal . . ."

Jack rushed up from behind. Clamping one hand over her mouth, he locked an arm around her waist, pinning Anne's arms tight to her side. Twisting her head, eyes wide in recognition, she struggled to break free from his grip, thrashing, kicking, her screams choked and muffled. They bumped into the chest and the lid slammed closed.

"Stop it!" Jack gave her a hard shake, as if she were a rag doll. Anne ceased her futile thrashing, her breasts rising and falling with deep indrawn breaths. "I know you wish me ill," Jack rasped into her ear, "but I can't imagine you'd wish anyone into a British prison. Let's come to a reckoning—promise you won't scream, and I'll let you go."

Anne nodded once.

Jack let her go and she spun around. Like a wild woman from a Norse saga, she bore a mean glint in her eye and an angry set to her shoulders. Her hair was a tangle about her head, and she spoke with teeth clenched. "What did you come here for?"

A loving look, a welcome kiss, a happy reunion . . .

"For the same favors you so freely dispense among the British cavalry," he growled. Pulling her into his arms, he groped at her breasts and tugged at her shift, burying his face in her neck.

Anne Merrick buried her knee in his bollocks.

Jack's world turned red for an instant. Cramped in a half crouch as a white-hot corkscrew twisted up through his stones into his gut, he blinked back tears. Concentrating on catching a breath, he heard the hammer cock back on a pistol.

"Get out!"

Jack looked up, his one eye squinched like Tully's. Anne Merrick stood with a dueling pistol leveled at his head.

"Get out *now*," she ordered.

"*Bitch* . . ." he spat, hobbling to the window. "Tory *cunt* . . ." He kicked at the chair, sending it in a scrape along the floorboards to bang into the wall. Jack managed to grasp the grapple and secure it to the sill. The hideous pain radiating in waves through his abdomen subsiding a bit, he tried to straighten to a full stand.

"Out the window now, or I will shoot."

"Shoot, then, for I am moving with as much speed as I can muster." Jack leaned against the sill, and drew in a deep breath. "I promise you, madam, your desire to have me gone is eclipsed by my desire to be away from you."

"You promise . . ." Anne sneered, swiping away tears with the back of her hand. "Like you promised to come back?"

"I'm here, aren't I?"

"Whoremongering reprobate!" The muzzle of the pistol began to waver, and she brought her free hand to steady her weakening wrist. "Sally saw you with Patsy at the brothel on Murray Street a sennight ago . . ."

"So what? You fuck Redcoats," Jack countered.

There was a knock at the door, and Edward Blankenship called out, "Are you alright, Anne? Is something amiss?"

Anne moved in on Jack, gesturing with the tip of her pistol for him to exit. She sang out in a bright voice, "I'm fine—don't worry—I'll see you in the morning, Edward."

After a pause, Blankenship answered, "All right, then . . . good night."

"*Don't worry, Edward. I'll suck your cock in the morning, Edward,*" Jack whispered, mimicking her tone. He tried to hoist a leg over the sill, and yet unequal to the task, lost his balance and stumbled forward, the spool of ribbon inside his shirt tumbling out onto the stack of paper-wrapped packages beside the desk.

"Get out!" Anne put the barrel end of her pistol to his temple.

Unmoved, Jack stared at the reams of paper draped in a length of grosgrain ribbon. Images and words flashed through his mind—Anne's garter, tied in a pretty bow above her knee—the ribbon Titus untied in the moonlight at the apple orchard. *The widow has become quite the Tory gadfly these days . . . Correspondence in the morning . . .*

Jack jerked to a stand. "Are you working for the Stitch?"

"Get out, Jack." Anne extended her elbows.

Snatching the half-cocked pistol by the barrel, Jack tossed it onto the chair, and grabbed Anne by the arms. *"Answer me, goddammit!* Do you gather intelligence for the Stitch?"

"You were the one who sent me to him," she lashed back.

Jack released her. He took a few steps back, bumping his head on the pitched ceiling. "He lied to me . . ."

"Who lied?"

"Hercules." Jack rubbed his sore head. "The day we came for you—me and Titus—we saw you kissing the dragoon out on the lane . . ."

"No . . ." Anne shook her head. "I know the day you're talking about and it wasn't like that. *He* kissed *me* . . ."

"Sent me mad regardless—the sight of it." Jack pinched the bridge of his nose. "Titus literally dragged me away to the Thimble and Shears—and Hercules dosed me with whiskey and led me to believe the worst . . . the absolute *worst*."

Anne stood rubbing her upper arms where he had gripped her so tight. "And you believed the worst?"

"I did . . ." Jack nodded. "And was made miserable for it. Titus didn't believe. Titus thought you might be courting the Redcoats for good purpose, but that bastard Irishman . . . *Goddamn him!*"

"I suppose Mr. Mulligan was protecting me . . ."

"A load of shite, that is." Jack's forehead knotted. "Lying to me has nothing to do with protecting your well-being, and everything to do with keeping us both in New York. It's all so clear to me now—you are his connection to Howe—and he needs me and Titus for his counterfeiting operation. These purposes would not be served if I had taken you away." Jack dropped to sit on the bed. "I knew Hercules for a fanatic, but I never figured him as one who'd misuse his friends so cruelly."

"Misused to further the cause of liberty, Jack. Don't judge the tailor too harshly, his motives being unselfish and true . . ." Anne took a step forward, hands on hips, chin cocked. "But what about you and Patsy Quinn? Sally saw you happy with her . . ."

"Patsy's working with us on the counterfeiting scheme. We all met once, on the brothel rooftop. I suspect that's what Sally saw, though I was nowhere near being happy—I haven't had a moment's happiness since seeing you with *him*"—Jack pointed ruefully to the floorboards—"the dragoon you keep beneath your bed."

The candle had dwindled to a snippet of black wick sputtering in a scant puddle of molten wax in the well of the candledish. Anne stood with her back to the open windows—her shift as sheer as a dragonfly's wing—and Jack ached to caress the curves of her silhouette beckoning in the flickering light. Swinging her waist-length hair over her shoulder, Anne came to stand before him, her whisper harsh. "If you believed me a whore for Redcoats, why did you bother coming here?"

"I'm here because you've caused me to lose what little wits I possess . . ." Jack looked up into her eyes. "I'm here because I'm desperate in love with you." He slid hands up beneath the hem of her shift, running his fingers along the length of her legs, her skin soft, smooth and warm, smelling of lavender. Hands at her waist, he pulled Anne close, and they rolled back to fall onto the mattress. Limbs and bodies entwined in embrace, hungry mouths met to finish the kiss begun months before.

She moaned in his ear. "I want you moving inside me . . ."

Jack rose up on his knees. He tugged his shirt off, his voice low. "I'm not one for reciting pretty poetry, Annie . . ." A wicked smile crinkled the corners of his eyes as he unbuttoned the straining buttons on his breeches. "But I promise I will carry you away—I will move you to ecstasy."

The candle sputtered out, and breathless, Anne reached for him in the dark, whispering, "I'm going to hold you to that promise . . ."

ob ob ob

Charles Spangler
Elijah Lewis
Reuben Bates
Rebels all. Sentenced to suffer Death. Hanged without Mercy for
committing the most heinous High Treason by levying war against
their Sovereign, the King of this realm . . .

Long past the midnight hour, but William Cunningham diligently scrived the meticulous record of the night's work by the light of the bayberry candle he'd lit against the stench of the Provost Prison. "Enter," he called in answer to the knock on his door, continuing to scratch away with his goose-feather quill in the orderly book, not deigning to look up from his task as Quartermaster Lemuel Floyd swaggered in.

Floyd was a handsome man—the youngest son of a prosperous draper in Ipswich. He'd enlisted in the British Army on a drunken spree, and soon found he was not suited to the lifelong discipline and rigor required of an infantryman. Good with figures, knowledgeable in trade, Lemuel proved himself better able to the tasks of negotiation and purchase than to the tasks of loading and firing a musket. With an ambition fueled by the need to make army life bearable, Floyd gained the most senior noncommissioned rank possible, and as quartermaster he kept himself plump in the pocket selling the goods he commandeered for military use. And for a percentage, the shrewd quartermaster acted as Cunningham's intermediary, selling the stores appropriated from prison rations to the market at large.

Floyd dropped down in the chair, pushed his tricorn back on his head, heaved a sigh and reached for the bottle of rum the provost kept on his desk. "I am spent!"

Cunningham snatched the bottle from his grasp. "You are late. Supper was at dusk, and the hangings were over an hour ago."

"Sorry to have missed your neck-stretching party, Billy, but I was busy taking care of important business."

"Hmph! Business." Cunningham cast a gimlet eye on the white facings on Floyd's red jacket, smeared carmine with rouge. Dipping his pen in the inkwell, the provost resumed his book work. "Moderation, lad. Your weakness for quim will be the end of you. Whores will steal your health and pence. Mark my words, if you don't temper your habits, you'll wind up a pauper, pissing pins and needles."

"Mounting the likes of Patsy Quinn is well worth chancing a dose of the French pox." The quartermaster winked, stretching out his legs. "By the way she was bucking and moaning, I'd say she more than enjoyed the ride."

"Don't be gulled. That clever cunt has had more pricks than a secondhand dartboard—and yours the least of them all, no doubt." The provost set down his pen. "Have you come to an arrangement with the bawd?"

Floyd reached once again for the rum, and this time Cunningham did not come between the quartermaster and the bottle. "She says her customer is ready to accept shipment Friday next. I've only to name the place of delivery. I'm thinking the shipyards . . ."

"What sort of goods is this customer looking to buy?"

"Goods the rebel army lacks most—wool blankets and canvas yardage for tents. The whore guarantees her man will remit payment in currency."

Cunningham opened his desk drawer and produced another bottle. "Colonials . . ." Leaning back in his chair, he fiddled with the bumpy scar above his ear. "Fucking greedy buggers, these so-called Loyalists. First they gouge the King's Army for every barrel of flour and meat, then they turncoat and use those profits to line their pockets even further, trading with the enemy."

Floyd raised his bottle. "Well, here's to bagging this one bugger."

"It is a crooked, fretful world we live in, Mr. Floyd . . ." The provost uncorked his bottle and took a gulp. "And we who are truly loyal to our good King are called to put a halt to these perfidious practices, and make an example of these quisling men."

ↄ ↄ ↄ

JACK forced a smile, and hooked the grapple onto the windowsill. "I'll see you soon . . ."

Anne fell back against the wall, sad and sleepy, clutching the sheet she'd dragged off the bed for protection against the early-morning chill. "When?"

"I have business to sort out with Mulligan—and I'll pass on the information you gleaned last night. If things bog me down, I'll send Titus with word—but both he and I have to be careful coming around in the light of day. The Crown and Quill is a haven for dragoons." He played the rope out the window, and double-checked the integrity of the grapple's grip on the sill. "There . . . don't forget to drop the hook down after I'm gone."

Anne nodded. "I'll stash it behind the cistern—for when you return."

Jack hated to leave. Waking beneath the warm weight of Anne's arm and leg—her head nestled to his shoulder, her scent in his nose—all brought him peace and well-being beyond measure. When he woke wrapped within his true love's sleepy embrace after a long night of lovemaking, he could not help but revel in knowing Edward Blankenship lay alone in his bed—right beneath the floorboards—with nothing more to comfort him but his poor, dry palm.

But the rooster's clarion call sounded the alarm, the sparkling stars began to dim as the square patch of black sky visible through the open window brightened to deep blue, and Jack forced himself to summon the will to leave his Anne once again. Afraid to take her into his arms for fear of not being able to let her go, he leaned in for one last kiss, bracing his hand to the wall.

"I love you so . . ." she whispered, just before her tender lips met his.

"And I you."

Jack went over the sill. Arm under arm, bootsoles walking the wall, he carefully descended, jumping the last eight feet to the ground. As soon as his feet met the earth, cold sharp steel met the hollow of his throat.

"Up wi' yer mitts, blackguard, afore I carve ye a new smile," Sally snarled.

Jack raised his arms. "Put by your knife, Sal—it's your ol' friend Jack Hampton."

"*Sally!*" Anne whispered, leaning out the window, waving her arm. "*All's well!*"

Sally eyed her smiling mistress, naked but for the bed linen clutched to her breast. "Yer most surely th' devil's get, Jack Hampton," she hissed, withdrawing her blade, "t' have charmed th' anger from tha' woman."

Jack spun around with a wide grin and a wag of his brows. "More than charm put the smile on your mistress's face."

"I swear t' Christ, lad." Sally gave him her fiercest redheaded, cutty-eye glare, pointing the tip of her carving knife toward his nether region. "If I find yiv caused our Annie a moment's grief, I'll slice off yer tallywags and shove 'em one by one down yer gullet."

"And if I were to commit such a crime, I would expect nothing less, Sal."

Taking off in a run, Jack bounded onto the table, grabbed a tree limb and swung onto the top of the wall. He turned and blew a kiss up to Anne, and in one leap disappeared.

CHAPTER NINETEEN

✿❧·❧✿

In short, Independence is the only BOND
that can tye and keep us together.

THOMAS PAINE, *Common Sense*

Thursday, June 19, 1777
Closing Time, at the Crown and Quill

SALLY urged the last customers out the front door, and spied the two-horse cariole turning onto the narrow lane. She called to Anne, "The coach is here!" then ran halfway up the stairs and shouted, "Captain Blankenship! Yer transport has arrived!"

A few moments later, the three dragoons came trouncing down, dressed in their brilliant regimentals—helmets polished, death's-heads glaring, swords agleam.

"Och! Verra braw, yiz are, gentlemen." Sally fanned her face with fingers. "Nothing like a cavalryman in full feather t' set a lass's heart aflutter."

Wemyss sucked in his gut, Stuart puffed out his scrawny chest, and Blankenship searched the room for Anne. "Where's your mistress, Sally?"

Sally cupped hands to mouth, shouting, "Annie! The captain's askin' after ye!"

Anne came scurrying out of the kitchenhouse, red-faced, straight-ening her ink-stained mobcap with one hand, digging in the pocket of her brown work skirt with the other. Arm outstretched, she of-fered the front door key to Edward Blankenship. "As Sally and I will no doubt be fast asleep on your return . . ."

"Don't forget to leave the door unbolted, Miss Sally," Wemyss reminded. "Lest we be forced to scale the walls . . ."

"Scale the walls!" Stuart laughed. "I'll be happy to see you scale your bed unaided."

The officers were on their way to a gala event being hosted by General Howe at the headquarters established at Mount Pleasant—the expansive Beekman Estate on the East River—a full hour's car-riage ride up the Post Road.

Edward slipped the key inside his pocket and took Anne by the hands. "I wish you would change your mind and come along. Run up and put on that pretty blue dress—I'll have the coachman wait . . ."

Anne pulled her hands free, and took a step back. "Edward, you know I'm committed to running the press tonight. This maiden job is crucial to re-establishing my printing business, and I must watch and ward over these new journeymen I've managed to hire."

The three dragoons turned and eyed the two men clad in leather aprons at work assembling a small engraving press at the back of the shop.

"The wee nyaff with the blue specs is an oddling, Mrs. Merrick." Stuart tapped his temple with his forefinger. "Two bricks shy of a load . . . if you ken my meaning . . ."

"On the contrary, Mr. Stuart," Anne declared. "The man is of very good substance—why, he's a Quaker."

The little man pushed his spectacles to the top of his head, and said, very loud, "Actually, mistress, I am a Deist . . . but I can assure you, I am in possession of all my 'bricks.'"

"Please mind your tongue, Lieutenant," Anne whispered. "Reli-able journeymen are few and far between . . ."

"Your other man—the squinty-eyed fellow—I'd say he bears

watching," Wemyss warned. "The rogue has a thievish look about him."

"Is that the coachman calling?" Sally exhibited her closing-time prowess. Linking arms with the two lieutenants, she hustled them out the door before Tully could cull up any umbrage to the lieutenant's astute observation.

Anne led the captain by the hand. "Enjoy the gala, Edward . . ."

"An impossible task, without you by my side." Planting a lingering kiss to Anne's palm, Blankenship climbed into the cariole.

The women stood out on the lane, smiling, waving and calling, "*Farewell!*" as the hired carriage rolled away. The very second it disappeared around the corner onto Dock Street, they scurried back into the shop. Sally slammed the door shut and shot the three brass bolts home. Anne closed the drapery and shouted, "All clear."

Jack came out of the kitchenhouse, doling out a belly rub to a very complacent Bandit, who was cradled legs-up in his arms. Titus followed after, munching on a triangle of shortbread. Anne marched to the back of the shop wiping her just-kissed palm to her skirt.

"Let's get to work . . . we've not a moment to spare."

Tully slipped off the leather apron he wore and handed it to Titus. "How much time d' ye think we have, missus?"

"They won't be back for at least six hours—perhaps seven, if the punch flows free and their luck holds at the faro table."

Jack set Bandit on his feet. "Sally, do you have a little something these boys can call supper?"

"Och! I've lashins and lavins . . . Take a seat and I'll bring yiz all a bite to eat."

"Aye that, Sal." Tully grinned. "High treason is best committed on a full belly."

The four men took seats around a pair of tables shoved together, and Anne helped Sally dish up a quick supper of fish chowder served with slabs of dense brownbread, butter and jam. While the men ate, Anne leaned back in her chair, arms crossed over her chest, eyeing with a measure of wonder the strange apparatus assembled at the back of her shop. She had not even known of its existence until

Titus unearthed it from the deepest depths of the closet beneath the stair—and there it sat, the machine they would use to commit the felonious act that, if caught, would earn them all a dance beneath the gibbet.

"Mr. Mulligan is very lucky, Jack, that you're not one to bear a grudge . . ." Anne said. "I doubt he could have found anyone else to operate that contraption."

The engraving press was quite different from the more common letterpress she was accustomed to. The device was equipped with a moveable bed, which carried plate and paper between a pair of heavy mahogany rollers, and was worked by turning a large wheel, much like the helm on a three-masted brigantine.

Parker's Press, where Jack had apprenticed and earned his journeyman status, had been outfitted with such a press that was used mostly for printing illustrations and maps. Jack reassured them all, and the engraver concurred, the difficulty in engraved printing lay in producing the copper plate. "And we are rich in this regard"—Jack and Titus tapped tankards of cider in toast—"for our ever-thinking Quaker has created not one, but two master works for our use."

Twilight loomed, and the counterfeiting crew could not afford to dillydally over their meal. Titus hung a series of oil lanterns to illuminate the press and compositor's table. Sally arranged ladderback chairs in a semicircle around the fireplace to serve as makeshift racks. Tully brought in a supply of wood and kindled a fire on the hearth to speed the drying process. The Quaker cut two hundred foolscap-sized sheets in half, and put the paper to soak in a large pan filled with clear water from the cistern.

Anne stood at the compositor's table preparing an inkball. She stuffed fluffy wool into the bulbous leather cover, and hammered home the tacks securing it to the wooden handle—all the while covertly watching Jack as he made the final adjustments to the press.

What a fine-looking man he is . . .

Every night since that first night when he'd climbed into her garret window, Jack had come flying across rooftops to share her bed, and the knowance they had of one another was built upon whispers and caresses in the dark. It was a different sort of pleasure—seeing Jack in the bright lantern light, happy amid the tools of his trade.

Like the day he'd first kissed her beneath the portico of St. Paul's, Jack was dressed in plain journeyman's garb—leather breeches, his linsey shirt open at the collar and protected by a leather apron, sleeves rolled to elbows. She admired the tight muscles in his forearms, bunching and twisting as he worked the wrench, his expressive brows furled in concentration, calibrating the space between the rollers to the perfect degree. Anne had touched every square inch of his hard body, but she only just now noticed the slight scar below his left eye, and she longed to swipe back the loose strand of hair escaped from the hasty queue he'd tied round with a length of twine snatched from the ream of paper. Handsome features tinged by the blue-black of a two-day beard lent him a rakish countenance Anne could only equate with the words *daring* and *courage,* and the wanton recollection of that rough, unshaven cheek scraping along the tender skin of her inner thigh sent a warm thrill spiraling up her spine.

Anne set the inkball aside, and pleated a sheet of paper into a fan to cool her sudden blush. Jack Hampton required no silver trim or fancy plumage to enhance his tall, strong form, and the very sight of him kindled a fire in her heart that burned beyond the bounds of all reason.

Jack put the wrench down and gave the big wheel a turn, his soft brown eyes intent on the motion of the rollers. Satisfied with the result, he came around and joined her at the composing table. Pressing a hand to the small of her back, he smiled and planted a soft peck on her cheek.

"So, my little devil, are you ready for your next lesson?"

Anne sighed. "Oh, yes."

Jack took up the spouted tin vessel Tully had diverted from a shipment destined for Rivington's Press, and drizzled a syrupy stream onto the inkblock, coating the bottom surface with a thin layer. "First we ink the plate."

The engraved copper plate was lying on a thick pad of newsprint, centered on the composing table. He situated the inkblock to his left, agitating the viscous substance with the spatulalike steel. To the right of the plate, he stacked two dozen quarter-yard swaths of tarlatan gauze he had folded into hand-sized pads. Next to the tarlatan he placed a small bowl of powdered chalk.

"You must be thorough in beating the ink into the etched lines." Jack coated the leather ball with sticky ink and daubed it to the engraved copper plate. "Just as in working a letterpress, proper inking is crucial to achieving a quality impression." Using the broad blade on the steel, he scraped the surplus ink off the plate, and took up a pad of the coarse, loosely woven gauze. "Apply the tarlatan with a light hand." He demonstrated, carefully wiping the face of the plate with small circular motions—cleaning the plate, but leaving the incised lines filled with ink.

"And then the final step . . ." Jack dipped the heel of his left hand into the bowl of chalk, clapping the excess away. "Mind—only a touch of chalk is required." He swiped his powdered palm across the face of the plate twice to remove any filmy ink residue remaining. "The handwipe ensures a bright result."

Anne picked up the plate by the edges. "Let's press a sheet and see how it pleases us."

"Gather round, mates, and see how it's done." Jack waved them all to the press. "With two plates, we will work in turn—while one plate is being run through the press, the other plate is being inked. With diligence, we will have three hundred impressions by midnight—three thousand pounds!"

"You and Mrs. Anne should ink the plates," Titus suggested. "Tully and I can work the wheel. Sally and the Quaker will see to maintaining a ready supply of paper, and to the drying of the finished bills."

Anne laid the inked plate upon the press bed, faceup. Titus positioned a sheet of damp paper square over the plate. Jack piled three thick layers of felt atop paper and plate. Tully turned the wheel, and the bed moved forward. The entire assemblage—plate, paper and felt—was wrung between the heavy rollers, squeezing the page to the incised design on the plate. Once through the wringers, Sally removed the felts, and the Quaker carefully peeled the paper free.

They all gathered around the compositor's table while Jack examined the finished ten-pound note with a magnifying glass. "Without flaw!" he proclaimed. "Let's get busy."

The team fell into working in concert, keeping the flow of inked plate, paper and press constant, turning out notes with such speed, Sally and the Quaker resorted to stringing a line across the width of the room, and hanging the wet pages with clothes pegs. Before the midnight hour tolled, over three hundred impressions had been struck.

"A good night's work!" Jack proclaimed. "Let's tidy up."

Sally rotated the few still-damp sheets closer to the heat of the fire. Tully gathered the few wasted and spoiled sheets and fed them to the flames. Anne and Jack cleaned the plates and the tools with a wash of turpentine, while Titus and the Quaker stacked the dry notes on the press, inspecting each through a glass for quality.

"Once trimmed and forged with the bankman's signature, it will take a better eye than mine to discern counterfeit from genuine." Titus slapped the Quaker on the back, knocking him a step forward. "You are a man of uncommon talent."

Jack agreed. "Our success has exceeded my hope, due in large part to the Quaker's skilled engravings."

The Quaker blushed and mumbled, and began to dig in his breast pocket, unearthing a leathern flask. "Armagnac," he said. "May I propose a toast to our mutual endeavor?"

"French brandy?" Tully rasped, throwing an enthusiastic arm about the engraver's shoulders. "We have ourselves a wet Quaker!"

"But I'm *not* a Quaker, wet or dry . . ."

Sally set six teacups out on the press, and the meticulous engraver distributed equal amounts of brandy into each, emptying his flask. He raised his cup high.

"I am a simple man—I lack a voluble tongue, and am not prone to flam or gasconade—but I will adventure to say this, my dear friends . . ." He gazed about the table, his eyes bright with pride.

"Man or woman, there is not a faint heart among you. May justice support what courage has gained! Here's to Liberty and these United States of America!"

"Hear! Hear!" Titus and Tully pounded fists to the press.

"To liberty!" Jack tapped his teacup to the Quaker's.

Anne and Sally aped the men, and to the cheers of their fellows, the women tossed back their spirits in one gulp along with much coughing and sputtering.

Tully began to douse the lanterns. "We best jump ship afore the bloodybacks come home and spoil our party."

Anne took a broom to the floor, and Jack stored the tools and paraphernalia. The Quaker wrapped the copper plates in a soft cloth, and slipped them into his jacket pocket. Sally packed three thousand pounds' worth of banknotes into a wooden box.

Titus and Tully were charged with delivering both the crate of counterfeits and the Quaker to the Thimble and Shears, where they would spend the rest of the night trimming the notes to size while the engraver added the finishing touch, forging the bankman's signature with red ink.

"I'll meet you at Mulligan's within the hour," Jack promised, bidding the men good-bye. Sally checked up and down the lane and determined Titus, Tully and the engraver might egress safely via the front door, rather than deal with getting the Quaker and the cash up and over the garden wall.

Holding the last lit lantern aloft, Jack came back to methodically pace the floor, checking for any printed notes that might have gone astray. "We can't afford to be careless . . ."

"Well, I'm to bed." Sally yawned. She unbolted the front door, left a lit candle on the newel post and headed up the stair. "Dinna tarry overlong, you two. The Redcoat bastards can be back at any moment."

"Don't worry, Sal." Anne paused in working her broom. "I'll be up as soon as I finish the sweeping."

"Aye." Sally nodded, and winked. "Finish yer sweepin' . . ."

As Sally's footfalls faded, Jack set the lantern on the press, and removed his apron. "Sal's right, Annie, we've no time to tarry." Smile wide, he opened his arms. "*Gather ye rosebuds while ye may* . . .'"

"You *do* know how to recite pretty poetry!" Anne laughed, putting her broom aside. She pulled the mobcap from her head, let her careless hair fall to her waist and skipped into the wonder of his embrace. Slipping her hands beneath his loose shirt, she pressed her ear to his heart. "Stay the night . . ." she whispered. "Titus will see to finishing the notes . . ."

Jack kissed the top of her head. "We need all hands at work to finish the notes in time for the meeting with Patsy's quartermaster tomorrow."

"I'll be very glad when we're done with this business. I'm grown weary of deception, tired of worrying and heartily sick of paying court to Redcoats." Anne heaved a sigh. "I just want to be with you . . ."

Jack found her lips with a warm and tender kiss. "After Friday, I will carry you away from here and we will be together always."

Anne leaned over and blew out the lantern. But for the candle Sally left behind on the stair, the shop was thrown into darkness. Her hands against his chest, Anne pressed forward two paces, pushing Jack back against the composing table. "Stay . . ." Her bold finger blazed a zigzagging path, connecting the two rows of buttons securing his drop-front breeches.

Jack grabbed her by the wrists as she undid the first few buttons. "*Annie* . . . there's no time . . . the dragoons are due back . . . we can't . . ."

"We *can*! We've plenty of time . . ." She twisted free from his halfhearted grasp, and slipped a questing hand inside his breeches. "They won't be back for an hour, at least."

Jack groaned, and grabbed her round the waist. Lifting and spinning around in one motion, he set Anne atop the engraving press. Their lips met in a fervent kiss, while Anne pulled at her skirts, and Jack pushed through the fabric.

Grabbing hold of Jack's shoulders, Anne dug her fingers into the recesses where taut muscle met hard bone. Big, strong hands found soft, round hips—pulling her forward as he pushed inward—and they joined as one.

In an exchange of haphazard kisses and stifled moans, the tin lantern inched along the smooth bed of the press, jostled forward by the motion of two moving in time, bodies parting and meeting again and again, until coming, at last, in an "Oh!" of sweet fury and wondrous release.

Gasping for breath, Anne relaxed her grip on his shoulders and leaned back on one palm, swiping back long swaths of hair from her face.

"I must say, Mrs. Merrick." Stumbling back a step, breathing heavy, Jack fastened his breeches. "You are, by far, the most accommodating devil I have ever worked with . . ."

"I should hope so!" Anne smiled, tugging at her skirts.

The shop door slammed open, and the three dragoons stumbled into the room, each with an arm thrown about the other's shoulders, they burst out in song:

> *"We always are ready, Steady, boys, steady,*
> *We'll fight and we'll conquer again and again . . ."*

Anne hopped down from the press, falling into a crouch beside Jack, knocking the tin and glass lantern to the floorboards at the same moment. Together, they lunged forward to stop the lantern's clattering trajectory. The crash put a sudden end to the merrymakers' song.

"What was that?" Edward Blankenship peeled away, taking a few steps toward the back end of the shop. In answer, Wemyss and Stuart struck up another loud chorus:

> *"We ne'er see our foes but we wish them to stay,*
> *They never see us but they wish us away . . ."*

"Pipe down, you drunken sods!" Blankenship ordered.

"*Wheesht*, Wemyss," Stuart chided. "Our brave captain's stalking a possible intruder."

Wemyss giggled, and began singing in an exaggerated whisper:

"They swear they'll invade us, these terrible foes;
They frighten our women, and our children, and beaus . . ."

"*Quiet!*" Blankenship ordered, the zing of sharp steel whisked from its scabbard shrill in the dark.

At the approach of the dragoon's boot steps, hard and brisk on the floorboards, Anne and Jack hunkered down, creeping around the engraving press, hiding in the deepest shadows at the short end.

Blankenship came to a halt with heels crunching on shards of glass at the opposite end of the press. He picked up the broken lantern and set it on the press, calling, "Stuart! Bring the light over."

The back of the shop brightened as Stuart drew near, candle in hand, and the glint of Jack's dagger being inched from his boot caught the corner of Anne's eye. She popped up to a stand, her hands flying up over her head.

"Pray, Edward—put by your sword!" Anne rushed around the press. "I had only just doused the light when your boisterous entrance startled me so—I dropped the lantern and . . . and . . ." She covered her face with her hands and began to sob, shoulders shaking, whimpering, "Friend or foe? I could not tell. Instinct bade me hide . . . Marauders, thought I!"

"My poor Anne," Edward sheathed his sword, immediately contrite. He moved in to encase her in consoling arms. "I thought—well, I am so sorry to have frightened you so . . ."

Jack's scent ripe upon her skin, and his seed seeping sticky from between her legs, Anne could endure the Redcoat's embrace for only the briefest moment. Pulling away, she snatched the candle from Stuart and led the huddle of Redcoats from the press Jack crouched behind, to the stairway.

"You all ought to be ashamed," she sniffled. "Officers in the

King's Army—reeking of rum—behaving no better than common enlisted men on a carouse."

"You are correct, madam." Blankenship offered her an apologetic bow. "Please accept our apologies."

Stuart grumbled, "It is Wemyss's fault—him and his singing . . ."

"Can you ever forgive me, Mrs. Merrick?" Wemyss blubbered. "I certainly meant no harm . . ."

"I am spent." Anne trod up the stairs, dragging along the trio of chastised, drunken dragoons. "It has been, all in all, a very trying day . . ."

Quick and quiet, Jack stepped to the back door and worked the latch, slipping out to disappear over the garden wall.

CHAPTER TWENTY

Society in every state is a blessing,
but government even in its best state is but a necessary evil;
in its worst state an intolerable one.

THOMAS PAINE, *Common Sense*

Friday, June 20, 1777
After Curfew, on the East River

SIDE BY SIDE amidships, Tully and Titus bent their backs to the oars, becoming the human engine that propelled their flat-bottomed craft upriver in the light of the rising moon.

At the back end of the pettiauger, Jack sat at the edge of his seat, his right hand light on the rudder, his left comforted by the smooth butt of the loaded pistol tucked into the satin sash at his waist. The breast pocket of the fine frock coat Mulligan dressed him in was bulging heavy with counterfeit banknotes—fifteen hundred pounds to purchase hard-to-come-by trade goods the Continental Army desperately needed if it meant to survive another winter.

Steering an upriver course parallel to the city's shoreline, the pettiauger cruised by a dark, saw-toothed skyline of steeples, pitched rooftops and ships' masts—the silhouette studded here and there by a pinprick of lantern light, or the soft golden glow of candlelit windows left open to catch a fair night wind.

The shush of muffled oars dipping into the water and the forlorn howl of a far-off hound enhanced the peaceful curfew-quiet. Soothed by a fresh breeze off the water, Jack tried for a moment to forget his city was overrun by a careless occupying force, and mired in a sickly stench of fish offal, rotting carcasses and pig dung simmering and stewing the day long in the summer sun. In truth, the omnipresent reek was far worse than any description he could ever contrive.

A bad smell . . . smells bad. Jack heaved a sigh, reminded of another, more bothersome indescribable gnawing at the back of his brain.

The counterfeits were printed and finished, and the particulars of the meeting were arranged to each party's satisfaction, yet something about the scheme did not smell right, and Jack could not shed the feeling that somehow, something had been overlooked. While donning his disguise at the Thimble and Shears earlier, he'd put a voice to his indefinable concern, only to be fobbed off by his fellows.

"Your nose is misguided, lad. We've been more than thorough in our planning," Mulligan asserted, tugging an old-fashioned gray periwig over Jack's jet-black hair. "I have checked and double-checked through my every connection—this quartermaster's corrupt nature is well-established within the black market. Once he sets greedy eyes on those banknotes, there's no reason to expect anything but an easy exchange of money for the goods our army is desperate for."

Titus agreed. "And the counterfeits are near perfect—but for the slight difference in paper quality, our false notes are practically indiscernible from true."

"I know, I know." Jack shrugged and slipped his arms into the frock coat Mulligan offered. "I can't say what it is—it's just that something seems off . . ."

The tailor stepped back to admire the disguise he'd devised for Jack. "Does he not look every bit the Tory merchant?"

"Aye, Stitch, he's as pretty as a new-plucked rose," Tully teased in his gruff voice, giving Jack a sound thump between the shoulder blades.

"Aw, Tully," Jack countered. "I bet that's what you tell all the boys."

"Haw!" Tully laughed along with the others, then hawked up a gob of phlegm, and spat it out the open window. "As to your problem, lad, I'll put a name on it—*woman*. Courtin' your widow has put a blunt edge to your blade, Jack. Gallivanting over rooftops . . . climbing through windows every night . . ."

"Not to mention what goes on once the window's been breached." Titus smirked and winked.

"Ah, love, true love . . ." The Quaker nodded with a wistful little smile. "I must agree with Mr. Tully. The love of a good woman has the power to temper the most reckless spirit. Therein lies the source of your unreasonable anxiety, Jack."

"Which reminds me . . ." Titus fished through his pocket, and tossed something over to Jack. "I've been keeping it for you—thought you might want to have it back one day."

Jack caught the item. "My lucky piece!" Happy to see his wise friend had rescued the half-crown he had discarded with such anger and bitterness, he looped the leather thong around his neck, tucked the token inside his shirt and grinned. "I could not want for a better friend than you, Titus." The scavenged scrap of cast iron served not only as a reminder of his devotion to Anne, but also his devotion to the cause of liberty.

At the outskirts of the city, Titus and Tully put good muscle to the oars, sending the pettiauger skirting past Peck's Slip in no time. Jack nudged the rudder to hug a course closer to the shoreline. "Keep your eyes peeled for the signal," he said. Relaxing the grip on his pistol, he sought the iron lump lying just beneath the neat bow-knot tied in the linen cravat he wore.

True love—the Quaker put his finger square on the problem . . .

Jack had spent the past few nights nestled with the woman he loved warm in his arms, whispering words like *marriage*, *home* and *children*—her head on his shoulder, his nose in her hair—both of them imagining a life together. Suddenly, Jack had something of consequence to risk—or maybe even lose—the prospect of happiness.

"There's our green light." Tully pointed.

Jack pulled hard on the rudder to aim the prow of the pettiauger at the one shipyard dock beckoning with a green glass lantern mounted atop the pilings—the agreed-upon signal.

Visible in the dim combination of moonlight and eerie green glow as they edged closer to the dock, a tall officer and two infantrymen armed with muskets rose to attention beside a mass of trade goods—bales of woolen blankets bundled in twine, and long rolls of canvas yardage—stacked in a man-high pile about fifty paces away, just where the dock met land.

"What a fine covey we have here, mates." Tully whistled low. "Three red birds ripe for plucking." Bringing in his oar, he half cocked the two pistols he'd brought and stuffed them into the leather belt at his waist, then retrieved his blunderbuss from under the seat.

Jack's fingers tightened to his pistol. Leaning forward, he whispered, "Stand ready to cut loose and row like the devil if aught looks amiss."

"Aye that, Jack," Titus answered. Adjusting the brace of pistols he carried in his belt, he drew a wicked-looking dagger from his boot.

Jack eased the boat in to thump up against the end of the dock. Titus put his knife between his teeth and leapt out to secure a line to the piling.

"Stay in the boat," Jack muttered to Tully, "and keep that good eye on us."

Tully slapped a hand to the stock of his blunderbuss. "Don't worry, Jack. If needs be, I'll kick up a breeze with my friend here."

As any slave would, Titus followed a half step behind Jack, marching the length of the dock in a quickstep. They were met midway by the curt-bowing quartermaster.

Jack returned the bow, and gestured to the pile of goods. "I take it, sir, you and I have business to transact?"

"Correct, sir." A tall, well-built fellow, the quartermaster was relaxed and did not exhibit the least nervousness. In contrast, the two ramrod-stiff grenadiers flanking him gripped their polished muskets with purpose, made even more malevolent by the odd green light.

The quartermaster ordered his men to stand down and step back. "A necessary precaution against rebel bandits," he explained, and then, very businesslike, launched into rattling off the details pertaining to the quantity and type of blankets and canvas yardage he had brought to trade. Jack agreed to the prices quoted, which did not vary from those Patsy had purported.

"Have you the currency?" the quartermaster asked.

Wishing he could just hand over the notes and be done with it, Jack knew no self-respecting merchant would ever remit payment without assessing the goods firsthand. "That will depend on the quality of the merchandise. May I?" he gestured to the pile at the end of the dock.

"Of course," the quartermaster answered, with a sweep of his arm.

After making a show of unfurling a few of the blankets, and fingering several bolts of canvas between thumb and forefinger, Jack proclaimed, "We can come to terms on this lot . . ." He reached into his pocket and handed over the banded stack of counterfeit notes. "Fifteen hundred, as agreed."

The quartermaster took payment, and instantly began counting the money, accepting the banknotes as genuine without question. Relieved the transaction was going as smooth as Mulligan had predicted, and anxious to be back on the river, Jack sent Titus running to bring the boat in closer for quick loading.

As Jack watched Titus head down the dock, the unmistakable jab of a gun barrel pressed between his shoulder blades was followed by the ominous clack of the hammer cocking back. Jack groaned. "Now, sir . . ."

"Up with your hands—"

Jack raised his hands, and fought to keep his voice reasonable. "If there is some misunderstanding concerning the amount, we ought . . ."

"Not another word." The quartermaster dug the muzzle of his

pistol into Jack's back as he reached around to disarm him. "Take the negro down," he ordered, and a grenadier appeared at Jack's left, leveling his musket.

"*Titus!*" Jack shouted and threw himself into the grenadier just as the trigger was pulled. Titus went flying into the pettiauger. The quartermaster pistol-whipped Jack across the back of the head, dropping him to his knees.

A half-dozen more soldiers came running out from behind the pile of trade goods, bootsteps rumbling the dock. Tully popped up with a flash and sent the Redcoats down to their bellies with a blast of buckshot spraying from his blunderbuss.

"Row, Titus, *row!*" Tully's gravelly voice sounded, and pistol shots flashed, zinging toward any Redcoat foolish enough to raise his head. Furious oars slapped the water, fading as the craft moved beyond pistol range. The soldiers sprang to their feet, and let off a volley.

"Fall back," the quartermaster shouted, jerking Jack up to his feet. "No use wasting lead on those flunkies. We've captured the quarry we were after. Shackle the bastard—and search him well. He'll stand before the provost in the morning."

⚓ ⚓ ⚓

SALLY rushed out the kitchen door with a full pot of coffee, darting over to the right to avoid colliding with Anne, who went spinning through the doorway, the empty tray she held swept up over her head like a gypsy's tambourine.

The Crown and Quill was a-bustle, as usual, on a Saturday morning, and Anne was glad for the distraction. The demands of the shop helped her to keep from worrying over whether or not Jack and the others had been successful in their midnight black market dealings.

"Dinna fash," Sally advised, as they dealt with the morning rush. "The Stitch would have sent word by now if aught went awry."

"You're right." Anne nodded. "But you'd think he'd send word that all went well."

"Men." Sally shrugged. "Na?"

Sally went on to serve her coffee, and Anne replenished her tray with the last of the scones and muffins. She headed back into the fray to catch up with Sally. Scanning the room, she found her at the table closest to the front door, pouring a cup of coffee for Tully.

News. Anne heaved a sigh of relief. Raising the laden tray on fingertips above her shoulder, she negotiated the tight path between the occupied chairs and benches.

Before she could reach the front of the shop, Tully tossed back his coffee like a shot of rotgut rum and rushed out the door. Sally left her pot on the table, snatched up her skirts and flew through the shop, blinking back tears.

Wemyss rose from his seat at a table nearby, tracking Sally's path to the kitchen. "Your squinty-eyed journeyman seems to have upset our Miss Sally . . ."

Anne fought the desire to run screaming after her friend. She lowered the tray into Wemyss's hands. "Could you mind the shop, Lieutenant, so that I may see to her?"

"M-mind the—of course!" Wemyss sputtered.

Anne stepped into the kitchenhouse. Sally huddled on the hearth, her face buried in her apron. Shutting and bolting the door, Anne asked, "What's happened?"

Sally looked up with fearful eyes. "The Stitch wants to see you right away."

"Why?" Anne grasped Sal by the upper arm. "What's happened?"

Sal shrugged. "Nae details. Tully said naught but it's bad."

"How bad? What's bad?"

"I dinna ken, Annie. He said, '*It's bad*,' and ran out."

Anne hopped to her feet, tearing at her apron strings. "I'm to the Thimble and Shears, and I need you to pull yourself together and see to the shop." She fumbled, trying to tie her bonnet ribbon beneath her chin. "Wemyss is out there wondering what's amiss. Make up some excuse to explain your erratic behavior and . . ." She squeezed her eyes shut and clenched her fists tight, fighting the wave of panic threatening to overcome her reason. She could remember feeling the same breathtaking despair the night the physician had advised her to bid farewell to her little Jemmy. Taking in a long, deep breath through her nose, she released it in a slow *whoosh*.

Sally stood, knuckling the tears from her eyes. "What should I say if the captain asks after ye?"

Anne's eyes snapped open. "Who? Oh . . . I don't care . . . tell him . . . tell him I've gone to market or some such."

ᘓ   ᘓ   ᘓ

Keeping her expression impassive, and her gait measured and steady, Anne strolled along Queen Street, her mind roiling with a hurricane of possibilities the very best of which were not much better than the very worst.

The doorbell tinkled bright when she entered the tailor's shop. "I've an appointment with Mr. Mulligan." One of the stitchers sitting on the worktable led her back through a long hallway, and directed her to a closed door.

"He's waitin' for ye in there."

Anne heaved a sigh, and pressed down on the lever handle.

They all looked up when she entered: Mulligan pouring out a round of whiskey, the Quaker in his blue spectacles sitting at the desk, Titus hugging his knees, sitting on the floor beneath a potted lemon tree, a bloody red stain beginning to rust around the edges patching his right shoulder, Patsy Quinn with eyes teary and swollen, slumped on a bench against the wall next to Tully. All gathered together.

All but Jack.

The Quaker relinquished his chair, and Anne stumbled to it, her every joint gone to jelly. To resist a sudden overwhelming urge to wail and rend her garments and tear her hair, Anne laced her fingers into a tight ball on her lap. Mulligan offered her a glass of whiskey.

"Just tell me," Anne managed to say. "Is he dead?"

"No," Mulligan said. "Not dead . . ."

"Not dead!" Anne felt it. It was palpable. Renewal—hope—thudding into her very being.

Titus said, "Jack's been arrested, Mrs. Anne."

"Arrested . . ." The word puffed out of her mouth, like a cloud of tobacco smoke.

"We were ambushed," Titus said. "Me and Tully got away. The meeting was a trap."

"A trap . . ." Anne glared at Patsy.

"It *is* all my fault!" Patsy began to blubber. "Floyd—the sodding bugger! I should have known better . . . I should have known he was playing me for a fool . . ."

"I should have done better than to leave Jack behind," Titus joined in on the chorus of regrets.

"Belay that—both of you." Tully laid a rough hand on Patsy's shoulder and gave her a shake. "Nothing to be gained by *shoulds* and *woulds*. Jack knows full well not a one of us meant to cause him harm."

Mulligan pressed a glass of whiskey into Anne's hand. "I learned from an informant that Jack's to be brought before the provost marshall with a charge of treason."

"For the counterfeiting . . ." Anne nodded.

"That's the rub," Titus said. "They've no idea about the counterfeiting. He's charged with colluding with the enemy in the sale of smuggled goods."

"The provost is nobody's fool. It's only a matter of time before he puts Jack to the question and wills out the truth." Mulligan shook his big melancholy head. "And once Jack breaks, we are all in danger."

Anne looked up. "Jack will not break."

"And he'd never inform on any of us." Titus rose to his feet.

"Tough as nails, Jack is," Tully graveled.

"Your faith in Jack is admirable, and aye, he was a good friend to all of us, but the provost is not known for kindness to those in his charge." Mulligan shrugged. "He'll have Jack talking by Sunday, and dangling on Monday."

"Jack is not dead." Anne stared into the drink in her hand, the amber liquid smooth as glass. "We don't have a lot of time. We need to come up with a plan to free him."

"Don't be daft," Mulligan snapped. "I brought us together to discuss how we can save our own skins, not Jack's. There is absolutely no way for us to get to him."

"You know Jack would come up with a way if it were one of us the Redcoats nabbed," Tully admonished.

"Could we bribe a guard?" Anne asked.

Titus pinched the bridge of his nose. "Noooo . . . the Stitch is right. There's no good way to get to him while he's in prison . . ."

"At last," Hercules exclaimed. "A voice of reason!"

". . . But we just might be able to get to him on his *way* to the gallows." Titus smiled.

Tully pounded his fist to his palm. "Ambush the bloody buggers just like they ambushed us!"

"I-God!" The tailor threw his hands up.

"Cunningham holds his hangings after dark," Patsy added. "Awful, drunken parties—Mother Babcock often provides the company keepers. I've never gone—there's not enough gold in Christendom to get me to lift my skirts for that lot—but my friend Molly, she's been to more than one of his hangings . . ."

Mulligan fell back against the wall. "You're all mad," he said, with eyes shut. "Each and every one of you . . . mad as hatters."

"Patsy, you must question your friend, and find out everything you can." Anne put the glass to her lips and downed the whiskey with one gulp. "We are going to do this thing."

ငာ ငာ ငာ

IT was impossible for Jack to keep pace with Quartermaster Floyd. The short span of chain linking the leg irons he wore rattled a rusty, arrhythmic tune as he struggled to mount the stairs into the Provost Prison. His hands were similarly bound in tight iron bracelets, the gritty shackles chafing his wrists raw and staining the cuffs of his shirt ocher. The impatient guard at his rear wielding a bayoneted musket was only too eager to speed Jack's halting progress up the stairs, and the fine linen across Jack's shoulders was punctured and dotted crimson with pointed encouragement.

"Enter!" the voice called in answer to the quartermaster's knock.

Manacles chattering, Jack shuffled into the provost's office, and was prodded into a position three paces away from a large desk, where Cunningham sat with head down, scribbling away in a large ledger. The quartermaster dismissed the escort, and took an at-ease stance beside Jack.

It was long past sunrise on a bright June morning, but the provost marshall kept a thick bayberry candle burning in a futile attempt to mask the unwholesome, rotten cabbage stench permeating the dreary brick walls. The open windows were veiled with a crisscross of iron bars, and the daylight streaming in cast checkered patches on the smooth floorboards at either side of Cunningham's desk. A ladderback chair—the only other piece of furniture in the room—was pushed into the far corner amid a herd of empty rum and whiskey bottles.

What I wouldn't do for a slug of whiskey right now . . . Jack peeked through the tangled periwig askew upon his head, eyeing the half-full bottle on the provost's desktop. His head ached—ears ringing a constant, shrill peal, as if it were Christmas morning over and over again. Shackles clattering, Jack reached behind to awkwardly finger the prodigious knot swelled up and throbbing on the bulb of his skull bone.

Cunningham set aside his quill, and pushed the ledger away. Just as he had been two weeks before, when putting an end to the brawl between Jack and the Brunswicker, the provost was bewigged and trussed into an austere, dark uniform. The silver gorget he wore strung on a bloodred ribbon reflected an eerie light onto pock-scarred skin drawn tight to the bone. The provost grasped the neck of the bottle with thin fingers bulging at the knuckles, and dosed himself with a swallow.

"Am I to take it, Mr. Floyd, this man has sprung our little trap?"

A trap for counterfeiters, and I stepped straight into it. Jack retreated farther into the ridiculous wig Mulligan had furnished him; keeping his eyes downcast, shoulders slumped, he shook a few more gray locks forward to mask his face, and tried to make himself small.

"He says his name is Shipton, from Elizabethtown across the river—" The quartermaster gave Jack a shove forward, and tossed the banded stack of currency onto the desk. "Fifteen hundred pounds he had."

Cunningham leaned forward and flipped through the banknotes. "You realize, Mr. Shipton, trafficking with rebels is high treason—a hanging offense."

Jack wavered a bit, struck by Cunningham's failure to reference counterfeiting. *Tread carefully* . . . Keeping his eyes downcast, he spoke, raising the timbre of his voice to incorporate a plaintive whine. "I know no rebels, sir. I was trafficking with your man—Quartermaster Floyd."

Cunningham hitched forward in his seat. "You are familiar to me, Mr. Shipton . . . have we ever chanced to meet before?"

"We have." Jack gulped back the dry lump in his throat, and nodded. "I confess to a weakness for faro."

"A gambler, eh?" Cunningham tapped the pile of notes, leaned back and took another drink from his bottle. "Mr. Floyd, what proof have you to support your claim of treason in this case?"

"My claim?" Annoyed by the shift in attitude, Floyd snapped, "You know we arrested this man for purchasing illicit army stores—what more proof do you require?"

Jack nodded in agreement. "I readily admit to the offense, Marshall. The same greed for quick and easy profit that leads me to your gaming table has led me to purchase contraband goods. For that crime, I submit to any punishment you hand down." He raised his shackled fists to his heart. "But as an ever-true and loyal subject to the Crown, I strongly protest the charge of treason."

The quartermaster folded his arms across his chest. "Shots were exchanged. He fired upon King's soldiers."

"The shots were fired by hired men in flight. I never fired a single shot. I committed no treason, nor did I ever plan to."

"You purchased a very large quantity of wool and canvas," Cunningham pointed out. "Who was your intended customer, if not the Rebel Army?"

Keep your wits about you. Jack raised his head, and blurted, "Germans."

"Germans!" Floyd leaned on Cunningham's desktop. "You hear that? Those Hessian bastards—giving us the short shrift and taking their custom to the black market!"

Jack wagged his head up and down. "The Hessian quartermasters pay in hard currency."

"Germans . . ." Cunningham sat for a moment, pinching the bridge of his hawkish beak. "Well, Mr. Shipton"—he slapped the desktop with both palms of his hands—"*I* am convinced, and am reducing the charge from treason to smuggling, which carries the lesser sentence of impressment into His Majesty's Navy."

A life sentence aboard a floating prison—better to be hanged. Jack inched forward, his hands clasped. "I have learned a rough lesson here, Marshall. I swear on all I hold dear, I will never again venture into illegal trade—not with Germans—not with anyone." Jack cast his eye at the stack of banknotes. "Could we not reach some sort of mutual accommodation?"

"Perhaps." Cunningham laced his fingers. "After all, we are sensible, are we not, Mr. Floyd, that greed can often drive a man down a road untraveled . . . but young men so led astray, can often be . . . redeemed."

"A wise and fair judgment, Provost." Floyd reached for the bottle.

Cunningham picked up the stack of banknotes. "As this is your first offense, I am reducing the sentence from naval service to payment of a fine—say fifteen hundred pounds?"

"Gladly, sir." Jack heaved a sigh. "Happily!" *Out the door to the Thimble and Shears as fast as feet will fly. Send Mulligan for Titus and Anne. Push off from these shores, never to return until the British are purged from the city . . .*

"*O'Keefe!*" Cunningham bellowed, slipping the stack of banknotes into his pocket.

The red-faced sergeant marched in and Cunningham ordered, "Strike this fellow's irons and see that he's released."

"C'mon, ye troublesome bollocks." O'Keefe took Jack by the arm and led him to the door. "What d'ye do this time? Wrestling with those green-jackets again?"

Jack shook his head no—pulling ahead of O'Keefe—the door was but two paces away.

"*Hold!*" Cunningham came rushing around the desk and snatched the wig from Jack's head. "His name, O'Keefe—do you recall what it is?"

"Hampshire . . ." The sergeant paused. "No. Hampton."

"Hampton!" Cunningham grabbed Jack by the arm and pulled him into the light near the window.

Jack could see the cogs and levers working the machine in Cunningham's mind—recognition triggering memories, memories turning the wheel, producing connections, parts and pieces tumbling into order in a heartbeat. "Hampton. Aye. You were there—"

"I don't know what you're talking about . . ."

In a sudden, frantic fit of madness, Cunningham pushed at the sleeves of Jack's shirt, forcing the fabric up to his elbows. "I remember you. A mechanic, with ink on your arms . . ."

"No, sir. You have me confused . . ."

Cunningham ripped off his own wig, exposing the thick pink scars worming along his skull. "See the damage you wrought. '*Let's get it done,*' you said." The provost had gone pale as a cadaver. "One of Isaac Sears's myrmidons you are—shoulder to shoulder with those fanatics. Admit it—you were there with them."

Jaw clenched, Jack met the provost marshall, eye to beady ferret eye. He drew himself tall, threw back his shoulders and said, "I was then, as I am now, a Son of Liberty."

Floyd and O'Keefe stood bristling with pistols drawn as Cunningham staggered back to his bottle, a mad jack-o'-lantern grin rupturing his face in two. "Take him away. Put the bastard in Cortlandt's Sugar House for the time being. Come Monday, I will put a period to his existence."

Jack turned to gaze out the window, pressing shackled fists against the iron token strung around his neck.

Oh, Annie . . .

Chapter Twenty-one

*The strength of one man is so unequal to his
wants, and his mind so unfitted for perpetual solitude,
that he is soon obliged to seek
assistance and relief of another, who in turn requires the same.*

THOMAS PAINE, *Common Sense*

Sunday, June 22, 1777
Almost the Supper Hour, at the Crown and Quill

M R. Wemyss!" The Widow Merrick hooked the pudgy lieutenant by the arm as he came down the stairs, and led him back
to the garden. "Might we have a word before supper?"

Anne left him at the table in the shade of the peach tree to fetch
over a draft from the firkin of cider keeping cool in the cistern.

Wemyss peeked in beyond the threshold of the kitchen door to
catch a glimpse of Sally bustling around the fire. "Something smells
good."

"Sally's preparing a special Sunday supper." The widow beamed,
sitting opposite him. "Split chickens spiced and broiled on a grate
over a clear fire, parsley sauce, corn pudding . . ."

"And dinna forget the gooseberry fool!" Sally came out of the
kitchen swiping off her head scarf, a pretty sheen of sweat glistening

on her freckled cheeks. She set a plate of hard cheese and savory biscuits on the table, and sat close to the lieutenant.

Wemyss helped himself to the cheese. "Now that I am suitably cosseted, perhaps you ladies can tell me how I can be of service?"

"You are very astute, Mr. Wemyss." Anne unfurled her folding fan, and beat the air near her face. "You must have noticed, our Sally has been suffering an upset of late, being in the throes of an unfortunate family . . . situation. As I am familiar with the bend of your sympathies in this particular regard, I have counseled her to ask for your assistance."

"I see." Wemyss reached for a biscuit.

Sally laid a hand on the lieutenant's knee. "I feel I can trust ye, sir, with this confidence . . ."

"A strict confidence," Anne added, "for reasons soon to be revealed."

"Of course." Wemyss nodded. "I am not one to bear tales. You have my word as an officer and a gentleman."

Sally folded her hands in her lap and took a deep breath. "My close cousin—my mother's sister's son—Jack's his name—has run afoul of the law."

"Apprehended and imprisoned," Anne said.

"Oh my!" Wemyss asked. "On what charge?"

"Smuggling"—Sally blinked tearful eyes, her voice dropping to a whisper—"for the damned rebels!"

Softhearted Wemyss took her by the hand. "Poor, dear Miss Sally!"

"He's a lazy rascal—Jack is—too smart for his own good." Sally sniffed. "But when the devil finds an idle man, he'll set him to work, na?"

"She's been fretful day and night," Anne added with a knowing nod. "The conditions in the prisons being what they are these days . . ."

"Of course," Wemyss agreed. "Simply appalling."

Sally heaved a shuddered sigh. "The provost will hang poor Jack on th' morrow, and I was hopin' ye might . . ."

Wemyss interrupted, "I'm afraid, Miss Sally, as a lowly lieuten-ant, I can bring no influence to bear in such a case."

"Och no, Mr. Wemyss," Sally cried. "I dinna expect ye t' interfere with the King's justice, but Jack's th' onliest kin I have to speak of on this side of the water. He was like a brother to me when we were weans, an' I'm compelled t' give him some ease, on these, his last days on earth." Sally buried her face in Wemyss's shoulder, and sobbed.

"Your help in facilitating the delivery of some small amenity to a condemned man will be of great comfort to our Sally," Anne added.

"There, there . . . please don't take on so." Wemyss patted Sally on the back. "I'm certain we will be able to sort something out."

∞ ∞ ∞

IT squeaked. "Wake up, mister."

Jack shrugged away the tug on his shirtsleeve. Sitting slouched against the wall beside a broken tumble of clay sugar cones, he groaned and covered his ears. A steady, resounding clank akin to a blacksmith's hammer striking an anvil was now accompanying the incessant shrill whine in his head.

"Get up!" Someone gave his outstretched legs a kick. "Can't you hear they're ringing us down for supper?"

Ringing us down . . . Jack was relieved to find the clank origi-nated from somewhere other than the inside of his battered brain. He pulled his shirtfront over his nose in a vain attempt to filter the wretched smell of piss, shit and death, which along with the noise was a constant intrusion upon his fitful sleep. *What a stink . . .*

"If'n you don't get up, you won't get your share," the squeaky voice persisted.

Jack did not want to, but he opened his eyes to view his tormen-tors.

Boys.

Hugging knees to chest, Jack buried his face in his arms.

The skinny boy squatting at his right began to poking him in the ribs. "C'mon, mister . . . your rations . . ."

"Leave me be." Jack uttered his first words since setting foot inside the prison, swatting at the sharp finger. "I don't care about any rations."

The taller boy standing beside the squatting boy gave Jack a shove to the shoulder. "Get up, you selfish old bugger!"

Jack jerked his head up, bared his teeth and snarled, "Shove off!" but the two were not impressed.

"You have t' claim your share," the squatting boy advised with a wise nod. "If you don't want 'em, your rations can be splits amongst them that are hungerin'."

"Selfish old bugger!" the other repeated.

Them that are hungering. Jack pushed up to a stand, and dusted his palms off on his breeches. "Alright, alright . . . I need to piss anyway."

"Best wait 'til we're in the yard for that," the older boy advised.

The younger boy pinched his nose, turning his squeaky voice into an odd nasal drone. "The shit tubs is overflowin'—ain't been emptied in days."

The taller boy led the way past rows of slow-moving men rising from beds of moldering, vermin-infested straw. The British held only a portion of the four thousand captured Patriot soldiers in this five-story building. Between the sick and dying men too feeble to rise and seek out their rations, and the stream of ill-kempt, cadaverous men funneling down the stairway in a slow shuffle, Jack had gauged that close to six hundred prisoners of war suffered the filth and deprivation of Cortlandt's Sugar House.

"We had our eye on you—saw that drunken bastard O'Keefe and the mulatto hangman bring you in yesterday." Bobbing along beside Jack, the smaller boy offered his hand in greeting. "I'm Jim Griffin."

Jack took the thin hand. "Jack Hampton."

It would be generous to say the boy was skin and bone. His wide blue eyes were a bright contrast to the rest of him, mired under a layer of grime from the top of his ill-shorn head to the chipped and cracked nails on his bare toes. A clacking pair of drumsticks and a wooden canteen were strung to a shred of burlap sacking tied at his waist. The sleeve on his tattered shirt was crudely mended at the shoulder with knotted bits of twine, and his filthy breeches had frayed away to expose scabby, bony knees.

Jack jerked his head toward the taller boy. "That pleasant fellow your brother?"

"Him and me are brothers in arms," answered Jim, giving his friend a slap on the back.

The taller boy turned with an apologetic grin and shook Jack's hand as well. "Brian Eliot, of Rawlings's Maryland Riflemen." He fell back to flank Jack. "Sorry 'bout being so rough on you. I find I don't have much patience for newcomers when my stomach worm gets to gnawing."

Brian bore in his voice the soft twang of a Southerner. He was year or two older and a few inches taller than Jim, but just as gaunt. His shoulder-length hair was drawn into a greasy tail, and tied with a strip of cloth torn from the filthy rifleman's frock shirt he wore gathered at his slim waist with a tooled leather belt.

Jack pointed to the foot-long piece of iron sheathed on Brian's belt. "That's a nasty looking sticker you carry, brother."

Brian smiled proud, and slipped his makeshift weapon out for Jack to admire. The young rifleman had somewhere scavenged a flat strap door hinge, and sharpened the decorative fleur-de-lis end to a menacing point. "Keeps the boy-buggerers and thieves away, don't it, Jim?"

"Aye that." Jim grinned. "Don't nobody bother us no more."

"How long you boys been in here?" Jack asked.

"Brian was amongst them who was captured at Fort Washington back in November," Jim said. "I've been here longer—I was drumming for Atlee's musketry battalion on Brooklyn when we was boxed in and captured by Cornwallis."

They shuffled down four flights of stairs to the main floor—past a square-jawed Hessian soldier beating his musket butt to a big iron sugar cauldron—and out into an open area within a tall palisade adjacent to the sugarhouse. A company of surly faced, blue-jacketed

Hessians guarded the enclosure and distributed rations. Jack joined the line waiting to collect a share for the week—a paper-wrapped packet of hardtack along with a dripping one-pound chunk of pickled pork.

A Redcoat sergeant accompanied by a drummer boy came in through the gate and addressed the captives. After marching up and down the line in an annoying spate of drumming, the sergeant called out, "Step up, lads, and volunteer! Reclaim yer honor and sign on to take the King's shilling. Put an end to yer misery—yer rebellion has been squashed flatter than a French pancake."

There was a bristling among the prisoners—eyes shifting to and fro—each man bolstering his fellow with a nudge or a glance, and not a single man taking up what was, under the circumstances, a very tempting offer.

"C'mon, lads," the sergeant urged. "I'll stand any man who steps up to take the oath to a pint."

"D'ruther drink my own piss, than drink with the likes of you," a lanky Virginian drawled.

A voice shouted, "Bugger off, ye wee lickspigot!"

"Aye," another yelled, "you and yer whole shitten army."

The recruiting sergeant rolled his eyes. "God rot yiz all, then—fools! Fuckin' stupid rebel sods." He gave his drummer a nudge, and they left the yard in search of a friendlier audience.

"Here you go, boys—" Jack handed off his rations, adding, with as much swagger as he could muster, "Wasted on me, seeing as how I'm due for a neck stretching on the morrow."

Neither boy hesitated. Jim took the hardtack, Brian took the meat, and Jack knew the friends would come to a fair reckoning in divvying up the extra food they'd earned for keeping a sharp eye on the comings and goings of the provost's minions.

"Thank you kindly, Jack." Brian slipped his rations inside his shirt.

"Me and him figured you for a goner." Jim pulled out a biscuit and sniffed it. "O'Keefe only deals with those destined to dangle. You fellas never seem to be very hungry." He cracked the hardtack in two. It was writhing with weevils. The boy broke up the biscuit and flicked out most of the vermin before sifting the crumbs into his mouth.

"What'd you do t' warrant a neck stretchin'?" Brian asked.

"I got caught trying to smuggle a boatload of British Army stores to Washington."

"A-yup." Brian nodded. "High treason. That'll do it."

"A good thing to swing for, I reckon," Jim said, uncorking the stopper on his canteen. "Cheers to you, Jack!"

Jack bid the boys farewell, and went off to join a long row of ragged scarecrows relieving themselves against the fencing. Finishing his business, and buttoning his breeches, he turned to find the boys waiting for him.

"We want you to come with us to our place," Brian said.

"C'mon . . ." Jim leaned in with a wave and a whisper. "We got something you'll want to see."

Jack followed the boys back into the building, through the river of men still flowing into the small yard for food and fresh air, to a narrow staircase leading down to the cellar.

"I don't know . . ." Jack stopped at the top of the stairs. "Whatever you're after, boys, I'd rather just hand it over than suffer a thump to the head or the business end of that sticker."

Brian crisscrossed his thumb over his heart. "We mean you no harm."

"I promise you're gonna like our place," Jim added. "You're a true Patriot, just like us."

Jack followed the boys down the stairs, where they negotiated the dank maze of corridors with the ease of nocturnal prowlers. He kept up with a grip on Jim's bony shoulder knob while his eyes adjusted to the darkness, careful to avoid stepping on the squeaking swarm of rodents retreating as the threesome pressed forward.

They came to a cobwebbed barricade made up of several big sugar barrels, a heavy, fallen-down ceiling timber and an old broken barrow. "There it is." Brian pointed out a half-hidden padlocked door.

"We found it when we were rat huntin'." He scooted under the downed ceiling beam. "Watch your head . . ."

"We tapped the pins from the hinges," Jim explained as Brian pried the door open at the hinge side with the flat end of his iron sticker. Jack followed them in, squeezing through the narrow opening.

Brian called out, "Hold still while I get us a light."

In the rustling darkness, Jack heard the comforting sound of flint striking steel. After a few failed, flashing attempts, the tinder—a frizzle of old burlap sacking—caught a spark.

"We found a whole cask of whale oil in here," Brian explained as he nurtured the flame and transferred it to a twist of paper to light the wick on a large glass-chimneyed oil lamp, bathing the small room in a golden, wavering light.

"We eats a spoonful once a week," Jim added, scrunching his face. "Brian says it does us good."

The boys unloaded their rations onto the same counter that held the lamp—a long wooden desk fitted with a series of cubbyholes still stocked with a dusty assortment of paper labels, tags and blank bills of lading.

The room was no bigger than ten foot square, and Jack stood in the center of the dirt floor, gazing in wonder about him. "My word! These are very fine . . ."

Jim elbowed Brian. "See, I knew he'd like 'em."

Jack wandered the perimeter of the room, examining a series of intricate scenes rendered in black on the smooth plaster walls. "Who drew them?"

"We did," Brian said. "Me and Jim—with chunks of charcoal we found in an old bin."

"Trying to make our room a pleasant place," Jim added. "Since there weren't no windows in here, we fashioned our own."

Windows into worlds far beyond these prison walls . . . The drawings were large, and each scene was framed in a heavy, broad stroke—a boy and a spotted hound running through a field of corn under a cloud-filled sky; a mother kneading dough before a cheery hearth, her baby asleep in a basket at her feet; two boys in straw hats lazing along a marshy shoreline, their hopeful lines cast; a family with hands joined in prayer, gathered around a table groaning with food.

The two drawing styles were distinct, but still, the subject matter was wrought with much skill, and Jack was struck by the beauty and peace conveyed in simple lines from the minds and hands of such young boys. The images were at once wonderful and painful for Jack to gaze upon. It broke his heart to think of the talent and dreams imprisoned and snuffed out in this awful place.

While the artists sat on the floor chewing on a supper of un-cooked meat and moldy, weevil-infested biscuits, Jack took in each scene. Smiling, he began to compose the "window" he'd draw, if he were lucky enough to own such skill.

My beautiful Anne, standing at the compositor's table, teaching our daughter to set type—our tall son beside me, working the press, a stew pot simmering on the fire . . . and . . . and it will never be . . . Jack lost his smile. *For I am a dead man.*

As if he'd been struck once again across the back of the head with a pistol butt, Jack was staggered by the admission. *I end tomorrow beneath Cunningham's gallows.* There was no bravado in the thought. Every hope, dream and desire he'd ever had would be strangled life-less by a hempen rope.

Jack clutched at the cast-iron half-crown around his neck, his breath stuck in his chest. He closed his eyes and imagined the other half in Anne's possession, lying against the creamy, smooth skin just beneath the hollow of her throat. Gasping a shallow breath, he could almost feel the soothing peace of her fingertips on his brow.

"We didn't mean t' make you sad, Jack," Jim said, in a quiet voice. "Sometimes, the pictures take you to a place you didn't mean to go to . . ."

Jack heaved in and puffed out a sigh, swiping tears away with his sleeve. "No . . . I'm glad I came. Really. Thank you, boys, for sharing your place with me."

Brian nodded. "Even if it's only in your mind's eye, and only for a smidge of time, it helps to wander away from this shit-stinking world, don't it?"

Rations were stowed into a small keg with a tight-fitting lid. The lantern was doused, and the three trudged back upstairs to slip back into the crowded yard just as the Hessians began to bark out orders and herd the prisoners back inside. Jack joined the despondent double file of men, moving through the doorway, shuffling along to the beat of consumptive hacks and groans.

It surely is a shit-stinking world . . .

"Hampton!"

Jack turned to his name. Through the moving crowd he could see a red-coated officer standing with a Hessian guard call out his name again.

"Hampton!"

Jack kept pace with the herd, all the while snatching glances over his shoulder.

Jim grabbed Jack by the shirttail, whispering, "What's that bloodyback want with you?"

"I suppose it's my gallows time . . ."

"No, sir." Brian shook his head. "They ain't allowed t' scrag anybody on the Sabbath . . ."

Jack shrugged. "The provost may have something in mind for me—more than just a hanging."

"Don't answer, Jack."

"Make 'em find you."

"Hampton! Jack Hampton!" the officer shouted, craning his neck. The Redcoat and the Hessian guard began to move up the line, and as they drew closer Jack could see the officer was cradling the distinctive brass helmet worn by the 17th Light Dragoons in the crook of his arm. In his other hand, he bore a loaf-sized rectangular package wrapped in rose-colored paper and tied with a blue, grosgrain ribbon.

"Here!" Jack shouted, stepping out with Jim and Brian on his heels trying to pull him back.

The lieutenant was one of the cavalrymen he had ridden with

when he had scouted for General Clinton . . . one of the three dragoons Anne quartered above the Crown and Quill . . . *Wemyss*.

"I'm Jack Hampton," he announced. "I'm him." Jack could see the reciprocal flash of recognition in the dragoon's eye—the lieutenant clearly hesitating before at last handing over the package.

"Your cousin has sent this small comfort for your last hours. Miss Sally bid me to tell you she made this cake special, just for you, and she will pray for your mortal soul."

"Thank you, sir . . . thank you so much." Jack slipped the package inside his shirt, and touched his fingers to his brow in salute. "Please tell my cousin I am most grateful for her kindness and her prayers."

Wemyss brought a kerchief to his nose to allay the stink and considered Jack for a moment with a furrowed brow. Then, turning abrupt on his heel, he marched away.

Jack tugged the boys back into the shuffling throng, and under his breath he said, "I need to use your light."

Both boys eyed the bulge in Jack's shirt, and nodded. They dragged their feet, making sure they were among the last prisoners lagging behind when the guards shut the big door. At the sound of the heavy iron bar dropping into its seat, Brian whispered, "Go!" and the three of them peeled away and skittered down the cellar stairs.

"Whatever you got there, it surely smells grand," Jim said, his nose twitching like a rabbit's as they pried the door open to the secret room. "What do you think it is?"

Jack pulled the package from his shirt and took a sniff. "It is definitely the finest soft gingerbread in all of New York. I'm hoping it is also a message from my woman."

"How'd your woman get a Redcoat to deliver it?" Brian asked, putting flint to steel to light the oil lamp.

"My Anne, she is a wonder." His heart was dancing a jig in his chest, and he fumbled so untying the ribbon, he threw up his hands and left it to Brian to accomplish the unwrapping.

The deep brown loaf was wrapped in four sheets of rose-colored foolscap paper. He spread the sheets out on the countertop, examining each one, front and back.

Seeing every page was blank, Brian sighed in sympathy. "It was probably too dangerous for her to write a message . . ."

"No. There's a message here. I know it." Jack set aside the two most grease-stained pages, and ran his fingertips over the surface of the two clean pages.

"Can we eat a bite?" Jim asked. On Jack's absentminded nod, the boys converged on the loaf, prying off two good-sized chunks.

"Looky here," Brian said, "there's somethin' in this cake . . ."

"Looks like the mate to the one you wear." Jim showed Jack the crumb-covered half-crown in the palm of his hand.

"'*Made it special* . . .'" Jack said, with a grin and shake of his head.

He removed the glass chimney on the lamp, held the paper to the heat of the flame and held his breath when the faint strokes of a pen began to darken on the page. "Here it comes . . ." He laughed. The script formed into full black, and he threw his head back and exclaimed, "Oh, Annie!"

The boys crowded on either side. "What's it say? What's it say?"

Jack read aloud the words rendered in Anne's fine, strong hand:

> "*Be Ready.*
> *We are coming for You.*"

CHAPTER TWENTY-TWO

There are injuries which nature cannot forgive;
she would cease to be nature if she did.

THOMAS PAINE, *Common Sense*

Monday, June 23, 1777
Supper Hour at the Red Lion on Broad Way and Murray

*E*IGHT *o'clock* ...
William Cunningham snapped the case on his pocket watch shut and waved the serving boys in to clear the table. But for a few scraps and bones congealing in greasy, bloody puddles, the platters and bowls were picked clean and the gravy jugs were drained dry. The boys carried off the remnants of the main course, and set out an impressive array of exotic sweetmeats and imported English cheeses. Brandy goblets were distributed, and the publican placed six bottles of Armagnac on the long table at regular intervals. The provost poured himself a glassful, and waited for his guests to ready their drinks.

The cut-crystal goblet weighed heavy in his hand. Pushing away from the table, his head swam a bit. *Too much claret and punch, and not enough meat and potatoes,* he thought. Of late, his appetite never seemed to match his thirst.

Cunningham fortified himself with a gulp of brandy, and rose to propose the customary toast. On this signal, chairs scraped back across the floorboards, and the group of merchants, bureaucrats and British officers whose favor he regularly curried joined him.

The provost held his glass high, and proclaimed, "His Majesty, the King."

Which was followed by the rumbled communal response of, "His Majesty, King George the Third." Crystal tinging, everyone took a good swallow.

Joshua Loring raised his glass and added, "The provost marshall—generous host of this glorious feast."

"Hear, hear!"

Cunningham accepted the accolade with proper humility, and as planned, Quartermaster Floyd put an end to the toasting, glass aloft. "Our wives and sweethearts—may they never meet."

The old jest drew the requisite amused guffaw, and the guests resumed their seats.

Wavering a bit, Cunningham remained on his feet at the head of the table. He could feel his new wig had slipped off-kilter, and the sharp tug he gave to right it sent it off to the other extreme. He grasped the table edge, and buttressed his stance with a deep swallow of French brandy, then launched into his speech.

"Trusted servants of the British Crown—not so long ago, this very room served as the gathering place for that nest of vipers known as the Sons of Liberty." He swept his arms up, inadvertently cuffing the servant boy who had ducked in to set a plate on the table, knocking a wheel of Cheshire cheese onto the floor.

The provost glared, waiting for the boy as he dusted the retrieved cheese with a grimy rag from his pocket and set it back on its plate. "Aye . . ." Cunningham continued, "*these* very walls bore witness as the scoundrels planned their nefarious treason. And around this very table . . ." He pounded his fist, rattling the nearby china and glassware. "Around *this* table, these so called Liberty Boys fomented rebellion and war.

"Loyal and valiant men! Your presence around this table is a testament to the rising tide of victory. Washington and his motley rabble are on the run, and soon the country will be swept clean of the rebel menace, and proper order will reign over the whole of His Majesty's Empire."

"Hear, hear!" The company broke into applause, and the ardent took to their feet.

Cunningham quieted the room with outstretched arms. "We have brought into submission one of the most pernicious, vile Sons of Liberty to have ever claimed that mantle. An unrepentant black-hearted whoreson, who will at the end of our party answer to the devil himself."

Joshua Loring offered up a weak, "Huzzah!"

Wincing at the solo bleat issued from one of his pandering sheep, Cunningham raised his glass one last time. "I invite you all to join me at the new gallows behind Bridewell at midnight, to witness as I send yet another rebel bastard to an aggravated damnation in hell."

The provost plopped back into his seat, brandy sloshing. "Until then, my friends, you're still my guests—doxies, dice and faro await in the public room."

⚓ ⚓ ⚓

TRUSSED into a red silk gown, Anne sat on the chest at the foot of Patsy Quinn's bed. Fists balled in her lap, she splayed a finger in time with every bong of the new bell at City Hall.

"Eleven o'clock already," Sally said, with a shake of her head.

"As if we hadn't noticed. Now keep your mouth closed." Patsy rubbed her pinky finger into the pot of lip pomade, and artfully applied the crimson paint to give Sally a proper streetwalker's pout. "There! My turn."

Sally relinquished her seat at the dressing table to Patsy Quinn, and went to sit beside Anne. "It takes some getting used to," she said, barely moving her lips. "All this paint and hair."

Afraid to upset the high-piled wig on her head, Anne thought better of nodding. She fiddled with the red ribbon tied at her throat, the layers of paint feeling much like a skim coat of plaster on her skin. "If I didn't know better, Sal, I'd never guess it was you."

"Nor I you—good thing we have some time to grow accustomed t' this gear," Sally said with a waggle of her head. "I'm like to burst out laughing every time I take a look at ye."

Patsy talked into the mirror above her dressing table, twirling her long dark hair into a knot at the back of her head. "The provost and the quartermaster transact regular with sporting girls. If our plan is going to work, the ruse must convince. You ladies might look the part—but you must play whore with some gusto or we'll all wind up dangling alongside Jack." Opening the front of her dressing gown, she used a little sea sponge to apply an even coat of stark white paint from forehead to chest.

"You're right, Patsy." Anne tried to relax her stiff shoulders. "It's really no different than flirting with our dragoons, I suppose."

Patsy mixed red and white paint into a garish pink color that she applied to her cheeks and nipples. "There's a difference dealing with men who pay good coin, and those who try to wheedle the goods for naught."

"Annie . . ." Sally eyed the nipple painting. "We ought plump up our bubbies a bit . . ."

The women helped lace Patsy into her stays, and pinned her into a red silk dress. After tugging on a big wig to match the wigs Sally and Anne wore, Patsy applied crimson lip pomade, and affixed a small crescent-shaped black silk patch to her left temple, near her eye.

Patsy passed the patchbox to Sally. "Put on a *mouche* . . . left is the Tory side, and the temple bespeaks passion."

Sally poked her finger through the assortment of black silk patches and chose a clover shape. "For luck!" Touching a dab of gum arabic to the patch, she mimicked Patsy, pressing the *mouche* to her left temple and passing the little box on to Anne.

Anne read the motto inscribed on the lid of the enamelware patchbox aloud. "*The hardness of your heart causes mine to ache and smart.*"

"The city commandant gave me that trifle himself—calls me Hard-hearted Patsy, he does—he's been after me to become his mistress." Patsy stood before the mirror, tying a red satin ribbon around her throat. "Bitch Babcock is all for it—says we ought pick the ol' lecher's pocket whilst he breathes—but I say there's more to life than money. I generally don't have much of a stomach for shriveled-up old men—old Tories in particular—" Patsy glanced over to Anne, adding, "No offense."

Anne chose a five-pointed star-shaped patch, and glued it into place. "None taken. I prefer a younger man myself—and it seems he prefers me as well . . ."

Patsy flinched and sat down on the bed, biting her lip.

"Annie!" Sally scolded, sitting down beside Patsy.

"I'm so sorry. That was cruel." Anne sank down to sit on the other side, taking Patsy by the hand. Her barb had shattered Patsy's protective shell, and Anne could see her for what she truly was, a young girl with a very broken heart.

Patsy shrugged. "Knowing Jack loves you don't stop me from loving him. I wish it did—but it don't. My poor heart just won't mind my brain."

Anne slipped her arm around Patsy's shoulders. "You must love Jack very much to risk all for him. When I consider if I would do the same if I wore your shoes, I think I would not. Your heart is far more brave and generous than mine."

"More foolish than brave." Patsy heaved a sigh and leaned into Anne.

"Yer nobody's fool, Pats," Sally argued.

"We're lucky to have you as a friend, Patsy—all of us."

There was a knock at the door, and Titus called, "Can we come in?"

The door inched open and Tully ducked his head in. "Uncle Tully has brung you girls a few trinkets . . ."

The women all leapt up, smoothing skirts and dabbing hankies to eyes, waving Titus and Tully into the crowded little room.

Dressed in his usual wooly cap and longshoreman toggery, Tully's lading hook dangled from his belt, and he carried a large bundle of sailcloth under one arm.

Wearing a seaman's checked shirt and striped trousers tucked into cuffed boots, Titus looked like the typical bullyback a madam might send along to protect her girls working the streets.

"Ye have the air of a pirate about ye, Titus!" Sally said.

Tully grunted. "He looks like a pimp to me."

Titus tipped the befeathered tricorn he wore over a red silk scarf tied about his bald head. A mean-looking cudgel was stuck in the sash at his waist. "I hope to confound the provost, lest he recognize me."

Patsy asked, "How do we look?"

The women lined up, shoulder to shoulder, each in a fair-haired wig, wearing a red dress and ribbon about her neck. When Titus suggested they dress alike, to not only add to their allure, but also to confuse men who would be addled with spirits, Patsy had immediately pounced upon the brilliance of the strategy. "Men go *mad* for a comely pair of twins. The quartermaster, for one, will not be able to resist a trio."

Of a same height and build, with faces painted, the only distinguishing marks were the patches adorning their temples. Titus nodded his approval, and Tully graveled, "As alike as peas in a pod."

"Have we any news?" Anne asked.

"We do." Tully set his bundle on the bed. "O'Keefe's been dispatched to fetch Jack to the gallows."

Titus added, "Our boy at the Red Lion says he's made the rounds to most of Cunningham's party guests, passing the message that the hanging's been postponed—just like we told him to."

Tully unrolled the canvas parcel, revealing their arsenal. "The pistols are all primed, loaded and ready to fire." Titus grabbed up the largest and stuffed it into his sash. Tully tucked one into his shirt, and handed a pistol to each woman. "Remember, cock the hammer all the way back, grip your weapon with both hands and aim at the biggest target . . ."

Titus pounded his chest. "The heart."

"Like we practiced, aye?" Sally brooked a two-handed stance and aimed her pistol out the window. Anne and Patsy slipped their guns into their pockets.

Tully handed them each a sheathed, double-edged dagger. "Never hurts to have a knife at the ready."

Patsy raised her skirts and slipped the sheath into the garter on her right knee. Anne and Sally followed suit.

"I only wish we knew exactly how many and who we might be tangling with." Tully whisked off his cap and scratched behind his ear, his squinty eye squashed to a slit. "When you dance in the dark, it's good to ken what might take you by the hand, eh?"

"We face many unknowables in this venture." Titus stowed his knife in his boot. "Best gather up your pluck, ladies and gents. As my good friend Jack Hampton would say, it's time to add a new wrinkle to the provost's arsehole."

♉ ♉ ♉

Surrounded and serenaded by his snoring brethren, Jack sat propped against the wall near a window, listening to the new bell at City Hall toll half-past eleven.

Almost midnight.

Something must have gone awry. He thought for certain Cunningham would have come for him by now. Since nightfall, he'd waited, anxious, expecting to be dispatched to the gallows at any moment.

Be Ready. We are coming for You.

For the thousandth time since he'd read the clandestine message written in Anne's hand, Jack's mind became embroiled in a whirlwind of hope and worries.

Could they? Should they?

As much as he did not want to hang, the danger posed to his friends staging his rescue was high, and the probability of success low.

The boys came tearing up the stairs, dodging around prone men huddled in their blankets. They skittered across the dark room and dropped down to their knees to sit on either side of him.

"They're here, Jack . . ." Brian gasped, his narrow chest heaving.

"O'Keefe and the hangman," Jim continued. "Coming up the stairs."

Jack stood, nodding. "I'm ready."

The bootsteps thudded up the stairs and a rough voice bellowed, *"Hampton!"* rousing the sleeping prisoners and touching off a wildfire of coughs, groans and complaints that spread from floor to floor.

Brian took Jack by the arm. "We'd better say our good-byes."

"Before I go . . ." Jack clapped both boys by the shoulder, and looked them each in the eye. "I want you to promise me this—next time the recruiting sergeant comes around looking for volunteers, I want you to step forward . . ."

"No!" Jim jerked away. "We won't swear false. We're Patriots."

Brian stepped back and crossed his arms. "We ain't no turncoats, Jack. We ain't!"

"Listen to me—*listen to me!*" Jack grabbed Brian by the shoulder and gave him a shake. "Dying in this shithole serves no purpose. Join the Redcoat army and then *desert*—you are both clever and brave enough to make that happen. Desert and find your way back to the Continentals." Jack snatched Jim up by the arm and gave both stubborn boys another hard shake. "Washington needs your drum, Jim—and your rifle, Brian. If you're the Patriots you claim to be, you'll do what you must to get back and fight for our cause—promise me now—*promise me!*"

Brian and Jim nodded.

"Good." Jack heaved a sigh. "Good men, you are."

"Hampton!" The call came from the story below, and a flickering light illuminated the rafters above the stairwell.

Jack gave the boys each a handshake and a bear hug. "Till we meet again, right?"

Standing side by side, Brian swiped his forearm across his eyes, and Jim fisted his tears away.

"We'll see you soon, Jack."

"Aye, that . . . good luck to you, Jack."

"Hampton!" The boys ducked down into feigned sleeping positions as a torch-bearing O'Keefe and the mulatto hangman came up out of the stairwell, followed by a sleepy-eyed Hessian guard bearing a bayoneted musket.

"Quit your caterwauling—I'm coming," Jack called. Picking a path through the field of huddled gray lumps, he made his way to stand before the sergeant. "You're a noisy little bootlick, aren't you?"

"Richmond"—the sergeant tossed him a coil of rope—"bind and gag the devil."

The mulatto came forward, his calloused bare feet scraping on the floorboards. Richmond fished a filthy rag from the pocket of his trousers, forced the cloth between Jack's teeth and tied the gag tight. With his long, matted plaits swinging, Richmond's practiced fingers worked the rope into strong knots, binding Jack's wrists tight behind his back, and hobbling his ankles with just enough slack to allow him to manage the stairs.

The trudge down four flights of stairs was made ponderous and painful by the hobbling and the point of the Hessian's bayonet. Once on the street, they shuffled in a silent single file down the long, deserted stretch of Broad Way. O'Keefe took the lead with the sputtering pine-pitch torch, followed by Jack, the Hessian guard and the witless hangman trailing at the last.

Turning into the yard behind Bridewell, Jack was at once riveted by the rope centered on the beam between the two gallows posts. Tied with a hangman's knot, the noose was fashioned from an unfrayed length of new rope, and almost seemed to glow in the light of half a dozen torches burning bright in holders mounted to the granite prison wall.

The gallows were built perpendicular to the prison, and parallel to Broad Way. Flanked by two circular iron fire baskets with flames leaping, the provost's improved gallows was three times the size of the one erected in haste on the Commons at the onset of the city's occupation. Built with an eye for volume business, it could easily accommodate three or four customers at a time.

Three men were waiting near the gallows. Jack spotted the provost immediately. Dressed in black, the silver gorget around Cunningham's neck reflected the flickering yellow torchlight up onto his craggy features. He fidgeted with his cane in a small huddle with

Quartermaster Floyd and a small portly fellow Jack did not recognize. Upon sighting the little parade, the provost snapped his watch shut. "Richmond," he ordered, "go fetch your wagon."

The hangman took off running across the field littered with tree stumps. Disheartened, Jack could see no vantage point from which anyone could launch an ambush or attack. Washington's Army had harvested the small grove of oak trees that once separated the prison from the soldier's barracks.

All that timber and back-breaking work spent to build useless fortifications . . .

O'Keefe gave Jack a rough shove. "G'won and stand your place beneath the gibbet."

The city bell began a doleful tolling of the midnight hour, and Jack was stricken with an overwhelming weariness, sapping the strength from his legs. The sleepy Hessian guard induced Jack onward with a halfhearted poke to the ribs, and he stumbled forward to stand within the frame of the gallows.

Small comfort for your last hours . . . the notion of a rescue.

The half-crown hidden in the ginger cake—the message but a distraction so he might wile away his final hours dwelling upon something hopeful, something other than his inevitable, lonely, inglorious demise at the hand of a despicable man.

The agitated provost checked his pocket watch again. "You both heard me say midnight, didn't you?"

The stout fellow wagged his head up and down. "It was probably a mistake to loose the whores on that lot *afore* the hanging."

"Christ, Loring, you can be such a dolt. That's how we've always done it—gambling and whoring before the hanging." The provost fished a flask from his pocket, and took a generous swallow.

What I wouldn't do for a drink of water . . . Jack's throat felt like it had been scoured with a sooty chimney brush. The dusty rag Richmond used as a gag tasted of turpentine, and absorbed every bit of moisture in his mouth.

"Of course, you're right . . ." Loring toadied. "They are a brood of ungrateful buggers."

"The bastards ate my food, drank my liquor and they are now fucking the cunt I paid for—selfish, greedy bastards . . ." The provost paced a few steps forth and back.

Loring threw his arms up. "The height of rudeness to say the least . . ."

Floyd shot an upraised eyebrow Loring's way before offering, "I can run over to the Lion and roust the bastards from their beds . . ."

Cunningham swayed on his feet, checked his watch once again. "No. Fuck 'em. I'm ready to see this man hang now."

Richmond drove a big two-mule dray into the yard. Jack shuffled over as the hangman backed the wagon in to sit with the tail end centered beneath the noose. Hopping down from the seat, the big mulatto grabbed Jack up like a sack of potatoes to sit on the wagon bed. Jack looked up at the noose, and his heart began beating wild in his chest as if it might burst.

Think of something else . . . something good . . . something kind . . . something beautiful . . .

Frantic to quell his panic, Jack closed his eyes, breathed in through his nose and out through his mouth, and tried to remember—the weight of Annie's leg tossed over his in the morning . . . how soft her cheek felt under his thumb . . . the blue of her eye when she said, "I love you . . ."

> *"I've got me boots, me nobby, nobby boots*
> *I've got boots a-seen a lot of rough weather*
> *For the bottoms' near wore out and the heels flying about*
> *And me toes are looking out for better weather . . ."*

Jack's eyes snapped open at the familiar scratchy voice singing the familiar ditty. Tully swaggered into the torchlight, bottle of rum in hand.

> *"Here's to the grog, boys, the jolly, jolly grog*
> *Here's to the rum and tobacco*

I've a-spent all my tin with the lassies drinking gin
And to cross the briny ocean I must wander . . ."

"Heigh-ho, lads!" Tully grinned and waved his bottle. Jack was grateful for the gag, for he would have surely given Tully's ruse away for the enormous smile on his face.

O'Keefe rushed up, grabbed Tully by the scruff of the neck and attempted to drag him away. "Drunken sot . . ."

Tully shook off his assailant, and in a thick brogue—no doubt aping his long-dead Irish mother—the longshoreman protested this rude treatment.

"Away and take yer face for a shite, you ugly little fart-sucker. I am able to perambulate on me own accord."

"Leave the man be, O'Keefe," the provost ordered.

"The bastard's drunk and past curfew . . ." the sergeant blustered.

"Curfew be damned," Tully shouted. "I've come to see a rebel be scragged."

"A man after me own heart." Cunningham swept his hand up. "Come on over, Dublin, and join the party."

Tully bowed. "Thank you kindly, sir."

Upon the provost's order to "Carry on," the hangman jumped onto the wagon and pulled Jack up to a stand. Like a player on a stage, Jack bounced on the balls of his feet, scanning his audience and assessing the lay of the land.

O'Keefe and the Hessian leaned on muskets off to his left. Directly ahead, perhaps twelve paces back from the wagon's edge, the provost stood with Loring and the quartermaster. Tully had positioned himself betwixt the two groups. Jack met his friend's eye, and they exchanged a barely discernible nod. But for the green glass bottle in his hand, Tully was apparently unarmed, but Jack knew better.

O'Keefe—musket. Hessian—musket. Quartermaster—pistol and sword. Cunningham—cane, perhaps a hidden sword. Loring—also apparently unarmed.

Richmond dropped the noose over his head. The heft of the rope around his neck caused Jack to shift his weight from one foot to the other, eyes darting about. *What is Tully waiting for?*

"You see that?" Cunningham pointed with his cane. "This bastard's the type who'll both piss and shit himself."

A peal of inane giggles rang out, and Jack heard Sally Tucker shout, "Hoy, lads! *Wait!* Wait for us!"

A trio of garish prostitutes and their bullyback came into the yard off Broad Way. The women linked arms. Skipping over to stand before Cunningham, they dipped in a florid, unison curtsy. Their disguises were so complete and so alike, Jack was only able to tell who they were by their voices.

"A special gift . . ." Patsy began.

"For the provost marshall . . ." Sally continued.

"Compliments of the captain," Anne completed.

On this cue the women threw their skirts up, offering a very brief flash of what lay under all that red silk.

Floyd grinned from ear to ear. Cunningham leaned in on his cane a bit wobbly, and actually smiled. "A lovely threesome! What captain sends such a *generous* gift?" he asked.

Anne put a finger to her temple, and squeezed her eyes tight in concentration. Snapping her eyes wide-open, she said with an adorable nod, "The captain at the Red Lion, sir."

Floyd pulled Sally into his arms. "Now this is what I call a hanging party."

"Aye." Sally brazenly drew a flask from the quartermaster's sash, and offered a toast. "Here's hopin' that rebel's not the only man who'll be well hung tonight."

Anne sidled up to Loring, and he squeaked, "Hear, hear!"

Patsy looped her arm through Cunningham's and gazed up at him with adoring eyes.

"You can go home to your madam." Cunningham waved Titus away. "I'll see these ladies are escorted back safe."

Titus bowed. "Yessuh!"

Cunningham shouted, "Get on with it, Richmond."

Jack kept his eye on Titus as he turned to leave, and saw him slip the cudgel from his sash as he skirted around behind O'Keefe.

Tully shouted, *"Now!"*

In the same instant, Titus dropped first the sergeant and then the Hessian with two fierce thwacks to the backs of their heads. The girls leapt back, pistols cocked and leveled. Tully drew a pistol and advanced on Richmond, shouting, "Up with your arms, hangman! *Up!"*

"You, too!" Patsy shouted. "Up with your arms!"

Cunningham groaned. Both he and Loring raised their arms.

"Patsy! By Christ!" Floyd struggled to pull his pistol from his sash.

"Up with yer arms," Sally warned.

Floyd freed his pistol, and aimed it at Tully, climbing onto the wagon.

Titus snatched up a musket and shouted, *"Shoot him, Sal!"*

Sally and Floyd pulled their triggers.

Sally's shot aimed steady and square to his chest sent the quartermaster flying back. His shot knocked Tully to the ground.

Richmond pursued his vocation like an automaton—tightening the noose, positioning the knot just beneath Jack's left ear. Taking up a leather quirt, he leapt down to stand beside the mules with arms folded, waiting for the signal from his master.

Cunningham shouted, "Scrag the bastard, Richmond!"

The hangman whipped the mules. The mules did not budge.

Titus fired a musket, hitting the hangman in the shoulder, staggering Richmond only for a moment. Titus leapt up onto the dray. Whipping his knife from his boot, he sliced through the binding at Jack's wrists.

Richmond continued to whip the stubborn mules. Tully pulled himself up and, leveling his pistol at the large target, sent the hangman flying with a ball to his chest.

Hands free, Jack struggled to loosen the knot behind his ear as Titus sawed away at the thick rope. *"Mrs. Anne!"* Titus shouted.

Anne turned to see the dray lurch forward and the rope grow taut, as Jack struggled to keep his footing on the moving wagon bed.

Tully staggered forward to try to gain control of the slow-moving mules. Titus leapt up and grabbed hold of the rope above the noose as Jack grabbed hold of the rope around his neck with both fists. The mules continued forward and the two went swinging.

"Hold on, Jack—hold on!" Titus gasped, hanging by one arm. Swinging to and fro, he sliced through the taut hempen cording. Jack struggled to breathe through the gag; he hung on to the loop around his neck, jerking his hobbled legs up to keep from strangling as the noose tightened, biting into his fingers.

Anne pressed her pistol on Sally and ran to catch Jack by the legs and lift him as best she could to relieve the pressure on his airway.

"There!" Titus cut through the rope, and they all tumbled into the dirt.

Tully managed to grab a harness and stop the animals backing them up a few paces. Titus and Anne lifted Jack onto the wagon bed, and jumped on. Tully pulled up onto the seat. Taking hold of the reins, he slapped the mules into motion.

Jack tore at the gag and pulled the noose loose, gulping and coughing for a breath.

"C'mon, c'mon!" Titus shouted to the girls, as Tully urged the trotting mules across Broad Way.

Tossing wigs to the ground, Sally and Patsy lifted their skirts and sprinted toward the wagon, leaving Cunningham and Loring fumbling for the pistols under their jackets. Sally reached the wagon first, tossing her pistol to Titus, who fired off a cover round as Anne pulled Sally aboard. The mules picked up speed.

"Take my hand!" Titus shouted to Patsy, who was struggling to catch up. She tossed her pistol away, and reached out. Titus grabbed her by the forearm. The provost gave chase, getting off a shot just as Patsy was pulled aboard.

Careening around the corner, the wagon clattered over the cobbles of Church Street, and Tully whipped the reins and drove like mad, straight into the heart of Canvas Town.

Patsy pulled up to a sit with her back against the driver's seat. "We did it!"

Anne and Sally used their knives to cut through the bonds at Jack's ankles. Jack tugged the noose over his head and tossed it overboard. Coughing and hacking, he clutched at his throat, and in a voice raspier than Tully's, he finally croaked out, "No man—could want—for finer friends . . ."

Tully tugged on the reins, pulled the wagon into a narrow little alley and came to a noisy stop. Turning in his seat with a wince, he waved them all out of the wagon. "We're on foot from here on. Can you walk, Jack?"

Jack nodded. "Can you?"

"Took a ball in the arse," Tully said. "I ain't gonna pay it much mind just yet."

Titus jumped down. "Better hurry. The provost will have Redcoats crawling all over the city in no time."

Patsy pushed off on her palms, and shifted forward to sit at the edge of the wagon bed.

"We've a ways to go yet . . ." Titus looked up and down the narrow corridor between two rows of burned-out and crumbling tenements. Their arrival had drawn the curiosity of more than a few furtive faces peeking out from behind draped canvas, and around dark doorways.

"Where're we going?" Jack asked.

Tully hopped down and picked up a piece of timber suitable for use as a club. "Fishmarket—the Quaker waits there with the boat."

"Fishmarket." Jack ran his hands over his hair. "Bound to smell better than Canvas Town."

"I never thought to hear myself say it, but I willna breathe easy till we're on the water." Sally scooted off the side of the dray.

Anne gathered her skirts and hopped down. "I never thought I'd ever look forward to going to Peekskill."

Jack debarked and, wavering, clutched at the wagon's side, stamping both feet to the ground to regain his bearings. "I guess a fellow needs to find his land legs after a dance at the gallows . . ."

Anne steadied him with an arm around his waist. "Maybe you need to rest a bit?"

He squeezed her hand. "I'll rest on the boat."

"Alright, mates—quick and quiet are the words. Let's go."

"You heard what Tully said—quick and quiet." Titus gave Patsy a nudge, and she slumped over on the wagon bed like a sack of beans. "Pats!" Rolling the girl onto her back, his hand came up dark and sticky with blood. "She's shot . . ."

Jack pushed Titus aside and tore at Patsy's dress, which was drenched in blood. "I can't find the wound . . ." He grasped her stays and ripped them apart.

Patsy moaned. "My legs, Jack . . . they're gone . . ."

"Nooo . . . nooo . . . your legs are fine," Jack whispered, grasping her by the hand. "Titus is just goin' t' roll you over a bit, so we can find the wound and stanch the bleeding, alright?"

"Uh-huh . . ."

Titus pulled her gently onto her side. In the moonlight, they both could see a ragged hole the size of a fist, torn in the pale flesh between her shoulder blades, pumping a river of dark blood.

Jack pressed a hand to the wound to no avail. Patsy's blood continued to pulse through his fingers with every beat of her heart. Titus looked at Jack, shook his head, and they rolled her back. Jack pulled the edges of her dress together, and whispered over his shoulder to the others.

"We—" Jack swallowed, choking back his tears. "We need to wait here just a bit—alright?"

Anne and Sally pushed past Titus to the side of the dray.

"I've cocked it all up . . ." Patsy breathed.

Anne pressed her fingers to Patsy's cheek. "Everything will be fine, Patsy, you'll see . . ."

"Ye just need to rest a bit, lass."

Patsy smiled. "We saved him, Annie . . ."

Leaning in, Anne stroked Patsy's hair. "We did, brave girl . . . We did."

Patsy sighed. "I'm dead, aren't I?"

"Nooo . . ." Jack took Patsy's hand to his lips.

"It figures . . ." Patsy looked up into his eyes, her words puffing out in gasps. "My heart . . . a big target . . ." Whispering a soft, *"Oh!"* her eyes fluttered closed.

Jack heaved a shuddered sigh, and folded Patsy's hands together. "She's gone from us."

Anne buried her face in Jack's shoulder.

Tully crossed himself. "God curse the man who fired that shot."

"My, my God . . ." Titus moaned, and bolstered Sally with an arm around her shoulders. They all stood stunned and the tower bell rang out once, as though to toll Patsy's soul onward.

"We'd better get moving, mate." Tully laid a hand on Jack's shoulder. "This ain't a very wholesome place—I fear there are desperate eyes and ears about us."

"I know . . ." Jack swiped away his tears. "But we can't leave Patsy—not here."

"I have her, Jack." Titus lifted Patsy in his arms. "We won't be leavin' Patsy to the pigs what live in this rubbish heap."

Tully groaned, shaking his head. "But we've got to move quick, lads . . ."

"We're near the churchyard," Anne said, "consecrated ground. We can lay Patsy with Jemmy, and she'll be safe until the churchman can see to her in the morning."

"Good," Jack agreed. "To Trinity."

Tully led the way, followed by Titus, Anne and Sally. Jack brought up the rear, armed with a stout club he'd picked up along the way.

Canvas Town came alive as they moved in its uneasy darkness. Odd whistles, footfalls and whispers followed them as they crunched through the ruins along mazelike paths created by the Tory denizens to purposefully confuse and entrap.

"There's a light ahead," Tully whispered over his shoulder. "The churchyard, I think."

Titus was stumbling and breathing hard, his burden grown heavy and cumbersome. Anne whispered, "Almost there, good friend."

They crossed Thames Street, and climbed over the short picket fence into the graveyard. Anne led them to a spot beneath a locust tree, whose rustling leaves cast feathery shadows in the moonlight. She pointed to the empty space to the left of Jemmy's little grave. "That's my place—lay Patsy there."

Titus laid Patsy out on the grass. Sally used the hem of her petticoat to rub the paint and blood from her friend's pretty face. Anne straightened Patsy's clothing, and combed fingers through her soft dark curls. Jack folded her small hands across her breast, and kissed her cold cheek.

"Be at peace, dear Patsy."

Shouts, and the unmistakable clank and creak of soldiers at the quickstep caught their ears, and Tully urged, "With speed, mates . . . across Broad Way—*now*."

Sally and Titus followed Tully to the churchyard fence that bordered Broad Way.

"Wait . . ." Anne fell to her knees and began picking and plucking at the dead leaves and twigs entangled in the grass on Jemmy's grave.

"Annie . . ." Jack took her by the shoulders. "We have to go . . ."

Anne stopped her frantic tending, and leaned against the stone marker, tipping her head to rest on the curve of the granite for a moment. She closed her eyes, and heaved a sigh. Rising to her feet, she took Jack by the hand and they ran to catch up with the others. Anne glanced back as they passed through the churchyard gate. "You think we'll ever come back?"

"Oh, we'll be back." Jack gave her hand a squeeze. "I promise."

cb cb cb

KEEPING to shadows and dark doorways, Jack traversed the familiar backstreets and alleyways, leading the group to the Fishmarket, evading the Watch, and the companies of Redcoats the provost had patrolling the streets. They scurried down to the very end of the dock and found the Quaker minding the pettiauger with a pistol in his hand, and Bandit asleep in a tight curl on his lap.

"Wonderful to see you all safe, Jack." The Quaker welcomed each of them, handing off his weapon to Titus. Bandit leapt into Sally's arms, panting and licking the paint from her face.

"Patsy's fallen," Jack said. "The provost shot her dead."

"Not Patsy!" The Quaker gave a sad shake of his head. "Oh, to lose a heart so young and brave . . ."

"We had to leave her in Trinity Churchyard," Titus added. "Tell the Stitch we depend on him to see to her burial."

"I will."

Before boarding the pettiauger, everyone took turns bidding a quick farewell to the Quaker and Bandit, who was being left in the Quaker's care. The women each gave the man a hug and a kiss on his pate.

The Quaker gathered Bandit into his arms, and began making his way up the dock, when Jack called soft, "For the record, Quaker—what *is* your name?"

"Elbert—" he said with a little waggle of his fingers. "Elbert Hadley."

"Farewell, Elbert."

"Aye," Sally said, "he's got the look of an Elbert, na?"

Anne and Sally climbed into the boat, and sat together on the cross-thwart nearest the bow. Jack set the oars into the locks. Titus rearranged the bags and parcels they had tossed into the boat with such haste earlier.

"How's your arse, Tully?"

"Don't worry about my arse, Titus. My arse'll be fine once one of you digs the lead out of it." Tully loosed the stern line and took the rudder.

Jack shot Titus an elbow as they took the oars. "Now there's something to look forward to."

Tully rasped, "Sally, loose that bowline."

Anne grabbed Sally by the arm. "Did you pack my brooch?"

"Yer brooch?" Sally's eyes grew wide. "I didna! I meant to, but something . . ."

Anne tugged on the bowline and pulled herself out of the boat. "I *have* to go back for my brooch. It's all I have of Jemmy—I'll be quick . . . I promise."

Jack scrambled out after her. "I'm coming with you."

"Annie! Keys!" Sally fished through a bag at her feet, and tossed up a ring of keys.

"Wait!" Titus dove under his seat. "Redcoats are on the prowl—arm yourselves." He handed up a saber in scabbard to Jack. Anne took the pistol Titus pulled from his sash and dropped it into her pocket. The two linked hands, and ran the short distance to the Crown and Quill.

When Anne put the key in the lock and turned the latch, she was relieved to find the inside bolts had not been thrown, and Jack would not be forced to scale the wall. Pointing to the burning candle Sally set out for the Redcoat officers, she whispered, "They are still out . . ."

"But might be back at any time." Jack slid the three bolts home. "I'll stand watch. If they come, we'll go out the back way. Hurry now and get the brooch."

Anne hiked her skirts. Taking the stairs two at a time, she ran down the hallway and pounded up the garret stair.

She had left her room in a complete uproar—but the laquered box was on the night table, where she always kept it. Anne pinned the brooch to the inside of her stays, and pressed both hands over it. Having it next to her heart brought her great ease. *Everything is going to be alright.*

Anne ran down the garret stairs and skipped down the second-floor hallway, calling out a merry, "I have it!" when the door to her old bedchamber swung open and she was grabbed hard by the arm.

Edward Blankenship shouted, "*Thief!*" and put his sword to her throat.

"Stop! Edward! I'm no thief—it's me—it's Anne," she blubbered.

The captain spun her around, lowering his blade. "Anne?"

He must have been readying for bed. In stockinged feet, his

shirttails were half-hanging and his hair was unbound. He had a pistol stuffed into the waistband of his breeches. She could smell rum on his breath.

"I thought I heard a noise . . ." she blathered. "I didn't hear you come in. Where are the others—Wemyss and Stuart?"

Sword in fist, Blankenship jerked her toward the doorway of his room where the candle cast a light on her disheveled costume and painted face. "What are you up to? Who were you calling to?"

"She was calling to me."

Blankenship jerked around, his boyish brow beetled, like a schoolboy at his ciphers.

Jack stood at the top of the landing. The week's worth of stubble he wore enabled the captain to put a name to a familiar face.

"Stapleton?"

"You have a good memory for faces."

"I have a good memory for rebel spies."

Jack moved forward. His filthy shirt was besmeared in blood, and dark welts were raised where the noose had burned his neck and fingers. He unsheathed his sword and tossed the scabbard aside. "Let her loose. She's going with me."

"Then she's a spy as well . . ." Blankenship pulled Anne close.

"Bravo, Captain." Jack laughed, inching forward. "You're a quick study, aren't you? She's the rebel spy you have brought into General Howe's home—she's the rebel spy who's passed along every secret you've been gulled into uttering."

Like a terrier with its quarry, Blankenship's grip tightened and he gave Anne a rough shake. "Not true . . ."

"She's been playing you for a fool all along—'*Soon, Edward*,' she says, right? Promising to come to your bed? Well, friend, *I* know the pleasure of her bed—every night—right over your very head." Jack pointed up to the ceiling.

Blankenship growled. Letting go of Anne, he drew his pistol and fired. The hurried shot went wide, splintering the doorframe. Anne ran to Jack and they flew down the stairs.

The captain barreled after them, meeting Jack at the bottom of the stairs in a clash of honed steel, while Anne fumbled with the bolts. The dragoon drove Jack away from the door.

A journeyman was certainly no match for a cavalryman, and Jack stumbled around tables and chairs, awkward in parrying the relentless onslaught of expert blows Blankenship rained down upon him.

"Rebel scum!" the dragoon growled, slicing his blade through to the bone on Jack's right forearm.

"Stop, Edward, or I will shoot!" Anne leveled her pistol, and brooked the shooting stance. Steadying her wrist like Titus had taught her, she held her breath and sought a clear target.

His right arm hanging useless, his left weakening, Jack flailed his saber, and was beaten back into the corner.

In total command, Blankenship smiled. "You, I will kill . . . a gut wound, I think." The tip of his angry blade lashed out and sliced Jack across the cheek. "And after my men have had their fill of her, your whore will hang for a spy."

"Anne!" Jack shouted. "*Shoot him!*"

Blankenship glanced back at Anne. Jack lunged forward with a backhanded swipe of his saber, and cleaved the captain across the face at the exact same instant Anne pulled the trigger, felling him with a ball to his head.

As suddenly as it all began, it was over. With a measure of disbelief, Anne and Jack gulped air, tasting the sulfur floating on the smoke. Anne whimpered, "I told him I would shoot."

An alarm was shouted. A dog barked in the distance. The saber slipped from Jack's grip and fell clanging to the floorboards. He skirted around the dragoon lying facedown in an ever-widening pool of deep red blood. Stumbling through a tangle of chairs, he reached out and took Anne by the hand.

"Let's go."

Anne slipped the pistol in her pocket, and together they ran out into the night.

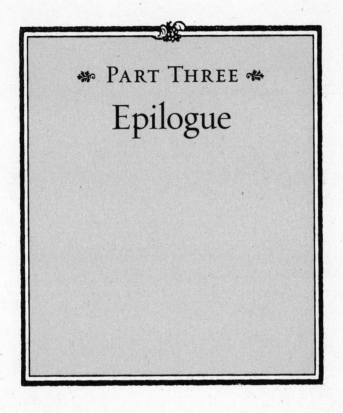

PART THREE
Epilogue

Monday, July 28, 1777
Peabody's Press at the Sign of the Oak and Acorn
Peekskill, New York

ANNE's father sat in a chair at the opposite end of the table, positioned to catch the lone shaft of fading light coming in through a west-facing window. With one leg crossed over the other, he held a copy of the *Peekskill Journal* at arm's length, reading the latest edition issued by his press, lips pursed in disappointment. "This composition looks very ragged, daughter—"

"I did the best I could with the poor type you keep." Anne looked up from the potato she was peeling. "It is a pity you don't have another daughter to exchange for a new set, isn't it?"

The rusty cowbell rigged over the shop door clanked twice as the door swept open. Anne leaned back in her seat to peer through the doorway between the living quarters and the small pressroom and smiled. "It's Jack!"

The bell brayed again as the door closed behind him, and Jack skirted around the ramshackle press to enter the room that served as kitchen and parlor in the Peabody home. Pale and thinner from a prolonged bout with fever, he carried his right arm in a sling. Anne cleared a space for him to sit at the end of the long table where she and Sally sat preparing root vegtables for the stew pot.

"Good day to you, Mr. Peabody," Jack said with a nod, taking a seat beside Anne.

Without bothering to glance up, Amos Peabody emitted a curt *hmmph*. Gathering his reading material, he rose from his seat and headed for the stairs. "Anne," he ordered over his shoulder, "have that girl bring my supper up to my bedchamber."

"'That girl' is Sally, and David will marry her no matter how you grumble or pretend not to remember her name," Anne shouted after her father, the timbre of her voice rising with his every angry stamp up the stairs. "Be assured, we here are more than happy to be relieved of your rude and unpleasant company, you miserable, old ba—" Anne stopped herself, heaved a sigh, and with a shrug to Jack and Sally she said, "My mother was the one who knew how to temper his willfulness. I should try to have more patience with him."

Sally stirred a bowlful of cut carrots into the pot of stew simmering over the fire. "Stubborn and proud, yer da is—and from what I ken, th' acorns dinna fall far from the tree."

Jack reached out and pressed the back of his hand to Anne's flushed cheek. "He'll come around. When me and Titus brought David home, your father was nothing but friendly and kind to us . . ."

"That was afore he knew ye were fixin' t' wed his daughter and rob him of his dower share," Sally said, with a shake of her spoon. "Yer a thief and a rogue, Jack Hampton, and I am a grasping Jezebel."

Anne laughed and leaned her head against Jack's shoulder. "But for you and Sally, I would have gone mad after one week under this roof."

"As soon as Hercules sends the money, we can marry and find a roof of our own."

"A home of our own and a printshop . . ." Anne added. She and Jack exchanged a soft kiss.

"And you won't have to put up with your father except for when he comes to visit his grandchildren." Jack winked.

Sally heaved a sigh. "Yer so lucky, Annie, t' have yer man at hand, safe and sound."

"He's not yet sound." Anne gave Jack a little nudge. "Move into the good light, and let me see to your arm."

"I'm all healed." Jack slipped his arm from the sling and rolled his sleeve up. "Four days since I last fevered—I'm sure the wound's no longer festering."

Anne unwound the bandage protecting the deep gash on his right forearm while eyeing the lighter wound on his face. The facial cut healed clean, and she knew Jack was pleased with the thin pink scar curved from his left eye to the corner of his mouth. "A swordmark lends an air of menace to a man, don't you think?" he had said, looking into a mirror the other day.

But she noticed he had taken to always wearing a linen neck-stock to hide the ugly story told by the abrasions around his neck. Anne doubted the rope scars would ever fade completely away. "Ooohhh . . ." She peeled away the pad of cotton lint. "Much better today, don't you think, Sally?"

Sally leaned in for a good look. "Aye—much calmed—tha' new ointment from the apothecary is doin' ye some good, na?"

Jack slowly flexed his fingers, opening and closing his fist. "The muscle is on the mend as well—feels stronger."

While Anne re-dressed his wound with fresh ointment and a clean bandage, the doorbell clanged, followed by a familiar voice calling, "Titus here!"

"Come on back," Anne shouted.

Titus plopped down beside Jack and fished a folded copy of the *Pennsylvania Gazette* from his pocket. "Bad news—Howe's finally left New York—over two-hundred and fifty ships heading for Philadelphia."

Sally groaned and sank into a chair.

Jack studied the newspaper. "It says here eighteen thousand men at arms are aboard those ships . . ." He whistled low. "And that's not counting the eight thousand in Burgoyne's army."

"Washington's shifting his forces as well. I saw a full corps of riflemen on the march toward Putnam's camp on the hill above town. They say the Putnam and Gates will be dispatched to try and stop

Burgoyne from reaching Albany." Titus puffed out a breath. "Looks like all hell's about to break loose."

The cowbell clanked anew and Anne went up front to find two dusty soldiers dressed in like fringed frock shirts and leather leggings, standing at the open doorway, squinting upward, trying to read the weatherworn shop sign in the twilight.

"Can I help you, sirs?"

"A-yup . . ." the shorter of the two took a step inside. "We're lookin' fer Peabody's Press . . ."

"At the sign of the Acorn and Oak . . ." the second soldier added.

"This is Peabody's Press . . ." Anne felt the comfort of Jack and Titus looming behind her. Sally scooted around to stand at her side, iron poker in hand.

The short soldier let the breach end of his long rifle thump to the floorboards as he drew forth a pair of sealed letters from inside his shirt. "These here are sent by Cap'n Peabody, Third Yorkers."

With a high-pitched yip, Sally ran up and snatched the letters from his hand. Saying, "One for you and one for me," she handed a letter to Anne and cracked the seal on the other, wandering back into the kitchen to sit on the hearth and read by the light of the fire.

"Can we offer you boys a meal for your trouble?" Jack asked.

"Smells awful good." The shorter man leaned in on his rifle. "I wouldn't oppose the notion of drawing a quick bite to eat."

The tall man shouldered his weapon. "We thank ye kindly for the offer, friend."

The soldiers were ushered to seats at the kitchen table. Anne dished up brimming bowls of stew served with crumbling hunks of cornbread and tankards of spruce beer.

Armed with spoons dug up from the depths of their possible bags, the riflemen grinned at the portions, the shorter one saying, "I don't hardly memorise the last time we et anything as fine."

While the unexpected but welcome guests smiled and slurped their way through their suppers, Anne brought a brand from the fire to light the four-wick oil lamp, and she sat beside Jack to read her letter:

> *Dear Sister,*
> *I am safe and well and hope this letter finds you the same. There may be reason to Expect a Tumult in the Universe. Please send our Father my Kindest Regards, and offer my Best Wishes to our very good friends J and T.*
> *Your Affectionate brother,*
> *David*

Anne glanced over at Sally, still immersed in reading her single foolscap sheet so covered in compact handwriting, she was compelled to rotate the page to read the sentences David crammed into the margins. Shrugging, Anne smiled at the three short sentences her brother scrawled in haste. "I suppose David hasn't much inclination to write after pouring his heart out to Sally . . ."

"Aahh, Pinkus." The short rifleman shot his companion an elbow. "Here we sit, noses buried in our feed, neglectin' t' pass along the cap'n's message."

"It's true—we're a right pair o' gluttons, miss," the taller man sputtered through a mouthful of cornbread. "The cap'n—he said for you to read between the lines of what he writ, as he always must guard agin a letter goin' astray into enemy hands."

Brow beetled, Anne looked at Jack. "Between the lines?"

"By Christ, I should have figured . . . afterall, he is *your* brother." Jack pulled the lamp close and set the glass chimney to the side. He took the page and held it to the heat of the flame. After a moment, words began to darken and form in the blank space between the second and third lines of the letter—

The General Requires Your Services.

"I don't know . . ." Anne looked at Jack, caught up in the excitement dancing bright in his dark eyes. "It seems our small dreams will have to wait while we work toward the larger cause . . ."

With a whoop, Jack pulled Anne into his arms and whispered into her ear. "Oh, Annie, you are the darling of my heart, to be sure."

"A toast!" Titus raised his tankard. "Here's to those who dare to be free!"

Monday, July 28, 1777
H.M.S. *Phoenix*
Bound for Liverpool, England

"Cook sent me down with a nice, clear broth, Abner." The cook's boy set the covered pot on the table. Stringy arms akimbo, he said with a shake of his head, "Sweet lamb o' Jesus! Would ye listen to the poor bastard moan? How can you bear it?"

Abner dipped a rag in a bowl of water and wrung it out. "A wet cloth to his lips seems to give him some comfort." The old seaman sat on a three-legged stool near the bunk, and dabbed the wet rag to his patient's lips—lips, nostrils and one eye being the only parts of his face not swathed in layers of pus-stained bandages. His moans quieted.

The boy came to stand beside Abner. "Cook says the poor bugger's face's mangled beyond repair."

"His face was near cleaved in two by a saber, and he has a rebel musketball buried in his skull bone," Abner affirmed. "And I should know. Ain't I the one what changes the dressings?"

"Cleaved in two!" The boy stepped closer to get a better look. "Cook says you're wasting your time—cook says this bugger won't survive the voy—!"

Quick as a cat, the bandaged convalescent reached out and

clapped his fist around the boy's bony wrist, causing him to near leap from his skin.

"Foh!" Ol' Abner cackled and slapped his knee. "Aye, lad. Ye can see the cap'n here has fire in him yet—a fire not so easily smothered."

Twisting and tugging, the boy tried to break free but the grasping fingers only tightened and pulled him inward.

One watery blue eye, red rimmed and shot with blood, stared out from an opening in the rusty bandages wrapped around the man's head. Crusty lips parted, and the boy heard him gasp out one word:

"Betrayed."

Let the names of Whig and Tory be extinct; and let none other be heard among us, than those of **a good citizen; an open and resolute friend; and a virtuous supporter of the** *RIGHTS OF MANKIND* **and of the** *FREE AND INDEPENDENT STATES OF AMERICA.*

THOMAS PAINE, *Common Sense*

Historical Note

In order of appearance, the following are characters appearing in this book who were drawn from the historical record. All other characters in *The Tory Widow* are drawn from the inner recesses of my brain.

- **James Rivington**, colonial printer, journalist, and apparent Loyalist.
- **Isaac Sears**, fanatic patriot and leader of the New York faction of the Sons of Liberty. He was also known as "King Sears" because of his influential role in organizing and leading the New York mob.
- **William Cunningham**, fanatic Loyalist, was mercilessly beaten and driven from town only to return after being appointed provost marshall of British occupied New York City. As provost, he was responsible for the most atrocious cruelties inflicted upon the American prisoners under his purview and for the deaths of thousands.
- **Samuel Fraunces**, owner of Fraunces Tavern, one of the few relics of old New York City still standing at the corner of Pearl and Broad Street.
- **Dr. Malachi Treat**, Professor of Medicine at King's College, eventually appointed physician-general to the Northern Army by Congress.
- **General George Washington**, commander-in-chief of the Continental Army, who engineered the nation's first network for gathering intelligence.

- **Major General Henry Clinton**, architect of the brilliant flanking maneuver that clinched victory for the British during the Battle of Long Island.
- **Major General Sir William Howe**, commander-in-chief of the British Army in America
- **Betsy Loring**, mistress to General Howe.
- **Admiral Richard Howe**, AKA "Black Dick," General Howe's brother and vice-admiral in command of the North American station.
- **Major General James Grant**, Howe's principal planner for the New York Campaign.
- **Oliver DeLancey**, Loyalist and member of New York's elite, he raised and equipped DeLancey's Loyalist Brigade.
- **Hercules Mulligan**, the Irish tailor to the British officer corps in occupied New York City and leader of the Mulligan Spy Ring.
- **Joshua Loring**, opportunistic Loyalist who exchanged his wife's favors for the lucrative position of Commissary of Prisons.

The following facts and events have been modified or altered for sake of this particular story and for dramatic effect:

- No official American flag existed at the time of the reading of the Declaration of Independence on July 9, 1776, and there is no documented account of the "Stars and Stripes" on display in the parade down Broad Way that day.
- Provost Marshall William Cunningham did see to the execution of convicted rebel spy, twenty-one-year-old Nathan Hale, on September 22, 1776, but the hanging and display of the corpse most likely occurred outside Dove's Tavern near the British artillery park located at present day Third and Sixty-sixth Streets, and not on the Commons.
- James Rivington's return from exile was accelerated to June from September of 1777.
- Though extravagant balls and gala events were common in British occupied New York City, there is no record of a ball cel-

ebrating the King's birthday occurring on June 4, 1777, at the Kennedy Mansion.
- There is no solid documentation to support the notion of British banknotes in use in the colonies in this time period.

Though my attempts to be true to history and geography in the telling of this story were undertaken with great diligence, *The Tory Widow* is still a work of fiction, written by a mortal being capable of error, misjudgment and inaccuracy, and I claim complete credit for any mistakes that may exist.

—CB

THE TORY WIDOW

By *Christine Blevins*

READERS GUIDE

1. A woman's marital status had considerable impact on the opportunities available to her in eighteenth-century colonial America. The same was true of widowhood. How do you think Anne Merrick's life changed as a result both of her marriage and of the death of her husband?

2. What specific events and experiences do you think caused Anne Merrick to move from political ambivalence to ardent patriotism over the course of the story? How do you think her life changed as a result?

3. American Patriots and Loyalists alike were adversely affected by tumultuous events depicted in *The Tory Widow*. Do you think the demands and sacrifices required of average Americans during the revolution compare to those of present day Americans in twenty-first century wartime? How so?

4. "Now there's another fine example of foolishness—they won't allow a black man to carry a gun or stop a British musket ball when it is clear they need every willing hand—more afraid of slave insurrection than they are of becoming slaves themselves." What would be the motivation for a black man, free or slave, to support the revolution?

5. Colonial Americans waged armed rebellion against the colonial system, which lacked representational government and limited economic growth. Can you imagine conditions or events that could drive contemporary Americans to revolt against their government?

6. "Our independence is won as much by lead type as it will be by lead bullets." What was the importance and the impact of the printed word during the time of the American Revolution?

7. The struggle for independence is a major theme of *The Tory Widow*. What stories of quest for individual freedom are interwoven into the larger backdrop of the fight for American independence from England?

8. Tarring and feathering and physical violence against private citizens, destroying private property, and firebombing naval vessels—all can be described as acts of terrorism. As a private citizen, does the goal of political change free Jack Hampton of any moral liability for his involvement in these acts?

9. The city of New York in 1775 convulses with sudden and violent change. How do the experiences of Jack, Anne, and the people they meet reflect those changes?

10. Describe the Anne Merrick we meet on her wedding day at the beginning of the book. Compare her to the Anne Merrick we've come to know by the story's conclusion.

11. We are introduced to the strong—in some cases, overbearing—personalities of Anne Merrick's father, husband, and brother. Little mention, however, is made in the story of female family members. How do you think Anne may have been affected by the relative lack of women in her family life?

12. How does the early death of Anne's son, Jemmy, affect the relationships she has with other characters in the novel?

13. Despite her low status as a common prostitute, Patsy Quinn was an ally both to Jack *and* Anne, and a fearless patriot. Compare Patsy's value and standing in society to that of Betsy Loring.